FIRST KISS

Liss sipped her wine, embarrassed by Wyatt's scrutiny. It made her uncomfortable to talk about her divorce.

"Liss, you are one helluva lady," he said. "Your husband—ex-husband—must have had rocks in his head to let you go." His voice was deep and husky. "You are beautiful . . . and sexy, too. I've been thinking about you since the first time I saw you. I've been wanting to kiss you. In fact, I want to kiss you right now."

Her voice shook when she spoke. "I'm not sure that's a good idea."

He stared into her blue eyes; she gazed into his darker blue ones, glittering with reflected light. She couldn't move as his head lowered toward hers.

His mouth brushed hers, soft and gentle. Her mouth softened; the kiss deepened. He took her glasses off and pulled her into his body, holding her close to him, learning the softness of her. She felt as if her bones had dissolved and flowed away, leaving her limp.

"Wyatt," she whispered, "no more. Stop." No matter how much she wanted to kiss Wyatt Harrow again, once had to be enough.

A LIFETIME OF LOVE

BONNIE HAMRE

ZEBRA BOOKS
KENSINGTON PUBLISHING CORP.

To my family, for personal reasons;
To my editor, Ann LaFarge, for professional reasons;
And to my friend, Jane Lewis, who knows the reasons.

ZEBRA BOOKS are published by

Kensington Publishing Corp.
475 Park Avenue South
New York, NY 10016

Zebra and the Z logo Reg. U.S. Pat. & TM Off.

First Printing: April, 1994

Printed in the United States of America

One

Liss Thayer snipped one of the fragrant roses she loved best, inhaled deeply, and placed the bud in her basket. "One more," she murmured, searching for the right bud.

Movement behind the tall pink and white oleanders marking her property line caught her eye. Myopic blue eyes narrowing, she squinted at the masculine profile that appeared and disappeared through the breaks in the greenery.

Focusing on the figure that came and went, she guessed he had to be Leona Greenley's new tenant. Liss didn't usually keep up with the "guests" who rented her ex-mother-in-law's remodeled carriage house, but this particular physique kept her staring until she realized that if she could see him, even without her glasses, then all he had to do was turn his head to see her. She frowned down at the oversized T-shirt she wore as a nightgown.

Torn between propriety and interest, she hesitated, measuring the broad expanse of tree-shaded lawn she had to cover before she could reach the safety of her house, then looked back at the hedge. Modesty dictated decorum, but curiosity demanded compromise.

While she considered her options, she walked right into the sudden spurt of the sprinklers.

"Damn!" she yelped, instantly drenched. She dropped the clippers; the business end missed the baby toe of her right foot by an angel's kiss. She leaped out of the cold arc, leaving the clippers behind, and shook the water out of her ash blonde hair. Soaked to the skin, Liss pulled the T-shirt away from her body and glared at the sprinklers.

A deep voice startled her. "Is somebody there?"

Liss threw a nervous look at the hedge. Seeing no one, she scooped up her clippers and quickly cut the nearest rose. She then grabbed her basket and sprinted through the slick grass, heading for the wide verandah that shaded three sides of her house.

"Was that you who yelled?"

Liss skidded to a stop, but her feet kept

going. Landing on her rump, she slithered into the flower border. She swallowed an embarrassed moan and pushed a dripping lock of hair out of her eyes. Glancing at the hedge, she couldn't tell for sure, but she thought she saw amusement on the face peering through the oleanders. The outlines were fuzzy, but by the amount of head showing above the tallest pink branch, Liss thought the owner of the voice had to be well over six feet.

"Not exactly the way to slide home, but it'll do."

The amusement in his deep tone made her feel warm all over. All at once, she understood the ostrich theory. She lacked the sand in which to hide her head, so she averted her face and tucked it into her shoulder as she turned her back on him.

"Need some help?"

She wished he'd disappear and take his smirk with him. The gazebo, freshly painted a brilliant white just last week, beckoned as a temporary haven. Could she reach that without her T-shirt playing show and tell?

"You always start the day with an outdoor shower?"

She peeked over her shoulder and blurrily saw his big grin. "Go away."

"Where?"

"I don't care. Anywhere!"

"Why don't you go inside?"

"Not with you there!"

He laughed, a warm, masculine sound that did nothing to ease her goose bumps. Or the humiliation of cowering like a schoolgirl.

That deep voice lingered by the hedge. "I'm not stopping you."

"Please, just go away . . ."

"If you insist."

She heard a door shut. Cautiously, she peered at the oleanders, making sure the man wasn't in sight. Feeling every one of her fifty-one years, she made a dash for the house, slipping and sliding over the wet grass, almost falling again in her haste. She galloped up the five wide steps and slammed the door behind her.

She muttered imprecations at the man next door, then chuckled at the ludicrous way she'd begun her Saturday. For the first time, she was glad she now lived alone and her house sat well back from the street. What would people think if they'd seen her scrambling around like that? *At my age, to be acting like a gawky kid.*

She laughed out loud and detoured into the laundry room, where she picked up a fresh bath towel and tore off the muddy shirt. Yanking it carelessly over her head, she was glad that she'd started sleeping in comfortable shirts rather than the long gowns her ex-husband had preferred.

Quickly, she reminded herself that she wasn't going to think of him any more. His preferences no longer mattered to her. She rubbed herself dry, she grabbed another towel for her hair, and wore both into her kitchen.

Her glasses lay on the newspaper she'd been reading before she went out to cut her roses. Impulsively, she put them on. Craning her neck, she waited, watching through the window until the man came out again.

Let patience have its perfect work, she fervently paraphrased the Bible as he reappeared behind the hedge. What had been a shapeless form became a clean-cut profile. Summer sunshine shimmered on his silvered hair. The brief glimpse of his red-shirted chest revealed well-muscled upper arms. She wondered if the rest of the body was as splendid. Intrigued, she forgot her dampness and watched him re-enter the carriage house.

Maybe she could call and ask after Leona's health, and casually work the conversation around to him. Instantly, she decided that was out of the question. All Leona needed was a hint that Liss was interested in a man and the phones would be ringing all over Oakmont.

Liss could imagine the gossips: "Imagine that, Liss Greenley—no, remember she took back her maiden name—Liss Thayer, so desperate for a man since David dumped her that she has to pick up strangers!"

She shuddered at the thought. Deliberately, she turned her back on the window and thought about the day ahead. Saturdays were busy, both at her antique shop and at the public library. On weekends, she had the browsers and the walk-ins, as well as her growing list of serious customers. She'd been in business less than two years, but she was beginning to make a reputable name for herself within the antique furnishings community and she welcomed an expanding clientele.

On days like today, with too many demands on her time, she almost regretted the impulse that had made her gather up her local memorabilia, much of it from her own family, and donate it to the library for an historical display which had become known as the Oakmont Collection. Granted, she'd been worn down and exhausted by dark emotions following the divorce, and in desperation had looked for something to give new meaning to her life, but she'd had no idea how the simple idea would snowball.

While she welcomed visitors to the exhibits she'd set up and maintained, the interruptions were making it harder for her to get the Collection ready to move to the new library.

Patrons ambling in and out were a steady distraction. It seemed that they all wanted to see the progress being made and speculate whether the governor would accept the invitation to attend the dedication ceremony two weeks away.

She planned her morning carefully. First, a stop at the shop to check with her assistant and best friend, Susan Powers, then on to the library for a few hours. If she worked through lunch, she could get back to the shop for the afternoon rush. She had some out-of-town buyers coming in at three and then she still had her bookwork to do. She hated the drudgery of it, but thankfully those books were at last showing some profit. It had been hard at first, competing with established businesses, but she'd kept at it.

And no matter what else she did, she had to make time to speak to Joe. After their argument yesterday, they had to get some things straight between them. He may be head librarian, but she was curator of the Collection and her decisions regarding the display were final. She had no intention of letting him ruin her vision of the Collection.

When she was ready, Liss drove through the tree-shaded streets of her neighborhood and turned onto the avenue where her antique store held pride of place on a newly renovated square. Admiring the combination of old red brick, white woodwork and black shutters on the buildings facing the square, she was glad she'd insisted on historical authenticity when the City Council had approved the project. Still smiling with satisfaction, she parked in the lot behind her store and used the rear entrance.

She went through the crammed storage area, noting that she'd have to make some space for the things she anticipated buying at an estate sale next week. Entering her office, she looked around with pleasure. She'd used a thoughtful selection of antiques, reproductions and up-to-date office equipment to create a comfortable niche for herself and Susan. She quickly made coffee, then took her roses through to the showroom.

She was just finishing arranging the freshly cut buds when she heard Susan's cheerful voice. "Morning, Liss."

She turned and smiled at the familiarly placid face of the other woman, liking the warm brown eyes, the ready smile and the deft way she had of dealing with the public. "Morning, yourself. Ready for another fun day?"

Susan's cozy laugh filled the quiet space of the office. "Fun? You betcha." She looked at the roses. "Are you going color blind? You have two reds and an orange. I thought you didn't like mixing colors?"

Liss carefully gave the orange bud a quarter turn. "Oh, I was in a hurry this morning and didn't pay attention." She swallowed a self-conscious laugh. "I got caught when the sprinklers turned on and I didn't wait around to choose the right rose."

A delightful smile spread across Susan's face. "So you got a cold shower. Getting soaked isn't too ladylike, eh?"

Liss grinned back, not minding that Susan teased her for her old-fashioned attention to decorum. Their friendship went back a long way. "Not at my age, it isn't. Especially in my nightie."

"How come you were out in that? Oh, of course." Susan's grin widened. "Your yard is sheltered. Somehow, I don't think your grandpa envisioned you scampering around in the altogether back there."

"It wasn't quite like that," Liss protested, before she remembered how naked she'd felt in her wet T-shirt, especially when she'd slid into the flowers on her fanny. She grinned and fibbed, "I did keep a stiff upper lip, though."

"I should hope so! The Thayers never give in to adversity."

"Right," Liss chimed in. "And women dew, men perspire—"

"—and horses sweat," finished Susan.

Liss laughed with her.

"It's good to hear you laugh again, Liss. It's been too long."

Liss glanced into her friend's approving brown eyes. "It has, hasn't it?" she agreed, feeling strangely excited, like a child anticipating a treat. "I promise not to be a grump any more."

"I wouldn't exactly call you a grump, not after what you've been through, but—"

"But it's time to pull up my socks and make the best of things? You're right. I don't know what I would have done without you, Susan."

The other woman's warm brown eyes glinted. "It just burns me up that you got the short end of the stick in this divorce. There he is, sitting pretty with that dolly-bird he married, and you're fighting to make ends meet."

"It's not as bad as all that," Liss protested. "I have to watch my pennies, but I'm not destitute." At the time of the divorce, David had made her a hefty settlement, partly out of guilt for his own actions and partly to buy her silence. It wouldn't do his fledgling political career any good to have certain things get around. She hadn't told anybody about the money, preferring to handle it discreetly. She'd made several arrangements about the settlement that were nobody's business but her own.

Not even Susan, her very best friend, knew the details. She wanted to keep it that way. And she certainly didn't want to talk about her ex-husband. "As long as we keep the store in the black, I'm okay."

Susan wasn't appeased. "I still think it stinks."

"It helps to have good friends and hard work." Liss took deep breath and continued, "Anyway, all that is past history. From now on, things are going to get better."

"Atta girl. I can tell you're feeling perkier this morning."

Liss smiled serenely, ignoring the fact that she'd felt anything but composed earlier in the morning. She'd felt gawky, like a graceless youngster instead of the mature, sensible woman she was. Amused now at the memory of her undignified gallop across the wet lawn, she turned her attention to the business at hand. "You'll be all right on your own while I'm over at the library?"

"Sure. After I spruce up the showroom, I'll check that inventory list again."

"I'm sorry to leave so much up to you. I

15

didn't think I'd be this involved in the Collection's move."

"Don't worry about it," Susan reassured Liss. "I knew what I was getting into when you asked me to work here. When you work with a perfectionist, you have to expect it."

"Maybe so, but who knew what you'd have to put up with. I had no idea Thayer's would grow so fast. Maybe we should think about getting some help. At least on the weekend?"

"Maybe. I could do with a little time off, but I don't know that I'd want anyone else in here. I like working, just the two of us."

Liss gave her friend a grateful look as she checked the contents of her briefcase. "Well, let me know if it gets to be too much. Don't want you overworked and complaining."

"Who's complaining?" Susan gave her a warm grin. "Go be a perfectionist over at the library and drive them crazy for a while."

Liss grinned back. "Sorry, no time to do that today."

"Dani says you work like a slave over there."

"Much as I love you and your family, Suze, it's a pity your daughter doesn't take after you. She's more into coffee breaks."

Susan ran a hand through already tousled gray hair. "I know. Her excuse is that she's just working there until something better comes along. She's hoping to get a job out at the plant."

"Intratec? I thought they weren't hiring."

Susan shrugged. "Tell her that. Besides, she's not too happy with Joe anymore."

Liss glanced up quickly. "How come?"

Susan shrugged. "She hasn't really said, but I think she's smarting from the last reprimand he gave her."

Liss said nothing, but she could see Dani's point. Even giving Joe the benefit of the doubt and laying the blame for his surly attitude on the stress of organizing the move to the new library, still, he'd been a bear to work with.

Susan looked at her boss carefully. "I hear he's been giving you a hard time, too."

Liss closed her briefcase with a snap. "I don't think it's anything more than jitters, but he keeps changing his mind. Talk about driving someone crazy! One day he wants it this way, the next day it's something else. Sometimes I think he's just giving me the runaround."

"Why would he do that?"

"Beats me. Maybe he doesn't understand my concept."

"Ah. You mean he's still dragging his feet about your display?"

Liss nodded. "We had a terrific argument

about it yesterday. He stomped into his office muttering at me. I was so frustrated with him I wanted to throw something."

Susan's eyes rounded. "How come he has so much time to get involved with your stuff? He's the librarian, you'd think he'd supervise the packing and moving."

"Actually," Liss confessed with a small shrug, "I prefer to do it myself."

"Well, watch yourself."

"I can handle Joe," Liss said firmly.

"If you can't, nobody can," Susan responded loyally. "Say, maybe if Dani quits the library, she could work here with us?"

"Ah—" Liss paused, looking for a tactful way of telling Susan that Dani wasn't the kind of employee she'd hire. "I don't think she's into antiques."

"Maybe not, but she sure likes a paycheck."

"Why don't we wait and see?"

"Okay. Got anything special for today?"

They talked shop for a few minutes, until, swallowing her last sip of coffee, Liss got up to go. "Call me if anything unusual comes up, but there's nothing you can't handle."

"Right," Susan grinned. "See you later."

Liss walked the several blocks to the red brick building that had housed the city offices and the library for over a hundred years. A growing need for space had gradually pushed all the non-governmental offices out; the library had a new, modern facility to move into.

Much as she looked forward to the new premises, Liss knew she'd miss the high-ceilinged rooms, the solid wooden floors and the tall doors of this building. She paused for a moment in the black and white marble tiled foyer, studying the mahogany double doors which opened into the library, feeling herself respond as always to the legacy her family had left this town.

Her great-grandfather had been the first to occupy the mayoral chambers on the second floor and every member of her family since then had been involved in Oakmont politics. Except her. Ah, but she had something much more worthwhile, something of lasting value to leave her home town. The Collection meant more to her than anything she'd done in a long, long time. She had plans for it. Big plans. Filled with a sense of purpose, she inhaled deeply, set her shoulders back, and entered the library.

Dani Powers came in just behind her, lugging a huge purse which she dropped with a thud on the reference desk. The bag tipped over, spilling out a toothbrush, toothpaste and a comb. Furtively, Dani scooped them up and shoved them back inside.

Liss recognized the clothes Dani had worn yesterday, but said nothing.

Dani, catching her look, defended herself. "Well, I had to do something to cheer Jack up—he's really down in the dumps. He says it's definite. Some honcho from headquarters is coming to close the plant down. Jack's going to have to find another job."

"That's for sure?" Liss asked, eyeing Dani's closely cropped black hair, the three earrings in one lobe, and the tight black leather skirt. Obviously, Susan no longer had a say in her nineteen-year-old daughter's wardrobe. Distracted by the image of Dani working at Thayer's dressed like that, she missed some of Dani's words.

". . . and he says he heard a couple of the big bosses talking—they looked pretty grim," the younger woman was saying, faithfully repeating her boyfriend's story. "It looks like they'll lay off a whole bunch more. Things are already tight."

"It's still just rumor," Liss reminded her.

"But, Jack heard them say—"

To put a stop to Dani's gossip, Liss looked around. "Where's Joe?"

"In his office, I guess."

Liss picked her way through the mess behind the desk to the office set aside for the head librarian. Although Joe Franklin had a small-town background, Liss didn't feel that he had any real appreciation for local history. Even after he'd worked closely with her on the display of the Collection, she sensed that he was merely humoring her. His attitude surprised her, since the Collection had earned excellent reviews in the California historical journals as well as good press for the library and the town of Oakmont.

She'd been nervous to meet the scholars who had come, maybe reluctantly at first, scoffing at the idea that an untutored small-town housewife could put together a collection with any historical import. She'd been delighted to see them change their minds after they'd studied the documents, journals and letters that formed the core of the Collection.

More than once, she'd introduced Joe as Head Librarian and seen him absently dismissed when he proved to have no detailed knowledge of the Collection. Maybe Joe resented being left out, or maybe he disliked giving up space in the new facility. No doubt he was just stressed out with the move.

Liss popped her head in through Joe's door. "Hi. Have you got a minute?"

Joe raised his eyes from his paperwork. "Didn't expect to see you here so early."

"Lots of things to do today. I'll be leaving after lunch."

"Whatever. Your time's your own."

Liss stepped into Joe's office and shut the door behind her. "Joe, let's settle this. We've got to come to some understanding."

Joe narrowed his eyes. "If you're referring to that display again—"

"I am. Why don't we just agree to disagree? You handle the library. I'll take care of the Collection."

"Fine," he shrugged, glancing away. "You do what you want. Anything else?"

Liss was taken aback by his unexpected change of mind. "No, that's it." Feeling she should make some gesture of peace, she added, "It'll all work out all right."

Joe shot her an unreadable look. "Yeah."

She lingered by the door a moment, baffled by his rapid mood swing. Yesterday he'd been adamant about getting his own way, today he seemed almost apathetic, almost agreeable. Was he showing signs of burnout? Perhaps she should suggest he talk to someone.

Considering the possibilities, she went back to her own cubbyhole. It was already too warm in the airless enclosure. She wished she'd worn something cooler than her blue linen suit as she settled behind her desk, reaching automatically for the paperwork outlining the moving schedule. Behind her conscious thoughts floated the memory of broad shoulders and a handsome profile.

She shook her head to dislodge the image and made herself concentrate on the sheet, counting with satisfaction the items already ticked off as accomplished, and moving ahead to the others.

Liss worked steadily through the morning, answering questions and checking the inventory of things to be moved against the articles already packed. By noon, when the library closed for an hour, she felt she'd made substantial inroads into her day's work.

Dani appeared in Liss's doorway. "Want to come to lunch with us?"

Liss looked up from a packing list. "No, thanks. I'd like to finish this before I leave."

"Bring you back something?" Dani offered.

"Thanks for offering, but I'll pick up something on my way back to the shop. Oh, leave the door open, will you?"

"But people might think the library's open and wander in."

"It's just too hot to close off the breeze."

"So don't you think we should get the air-conditioning fixed?" Dani complained. "No, don't answer that—I know it's not worth the expense since it's only two more weeks, but still, the corridor out there—"

"I'll keep an eye on things," Liss promised. "Go on. The restaurant will be cool."

Dani left with the others, and Liss settled back to work. She'd just roughed out a genealogy display when the sound of footsteps disturbed her. Lifting her eyes reluctantly from the plan, she took off her glasses and listened as the footsteps came closer. Annoyed at the interruption, she went out into the main room to shoo the would-be patron away.

In mid-step she tensed, inhaling involuntarily. There was no mistaking those broad shoulders or the silver hair of the man who had his back to her. She moved nervously toward him, wishing instead she had a handy place to hide. "I'm sorry. The library's closed."

He turned.

Liss felt her eyes widen.

Two

He was younger than she'd expected—not much older than she. His dark blue eyes widened in response as Liss stared. Her gaze took in a rugged face, lined around the eyes and the mouth which had started an amused smile, and a strong chin. His hair was gorgeous—up close, it just begged to be touched. She wondered if it could possibly be as soft and silky as it looked.

"I'm sorry," she said when she became aware of his amused expression. "It's rude of me to stare . . ." her words drifted away as she replaced her glasses and gazed at him. The rest of the body *was* as splendid as the head and shoulders.

It ought to be a crime, she thought disjointedly, *for a man to be so well built.* He'd changed into a light blue cotton shirt, open at the neck. His upper arms stretched the sleeves; she

25

wondered if he'd lifted weights as a young man. She looked up again, past his well-defined torso, and nervously felt the open interest of his return perusal.

What if he recognized her? He didn't appear to, but she felt sure there was more than curiosity in his gaze. She smoothed back her hair, making sure no errant strands escaped her chignon, glad now that she'd worn her blue suit, and more than anything else, glad the library staff wasn't here to witness the spectacle of Liss Thayer ogling a man.

Feeling anticipation build, waiting for him to speak again, she schooled herself to be poised and professional. Would he mention this morning?

He continued to study her, his eyes bright and interested. "If it's closed, how come the door's open?"

Oh, thank goodness! He hadn't made the connection. His voice, deep and melodious, was as perfect as she remembered.

"I left it open for air," Liss heard her voice flutter. She made an effort to bring it under control. "As long as you're here, can I help you with something?"

He glanced around at the mess. "What's going on?"

"We're getting ready to move into new facilities. Is there something you want?"

His eyes shuttered, and he turned slightly away from her.

Feeling rebuffed, Liss wondered if she somehow inadvertently offended him. Maybe he recognized her after all and was pretending not to?

When he turned back a moment later, his expression was pleasant, even affable. "Not really. I'm just looking around."

"Oh?" Liss was more puzzled by his manner.

"I have an appointment with the mayor, but I'm early."

"Today?" She wrinkled her nose in surprise. What could be so urgent that Howard Upjohn would give up his Saturday golf game? "I didn't think the mayor gave appointments on the weekend."

"Special arrangement. Do you mind if I browse while I wait for him?"

"Not at all," she answered honestly. She wouldn't mind another chance to look at him. Surprised by her own interest, she tried to remember the last time she'd noticed a man as a man. Oh, she saw plenty of them, and some of them even wanted to see more of her, but she couldn't remember the last time she'd been so aware of masculinity.

"Thanks," he said, making no move toward

the books. "I'm not keeping you from anything, am I?"

Liss thought of her tight schedule. "No."

He settled a hip comfortably against a large oak table. "Tell me about the move."

Her gaze skimmed over the blue and tan canvas and leather belt at his waist, lingered on the slim hips under tan chinos, and roved down long legs to glance at burnished loafers. She caught herself on the return upward trip. What was she doing, checking him over as though he had something to sell? Did he know that she'd stared at him just as hard earlier this morning?

She could feel a blush rising, and made herself look away. She gestured around the room. "Well, as you can see, the library is cramped for space in here. This was fine when Oakmont was much smaller, but no longer."

"What's your connection here?"

"I'm Liss Thayer. I do volunteer work with the historical display."

"And when you're not volunteering?"

She paused, wondering if he remembered her soaking wet. "I own Thayer's, an antique shop."

"Just one name?"

"Everybody knows it." She smiled.

28

"Oh?" He raised an eyebrow at her confidence. "Doing well?"

Her smile faded a little. If the plant did close down, she'd lose a major portion of her clientele. Lots of the families who had moved here more recently had bought the older houses built when Oakmont was a thriving agricultural community and discovered that their modern furnishings were out of place. They wanted appropriate decor for those big old Victorian homes, and she was happy to supply them.

She hoped she could continue to do that. Maybe she'd been premature talking to Susan about hiring some more help. Shrugging, she answered noncommittally. "I get by."

He eyed her classic blue suit, cut simply from expensive material. "Evidently. You're using the library to show your stock?"

"Oh, no!" she said, shocked that he'd think that. She hastened to explain. "A lot of documents, family history, memorabilia, even old clothing, that sort of thing, comes my way. I could sell it or give it away, but that seems shortsighted, when most of it has to do with Oakmont. I created a display here. People are fascinated by it. There's a lot of interest in discovering our roots."

He nodded. "I've heard that. I know some people who are tracing their ancestors."

"We've had a lot of researchers use our material."

"Maybe I'll have a chance to see it . . ."

"I'm sure you'll enjoy it, Mr.—?" she asked, definitely pleased that she didn't have to plot how to meet him. And even more pleased that he was so easy to talk to.

He extended a large hand. "Wyatt Harrow. New to Oakmont, as of this morning."

She could have told him she knew to the second what time this morning he'd moved in, but she smiled instead, light-hearted and expectant. If he wasn't going to mention their earlier meeting, neither would she. She took his hand, liking the firmness of his handshake. His long fingers lingered on hers for an extra heartbeat.

"Welcome to town," she murmured, taking back fingers which still tingled from his touch. "I hope you'll like living here."

"I guess I gave you the wrong impression. I'm just here on business."

"Oh? What do you do?" She tamped down a feeling of disappointment.

"I'm with Intratec."

"Are you an engineer?" A suspicion surfaced as she felt her throat close. Was this the honcho Dani's boyfriend feared?

"Used to be."

"Now you're an astronaut?"

He chuckled, as if amused by her persistence. "Now I'm vice president of manufacturing operations."

"I didn't realize the plant here is big enough to warrant a vice president," she probed, her uneasiness building.

"It's not. I'm here to tour the facility—"

"You're the one who's going to close down the plant?"

"Where did you get that idea?"

Liss heard the surprise in his voice, overlaid with suspicion. "There's been a lot of talk about Intratec."

He waved a hand dismissively. "You must have an overactive rumor mill around here."

She ignored the gesture. Something about the way his dark blue eyes narrowed, deepening the fine lines around them, made her sure she was right. He seemed to close in on himself, to present a No Admission sign to outsiders. It made her wonder what he had to hide. "No faster than anywhere else, I'd bet. Especially when people's jobs are at stake."

"What do you know about it?"

"Enough to know that people are worried and upset. Why would you close down a plant that's only been operating a few years?"

He regarded her for a moment before answering. Liss had the feeling he was deciding what he wanted to tell her. It wasn't any of her business, of course, but did he realize what he'd be doing to Oakmont if he shut the plant doors?

He spoke blandly. "No decisions have been made."

"That's not an answer. That's executive gobbledy-gook."

Surprisingly, he grinned at her. His expression opened and made her want to grin back, to share that smile. "It may not be cost effective to keep it operating as is."

"But that's hundreds of jobs! How can you justify firing all those people?"

Before her eyes, he changed; an impassive look, effectively masking his earlier flirtatious grin, settled over his well-chiseled features. She imagined him dressed differently, out of the informal blue shirt and chinos into a dark, well-cut suit. Something expensive, a power suit. He'd be even more of a force to reckon with then. She bit her lip, imagining the power of his will, the deep command of his voice.

When he spoke, however, his tone was soothing and practiced. "If it ever came to that, it's not firing, it's down-sizing."

"Same thing."

"We'd transfer some employees to other plants."

"Who? Any besides those few who came

here with Intratec in the first place? What about all the local people working there?"

"Look, nothing is decided yet. I shouldn't even be discussing this with you." He spread his hands in a gesture she recognized as a truce symbol.

"Why are you going to see Howard?"

"Mayor Upjohn?" He blinked at the rapid change in subject. "Just a courtesy call."

"Howard won't take the news well. He's proud of the business he brought to town."

"You're imagining things." His tone was curt.

"Now you're angry. Look, I know it's none of my business, but Intratec is the largest employer in town. A lot of people depend on their jobs with you."

"I know that," he said quietly.

"Other people depend on the plant being here." *People like me,* she added silently. "Does it make you feel omnipotent to hold people's livelihoods in the palm of your hand?

His mouth thinned. "Far from it."

Touched, she felt she'd just glimpsed the hidden man—one who wasn't happy with what he had to do. Her anger abated as she realized what a difficult decision he had to make—even if he wouldn't admit that was why he was here. What would she do in his place if she faced the same choices? Dollars and cents or people? What would *he* do?

He gave her a measured look. "Look, I wish we hadn't gotten into this. I ask you to keep your ideas to yourself."

"Why?"

"For one thing, you'd be spreading rumors, and—"

"Don't you think people have a right to know their jobs are at risk?"

"You're jumping to conclusions."

His response angered her. She forgot her attraction to him, forgot that moment when she'd seen under his businesslike manner. "Don't you care what will happen?"

"I care."

"But not enough to change your mind."

"Look, Liz—"

"Not Liz. Liss."

"Liss? That's unusual."

She said nothing, not wanting to be side-tracked with a discussion about her name.

He exhaled. "I've got a job to do, Liss, just like you do. Sometimes we have to make unpleasant or unpopular decisions, right?"

"Don't patronize me, Mr. Harrow."

"Wyatt, please. And I wasn't patronizing you. I'm asking if you haven't ever had to make a decision you didn't want to make?"

"Yes, of course I have, but—"

"And that decision was for the good of your business or—"

"This isn't Ethics 101 here, Mr. Harrow. We're talking about people's jobs, about paying bills and putting food on the table."

He began a quick retort, then stopped, visibly controlling his own anger.

Liss was chagrined. Her temper cooled as quickly as it had flared. Whatever this man was in Oakmont to do, she shouldn't be shrilling at him like a fishwife. "I apologize. I spoke out of turn."

He looked at her curiously. "You evidently feel quite an attachment to Oakmont."

"You could say that," she said slowly, thinking of her family's long involvement with the town. Since the first Thayer had come to the fertile San Joaquin Valley after striking out looking for gold, one after another of her ancestors had managed to poke a finger into the political pot. She wondered what they'd say if they knew she kept her hands to herself. Amused by her thoughts, she couldn't help a smile.

"Well, truce then?" he asked, with a hint of a responding smile.

Making peace implied possible other meetings between them. Liss felt a thrill of anticipation again, then remembered why he was there. "How long will you be here—uh, investigating?"

"I'll be meeting all next week with our people at the plant and with the local—"

"You'll be here only a week? Isn't that an awfully short time to make a decision?"

"If I need more time, I'll take it."

For a long moment, they looked at each other. Liss saw strength and honesty in his face. She believed his statement that he'd take his time, but was she reading more into it than he meant? Was she only imagining a certain reluctance to make the decision in the first place?

Wyatt spoke first. "Can I rely on your discretion?"

She paused, worrying at her lower lip. Dani's voice announced her presence seconds before she entered the library. Liss took a step backward, away from Wyatt.

Watching Liss, Wyatt saw her face become still and composed. Serenity suited her, he thought, still baffled by the way he'd argued with her almost as if he knew her. It didn't say much for his tact or his discretion, but she'd gotten under his skin and touched a nerve. It still smarted.

He checked his watch. "Well, the mayor should be here any minute." He spoke in a louder, casual tone, aware of the curious looks he was getting from the group standing beside the big mahogany door. "Thanks for your time, Liss."

"You're welcome." She paused, and then added softly, for his ears alone, "I won't spread any rumors."

A small smile touched his mouth. "Thanks, Liss. See you again?"

She returned the smile, hugging to herself the knowledge that they were neighbors, and she'd be very sure to see him again sooner than he might imagine. So long as he didn't mention wet T-shirts, she'd be glad to see him again.

Slowly, she murmured, "Oakmont isn't that big—we're sure to run into each other somewhere."

Three

"I'll look forward to that." Turning, he walked briskly out the door. She heard his heels on the old wooden staircase leading up to the city's government offices above and wondered what Howard would make of him.

Dani had watched him walk out, too. Turning, wide-eyed, to Liss, she gasped, *"Who* is that?"

"Someone who wandered in."

"Wandered in? That guy just wandered in?" Dani paused, pursing her mouth. "For an old guy, he's not half bad." Suspicion grew in her sparkling dark eyes. "Or were you expecting him? That's why you didn't come to lunch."

"You're way off, Dani. I've never seen him before today."

"You two were having a pretty serious conversation when we came in," Dani persisted. "Did I interrupt anything?"

"No," Liss said slowly, although she had felt a certain connection with Wyatt Harrow. How odd. She didn't involve strangers in arguments. "We were talking about Oakmont."

"I have the feeling I'm not getting the whole story here."

Liss evaded Dani's questioning gaze and ended the conversation by going into her office. It's not fair, she thought, unconsciously making a face. For the first time since her divorce she'd met someone who truly interested her, and he was only going to be in Oakmont for a week.

Hours later, Wyatt turned off his tape recorder, remembering how he'd taken the stairs, two at a time, up to the mayor's office on the second floor above the library, thinking that maybe this wouldn't be so bad after all.

He'd protested leaving Sunnyvale, claiming schedule conflicts, production problems, anything he could think of to get out of making this particular decision. He mentioned that his transfer from the Dallas facility was so recent he hadn't yet had time to get a handle on the situation. Dick Fields, his boss and president of Intratec, had just given him that flat look and reminded him that, inherited problem or not, Oakmont was his responsibility.

Now, he was almost glad he'd come. Meeting Liss Thayer had certainly brightened things up. Only fair. If he had to be in Oakmont, at least there should be some reward in it for him. Even though she'd given him a hard time about the plant—how the hell did she know about that? This whole thing was supposed to have been kept quiet. He'd have some investigating to do, and then he'd take care of the big mouth. Anyone who couldn't adhere to company policy was number one on the layoff list.

At least his meeting with the mayor had gone smoothly, since all he'd done was introduce himself and announce his intention of reviewing the Oakmont assembly plant.

Mayor Upjohn had beamed. "Now, that's real nice. It says good things about your company that you'd make a special effort to come in and say hello. Always glad to meet with your people."

"Good of you to see me on a Saturday. Hate to take you away from the links," Wyatt said, acknowledging the other man's golf outfit. "Good course?"

"Passable, passable. You play? We could maybe round up a foursome, see how we do."

"I doubt I'll have time. Maybe next trip,"

he said. One visit to this nothing town would be all he could stomach. He'd make the decisions, then leave it up to some young hot-shot on his staff to take care of the details.

"Always glad to show you boys a good time."

Wyatt had managed to keep a straight face, inwardly wincing at both the mayor's folksy manner and the possibility that future meetings wouldn't be as cordial.

Amazed that he'd gotten through the meeting without giving anything away, he sobered and pressed the record button again, taping his daily journal. "After meeting with Upjohn, who still doesn't know why I'm here, I spent several hours at the plant, this afternoon." He paused to reflect. "The problem is bigger than we'd estimated. It's going to take me longer than a week just to clear up the existing mess."

He sighed, not looking forward to rubber stamping a decision with which he couldn't agree, and leaned back against the comfortable easy chair Mrs. Greenley had provided. He stretched and put his feet up on the leather hassock, recalling his difficult meeting with the management team at the plant. "Lord knows how, but Pete Dodge was already aware their jobs were on the line. I called the first session on Saturday to keep it quiet, but the word was already out. I'll have to have a word with Dodge about security. We'll need to keep a tighter lid on things if we're going to make this work. The meeting went from bad to worse when Pete walked out." Grimly, Wyatt thought about the expression on the plant manager's face. "It's going to be tough convincing him."

Normally, a visiting vice president would be asked to dinner, he thought wryly, but no one wanted to spend any more time with him than was necessary. *Can't blame them, who wants to eat with the guy who can take away your paycheck?*

Well, another solitary meal wasn't going to kill him. He was used to it, traveling as he did, spending more time in hotels and on planes than he did in whichever apartment he called home, but sometimes he wished he could sit across from a friendly face and talk about something besides work.

The image of ash blonde hair and brilliant blue eyes teased him. He wasn't pleased to be here—not at all—but meeting Liss Thayer was one good thing to come out of this. He grinned, amused at the quick way she'd taken him on. Even in high heels, she was a hell of a lot smaller than he, yet she'd stood right up, nose to nose, telling him what for.

He remembered how Liss had stared at his hair. He was used to it by now, but her interest had amused him. She'd apologized so nicely for staring then gone right on doing it—even put on her glasses to get a better look.

Surprised at his own reaction, he'd stayed, when his instinctive response to aristocratic-looking blue-eyed blondes with delicate features and satin skin was to turn and run, just the way that sopping wet woman had done this morning.

He grinned, remembering how she'd loped across the lawn, long slender legs shimmering, sodden T-shirt riding high on her thighs. He hadn't minded the way it had hugged her breasts and flat midriff, either. He supposed he shouldn't have headed for the window the minute he entered the guest house, but how else could he have enjoyed the view? At his age, reduced to being a peeping Tom. Or did that qualify if he was inside, looking out a window and through a bushy hedge? The glimpses he'd had of her were just enough to tantalize him as he remembered them throughout the day. When would he see her again? He looked forward to that a moment longer, then his mind returned to the greater impact Liss Thayer had made on him. Although the barefoot stranger this morning had delighted him, cool, poised Liss Thayer this afternoon had fascinated him.

He'd almost walked away, until the temptation to stay and make her smile again overcame his reluctance. He wanted to forget that he was attracted to women who were aloof and polished on the outside and warm on the inside. Since their divorce, he'd stayed away from women who reminded him of Elaine. He'd been badly hurt. Never again. His relationships, short as they had to be, were with dark-eyed women who laughed easily.

Did Liss like to laugh? Her smiles, reluctant and all too infrequent, made him think her laugh would be special. Something about her, more than her obvious resemblance to Elaine, teased him. Wyatt speculated what it was about her that seemed familiar. He'd stared at her in the library, trying to place her until the surface likeness had faded, and he'd lost whatever it was that had made him think of someone else.

He was glad he'd stayed and talked with her, for Liss's expressive face had betrayed her moment of confusion before she'd schooled her reactions. He hadn't been able to restrain his response to her cool beauty once she'd shown him that, under her reserved exterior, she was deeply involved with the things that mattered to her. She'd been angry with him, her eyes flashing fire though her voice was controlled.

He'd respected her anger, even as he'd

studied her hands, wanting to touch, looking for a ring, absurdly pleased when her left third finger was bare. He wished he could have gotten closer to her to identity the perfume she wore. Something ladylike and traditional, he'd bet.

She'd attracted him, fascinated and charmed him into staying. Instead of provoking anger, her outspoken disapproval of his mission had triggered the desire to see her again. He wanted to see if he could spark the quick intelligence and lively humor.

Hell, who was he fooling? He wanted to see if he could incite the feelings that colored her cheeks and made her breath quicken. Unless he was completely mistaken, she'd been just as interested in him.

When could he see her again?

His stomach growled——he hadn't eaten since a hurried breakfast on the road. He'd seen several fast-food places and stopped at a mini-mart for a six-pack of beer on his way back to Mrs. Greenley's, but he'd have to stock his small efficiency kitchen and find someplace that didn't offer grease as the main item on the menu. He swallowed the last of his beer and got to his feet.

Car keys in hand, he walked down the long driveway to the street, planning to cruise around, get the feel of the town, and find a restaurant. He had his car door open when an older model white sedan with a blonde at the wheel turned into the driveway next door.

He recognized her immediately. So—prim and proper Ms. Thayer lived here. Interest stirred in him again. Could she be the T-shirted hoyden he'd fantasized about all day?

A smile breaking across his face, he shut his car door and ambled over to the Buick. A nicely turned leg, with a light blue skirt riding high on the thigh, emerged from the car, followed by the other trim leg and the rest of a slender body. Wyatt watched with pleasure until she straightened and saw him.

"Hi," Liss said, self-consciously tugging her jacket over her hips.

"So, neighbor." He grinned, enjoying the slight bloom of color that tinged her cheekbones. "I didn't realize who you were earlier. You're dressed differently."

"I recognized you," she said in a rush, heading off any remarks about her wet T-shirt.

"Why didn't you say something? I didn't make the connection until just now." He grinned again, flirting. "Although, with your hair dripping down your back you did look a little different."

The color in her face deepened.

Wyatt was entranced. How could any woman

of her age still blush so delightfully? "I'm sorry our meeting went wrong."

She smiled the smile he'd been hoping to see. "I apologize, too. I don't always act like that."

He returned the smile. "Like what?" he asked, wondering if she referred to the instant attraction between them.

"Losing my temper with strangers."

He bit back a momentary flash of disappointment. "Think nothing of it."

She blurted out the question that had niggled at her all day. "Why did you move in so early?"

"I woke up before dawn, so I thought I might as well miss some of the traffic. Besides, the sooner I take care of things, the sooner I can get back on schedule."

"Oh," she murmured, wondering if he was always so precipitous in going after what he wanted. Probably. That's the way things were done everywhere but Oakmont. She gestured to the open door of his car. "Don't let me keep you."

"I was just going out to eat. Can you recommend a good restaurant? No fast food, though."

She thought for a moment, concentration darkening her clear blue eyes. She named three restaurants and gave him directions. "They're all good."

"Thanks. I'll try one of them." He rubbed the toe of his loafer against the grass. "Guess I'd better get going."

"Yes," she said, thinking he certainly didn't look like a high-powered executive just now.

He lingered. "Ah, Liss, if you have nothing else planned, would you join me for dinner?"

"What?"

"Dinner?" he repeated, smiling a little at the puzzled look in her eyes. For a moment, she looked like a young girl, unexpectedly facing a situation she didn't know how to handle. The thought was crazy—a good-looking woman like Liss must have known from her playpen how to respond to a man's overt interest.

"Oh," she said, thinking fast. Surprised by how much she wanted to see more of him, she bit her lip in confusion. There was nothing she'd rather do than sit next to him, talk, get to know him better. But there was no point—he'd be gone in a few days. "Thanks, but I already have plans," she fibbed, willing her disappointment away.

"Another time?"

"Perhaps," she answered, knowing there wouldn't be another time.

Four

Breathing quickly after his run, Wyatt turned up the driveway to his rental quarters. Something about the clean soft air, with more than a hint of the heat to come, had reminded him of his meeting with Liss and distracted him enough to keep him off pace. He'd had a hard time with the easy stride he'd set himself and had finally given up.

Maybe it was the different streets, the anticipation of seeing Liss again, or worry that kept throwing him off stride, but he'd cut his run short and turned back.

Regretting his late start after a rough night, he stopped, then bent to brace his palms against his thighs. As he straightened, he caught a glimpse of blonde hair through the oleander hedge, and grinning, he pushed a branch out of the way to have a better look.

Ms. Thayer was gone. The barely-dressed

woman was back. Intrigued by the changes in her, he watched to see what had her so occupied.

Dressed in faded cutoffs and a diminutive pink halter top, Liss was on her knees, grubbing in the dirt. Again feeling like a peeping Tom, he watched her wipe her forehead. The gardening glove smeared dirt, making her look more like an urchin making mud pies than the cool, sophisticated woman he'd met yesterday.

Well, he amended, *met properly,* remembering her wet and embarrassed as she'd been earlier in the morning. He recalled the chagrined note in her voice, thin and high, almost girlish, and contrasted it to the low, throaty tones that had piqued his interest later.

Add the differences in her voice to the change in her appearance, and no wonder he hadn't recognized her. He wouldn't make the same mistake again.

Smiling, he jogged back down the driveway and followed it under the porte-cochere into her back yard. He'd spent a lot of sleepless hours last night wondering about her, deciding that he'd see no more of her. He recognized a brush-off when he got one, and even though it smarted, he realized she was right. He was here to do a job.

Socializing with the natives, even one as delectable as Liss Thayer, was the last thing he had time for or needed, for God's sake, but now, remembering the sweetness of her smile, he could hardly wait to see her again.

He took a deep breath, released it slowly. "Good morning."

Startled, Liss sat back on her heels and looked up, forgetting her intention not to see him again in the quick burst of pleasure that surged through her. She lowered her eyes quickly to her trowel, hiding her face from him, afraid he'd see too much, and then, unable to resist, flickered a glance at him.

Bare feet in running shoes gave way to ankles, calves and knees, all tanned the most glorious shade of golden brown she'd ever envied. Silently sucking in her breath, she let her gaze follow the legs up to muscular thighs that disappeared into blue nylon shorts. Above his trim waist, a blue and white striped tank top left no doubt about his chest. The shoulders were as marvelous from this angle as they'd been yesterday, and his biceps would be the envy of any body-builder.

When she reached the grin, she pushed her glasses back up her nose and grinned back. "You know it's illegal to come sneaking up on someone in her back yard."

"You call this sneaking? Sneaking is eyeballing you through the shrubbery, like I did before," he protested. "I'm being real up-front here."

Flushing, Liss lowered her eyes, recalling the way the wet T-shirt had clung, revealing far too much of her. Then her gaze fell on what she was wearing now and her cheeks bloomed a brighter pink.

Since the divorce, she'd started wearing what she felt comfortable in, not what was expected of her. David had always liked to see her in clothes that enhanced his image of themselves as Oakmont's aristocracy, as if her style would reflect on him, making him more important. As if he'd needed her to do that! The Greenleys were as equal to the Thayers as equal could get. Yet David had always liked being a little more equal than others.

Since she no longer had to please him, she'd experimented with what appealed to her, never thinking anyone would see her in some of her more outrageous outfits. Looking down at herself now, she felt self-conscious and uncomfortable. How skimpy her clothes were; more appropriate for a woman half her age.

He looked down at her, seeing the fragile curve of shoulder, the delicate line of her arms. The tiny pink halter top had just enough fabric in it for modesty, but not enough to stop him from staring at the curve of her breasts.

"What's illegal is that outfit you're wearing," he drawled, rewarded with another swift rush of color that stained her face and her slender throat, reaching under the top of the halter.

"Well, I wasn't expecting company," she protested with one quick glance at his face before she looked down again.

"Am I company? I thought neighbors could drop by any time. Borrow a cup of sugar and all that?"

It seemed to him that she looked down at the weed in her hand rather than let him see her reaction to his being neighborly. Something about her posture, her slumped shoulders, her bent head, and her steadily downcast gaze, belatedly told him how uneasy she was. *Jerk.* He hadn't come over here to make her miserable. "Would you rather I leave?"

Her fingers tightened around the trowel. This was her chance to say something polite but pointed. Something about being too busy to chat. Maybe throw in a reference to her lack of free time. She said nothing.

"Liss? Do you want me to go?"

She had to answer him. She lifted her eyes, shading them from the glare with the palm of her hand. "No." Where had that come from? She'd meant to send him away! Dismayed, she lowered her head and studied the ground as though the answers were written in the moist soil.

"Good."

She made no reply. He let the silence grow while he studied her, noting by the tension in her now stiffened shoulders that she was aware of him as he was of her. He saw the peek she gave his kneecaps, then the quick surge of color over the nape of her neck. Wanting to lay his palm over the fragile-looking skin, he spoke instead, keeping his voice casual. "So—what's to do in Oakmont?"

"Well . . ." She relaxed, once she realized he wasn't going to push the moment of awareness. "Apart from watching the grass grow, there's not much."

He groaned and hunkered down next to her. "That's what I was afraid of."

Suddenly, without knowing why, her constraint vanished. With him down at her eye level, without his masculine form towering over her, she felt relaxed and at ease with him, as though they hadn't met just yesterday, as though they were friends. "Sometimes for a change we watch the birds fly by," she added with a quick grin, daring to tease him. "Sometimes, nothing at all."

Wyatt gave her a horrified look. "You *are* kidding, right?"

"What do you do on Sundays, Wyatt?"

"Go into San Francisco, see a museum, art gallery, maybe go to a concert, a ball game, who knows. Out to dinner."

"You can do all that right here."

He reached out and lightly tugged her pony-tail. "Yeah?"

"Yeah," she mimicked, wishing she dared touch his hair in return. In the sunlight, the thick silver strands glistened silkily. Mussed now from his run, with a lock lying casually over his forehead, his hair looked even more inviting than it did when combed and styled. The urge to reach out, push that hair back and let her hand run down its length, was so strong that she had to put both hands between her knees to hold back.

"Want to show me?"

"Show you what?" she echoed, as if lost in her private battle.

"Around Oakmont. It's Sunday, isn't it?" he challenged, intent on her answer, wanting her to accept. What he didn't want, he acknowledged ruefully, was to analyze why her acceptance was suddenly so important to him. He just wanted a chance to get to know her, maybe push a little, see what developed.

Liss appeared to consider that. "I could

show you all that, but I'd rather show you a different side of Oakmont."

He heard the serious note in her voice and hesitated. He wanted a light, amusing day with her, a little fun, not an all-out campaign to keep Intratec in town. Was she going to try a soft sell on him? Show him how many houses belonged to Intratec employees? "No propaganda?"

She smiled. "No brainwashing either. Just take a look at Oakmont through my eyes. We won't even discuss what you're doing here."

"Okay. When?"

"Half an hour? I want to change first."

"You're on." He rose easily to his feet.

She stripped off her gloves and extended a hand. "Help me up?"

He pulled her up effortlessly, breathing in the scent of fresh dirt and earthy woman. Her hand was warm and soft; he felt the heat of her skin and ached with the sudden desire to put his arms around her and taste her parted lips. He commanded himself to keep a grip.

Liss inhaled. For one intense, tempting moment, Wyatt thought she'd let herself lean forward.

"Liss," he said, breathing faster.

She pulled back. "I'll see you shortly. If you want to wait, there's coffee in the kitchen."

Wyatt wanted nothing more than to follow

her inside, but he shook his head, putting distance between them. "I'll be back. I should change, too."

Liss made quick work of her shower, then stood in front of her closet considering one outfit after another. While she rummaged, she scolded herself for her involuntary response to him.

"That's what you get for getting carried away," she muttered as she pulled on a sleeveless raspberry knit sundress with a keyhole neckline and soft full skirt. "Acting like a brainless fool all because he got too close." She put on a little lip gloss and mascara, dabbed White Linen behind her ears and on her wrists, then slipped into white sandals.

"Cool and collected," she reminded herself. "No reason to be nervous. Nothing really happened, after all."

She came downstairs just as Wyatt walked across the verandah to the front door. "That's good timing," she said as she opened the screen door, admiring the freshly showered look of him in dark blue slacks and a white Polo shirt.

Wyatt smiled and pretended he hadn't been counting the minutes—exactly thirty-four and twenty-five seconds. "You're a beautiful woman, Liss. I like that dress."

"Thank you."

"Why are you blushing? I can't be the first man who's noticed—"

"No," she cut in, as if she didn't want to linger on that topic, "It's just that I blush easily. I'll probably still be doing it when I'm ninety."

"Ah," he said, delighted with her, wanting to wrap his arms around her and provoke that delightful bloom across her cheeks again.

Instead, he gestured toward the cars. "Shall we go?"

"Sure. I'll drive."

"No, I will."

Liss looked at him. "Are you one of those men who won't let a woman drive him?"

"If I drive, I'll learn my way around better. You navigate."

She nodded and let him guide her toward his silver Acura Legend. "Nice car."

He smiled his response while she slid in and did up her seat belt buckle.

He climbed in behind the wheel and smiled at her again.

Liss's heart did a somersault, but she kept her voice steady. "Where to?"

"You're the tour guide—lead on."

"Mmm, okay." She directed him through her neighborhood, pleased to show off the wide, amply shaded streets and the attractive homes set far back in quiet, expansive gardens. "This is old Oakmont. Most of these houses have been here since the turn of the century, some a little longer. Mine was built in the late 1880s."

"It's in great shape for being that old."

"It's been looked after. Some of these, like that one over there," she said as she pointed out a Victorian painted a jaunty yellow, "have been restored. A lot of people like older houses."

"H'mm," he murmured, but she could tell he wasn't particularly impressed. He probably had a condo, professionally decorated, where he entertained like they did on TV. Should she tell him that the newcomers to Oakmont, particularly the highly paid people coming from the Bay Area with Intratec, were buying up those old houses as soon as they came on the market?

No doubt he'd think she was trying to influence him. They turned a corner and drove down another street of lovingly restored homes. "It's like the downtown area—carefully preserved, but not very lively."

"It's bigger, older than I thought it would be."

Liss gave him a brief history of the town, from its initial incarnation as a supply depot for the outlying ranchos when California still belonged to Spain, through the Gold Rush days, up to the present. "A lot of the houses in this area were built by the miners who made a strike and settled down—"

"Here? Why not San Francisco?"

She laughed. "They figured out that San Franciscans like to eat, too. They could make more selling produce than digging for gold. Besides, they didn't get bushwhacked for digging up vegetables."

"Makes sense."

They cruised the business section of town until she directed him to the old plaza and pointed out her business. "Do you mind if I stop at the shop for a moment?"

"Not at all." He studied the simple facade, the white enamel door and the bow window with Thayer's written discreetly in one pane. He eyed the black lettering and thought it right—like her, elegant and understated. "Can I come in or will I distract you?"

"I need to check with my assistant, but come on in. Look around."

He held the front door open for her, savoring the faint aroma of potpourri and lemon oil that wafted out into the hot air. An overhead bell jingled and announced their entrance.

She paused. "Why don't you browse while I talk to Susan?"

"Sure," he said and moved forward, drawn by an arrangement of antique dueling pistols.

Liss headed for the rear of the store and met Susan coming from the office.

Susan's eyes were drawn to Wyatt. "Hi. Didn't expect you today. He with you?"

Liss nodded. "How's everything?"

"Very quiet. I was just thinking that if we don't get someone in soon, I'll close up shop. Go home for a swim."

"Sounds fine. Give it another hour, okay?"

Susan nodded, more interested in Wyatt, who'd moved on to a display of territorial maps. "Who is he?"

Liss shushed her. "My neighbor. I'm showing him around."

Susan grinned but obediently lowered her voice. "First time I've known you to do the Welcome Wagon routine. Been saving it for someone that good-looking, huh?"

Liss made a gesture for Susan to hush. "Well, if there aren't any problems, we'll be off."

"I want the whole story, tomorrow," Susan whispered.

Wyatt looked up and moved forward to join Liss. She made introductions, ignoring the way Susan grinned mischievously.

Wyatt cocked his head back at the map. "I

like those. One would look good hanging in my office. I'll take one of the framed ones."

"Sure. Which one?" Susan stepped forward.

Liss hung back, supposedly checking her messages but in reality uncomfortable about making a sale to Wyatt. The idea of accepting money from him, even for a business transaction, rubbed her the wrong way.

When she saw him replacing his gold card and Susan handing him the wrapped frame, she rejoined them. "I hope you enjoy the map."

"Thanks. I will. A souvenir of Oakmont."

With the reminder that he was only in town for a short stay, Liss nodded briefly and walked toward the door. "Ready to continue?"

Wyatt followed and Susan called after them, "See you tomorrow."

Liss waved back without answering.

Wyatt spoke casually. "She seems nice."

"More than that. She's my best friend."

He grinned. "That's why you're in for the third degree tomorrow?"

"You weren't supposed to hear that."

"Will she want my résumé? References?"

Humor restored, Liss laughed out loud. "I think she'll settle for a detailed description of what we do today."

Wyatt's grin widened, as he thought of several things Liss would probably edit out. Still smiling, he opened the trunk and carefully stowed the map. He unlocked the car door for her, helped her in, and whistling off-key, walked around to his side of the car. Once he was settled behind the wheel, he turned and looked at her.

Instinctively, Liss braced herself. Wyatt's look held questions, ones she knew he probably had a right to ask, but if she answered those, would he move on to the ones she didn't want to answer?

She fastened her seat belt. "If you'll turn left at the next corner, you'll see more of the downtown area we've been renovating to look as it did at the turn of the century."

Wyatt made no move to start the car. "Why did you agree to come with me today?"

Liss flickered a glance at him. This wasn't too bad. She'd expected something different. "I thought if I showed you around, you'd understand a little more about Oakmont."

"And?" he prompted.

"Why does there have to be more?"

He leaned back in his seat and looked directly at her. "Because there always is."

"Not in this case," Liss retorted, wondering who she was trying to convince.

He chuckled. "You'd be the first woman in

creation not to have more than one reason for doing something."

"And men don't have ulterior motives?"

"Of course we do. Want to know mine?"

She looked at him then, truly looked at his open expression, his affable smile, and his dark blue eyes. "I don't think so," she demurred, feeling she should open the car door and run for it while she had a chance. If she stayed, she ran the risk of making a mistake she wouldn't easily forget.

"I would never have taken you for a coward, Liss," he said softly as he gently ran a fingertip down her forearm.

She drew her arm away and crossed both in front of her.

"Well, since you won't ask, why don't I just tell you that I thought about you most of the night and couldn't wait to see you again."

"Don't say that!"

"Why not? Do you want me to tell you lies?"

She thought about the lies she'd heard before. She shook her head. "I don't want you to get the wrong idea. I'm only showing you around. Nothing else."

He sighed and turned the key in the ignition. "If you say so."

"Maybe we should forget this," she suggested. "Someone from the plant could probably do this for you."

He rolled his eyes. "I'm probably going to see more of those people than any of us wants. Do your civic duty and give them a break, huh?"

Liss laughed despite her qualms. "Okay, so long as you realize I'm doing this for your employees."

Wyatt laughed with her. "They'll award you a certificate of merit for rescuing them."

Responding to his good humor and feeling slightly more at ease with him, she next led him through the growing outlying areas, through neat subdivisions where more Intratec employees lived. "Breathe deeply—you can almost smell the new paint," she said, pointing at a new elementary school. "This is probably more what you're used to—"

"God forbid!" Wyatt cut in.

Liss eyed him speculatively. "You don't have children?"

"One," he admitted. "Toby. She lives in Dallas."

"Oh." It took her a moment to visualize him as a father. Somehow little toddlers at his knee just didn't fit her image of him. Curiosity prompted her. "How old is she?"

"Twenty-five. She works for the Intratec division there."

"Ah. But when she was in grade school, wasn't she in something like that?"

"No. We lived in Boston then." He paused and gave her a sly smile. "We loved living in the city."

"You prefer to live in smog and traffic and noise?" she asked, to cover her reaction to his statement. *We* had to mean his family. She was displeased to note how her stomach had clenched as he said it. "Is your wife in Dallas with your daughter?" she asked, hoping he didn't notice how hard it was for her to ask.

How could she have gotten to this point with him and not found out if he was married! After living with David's infidelities, she was never going to put herself in the same position. Never!

"Elaine—my ex—lives in New York. With her second husband, the stockbroker."

"You all must like cities," she said, her breathing suddenly calmer.

"It's where the action is," he teased, not missing her stiffened posture. Liss was a smart, chic woman, he thought. How could she bear to bury herself out in the middle of farm country?

She wondered how he could bear to be cooped up with a zillion other people, all breathing down his neck. "Well, let's hope you survive your hardship tour in Oakmont."

He chuckled. "Lead on, show me more of the local wonders."

She did just that, taking him on a guided tour of all that Oakmont had to offer, including the new high school and the river-front park. She kept up a light patter of conversation, pointing out historical markers and points of interest, until at last they reached the industrial area where Intratec occupied a sprawling modern facility whose stark angles and walls of glittering glass overwhelmed the surrounding countryside.

She noted Wyatt's sour look. "That's definitely a showplace. Don't you like the buildings?"

"Not much. What are those trees over there?"

"In the orchard? Peach trees—they're not ripe yet." The motion of her head, as she turned to look, released her fragrance into the car.

He breathed in, taken with her, wondering what the hell was happening to him. He had no business thinking of her as anything other than his temporary next door neighbor, but here he was speculating about her private life, wondering if she'd make room in it for him. On a short term basis, of course.

"Liss, how come you're not busy with other

things today?" The words were out of his mouth before he could stop them.

She glanced at him. "I was busy—weeding my yard, if you remember."

"No, I mean with other people. I could tell you weren't too sure about letting me stay." He saw her uneasiness and persisted anyway. "How come you were alone? Surely there must be someone—a date or something? Hell, Liss, what I'm asking is, how come you're not married?"

Her quickly indrawn breath gave her away. Wyatt looked at her more closely. "Did I touch a nerve? I'm sorry."

"Don't worry about it. I'm divorced."

Wyatt's eyes widened. "You, too? I'd have thought widowed, maybe, but not divorced. Do you have children?"

Her throat closed. "No." She sensed more than saw the way he looked at her, his deep blue eyes mirroring his wariness, his not-quite-sure expression. To save him as much as herself, she half-turned, keeping her gaze carefully averted. If there was any subject that she would not discuss, this was it.

She breathed a little easier when he snorted, "He must be an idiot to let a woman like you get away."

She felt the tautness within uncoil and disappear. It didn't matter that she'd heard the

68

same words from other people and had discounted them as flattery, as an insincere compliment meant to bridge an awkward moment. Hearing those words from Wyatt made her feel better. With a wry smile, she slanted a glance at him. "Don't get me started on that subject."

He chuckled. "Well, it's my good luck. So, how come you're free on a Sunday?"

"I usually keep my Sundays for myself. Quiet time, just for me."

He stared at her. "Why?"

She fiddled with the strap of her straw bag. "During the week, I see so many people. I prefer to relax, unwind, I guess."

His voice deepened. "I'm honored then, that you'd spend it with me."

She colored faintly. He didn't have to know that for months after the divorce, she'd retreated into her house, using the protection of her home to hide from raised eyebrows and sympathetic looks. It didn't help that most people felt outraged at David's dumping her for a much younger woman.

It should have made her feel better to hear the nasty things they said about him, but instead it made her feel worse. How could she have lived with him and not seen the changes? Or known that something was going on? How could she not have recognized the signs of yet another affair?

She still felt soiled at the thought of sharing a bed with him while he had been sharing increasingly more of his life with . . . she couldn't even bear to think of his new wife's name.

Closing her eyes to blot out the image of them together, she missed Wyatt's question.

"Pardon?"

"Where to?" he repeated.

She directed him to the other side of town where the new library occupied pride of place on a small knoll. The redwood and brick building still looked raw, sitting on bare ground, but Wyatt could imagine how it would look once the newness had worn off.

"You see how the architect and the builder worked together to keep to the style of the area?"

Wyatt didn't need a guide to tell him she didn't want to talk about herself. "Yeah," he agreed, falling in with her wishes. Scanning the building nestled between large old oaks, he commented, "Looks like prime real estate. Must have cost a chunk of cash."

Liss was silent, and then said slowly, "The city was able to buy it for a dollar an acre from an interested party."

He whistled between his teeth. "Interested, or crazy? That was giving it away!"

She colored and turned from him to hide her expression. She was too late. "What did I say, Liss?"

"Nothing," she demurred, but she still wouldn't meet his eye.

"You wouldn't know the person who gave that land away, would you?" When she said nothing, he guessed. "Or did you do it? How come?"

Feeling defensive, she met his dark blue gaze. "Oakmont needed a new library. I had the land, so I made a donation. Don't make such a big deal out of it. Besides, it helped my taxes."

"I'm impressed. I had no idea you were so involved in local doings."

"I'm not, really. It's just that I happened to have that piece of property and saw a need for it." She played down her role, saying nothing of how she'd mounted the campaign to get the funding for Oakmont to be able to build.

Nor did she tell him that she'd donated the major part of the hefty settlement she'd gotten from David to the fund. That she'd used the money to make herself feel better about the single most traumatic event in her life was nobody's business but her own.

If she thought privately that she'd used the money to buy herself some peace, then that was her affair. No one else needed to know that she considered the new library was hers, deep down, privately hers, and if she got pleasure from seeing it grow and develop, so what. She'd never tell anyone how proprietary she felt about the library, how she felt a piece of herself in every brick and length of redwood. It was enough that *she* knew.

Shrugging, she said, "It's only business."

Wyatt said nothing, but studied her more carefully. Despite her throw-away manner, he could tell that this building and everything it symbolized was very meaningful to her. It seemed as if the library meant more to her than a building and books.

Her cool, blonde looks and porcelain complexion had initially drawn him, he had to admit. He was a sucker for the type, no two ways about it, but now he began to wish he had a lot more free time to spend with her. He wanted to get to know her better. He certainly wished she'd tell him more about herself. He didn't want to know details about the ex-husband, but how could any man turn his back on a woman like this?

When she moved restlessly under his gaze, he turned back to the library building. "Who's the architect?"

She named the firm. "A local firm. A couple of young guys who moved here from Los Angeles, but aren't big city at all."

He snorted. "I'm surprised you let them set up shop."

She threw him a startled look, then burst out laughing. "If they'd wanted to put up a high-rise, then we'd have run them out of town on a rail."

He chuckled, impressed with her quick riposte. "And the builder? Also someone local?"

"Of course."

"You ever have anything to do with someone who's not local, Liss?"

Five

She'd been expecting a discreet innuendo, but nothing this blatant.

She flashed him a warning look.

His small smile held curiosity, and something else which made her cheeks feel warm. She swallowed, uneasy again with the turn in the conversation, and edged closer to the door. She gestured at the library. "They did a good job, didn't they?"

He seemed to accept the change of subject. As he looked back at the building, Liss followed his gaze. The brick and warm wood, punctuated by shaded windows, looked inviting and comfortable.

"Yes. It looks like it belongs."

"Solid, unpretentious, but you should see it inside."

"I'd like that. Maybe you could show me around one day?"

Reassured that he hadn't pursued his not-so-subtle questioning, Liss made a quick decision and dug in her purse for the keys. "Why not now?"

"How come you have the keys?"

"I've been coming and going so often, it just made sense. Want to go in?"

In answer, he pulled into the recently paved parking lot.

She unlocked the door, turned off the security alarm, and motioned him in. "As you can see, it's a mess yet, but isn't it marvelous?" Her voice echoed through the empty building where the air seemed to hover, waiting for people to bring it to life.

He stood in the tiled foyer, glancing around at the empty walls, at the skylight above. "Wasted space?"

"Not at all. This is the gallery. There'll be local artists' work displayed here, but for the opening I'm putting together a visual history of the town. A retrospective—how we got here from there. It will tie into the Collection."

"The famous Collection?"

"You'll see," she promised.

"He was impressed by her air of competence. "When will all this be open to the public?"

"Two weeks from today. It's going to be quite an opening. We've invited a lot of state officials, even the governor. The high sch-

band is rehearsing like crazy. It will be a big day for Oakmont."

He heard the excitement in her voice and noted how her eyes brightened with anticipation. With the delicate color in her cheeks, she looked like a young girl waiting for the prom. Idly, he wondered at her age. She had to be forty or so, yet he saw in her glimpses of a charming young girl.

Why hadn't her husband given her children to care for, to pass on the joy she so obviously felt? He suddenly regretted that they hadn't met years ago. What would it have been like to see her bloom with maturity? To have been a part of her life?

He lagged behind as she led the way into a large empty room. "This will be a meeting room for local groups. And over here," she gestured into an adjoining area, "is a reading room. There'll be the latest periodicals, magazines, tables, and comfortable seating."

"What else?" he asked politely, his mind still on her.

She sensed his distraction as she walked him through the empty stacks. She became increasingly conscious of being alone with him in the vacant building. The feeling was stronger here than in the car, making her ☐ : as tiny currents sparked along ☐ ndings.

She was too aware of him, of his size and his masculinity, making her in turn feel somehow small, very womanly and vulnerable. She chided herself. A divorced woman her age shouldn't be feeling these things, shouldn't be so aware of the sound of his breathing.

For a moment or two, she tried to remember what it had been like years ago, with David, but somehow it hadn't been quite like this.

She couldn't recall feeling this ill at ease, almost breathless, on the verge of something extraordinary. She couldn't remember being overly sensitive to the warmth of David's body when he stood too close to her. Whatever she felt now, she recognized Wyatt as the source.

Unnerved by his proximity, she inched away until she stood several feet away. At his look of curiosity, she threaded the way through carton after carton of books and other materials until she came to another locked door. Opening it, she let him into an outdoor amphitheater set into the curve of hill. She inhaled, taking in a deep, calming breath of the hot afternoon breeze. Her senses rearranged themselves into a nearly normal alignment.

She gestured at the stage. "For our local theater group, or anyone else who wants to use it."

"You're getting your money's worth. Is there more?"

"Come and see."

Indoors again, she showed him the children's reading room, where everything was in miniature, including rocking chairs and several sofas. She then led the way into a corner room.

Wyatt glanced out one window toward a long vista over fields sprouting something green he didn't recognize. Turning back to face her, he took in the big display cases, the shelves, the big table and chairs in the middle of the room, the comfortable old leather armchairs by the windows.

He knew without her telling him that this room was special to her. "And this is?"

She paused before answering, visualizing how the exhibits would look. She tensed, anticipating his reaction. "The Oakmont Collection will be in here."

"Well, tell me about it. How'd you get involved?"

"It just happened," she replied, wondering how much she could tell him. "After the . . . divorce, I needed something to keep me busy."

"I would have thought your antique shop would have kept you busy enough."

"I didn't have it then. I opened it afterward."

"Is that how you measure your life these days, Liss? As before and after your divorce?"

She sucked in air, astounded that he'd ask her such a question.

He heard her and she saw his eyebrow go up, in the gesture she was beginning to know. Steering the conversation back to safer waters, she said, "I started putting in some hours at the library. They didn't need any more volunteers, not for the time I was willing to put in, so I looked around for something else to do.

"I had all these antiques at home, crowding me out, so the idea just grew." She relaxed now, feeling at home, in her space. In control. "I looked around, found the right location, and went on from there."

"Where did you get all those things?"

She looked around with satisfaction, and a trace of sadness. "My family used to be a big one, lots of branches, most living locally. They were ranchers, farmers, in real estate, trade. Some traveled the world over and brought back curios and reminders of their travels. Over the years they made a lot of money, and lost most of it."

She picked up an ornately carved tea caddy and put it back carefully. "No matter how much money they lost, they never got rid of their possessions. You should see what pack rats some of them were! After all, how many butler tables can one person use?"

"Beats me. What if you don't have a butler?"

She laughed. "That was just an example. I was glad to get rid of some of it."

"How did you wind up with it and not somebody else?"

"Attrition." Glancing at him, she saw his interest and continued, "By the time I was born, the family was down to just my parents and one maiden aunt. I'm the only one left, so I inherited most of what was left of their property. I sold most of the real estate to pay their back taxes, but I kept the furnishings.

"The best of that went into the antique store, some of it I gave away to Goodwill and such, but I didn't know what to do with the documents—family Bibles, letters, ledgers, that sort of thing. Even scraps of wallpaper. I couldn't throw it away—it seemed like I would be tossing out my past."

She slanted another glance at him and then turned quickly away from the speculative look on his face. "So many other things in my life were changing at about that time. I couldn't bear to lose anything else."

He nodded. "That's understandable. It couldn't have been easy for you."

She studied her hands. "No. Anyway," she said on a brisker note, "I displayed some of it in the shop, but there was too much of it. I wanted to keep it all together, so I talked the librarian into giving me some space."

When she paused, Wyatt asked, "What happened then?"

"It was amazing! News of the display got around. Some people from the university in Sacramento came by and studied the papers, used some of them for their research work. Students did a thesis or two, and gradually the Collection became well-known. I have people coming in from all over California now, and even from other states. It takes a lot of maintenance."

"And you do all that?"

"Not all. The library staff does a lot of it, but any day now it will outgrow us." At his raised eyebrows, she went on. "It keeps growing, you see, as people donate more material. We've needed special display cases to keep the temperature and humidity at the right levels to preserve the documents."

She added, her voice filled with enthusiasm, "You wouldn't believe what I've had to learn to be able to take care of things! In the beginning, I thought all I had to do was keep the papers out of people's reach, but there's so much more. I've had to learn about authentication, provenance, restoration . . . so much! It's helped me with the shop, too."

"You've become an expert."

She heard the admiration in his voice and once again felt uneasy under his scrutiny. "I'm getting carried away again. Sorry."

"Hey, if you don't toot your own horn, who will?"

"Most Thayers don't toot," she said with a grin. "They lead the whole brass band."

"If that's so, how come you call it the Oakmont Collection and not Thayer?"

Her grin turned self-conscious. "I must be the exception. Anyway, it's not just my family's history, but the way the town grew up with them. And other families have donated things as well."

"Don't you get a lot of junk?"

She laughed. "Do I ever! Anything that no one wants to throw out, they give me. Atrocities old Aunt Gertie had up in the attic . . . I've had to be pretty ruthless in sorting out the good stuff, otherwise the Collection wouldn't be as historically interesting as it is."

"You've done a great job. I look forward to seeing it when it's all back together."

Through the quick rush of pleasure his words gave her, she wondered how he could do that if he intended leaving Oakmont in a week. Still, it was enough that he'd said it. "Thanks. This is important to me."

He reached out for her hand. "You've put a lot of yourself into this, haven't you?"

She nodded, a little shy under his approbation, yet pleased that he saw the room through her eyes. She let him keep her hand. "It's my baby. I live and breathe Oakmont history."

"How come?"

"I told you," she waved her free hand. "I grew up with family history all around me. My ancestors were responsible for a lot of the growth in this area."

"And now there's just you?"

"Just me. The last of the Thayers."

He heard the change in her voice. "Does it bother you?"

"Sometimes," she answered quietly. "I see other families, still going strong. I miss having that, but there are compensations."

"Like what?"

"My shop. The Collection. Good friends, my house."

Any other woman by now would have whipped out stories of her children's accomplishments. Instead, she'd shrugged and turned away from him, concealing her face. The movement of her shoulders drew his attention. He looked at the delicate curve where slender neck met shoulder and longed to trail his fingers over her skin. "Aren't you lonely?"

She sucked in a surprised breath. Looking at him in disbelief, expecting a sexual innuendo, she saw instead interest and growing amusement as he read her reaction. She shook her head and pulled back her hand.

His fingers tightened around hers to stop her retreat. "You've lived alone since the divorce?" he asked, his expression changing as a slow, seductive smile took over his mouth. His thumb caressed the soft flesh between her thumb and index finger. "Is there anyone special?"

Blue eyes widening, she could only stare. Again, she felt his closeness, his maleness, and felt a sudden frisson of fear. He seemed to take up much more than his share of the oxygen. She breathed quickly and shallowly as she looked up at him. No matter how attractive, how attentive, he was still very much a stranger.

Her earlier nervous feeling returned with a rush. She didn't want this, didn't want to be reminded of what she had lost . . .

"Did I go too fast, Liss?" he asked softly, moving his hand from hers to stroke the silken skin of her arm from wrist to elbow.

Feeling her muscles tighten, he smiled and clasped her upper arm, bringing her close to him.

She resisted.

He persisted a little until her breasts were only a deep breath away. "Don't be frightened of me. There's nothing to be scared of."

"I'm not scared of you," she whispered tremulously, telling the truth. She realized she wasn't scared of him, but of the feelings he provoked in her—of that quivery sensation in the pit of her stomach. Of that insane, impulsive yearning to cast aside her inhibitions and explore her feelings as though she were young, and not a discarded wife.

For a moment she was tempted. Why not? Why shouldn't I? And then all the reasons came flooding back.

She was Liss Thayer, fifty-one years old, on her way to becoming an independent person for the first time in her life. A quick fling with a stranger just passing through wasn't her style. She steeled her voice and repeated, "I'm not afraid."

"I'm glad. I don't want to scare you. I want to get to know you better—much better."

His meaning was unmistakably clear. She saw him as a man used to being in charge, getting what he wanted. She caught another quick glimpse of the hidden man, of the power he was used to exercising. Liss swallowed and belatedly recalled that she was also used to using her authority.

She looked squarely at him. "You *are* going too fast. In fact, you're out of line."

He said nothing, merely looked back at her, watching the emotions flit across her expressive features. Apprehension, self-consciousness, misgivings, longing and shyness came and went, until the remaining emotion on her face was doubt.

"I won't do anything rash," he promised, "but tell me—are you involved with anyone?"

"Involved?" she repeated, running her tongue over suddenly parched lips.

He eyed the movement of her tongue, unconsciously mimicking her, wanting to lick her lips himself. He nodded. "In a relationship? Something I should know about?"

"No-o," she admitted in little more than a whisper. Those annoying and regular proposals from Howard Upjohn didn't count.

He smiled, satisfied. "Good."

She regarded him intently, wordlessly demanding an explanation. "I'm not involved, either," he said, giving her a partial answer.

After all this time, after she thought she'd become immune to the demands of her body, to find out that she was just as vulnerable as she had been years ago left her feeling shaky.

Remembering at last that she couldn't condone affairs, she took back her hand and addressed him with a brisk change of tone. "The tour is over."

Six

"Not so fast!" Wyatt exclaimed. "You still haven't convinced me that Oakmont is the center of the universe."

She looked at him coldly for a moment, searching for just the right words to refuse him.

He pre-empted her. "We somehow got off the track, right?"

"Yes."

"I'm sorry, Liss. I should have realized I was making you uncomfortable."

Liss hesitated. She didn't know what magic he used to get around her like this, but it certainly worked. She should insist they stop right now before either of them got any ideas—any more ideas, she corrected herself.

After all, it wasn't as though she hadn't taken part willingly in the exchange, even though Wyatt was gentlemanly enough to assume responsibility.

She fished in her purse for a tissue and slowly polished her glasses. With them off, Wyatt blurred into an indistinct form. It was as though the easing of the distinct, hard lines of his physique also relaxed her uneasiness.

"I have to admit I'm feeling a little pressured," she began, unsure about talking with him like this. "I don't have much experience with this . . . sort of thing."

"Can you forget I said it? I feel like a jerk."

Impressed and awed by the executive as she'd been before, she liked this side of him. Who could have guessed that under the arrogance lay a man who could apologize—and actually sound as if he meant it. Liss checked herself.

It wasn't fair to Wyatt, no matter if she was upset with him, to take out her bitterness on him. He had nothing to do with the breakup of her marriage, or the fact that David had never learned to say "I'm sorry."

Watching Wyatt, she realized he wasn't anything like David. Not in looks, personality or style. There was so much more to him. Even though she was leery of him, she was also intrigued by his flashes of humor and the way he could create a lighthearted mood so easily.

It surprised her to realize how much she wanted to get to know him better.

Hoping she wasn't making a big mistake, she murmured, "Very well. The tour will continue."

He spoke simply. "Thanks, Liss."

He was pleased with her blush, realizing that under her teasing, she was nervous and was as aware of him as he was of her. His gaze skimmed over the raspberry sundress. The knit fabric clung to her breasts and waist before it swirled away around her hips. Her figure was gently rounded. She no longer had the slenderness of youth, but had something much more appealing and feminine.

She had the womanliness that comes with maturity, an unaware and unselfconscious familiarity with her body. That she didn't use it to taunt and provoke only made her more female and alluring. Mud-streaked and scantily clad this morning, she'd evoked instant, aching need. This afternoon, flirty and charmingly seductive, she made him think of long and leisurely lovemaking.

Liss pointed out a few more interesting features while Wyatt followed, nodding his head when necessary, deeply involved in making love to her in his fantasy.

When they left the library, Wyatt drove through town, passing the new shopping malls which looked as though they could have been transplanted from any other suburban setting.

She flashed a mischievous glance at him. "Want to cruise the mall? That's a big week-end thing—"

"Bite your tongue," he commanded.

She laughed.

The sound was giddy and youthful. Charmed, he burst into laughter of his own.

Wyatt pulled in at a Dairy Queen. Liss stood in line with him and asked for a root beer float while he ordered coffee. Taking their drinks outside, they sat in the shade of a plastic umbrella.

"You know what you've done, don't you?"

"What?" asked Wyatt, watching her swirl ice cream from the edge of her mouth with the tip of her tongue. His tongue mimicked the motion. He could almost taste the cool cream against the heat of her lips.

"You've participated in the most traditional of small-town Sunday afternoon occupations. Do you know what that is?" She hesitated, deliberately drawing out the moment. This was so unusual for her, this light flirtatious manner, that she felt giddy and playful.

When she felt she'd prolonged the suspense as long as she could, she whispered, "You've gone for a drive—and wound up at the Dairy Queen."

Wyatt looked startled, then grinned. "Yeah, but it's okay because I didn't enjoy it."

Her face fell. "You didn't?"

"Don't be silly, I'm teasing you." He reached over, took a sip of her float, and made a face. "How can you drink that?"

"Easy. Like this." She polished off the rest of the drink.

Watching her throat muscles move as she swallowed, Wyatt could almost feel the way her skin would taste when he put his mouth on the small hollow where her pulse beat.

He shifted uncomfortably. "*Now* what do good Oakmonters do?"

She consulted her watch. "They go home, have supper, and—"

"I like the 'and' part—but supper?"

"What do you call the evening meal? What you eat before you watch the Sunday Night Movie on television?"

"Dinner, and it's much too early for it. And I don't watch much TV."

"No?"

"No," he said firmly, wishing he could tell her what he really wanted, but it was much too soon for that. Particularly since he didn't know how she'd react to his suggestion. Was she still emotionally attached to her ex? Or could she be lonely enough to welcome an affair? If she was still hurting after the divorce, would she want to get back at her ex-husband any way she could?

The thought rankled.

Yet he didn't think he'd have to worry about that. For all her lighthearted behavior this afternoon, he knew in his gut that Liss was not a frivolous or vindictive woman. Under the laughter, he could feel her pain and he hurt with her.

It bothered him to feel this way, yet he couldn't help wanting to do something for her. Would she let him help her through it? And was he up to it?

"What do you do?" she asked, interrupting his thoughts.

He didn't answer directly, but she could guess what he'd been thinking. He missed someone, some woman with whom he'd share a late dinner, some sophisticated entertainment, perhaps at a jazz club, and then more intimate pleasures.

The thought annoyed her, and hooking the strap of her bag over her shoulder, she rose.

"What's the matter?"

"It's late. I'd better be getting home."

Wyatt's eyes narrowed, but he gathered up his keys and followed her to the car.

He drove silently back to her pleasant street

and parked in her driveway, then got out and opened the door for her. "Thank you, Liss. I truly enjoyed the tour."

She got out of the car, shoulders back, making sure no part of her body accidentally touched him. "You're welcome," she said stiffly. She didn't want to end their time together, but how could she keep him with her when he was obviously thinking of better things to do?

"I have a much better overview of Oakmont now."

"Good." She inclined her head slightly.

Wyatt thought furiously. He couldn't let the afternoon end like this. It was early evening already; the thought of another long night by himself was abhorrent.

He wanted more time with her. "I'm sorry if I said anything to offend you, Liss. I was just teasing—Oakmont must be a great place to live."

Liss gave him the briefest of looks, the only indication that she'd heard him.

He stretched his shoulders.

The motion caught her attention. She looked, riveted by the flex and play of muscle. Her mouth suddenly dry, she kept her face composed with an effort. "You didn't offend me," she said at last

His relief was quickly wiped from his face,

but not fast enough. Liss saw it and felt both better and worse.

"Well, good," he said. "I guess I'd better go . . ."

The words were out of her mouth before she knew she was going to say them. "Would you like to stay for supper—dinner? There's plenty." She stopped abruptly, as though she could pull the words back.

Wyatt paused, eager to spend more time with her, yet wondering about the wisdom of it. "Are you sure?" he asked, knowing his question meant much more than she realized.

"Yes." Strangely, the stiffness between them had disappeared once he seemed to acknowledge her reluctance to spend more time with him. "Come on in."

"Thanks." He followed her up an old brick pathway to the wide verandah. Waiting while she unlocked the door, Wyatt examined the white wicker furniture, the potted plants, the baskets trailing greenery. If he'd had to choose an architectural style, there was no doubt in his mind that he'd have selected something in redwood and glass, yet her home appealed to him. It was gracious and yet reserved.

He followed her into the wide entryway, walking over glossy parquet, glancing into an old-fashioned parlor furnished with antiques.

He lingered for a moment, studying the luxuriously ornate furnishings. "You live in a museum, Liss?"

She smiled at his surprise. "I never thought about it quite like that. My family's lived here for over a hundred years."

He was silent, absorbing the fact that families actually stayed in one place that long. Finally, he murmured, "I guess I didn't realize what that meant."

She sent him a questioning glance.

"You really get into this old stuff, don't you?"

"I grew up with it," she answered simply.

He made a gesture that took in the whole room. "This all stems from your family—the people you talked about earlier?"

"Exactly." She was pleased that he'd remembered, that he had really been listening to her. "Old Arthur—that's his portrait over the mantel—brought a lot of it when he settled here."

Wyatt studied the portrait; the fierce mutton chop whiskers, the grim unsmiling pose. "Arthur looks like he was a sourpuss."

Liss laughed.

Wyatt was reminded of the clear temple bells he'd heard the last time he was in Singapore. He wanted to hear the sound again and again. "It's a good thing you don't take after old Arthur."

"No, I look like Louisa Alice, his wife."

"Who?"

"I know, it's a dreadful name, but she was a Southern belle whose family lost everything and gradually made their way out West."

"She must have left a trail of broken hearts behind her."

"You seem to have a trace of Southern gallantry, yourself, sir." She pronounced it "suh," making him smile.

"No," he said, turning the conversation away from himself. "Tell me more about your family."

She tossed him a questioning look. "You really want to know?"

"Sure."

"Well, come with me while I start dinner."

"Anywhere," he murmured, but she was already walking away from him. He followed, fascinated by the swing of the sundress below her hips. He made himself look away, glancing into two more large rooms, one a formal dining room overcrowded with mismatched heavy oak and masses of crystal, and the other bare. The floor was rough in one area, partially sanded in others.

"Hey, you know you've got an empty room here?"

She stared at him, her eyes big and round. "Really?"

He grinned, amused by their banter.

"I'm redoing the floor. Dav . . . my ex-husband used it for an office, but originally it was the morning room."

Deliberately, he ignored the reference to the man who had shared this house with her. He didn't want to lose the mood. "The what?"

"The room the women used in the mornings, for letters, sewing, whatever they did. See, it faces east to catch the sun."

His amazement showed on his face. "A special room according to the time of day?"

"Sure. Afternoons, they sat in the parlor where it was cooler. The ladies accepted callers and had tea and probably gossiped about everyone they knew. In the evening, the family used it for after dinner polite conversation. If the gentlemen wanted to smoke, they had to use the verandah."

"Nasty habit. What are those white things on the backs of the chairs?"

She gestured at his head. "Antimacassars. Back then, men used oil on their hair. It left a terrible stain. I've often wondered why their wives didn't insist they stop using that stuff."

He rubbed hand over his glistening silver hair. "Good thing I don't use it."

Her gaze lingered on his hair, then she lowered her eyes and looked at him severely. "You still might not get to sit in my parlor."

He looked sufficiently threatened, yet the light dancing in his eyes gave him away. "Even if I promise to behave myself and talk politely?"

She sobered. "I think you usually get what you want without that."

"What does that mean?" His amusement faded as he caught her pensive expression. The silly, light-hearted mood they'd shared seemed to have disappeared.

"Well, you've obviously learned to use all sorts of skills to get where you are."

"Which is where?"

"Come on, Wyatt. No one gets to your position without knowing how to negotiate, give something here in order to get something else there."

"Are you accusing me of being underhanded?"

Her gaze examined his dark blue eyes, the creases around them proclaiming his ability to laugh, the integrity in them shining forth without a flicker of doubt. "No," she answered honestly. "But if you weren't good at your job, why would you be here in Oakmont? You and not somebody else?"

He studied her in turn before answering.

"Okay. I can buy that. Just so you know, I keep my hands clean."

She reacted more to his posture than to his words. "I apologize if I offended you."

"Maybe I was too thin-skinned." He smiled slightly, in deprecation.

Liss thought they were being too susceptible to one another. She knew she was definitely extra sensitive where he was concerned. Even as she recognized that, she felt other emotions; awareness of him as a man, and a wariness almost developed enough to be apprehension. She felt his intense magnetism, and feared the pull of his masculinity.

She smiled faintly, not sure how to back away from this turn in the conversation to the safer ground they'd stood on earlier. "Let's forget it, shall we?"

"Okay," he agreed promptly. "Will you show me the rest of your house?"

She nodded and spoke as though there had been no interruption in mood. "Gentlemen callers were restricted to the verandah, the dining room, and the parlor. Unmarried women were never left alone with them."

"How could they . . . ah, do any courting if they couldn't get away from everybody?"

"They must have managed," she said dryly. "In spite of families being a lot bigger back then."

"Yeah," he grinned. "Not much privacy, though. Tell me, Liss . . . where do you do your courting?"

She laughed at his unabashed interest. "Not in the parlor, that's for sure. I spend most of my time in here," she said, motioning him into a large kitchen and family room area which was totally modern, totally white, with only splashes of color to soften the severity.

"Somehow I can't see Arthur and Louisa Alice in here."

"Neither can I. I barely remember it, but the old kitchen was dingy. Very dark and utilitarian. My mother had walls taken down, combining several smaller rooms, and I did the rest after I married."

"And you stayed on in the house?"

"Of course," she said simply. "This is my home. I've never lived anywhere else." She didn't mention that she was busy erasing all traces of David as fast as possible. Soon, she'd have the house back to the way it was before David, and she'd never again have to sense his presence lingering like a stale odor in the rooms they'd shared.

"This is very nice, Liss." He looked around, seeing another side to her personality in the bright functional room, the nook she'd set up as an office. He stepped closer to her desk and looked out over her back lawn, glimpsing her view of the Greenley house next door. He looked back at her. "Close enough for us to keep track of each other."

This was not a subject she thought it wise to pursue. "Would you like some wine before dinner?"

"If you're having some."

Relieved to have his attention away from the window, she set two crystal glasses on the counter and poured. "So, Wyatt, how come you're at the Greenley's, instead of a hotel?"

"My secretary couldn't find me a decent hotel. I can't stand motels—all the traffic outside my door. She knows my habits, so she asked around. Someone at work recommended the place next door. Angie set it up for me." He gave her a slow grin. "I'm glad she did."

Liss ignored the grin and the effect it had on her while she bit back the question she really wanted to ask—*how* did his secretary know about his sleeping habits? "Oakmont has a very fine hotel downtown," she said stiffly.

"I'm very happy with the arrangements Angie made."

She frowned, visualizing a slinky brunette. "She's your secretary?"

"Angie's a grandmother three times over," Wyatt grinned.

Liss looked away.

Wyatt chuckled.

She looked back, daring him to say anything. "More wine?"

They sipped, looking at each other, until finally Liss broke eye contact and began busying herself in the kitchen. She prepared dinner simply and quickly.

Wyatt rested a hip on a stool. "You cook like this for yourself all the time?"

Liss kept her gaze averted from the pull of fabric across his thigh. "Not all the time. It's nice to have someone to cook for."

The word "again" lingered in the air between them.

Wyatt knew it wasn't the time to ask for more details, but he couldn't help his next question. "You don't mind being all alone here? It's an awfully big house for one person."

She paused. "Yes, it is."

"You don't mind living here by yourself?" he persisted.

"I'd rather not go into that. Another time, perhaps."

Pleased that she'd indicated that they'd see more of each other without his prompting, Wyatt said easily, "Sure. Didn't mean to pry."

"No problem," she said, and meant it, surprised that the evening was turning out so well. After their earlier tension and near-argument, who would have guessed that she'd ask him to dinner, and enjoy every minute of it? She couldn't remember the last time she'd done something impulsively.

"So who owns the big house next door?"

"Leona Greenley, my ex-mother-in-law."

Wyatt's eyebrow shot up. "Isn't that a little too cozy?"

"I don't see much of her," Liss replied flatly. "Have you met her yet?"

"No. Angie fixed everything up. I suppose I should introduce myself."

"Better do it fast—she's going to Europe on Wednesday."

Wyatt raised an eyebrow, deliberately this time. "I'd better see how much I'm paying for those guest quarters. You suppose she's using my fees to finance her trip?"

Liss chuckled. "Whatever you're paying her would last Leona about a day or two. Her family is old money—her great grandpa was luckier than mine."

"Could have fooled me—why does she rent out that little house, then?"

"It's called the carriage house. It once held the carriages for the family. The story is that Leona's grandfather used it as an art studio in his wild and crazy days."

"What's so wild about an artist?"

104

"Nothing, if he'd been painting landscapes. Supposedly he had a number of models who posed for him. Wild parties, that sort of thing. Leona's grandmother burned all the paintings and wouldn't let him touch a paint brush again."

Wyatt's lips twitched. "Or a model either, I'll bet."

"Leona would be upset if she heard you laughing about Grandpapa."

"Guess it's a good thing she's going to be somewhere else, huh?" Nonchalantly, he scratched his jaw. "How long will she be gone?"

"Oh, however long she wants," Liss answered breezily.

Wyatt's eyes lit up.

Heartlessly, she added, "But my neighbors across the street keep a close watch on the neighborhood. Nothing much happens in a town like this without everybody knowing about it. Right now, my neighbors probably have an eye on the house, wondering what's going on in here."

"Want to give them something worthwhile to talk about?"

Despite herself, she laughed. "Don't you ever give up?"

"Where would a guy be if he gave up too soon?" He frowned, then grinned.

Liss thought he'd considered an alternate approach, but he surprised her by changing the subject. "Liss. That's an unusual name. Where did you get it?"

"From David. When he was little, he couldn't stay Alice, just Liss."

"Alice?"

"Alice Louisa, that's me."

His laugh boomed through the kitchen.

She threw a pot holder at him.

He picked it up and returned it to her with a small bow. When she reached for it, he took her hand, turned it over, and placed a gentle kiss on her palm.

His mouth is so soft, Liss thought. So warm. So tender. Images of his mouth on hers, and on other parts of her body, tantalized. For a moment, she let herself dream. She might be an old divorced lady, but she was still alive. Still susceptible to handsome men paying outrageous attention to her.

Reluctantly, she withdrew her hand. "What was that for?"

"Compliments for the chef, Alice Louisa."

She frowned, her eyes teasing. "You call me that again, and you'll go hungry." She gathered up utensils to set a table on the back verandah.

Wyatt followed her back and forth, getting

in her way, until finally she handed him the plates and shooed him out of the kitchen.

When the meal was ready, he carried out the salad bowl. He snitched a slice of tomato on the way. "This tomato is delicious, Liss. Where do you buy them?"

"At a little produce stand outside town."

"Oh. That's a little out of my way. Too bad."

"It might be worth your while."

He doubted it. He wouldn't be here long enough to make shopping for tomatoes a priority. Aware that she was waiting for a response, he offered, "Thanks for saving me from another restaurant."

She slipped her apron off. "Do you eat out a lot?"

"Too much, since I'm not a great cook and I'm rarely home."

Before she could stop them, the words blurted out. "Too busy shutting down plants?"

He looked down at his plate. She saw his knuckles whiten around the stem of his wine glass.

Chagrined, she said quickly, "I'm sorry. That was uncalled for."

He was silent.

Uncomfortable with the tension between them, she added, "I shouldn't have said anything."

"Believe me, Liss," he said at last, his voice heavy, "I'd like to talk to you about it, but I can't."

She turned her attention to her now tasteless dinner. "It's none of my business, I know that." She set her fork down and stared at her plate. "I just can't help feeling sorry for the people who are going to lose their jobs."

"I wish I could assure you that everything will be all right. Damnit, I don't even know what the situation is yet."

She raised startled eyes to his. Was that frustration she heard in his voice? "I thought it was all decided. All over bar the shouting."

"I won't lie to you. A lot of work has already gone into this—cost analyses, manufacturing results. I wouldn't be here if there weren't a job for me to do."

"And you're good at your job, aren't you, Wyatt?" she asked hesitantly.

He didn't mince words. "Damn good."

"Somehow, I already knew that." She sighed. She'd known it all along. Even though he'd said he was a vice president, it took someone expert to do what she feared he'd come to Oakmont to do. How did he come by the skills he'd need for such a project?

She didn't like the idea that he was a hatchet man. Had he closed down other plants? Hesitantly, she asked, "I know I have no right to do this, but will you promise me something?"

He held her gaze. "If I can."

She moistened her lips nervously before she spoke. "Will you consider all the possibilities before you make your decision?"

He answered simply and honestly, "Yes."

"Thank you, Wyatt."

He touched her hand. "Will you do something for me in return?"

She felt the intensity of his question as though it flowed from his hand to hers. She looked at his long, tapering fingers, then up into his eyes. Her voice was quiet. "What is it?"

"Will you put this whole thing about my work to one side and just let us enjoy each other's company?"

Her gaze dropped again to their hands, one on top of the other. His, darker skinned, a few dark hairs dusting the knuckles; hers, pale and delicate in comparison. She studied the differences, seeing more than mere physical details. His hand spoke of contained strength, of purpose, of hard work, while hers looked small and ineffectual.

Appearances, though, were deceptive. She knew how hard she'd worked those hands, and she'd seen his tenderness. How could their two hands, barely touching, raise her awareness of him to such a degree?

When she lifted her eyes to his, Wyatt saw her bewilderment. He spoke gently. "Shouldn't I have asked that?"

"You're confusing the issue. I'm not part of your job here."

He curled his fingers around hers. "Not part of my work at Intratec, no. But I think you make a difference, just being here."

She withdrew her hand. The warmth of his fingers lingered on her palm. She placed her other hand over it to prolong the glow.

"I'll still be here after you've finished your work."

There was a pause as Wyatt took another bite of his food. He looked out at the gazebo, gleaming whitely in the deepening dusk, and asked, "You've always lived in Oakmont?"

"Are you changing the subject?"

"Indirectly, maybe. I'd like to know how you have such deep feelings about the town."

"Wasn't that obvious from this afternoon?"

"Humor me, Liss. Talk to me about Oakmont. I don't know much about small towns. I need to understand how things work."

"Will it make a difference in the way you make a decision?"

He heard the hope in her voice and

couldn't bear to disappoint her. "You never can tell."

"If it will help . . ."

"I know I can trust you to give me a fair picture."

"Oh? How can you be sure? I might be tempted to sway you any way I can."

He picked up on that immediately, and grinned at her wickedly.

Uncomfortable with his brazen perusal, Liss stumbled over her words. "I didn't mean that the way it sounded . . . I mean, not the way you think I did."

Still grinning, he repeated, "You've always lived here?"

Grateful to him for letting her off the hook, she answered quickly, "Yes. Except when I was away at college, of course."

"You didn't want to live someplace else?"

She shook her head. "I've thought about it . . . but this is my home. I'm happier here than anywhere else."

"So you came home and married the boy next door?"

"Something like that."

"And lived here, in your family home. Didn't he want to live somewhere else?"

She hesitated, remembering the arguments, the decision to stay with her ailing mother. "It worked out better this way."

He noted her colorless voice. "And now it's just you alone here. How do you manage?"

Wyatt was touched by her faint, sad smile. When she spoke, however, her voice carried no melancholy. "I like living here. My family's always been big on traditions, even if it's hard to carry them on all by myself."

He was struck by the disparity of their situations. "Our lives are so different," he commented. "I'm on the go a lot. Living out of suitcases."

"That must be hard on you. Have you always done it?"

"For the most part. My job keeps me traveling . . . troubleshooting, that sort of thing," he added before she could ask. "It seems I no sooner get home than I get a call from some other plant and I'm off again."

"It must have been hard on your family."

"Yeah. On Elaine especially."

"Oh? I'd have thought it would be harder on your little girl. What's her name—Toby?"

"Yeah, Toby. Only she's not so little any more. She does her own traveling, now."

"Like father, like daughter? Does she like it?"

Wyatt nodded. "She seems to."

"Maybe it would be different if she were married," Liss suggested. "She's not, is she?"

"No. I sometimes think she's too much like me."

"Why? I don't understand."

He shrugged that off. "Not much good at staying in one place long enough. It's what happened with me and her mother. Elaine finally decided she wanted a husband she could count on to be home for dinner. And to help with Toby."

"That's sad," Liss murmured. She didn't understand how families could splinter and fall apart. Even though it had finally happened to her, she'd fought the battle for years. On one hand, she'd denied anything was wrong, even when her relationship with David had deteriorated to the point where they hardly spoke.

Despite the fact that he virtually ignored her, she'd continued to cook a good dinner, set it out attractively, and then eat it alone when he failed to come home. Again. She'd tried everything she knew to keep her marriage going.

"You must have married very early if you have a daughter in her twenties."

"Elaine and I met in college, and married the summer between our sophomore and junior years."

"Gracious. So young! That must have been hard. Financially, at least."

"Not so bad. I had a scholarship, so as long as I kept my grade point average up, we were okay. Elaine's parents continued to pay her expenses. We managed."

"Oh," Liss murmured, unable to contrast their experience with her own.

"We were lucky," he added. "But in the long run, it didn't make much difference."

"No . . ." she agreed. "Sometimes, no matter how hard you try . . ."

"Don't worry about it."

She sipped her wine, wondering at how he seemed to be able to read her mind. Was he talking about himself or her? Either way, both situations saddened her. "You must be a very lonely man."

He shook his head. "I haven't got time to be lonely."

"Time has nothing to do with it," she answered in a fragile voice.

He had nothing to say to that. "It's getting late. Thanks for dinner. I enjoyed having some home cooking again."

She rose with him. At the verandah steps, he paused, absorbing the quiet summer night, the sweet-scented closeness of her body standing inches away from his. "I'll say good night. Thank you again."

"You're welcome. I'm sorry we argued."

"I'm not."

Startled by his swift answer, she slanted a glance up at him. His face was serious in the dim light, and she felt his gaze on her.

His voice was deep and husky. "Sometimes arguments clear the air. We know each other better now."

She felt herself tremble a little.

"Liss, I get the feeling that your husband—ex-husband," he corrected himself harshly, "really hurt you. Am I right?"

She said nothing. It was answer enough for him.

"I don't know why you divorced, but if there's any question at all in your mind, let me tell you this. You are one helluva lady. The guy must have rocks in his head."

Color flooded her cheeks. Speechless, she could only stare at him.

"You are also beautiful . . . and sexy. I've been thinking about you constantly since the first time I saw you. I've been wanting to kiss you. I want to kiss you right now, Liss."

Her voice shook. "That's not a good idea."

He stared into her blue eyes, asking. She gazed into his darker blue eyes as if mesmerized. She couldn't move as his head lowered.

His mouth brushed hers, soft and gentle against her firmly closed lips. Heart beating wildly in response to something new, something frightening, something exciting, she kept perfectly still, letting him kiss her without responding. His lips played with hers, coaxing, teasing, asking, not demanding, until, without volition, the stiffness left her and her mouth softened.

The kiss deepened. She parted her lips, allowing his tongue to taste more of her. He gently took off her glasses and pulled her into his body, holding her close to him, letting her feel him, learning the softness of her body where it strained against the firmness of his. Without her knowing quite how, her bones dissolved and flowed away, leaving her limp.

He shifted slightly. She was immediately aware of his legs straddling hers, propping her up. At last, she gave in to temptation and raised her arms to run her fingers through his silver hair. It was even silkier and softer than she'd imagined.

He groaned and lessened the force of his kiss, easing his mouth from hers to press heated kisses down the column of her throat, resting for a long moment at the base where he suckled as though he'd draw her very essence into him.

She stiffened, struggling against the need to ask for more. "Wyatt," she whispered huskily. "No more. Stop."

Instantly, his hands fell away. He stood back, breathing heavily, then leaned down and kissed her cheek. When he spoke, it was in an intimate whisper. "I won't apologize."

"No . . ."

"I'll see you very soon, Liss. Good night."

She watched him walk away, moonlight on his silvered hair. What a fool she was! How stupid to have given in to temptation when it only made things worse.

No matter how much she'd wanted to kiss Wyatt Harrow, and how much she'd like to kiss him again, once had to be enough.

Seven

Liss lay flat on her back, arms outstretched at her sides, completely awake. On her bedside table, the clock kept pace with her heartbeat, three-fifteen and forty seconds, three-fifteen and forty-one seconds, and on, while her mind raced and she cringed, recalling what her body had demanded.

She made herself think about work, counting off again the completed items from her to-do list, wondering what to wear tomorrow, if she'd have the Collection ready for the library's grand opening. When that palled, she wondered how Oakmont would handle the plant shutdown if Intratec pulled out.

She worried about the people who would lose their jobs, about the potential loss of her own income when she was already cutting it close to the bone, and—

Face it. Liss! You're worried how you're going to face Wyatt after tonight.

She rolled to one side and then the other, her body overheated in the air-conditioned coolness of her room, and tried to forget how she'd come undone in Wyatt's arms. How could she explain her behavior, make him understand that she was ordinarily circumspect and too restrained to indulge in frivolous displays of affection?

Would he think she was lonely and deprived? A divorcee looking for a replacement? She recalled the hungry, desperate look she'd seen in some other late-life divorcees—that urgent need to reassure themselves that they were still young and attractive to men.

Oh, sweet heavens, did Wyatt think she was like those women? Did he think she was ripe for an affair, or worse, a one-night stand, just because she'd enjoyed kissing him?

Embarrassed that she'd waited so long to stop that kiss, she kicked off the sheet, plumped her pillow savagely, then burrowed her head under it, wishing she could fall asleep and wake up in another dimension where she wouldn't have to see Wyatt Harrow ever again.

* * *

Across the oleander hedge, Wyatt slept, enjoying a dream in which Liss played the key part in satisfying his most erotic fantasies. Sprawled across his bed, sheet tucked under one bare hip, his hand moved in tandem with the way he dream-stroked her porcelain skin, bringing the heat to the surface, coloring it with desire.

He woke rested and satisfied.

She woke tired and jumpy.

Not wanting any more unforeseen events, she made sure the sprinklers were off and Wyatt was nowhere in sight before she skimmed across the lawn, snipped three pale yellow rosebuds, and raced back to the house.

Leaving her breakfast uneaten, she went out to her car, determined that when she saw Wyatt again, she'd be cool and composed. She'd explain, if the subject came up, that she was sorry if he had the wrong impression, but she wasn't that type, and he would just have to go and peddle his papers elsewhere.

She was rehearsing the part where she sent him away—nicely of course, without hurting his feelings—when his deep voice, slightly breathless, resounded too close to her left ear. "Hi. Sleep well?"

Startled, she turned to face him and felt a blush rise. The sight of him in almost nothing but sweat and brief running shorts made her

120

swallow. Her gaze centered on the expanse of his lightly furred chest. His entire body glistened in the early morning sunlight. Her mouth turned dry. Licking her lips did nothing.

He gave her that slow smile which had done her in yesterday, and leaned forward. At the last moment, she turned her head away; his lips grazed her cheek.

He withdrew an inch. "You smell great."

"You're sweaty," she blurted, not at all cool or composed. Feeling unexpectedly gauche, she stood rooted to the sidewalk, eyes intent on a root bulging up under the old paving. How on earth had she gotten herself into this?

"I've been running," he explained needlessly.

"I've got to go to work."

"Me, too." He indicated her pale lemon yellow dress. "You look like one of those rosebuds. See you later?"

"I don't think so. I'm very busy . . ." She fidgeted, wanting to get away from him, unable to look him in the eye.

"Too busy for dinner?"

"Ah, Wyatt, look. About last night. I'm sorry if I gave you the wrong idea . . ."

He stepped back a pace. "What idea is that?"

She hated the wash of color that stained her cheeks, but made herself go on. "I got carried away last night. I don't want you to think I do that all the time."

He said nothing, merely looked expectant.

She forged on. "You'll be very busy while you're here, and I'm totally involved with work and the historical display, so there's really no way for us to spend time together . . ."

Wyatt listened, hoping his face didn't betray his dismay. When she stopped, he kept his tone positive. "I don't see that we have a problem."

"I do."

Watching her drive away, Wyatt felt like kicking himself. He'd handled it all wrong. Hell, he'd handled *her* all wrong! She'd given him his walking papers just as he was planning long intimate evenings alone with her. How could he have been so wrong?

Last night, she'd surprised and thrilled him with her reaction. The way Liss had responded to him had been gratifyingly and excitingly genuine.

What made her so cold this morning?

He puzzled over it as he, too, prepared for work, thinking more about her than what he was going to do with Intratec. Driving to the company facility, with hardly a glance at the town or the peach orchards surrounding it,

Wyatt regretfully set the situation with Liss aside for later consideration and turned his thoughts to the problem at hand.

Talking with Pete Dodge, however, he had to make a conscious effort to concentrate on what the plant manager was saying.

"Listen, Wyatt, I owe you an apology for walking out of the meeting like that."

"Forget it."

"No, I mean it," Pete rumbled. "Closing down, after all the effort we've put into the plant, just gets to me."

"We don't have much choice."

"I tell you, Wyatt, there's gotta be a way to keep the place open. Hell, everybody knows that Far Eastern assembly operations aren't as profitable as they used to be."

"Maybe not, but the numbers are still good."

"Good enough to throw people here out of work? Where are they going to find another job these days?"

If there was one aspect of his job that he hated, it was this. No matter that a decision had been made after months of looking at all the options, when people heard about it for the first time they always had to question the logic, rehash the reasons. He could cope with that, but he hated to see the human effects caused by such a change.

Especially with someone like Pete. It was obvious that the older man put a lot of himself into his job. Nevertheless, it had to be faced. Wyatt looked straight at Pete. "What we're talking about is the bottom line."

"So what's the answer? I can't see how we're going to cut back any more than we already have. We've had so many twenty percent reductions that we're at nominal strength as it is."

"Let's go over the figures," Wyatt said, but the figure that came to mind was feminine, slender and fragile. He shook his head to clear his memory of how small and delicate she felt in his arms.

Did I scare her away? Damned fool. A blind man could see that she's still hurting, and you come on like some randy teenager. Why'd you have to go so fast?

Pete and Wyatt bent their heads over the computer printouts, intent on the projected operating expenses. Pete ran a large, veined hand through his salt and pepper hair, disarranging a strand combed carefully over a freckled bald spot.

He argued, determined to save the plant.

Wyatt pointed out facts, offered what consolation he could.

They called up more figures on the terminal in Pete's office, but got nowhere. Two hours later, trusting his calculator more than the spreadsheet equations, Pete refigured some of the totals, then shook his head. "I hate to admit it, but I just can't see a way. Lord, I hate to be the one to tell everyone we're closing."

"You won't have to, Pete. That's my responsibility."

Pete looked momentarily relieved, then he shook his head. "No, I'll do it. I've gotten close to people since I took over the plant. The wife and I like it here. These people are our friends."

"How do you feel about transferring back to headquarters?"

Pete paused a moment and ran a hand through his grizzled hair. "Tell you the truth, I don't like the idea at all. I'd rather stay here."

"What will you do?"

"I was gonna retire soon. Do it sooner, that's all."

"Retire and stay in Oakmont?" Wyatt asked, not bothering to hide his skepticism.

The older man smiled. "Place kinda grows on you. It's good for our grandkids." He saw Wyatt's look and his smile broadened. "Now for you young hotshots, Oakmont may seem a little tame, but it's a good place to live. Shutting down the plant is going to hurt this town."

Wyatt grimaced at the label. Young hotshot, indeed. It was days like this that made him feel older than Adam. And the thought of shutting down the plant rankled him. He just couldn't admit it out loud. "Well, if you're sure about it, we'll see what we can do for you."

"No more than my due. I don't want anything more than I've earned—especially since we'll be laying people off."

Wyatt nodded, impressed by Pete's integrity. Intratec would be losing a good man. "Okay. Let's go over the schedule and get the Human Resource people involved, get the paperwork started. Set up some meetings with the department heads, will you? God, the next few days are going to be rough."

Pete briefly closed his eyes. Watching him, Wyatt was struck by how hard Pete was taking this plant closure, as though it were a personal affront, a failure of some kind, rather than a dollars and cents business decision.

Uncomfortable with his role in this, Wyatt wished he hadn't accepted the assignment. Nuts and bolts he could handle with no problem, personnel decisions he could make easily, production schedules were a snap. But this was difficult.

* * *

In the old brick building that would house the library for only a short time longer, Liss frowned at Joe Franklin. "But that's not what we agreed. You said I can do whatever I want. Now you're telling me you don't like the Collection's displays."

"It'll be better my way. If you scatter all those papers, you lose the visual impact—"

"I've sorted them according to family and dates—"

"Maybe so, but grouping them all together will show how many more there are."

"That doesn't make sense, Joe. We're not selling them by the baker's dozen."

Joe grimaced. "I told Don that you wouldn't like it—"

"You discussed this with Don Simpson before you talked to me?" Liss heard her voice rise, and controlled it.

"Hey, don't get mad. The subject just came up, and—"

"And what? And when?" Liss cut in, exasperated that Joe would discuss something so trivial as the number of documents in one case with the chairman of the library board.

Joe gestured airily. "Last week, remember? You were busy with the carpenter when I was showing Don around. Hey, it's not my fault if he wants the display changed."

"Honestly, Joe! Haven't we got enough to do with getting ready for the grand opening? As it is, I'm already cutting into time at the shop. I don't have the extra time to keep running back and forth changing things."

"You don't have to do that. In fact, you could cut down on the time you spend here. We could do it for you."

"Thanks for offering, Joe, but I want this done just so." She eyed the man across from her. With his sparkling eyes and rounded pink cheeks, he looked almost angelic.

She'd heard him despair of the baby-faced image that made him look like a school kid instead of a highly professional degreed librarian, but right now she wanted to give him a good shake. She resisted the temptation to give in to his boyish grin. "It's too late to make changes."

"Uh, no, not really. I rearranged it all this morning."

Anger surged through her, propelling her to her feet. She restrained the urge to pace, and made herself stand still. "Now, listen here, Joe. That display is *my* project. I donated all the resource material, paid for the display cases, and I'm donating my time."

Control kept her from blurting out the fact that if he wanted to get technical, she owned a large piece of the library. She'd spent herself almost dry in her efforts to get it built. "I want the display left the way I arranged it. Understand?"

Like a small boy chafing under a reprimand, he shifted in his chair and looked away from her. Surly now, he nodded.

"Good. Now, how's the schedule? Will the movers be here on time?"

"Yeah," he mumbled.

"What?"

"I said we're done. Except for the exhibit you want for the foyer."

His grumble alerted Liss. "Are you still upset because I chose to do a retrospective?"

"This is a new library, Liss, we need to look forward, not back."

"I don't agree with you. This community is very proud of its roots. We like knowing that we're here to stay. Oakmont has weathered a lot of things over the last 130 years—"

"That's just it! You're catering to the old fuddy-duddies instead of the young people who—"

"I guess that makes me a fuddy-duddy, then."

Joe's ears reddened. He looked away.

Liss sighed. She really didn't have time to get into the old argument, but she had to make Joe understand. "Look at it this way: the people who come to Oakmont to live—

for whatever reason—become part of the community. More than one newcomer has told me that a big drawing point is the sense of tradition we have, of the past meshing with the present. It gives us all a sense of . . . oh, what would you call it? Of home, of belonging. Don't tell me you haven't felt it, too?"

Joe muttered something about his wife, Wendy.

"She likes it here, doesn't she? At the baby shower, she talked about raising children, feeling good about the town, saying she feels like staying for good."

"Yeah, well, Wendy was raised in a small town."

"So were you," Liss pointed out.

"So, okay. Maybe I want more for Oakmont than just contentment with the way things are. I want to see this place move forward."

She settled a hip on the edge of his desk and spoke firmly. "I do, too, Joe. That's one of the reasons I agreed to give the Oakmont Collection to the library—you and I see eye to eye on a lot of things, but we don't have to shove the past out of the way to move into the future. They're not mutually exclusive, you know."

He shrugged, looking sheepish but unconvinced. He started to say something, then checked himself.

Liss went right on. "Besides, there's a lot of interest, both for and against us. You know you got a new library only after we persuaded a number of people that we weren't going to ignore all the values they associate with Oakmont."

"Jeez, you make it sound like this town has mystical properties."

Liss had to smile. "Not quite. But I have to admit, I've never wanted to live anyplace else."

"Never?" He seemed to consider that. "How about when you went to college? Didn't you get a taste of the big world beyond Oakmont then?"

Her amusement faded. Slipping her glasses off, she rubbed the bridge of her nose, wondering if she could explain the complex feelings she'd experienced when after only two and a half years at college, working toward a degree in Business Administration, she'd returned home to look after her ailing mother.

She preferred not to remember how hurt and resentful she felt when a temporary absence turned into a permanent one. After her mother died, she could have gone back to finish college, but by then she and David had been married for almost a year and he didn't want a part-time wife.

She'd stayed home voluntarily of course, thinking at first she was just putting her education on hold, that once things were settled, she'd go back to get her bachelor's and then her master's.

But somehow one thing or another got in the way, and her life had evolved in a totally different pattern. Not like Wyatt's, she mused, then caught herself. Why did his marriage pop into mind? Resolutely, she tried to put him out of her thoughts, but his presence lingered, as did the memory of that devastating kiss.

"Liss?"

"Oh, sorry, Joe," she blinked. "I guess I was day dreaming. You were saying?"

"I'm just curious, that's all. Why did you decide to come back here when you could have gone anywhere, done anything?"

She shrugged. "It was a long time ago. Everything I want is here, now." Her laugh was spontaneous. "I guess I'm becoming fossilized."

Joe didn't laugh with her. He looked at his once-white athletic shoes and scuffed one toe against the floor. "You're too involved with the Oakmont Collection. Maybe you should get into the local political scene . . . didn't I hear that your family pretty much ran the joint over the years?"

"I don't know that I'd phrase it just that way, Joe," she said wryly, "but my contribution to Oakmont is limited to the Collection. My shop keeps me busy. I don't want or need to be involved with local politics."

"But your family, even your husband—"

"Ex-husband," she interrupted firmly. "Just because my—" she broke off, determined she wasn't going to talk about David. "I don't need to get involved with everything that goes on in this town. I'm perfectly happy with my life just the way it is."

Joe studied the worn linoleum under his foot as though he was attempting to memorize the faded pattern. "Maybe you *should* get more involved," he persisted, looking away from Liss.

"Why?"

"Just seems you'd want to use your influence to get things done, that's all."

"I used all the influence I had to get you the new library," she said, still wondering why Joe was so insistent she take on more when she had her hands full already.

She knew him well enough to know that he had something more on his mind than the desire to see her active in Oakmont politics. What could he be referring to?

"Uh, well . . . yeah. I guess I'd better get back to work."

Determined that she'd get to the bottom of this when Joe wasn't being quite so moody, Liss replaced her glasses and checked her watch. Keeping her face calm in spite of the uneasy feeling their talk had left her with, Liss collected her briefcase and left the library for her shop.

On the way, she picked up a deli sandwich to share with Susan.

As she entered her shop, Susan looked up from the crystal she was dusting. "If you'd gotten back ten minutes ago, you could have gone to lunch with that hunk," she said, with a knowing grin.

"What?"

"That guy you brought in here the other day—you know, the gorgeous one with the hair—sorta dropped in, all casual. He looked real disappointed that you'd already gone to lunch."

"Damn." Liss had managed to avoid thinking about Wyatt for most of the morning, and with just one reference to his splendid silver hair all her effort became uselessly expended energy.

Susan looked amused. "That's exactly what he said."

"I didn't mean it that way—I'm glad I wasn't here."

"Why?"

Liss ignored that and opened the white paper bag. "Ready for lunch? I got turkey and avocado on wheat, extra pickles."

Susan waved it away. "First things first. Why don't you want to see that man? It's clear as day that he's interested in you. All he did was watch you when you brought him in here. What's he like? As yummy as he looks?"

"Forget it, Susan. Let's eat, okay?"

"Fess up. What happened?"

"Well, it's just that . . ." Liss sighed and put down her sandwich. Once Susan got into her inquisitorial mode, she might as well confess everything. "I had him over to supper— only he calls it dinner—and it didn't go very well."

"No?" Susan's face creased with concern. "You had a fight?"

"Not exactly. I mean, we . . . well, I made a fool of myself and . . ."

"And now you're embarrassed?" Susan's face cleared as a smile took over. "What did you do—play strip poker?"

"No!" Liss burst out, chagrined that her best friend understood so easily and quickly.

"What then?"

"I kissed him."

135

Susan laughed. "Good grief, Liss. So what? You don't have to answer to anyone but yourself. You're single, remember? You can kiss a man if you want to. Kiss him again, if you liked it."

"You don't understand. I was practically all over him."

"So what? if I were twenty years younger and didn't have Tom, I'd be all over him, too."

"You don't understand," Liss repeated.

Susan assumed her earth mother face. "You want to talk about it?"

Liss tried to sort out her confusion and wound up telling Susan a short but graphic version of her experience with Wyatt.

"What are you worried about? The fact that you enjoyed it too much?"

"Suze!"

"What else did you do?"

"Nothing! That's just not the way I behave . . ."

"You're entitled to have fun. Loosen up. Just because David did a number on you, you don't have to resign from the world."

"I'm not doing that," Liss protested, but even to herself, her voice sounded weak.

"Oh? Could have fooled me. You and David got a divorce. That may be too bad, depending on the way you look at it, but it's not the end of civilization as we know it. You don't owe him an ounce of loyalty, not after what he did to you."

"It's not that," Liss began in protest, but Susan went right on.

"Since we're talking about it, and before you shut me up, I want to say something I've been choking on for the last year—" she broke off to wag a finger at Liss. "Don't give me that look."

Liss edged away.

"Sit down," Susan said firmly, and waited until Liss sat warily. "You gave up your own life to be the perfect wife for David and what have you got to show for it?"

Liss opened her mouth to speak.

"You let me finish. So you're divorced, so what? It isn't the end of your life. After years of putting him first, of spoiling him rotten, you need to think of yourself now. Forget that man and get on with living. Look at you, walking around as if you're only half there."

Liss murmured a protest which Susan ignored. "What about *your* needs? You're still young. Alive. You're letting David mess with your life as much as he did while you were married."

"Don't be silly, Suze."

"There's nothing silly about this. He's getting on with his life, him and his new wife and the baby." At the stricken look flashing over Liss's face, Susan stopped. "I'm sorry, I didn't mean to remind you of that."

Liss made a half-hearted gesture. "It's okay. Nobody died. You don't have to tiptoe around."

Taking her friend at her word, Susan put her fists on her ample hips. "Look at you. Crying your heart out because David gave another woman the baby which should have been yours."

Ignoring the pain in her friend's blue eyes, Susan continued. "What about your own happiness? What are you going to do for yourself? Don't you want to get married again? Are you going to live in that big old house by yourself forever?"

"No, but—"

"But what? You don't date—no, don't say you've gone out with Howard, everybody knows he's not the man for you. You won't go out with any of the other men who ask you, who could mean something in your life. What are you waiting for?"

Liss blinked. "I—"

"Don't answer that. I know exactly what you're going to say. You made a mistake. You don't want to make another. All right. Maybe you're entitled to be a little gun-shy," Susan said firmly, holding up her hand like a traffic cop when Liss started to protest. "After all, you married David Greenley when you were both kids and he did you dirty. At least twice."

Liss looked so startled that Susan softened her voice. "Everyone knows he was unfaithful to you before he met what's-her-face and got her pregnant. Who's to say how many other women he played around with? So when are you going to get over that jerk?"

Liss's face burned. "I don't want to talk about him."

"Okay by me, but put him out of your life. He's not worth one more minute of your time. Find someone like that hunk—"

"His name is Wyatt Harrow," Liss said without thinking.

Susan didn't lose an ounce of steam. "Find someone like that hunk Wyatt Harrow and see what happens."

"Aren't you getting things a little out of proportion here?"

"Who, me? It's not me walking around in a tizz today."

Liss had to laugh. "You're making an awful lot out of one kiss."

"That's all it was, wasn't it? A kiss?" Susan laughed, too. "Or did you two promise to love and cherish forevermore?"

"Of course not."

"So stop making such a big deal out of it. Relax. Learn to trust your instincts again."

Liss bit her lip. "You make it sound so easy."

"How do you know it isn't? You're divorced, Liss, not dead."

"I'm not sure how to act any more. Everything's changed so much since I was single."

"All the more reason to go out and learn what it's all about. Have fun. Enjoy yourself without any strings attached. Get out more."

"With whom? Howard?" Liss shuddered.

Susan chuckled. "Is he still hanging around?"

"You'd think he'd get the idea. Suze, I'm rude to him! He just won't go away."

"He knows a good thing when he sees it." Susan stood back and surveyed her boss. "To be honest, Liss, it's not just you he wants. Not that you're not holding your own, but he wants your name, your standing in this county. You'd give him class, smooth off the rough edges, make him more acceptable. He could show you off before the voters . . ."

"Not likely! After I've seen him, I always feel I have to count my fingers, to make sure they're all there."

"All right. So Howard is out. How about the guy who's putting those stars in your eyes? Spend time with him."

Liss frowned. "It's tempting, but I can't do that."

"Why not?"

Blinking at her friend's bluntness, Liss tried to explain. "He's a stranger. He'll be gone in a few days. And if that's not enough, I don't like what he's here to do—how can I spend time with him if he's going to put a bunch of people in this town out of work?"

Susan snorted. "I know an excuse when I hear one."

"Well, this time you're hearing things," Liss retorted. "How could I . . ." she paused, searching for the right word.

"Consort with the enemy?"

"Stop making light of this. It's serious."

"Lighten up, Liss. That isn't your problem."

"Maybe not, but how about you? You hear Jack and Dani talking a lot more than I do—you're closer to what's happening at the plant than I am."

"If Intratec closes down, we'll survive."

"But I can't just sit by and let that happen!"

"Liss, stay out of it. Let Howard and the city council handle it. Let David take care of himself—you don't have to worry about his job anymore, or making sure he gets ahead."

Susan paused for breath. Her voice turned coaxing as she said, "Stop using the thing with Intratec as an excuse for not getting to know that guy better. You have your whole life ahead of you. Why don't you do what *you* want for a change?"

Such a simple question. Liss wished the answers were as simple. She'd spent so much of her life pleasing others, first her parents and then David, that she'd never learned to put herself first. She'd tried so hard to make things better for other people that she didn't know how to consider her own needs.

A tiny warmth stole through her when she reflected how that wasn't strictly true anymore. She'd already started pleasing herself. She was reclaiming her home as money allowed and doing things to suit herself.

She'd started up this shop and if antiques continued to sell well, she'd wind up with a profit at year's end. She had her work at the library and the Collection. If she could do those things, why not do more?

Smiling at the thought, she stood and wrapped her arms around Susan's full figure. "You're too much, you know that? Thanks for the pep talk."

"Well, did you learn anything? Are you going to see him again?"

"Why don't we see what happens?" Liss

smiled mysteriously and disappeared into her office, cheered by her conversation with Susan. She *had* been making too much of one kiss. It was only because she wasn't used to kissing, that was all. If she saw Wyatt again, she'd be cool and distant, as though nothing unusual had happened.

Settling herself at her desk, Liss took a deep breath and put Wyatt out of her mind. All afternoon she worked steadily, but as the hours went by, she noticed that her concentration kept slipping. Wyatt flickered in and out of her mind until she stopped working on her inventory and let her thoughts dwell entirely on him. Despite her earlier resolve to be cool, she alternated between anticipating the thrill of seeing Wyatt again, and a nervous dread of doing just that.

Forcing her mind away from the memory of his body pressed so close to hers that she could hardly breathe, she made the mistake of brushing her lips with her fingertips. Instantly, the feel of his mouth on hers, sweet and tender one moment, then hungry and demanding the next, overcame her resistance.

Closing her eyes, she remembered every second of that kiss.

She leaned back in her chair, caught up in the sensations she'd felt last night when she'd loosened all restraints and had just let herself feel. It wasn't so bad, she reassured herself. *Susan's right—I just made too much of the whole thing.*

Wyatt himself hadn't seemed to think less of her this morning. If he didn't think of her as a man-starved divorcee on the prowl, why should she feel guilty for enjoying his kiss?

Armed with her new attitude, Liss closed the shop at five and started home. Halfway there, she reversed direction and drove the few blocks to the grocery store. It wouldn't hurt to have a few things in the house just in case . . .

Lighthearted, she took a cart and pushed it down the aisles. Coming around the corner of one aisle, she looked down the next and abruptly stopped. Her cart bumped a display of disposable diapers.

She paid little heed to the top level of the display swaying dangerously as every bit of her attention focused on the young woman halfway down the aisle.

Liss stared, her throat dry. There she was—the new wife! With the baby. Liss didn't want to look but she couldn't tear her gaze away. Tucked securely into an infant seat, the baby waved his arms and legs in the air, cooing to himself. Liss knew his name: Davey.

David Greenley, III. His reddish hair was like his mother's, only she had hers pulled back in a pony tail that jounced against her slender shoulders as she reached to grab a jar of baby food. With her short denim skirt, off-the-shoulder blouse, and long, bare legs, she looked casual and no different than any of the other young mothers in the store.

Retreating, her heart beating so hard that she thought others would hear it, Liss abandoned her grocery cart and almost ran for the exit. She had to get out of there before someone saw the state she was in.

Oh, God, to run into that woman now and here! Was she never going to get used to the fact that David had married that . . . that . . .

Her hands trembling, she had to try several times before she could get the key in the car door. When at last she did, she tumbled into the safety of her car and looked all around to make sure she wasn't being watched.

Seeing no one, she let her forehead drop against the steering wheel and she sat there taking deep breaths until she felt more like herself. At last, with a shaky inhalation, she raised her head and stared at the key still in her hand.

A few minutes later, she turned into her own driveway. Wyatt's car wasn't parked next door. Thank God. She couldn't face him now, not feeling as haggard as she must look. She had to get inside, safely away from nosy eyes.

She had to get hold of herself. Only one thing had proved strong enough to do the trick. Over the months, she'd lost herself in hard work. That was the only way to keep her mind off the things she didn't want to think about. Exhausting herself was the only thing to do. Resolutely, she marched up her front steps and let herself in.

Talking to herself, she stormed up the stairs and changed into her work clothes, then pulled out her heavy upright power sander and got to work. She'd already stripped the floor of the morning room and sanded it down over and over again until the old oak was as smooth and clean as it had been the day it was put down over a hundred years ago.

The marks left behind by David's heavy desk and file cabinets had turned to sawdust and had been swept away days ago. With each new stroke of the sander and the broom, she felt better, as if by erasing his presence in her home she was ridding herself of unwanted dross.

With every swing of the sander, she blotted out the image of his wife and baby.

With every muscle straining, she had no time to feel her heart ache.

Little by little, her home remedy began to work. She took a break, long enough to get something to drink and to turn on her compact disc player. With the music turned up loud enough to hear over the whine of the sander, she returned to the morning room and resumed her work.

More relaxed now than when she'd begun the job, she hummed along with the music while she went over the floor with fine grit sandpaper.

Abruptly, the sander stopped. She clicked the switch several times, but the machine was dead. Frowning, she looked back to see if she'd pulled the plug out of the wall. Her gaze followed the cord across the dusty floor and up the wall to the hand of the man leaning nonchalantly in the doorway.

"I rang the doorbell," Wyatt shouted over the music. "I rang it several times. I knocked. I yelled—what on earth are you doing?"

Liss stared at Wyatt, dressed casually in chinos and with a black knit shirt stretched snugly over his chest. Aware of her own appearance—her Oshkosh overalls torn at the knee and gaping at the waist where she'd lost the metal button—she pushed a droopy strap up over her shoulder to cover what the strapless red bandeau didn't.

"Wyatt!" she finally managed to say. "You scared me! I didn't hear you come in. What are you doing here?"

"I came to see you."

"Why?"

He grinned. "Maybe I wanted to see what all the noise was about. Can we turn that down?"

She gestured behind him. Wyatt turned and disappeared down the hall. A moment later, the house was silent. His footsteps warned Liss of his approach as she tried unsuccessfully to tuck herself back together.

Of all the times to just pop in, when she was wearing her oldest clothes, the ones she wore because nothing could hurt them or make them look any worse. Besides, she wasn't ready to see him when she was still upset over the near-encounter in the supermarket.

He leaned in the doorway again and looked her over from the top of her dusty hair to the soles of her shabby sneakers. "That's better. What *was* that awful noise?"

"You call Strauss waltzes awful noise?"

"You like that classical stuff?"

"I do," she responded firmly. "I also like Dwight Yoakum and Mary Chapin Carpenter."

"Country music, huh? Somehow I thought of you as the soft mood type. You know, lots of violins and piano."

"No more."

He arched an eyebrow to invite her to

elaborate, but she turned away. How could she explain her almost fierce desire to do all the things she hadn't been able to do while married?

If she wore too-young-for-her clothes around the house, experimented with different kinds of music and interests, who cared? She had no one to answer to now but herself. She could be any woman she wanted to be.

He grinned. "Every time I see you, you're a different person. Who are you now? Shall I expect Superwoman next?"

Startled by the way his thoughts reflected hers, she slanted a glance at him. "Superwoman? Hardly."

"Well, what are you doing?"

"I'm redoing the floor. I'm almost ready to varnish."

He looked around and whistled under his breath. "Good job. You've done all this yourself? I thought you had someone coming in to do it."

"Oh, no, I can't afford that! Besides, I prefer to do it myself."

He blinked. She lived in this huge house with a fortune in antiques cluttering up every inch and she couldn't afford to hire someone to refinish her floor?

He eyed her speculatively. "Why? Apart

from saving money? Why do you want to do it?"

She could have told him she was purging any trace of David from her house, little by little, room by room. She could have told him hard physical work was better at exorcising her demons than any therapy would have been, but instead she shrugged. "I like to see things done right. I enjoy the work."

He eyed the strap that slipped down her upper arm and imagined running his finger up her arm under the guise of replacing it. Better still, he imagined slipping it off her entirely, then peeling down those tattered overalls and discovering the woman beneath. His breath quickened.

When the silence between them grew obvious, he gestured at the floor. "You're going to varnish it, too?"

"Sure."

"That's hard stuff to work with. Takes forever to dry. You've done it before?"

"Look at your feet. I did the foyer a couple of months ago."

This time he whistled out loud. "Looks damned good. Need any help?"

"You?"

"Oh, lady, if you could see my calluses. I used to work in a marina, on the wooden boats, when I was in college."

"You did?" She was delighted, and gestured at the floor. "I'm going to use marine varnish."

"Perfect." He rubbed his hands together. "When can I start?"

"You sure you want to?"

He nodded. "I like working with my hands. It relaxes me."

"Me, too," she said, and then wondered too late if his words had a double meaning.

"Hard day?"

She shrugged, then quickly scooped up her errant strap, pretending not to notice how his gaze traveled the length of her bare arm from wrist to shoulder and then moved on to linger at the mark he'd made on her throat the night before.

In response, her heart rate moved into double time.

She was sure he'd see her pulse pounding, the way he was staring. "Uh, what?"

He dragged his gaze away from the curve of her breast just visible under the bib of her overalls, wondering how on earth he could be attracted to a sweaty, sawdusty handywoman with wisps of blonde hair spilling out of a once-smooth chignon.

He liked chic, imperturbable women, women perhaps a little hard around the edges, women who knew how to play the game and weren't looking for commitment any more than he was.

What was he doing, offering to perform manual labor for a woman who looked as though she didn't understand the rules?

For damned sure, if she'd been married any length of time, the divorce had left her vulnerable. In his experience, divorcees usually needed a man to reassure them that they were still desirable, still admired. Liss may be a couple of notches above those other women, but if he had any smarts at all, he'd make polite excuses and get the hell out of there before he gave in to the urge to make things better for her. He wasn't in the heart-mending business.

He saw her interested gaze and swallowed a groan. He might have had a chance of getting away if she hadn't looked at him quite that way. His resolve wavered. A few more minutes wouldn't hurt. What on earth had they been talking about? Oh, yes . . . "I asked if you'd had a hard day?"

"Oh," she said breathlessly, looking at his muscles tautening under her gaze, responding as they had last night when she'd run the flat of her palms down the hard lines of his torso. "Probably not as hard as yours. How are they taking the news at the plant?"

He stiffened. "I can't discuss Intratec business."

"Sorry, I forgot." She grinned. "Maybe I'd better mention that someone I know is dating a technician at Intratec. I get the inside scoop."

"Who is he?" Wyatt asked sharply.

"I can't discuss personal business."

He looked grim, then wiped his face of all expression. Again, she saw how he would be at work. Determined, analytical, intent on business. Ruthless when he had to be. He'd be a formidable opponent, she guessed, but just as tenacious an ally.

Unexpectedly, he gave her that slow smile again. "Well, since we can't talk business, we'll have to talk about us."

"Us? What do you mean?"

He advanced into the room, leaving Topsider footprints behind him in the dust. "Us," he said softly, forgetting his intention to leave under the determination to push just a little more, just enough to test her awareness of him. She had to have felt something last night. He couldn't have been that mistaken. His voice deepened as he continued, "You and me. Kisses that—"

"Stop right there."

He stopped. "I'll wipe my feet."

"That's not what I mean, and you know it! There is no us."

He smiled as Liss gripped the handle of the power sander as though it were her lifeline and she was going under for the third time.

Wyatt came closer. Reaching out, he ran his index finger down the line of her jaw, smiling at the trail it left in the fine powdery residue on her skin. "I couldn't stop thinking about you today."

She closed her eyes against the feel of him. Against the way his deep melodious voice plucked at inner strings and made her body hum.

Wyatt's breath was warm on her face. He took her glasses off, looked through the dusty lenses and then polished them with his handkerchief, all the time talking to her. "I kept remembering how you felt when I kissed you. How attracted I am to you, how glad I am that you feel the same way—"

She quivered as he replaced her glasses and checked the fit. His fingers lingered at her ears, then slid down her throat. She tried to ignore the sensations he was causing. "I do not feel the same way."

"No? You're going to pretend that you don't feel the heat between us?"

She looked away, afraid her face would betray her lie. "There's nothing to feel."

His fingers gently turned her chin back, until she was forced to look up into the dark blue eyes smiling knowingly at her. "You're forgetting how your body talks to mine—in my book, that makes it damned obvious that there's something between us. Something good. Something we can't ignore. The question is, what do we do about it?"

"Nothing," she whispered, fighting her instantaneous response to him.

His mouth barely brushed hers. "Yes. Make love with me, Liss."

Eight

Liss jerked back quickly, pulling her chin away from his finger. She retreated a step, holding out a hand to ward him off. "Make love with you? Don't be ridiculous! I don't even know you."

Wyatt reached for her again. "Sure you do. Enough to know that it'll be good between us."

She stepped behind the power sander to evade him. "Let me make something very clear," she said firmly, even as her senses frolicked with the possibility of meshing with his. "No matter what happened between us last night, I'm not in the habit of making love with strangers. I do not have affairs. Even if I lost my head and . . ."

"And made love with me?"

Her lower lip trembled with anger, but she managed to keep her voice clear and steady.

"If you're thinking that just because I'm divorced, I'm an easy mark, let me tell you—"

"That's the last thing I'd think about you," he cut in forcefully, his temper rising to match hers.

"—I'm not in the market for a lover."

"You make it sound like a one-night stand. I don't go in for those myself."

Taken aback by the harshness in his voice, she asked, "Well, what are you talking about, then? A two-night stand? A fling? A temporary liaison?"

"Do we have to put labels on it? Couldn't we go with our feelings and see what happens?"

The strong temptation to do just that shocked Liss. She'd only made love with one man in her entire life, and here she was considering jumping into bed with a stranger. Even if her marriage had fallen apart after thirty years, how could she forget the tenets of a lifetime?

Oh, Lord, what was happening to her? How could she be tempted to give in and indulge in an affair?

The word as much as the thought slithered through her consciousness, making her feel slimy and dirty. She hated affairs. Though she'd never had one, she'd lived with the consequences of David's infidelity.

An affair was indelibly and forever branded into her mind as the lowest, most unforgivably dishonest and heartless act someone could engage in.

Her mind reeling, she hung on to the one thing she knew for a fact. "You'll be gone in a few days."

Wyatt looked thoughtful. A traditional woman, with old-fashioned values in a delightful contemporary package, Liss sounded almost desperate in her denials. And then suddenly, he understood.

Her husband must have been running around on her. God, no wonder she looked at him that way. He stood still, considering the situation, wondering what he should do now.

Understanding at least part of her reservation, he couldn't dispute her reasoning. He should do the smart thing and walk away—as she said, he would be gone in a few days. But how could he leave Oakmont without understanding what it was about Liss Thayer that kept him buzzing around like a bee to her special fragrance?

Faithful to his wife during their short marriage, and selective about the women he'd seen since their divorce, he hadn't felt like this, uneasy and restless, powerful yet powerless against the needs of his body, for a long time. With her strong reasons against an affair, Liss might not accept the idea, but there was a special feeling growing between them.

He intended to explore it to the fullest. To do that, he had to go slow, convince her he meant her no harm . . . but how?

Lost in contemplation, he almost missed the nuances of what she'd said. Smiling at the notion that she'd use the sander to hide behind, he asked for clarification. "It would be different if I were going to be here permanently?"

"Well, who knows?" Liss paused, listening honestly to her feelings. Echoes of Susan's exhortations blended in with her own deeply felt need to find out for herself what kind of woman she was. Even at this late date, with years of living behind her, she felt like a girl on the threshold of some grand adventure.

Getting to know him better didn't automatically mean they had to have an affair, did it?

Cautiously, she explored the possibilities. "I mean, if you lived here, and we got to know each other over time, became friends—"

"You'd sleep with me if we were friends? You don't want to be lovers," he asked, not sure he was hearing her right, "but friends who sleep together?"

"Of course not! The idea is preposterous."

"It's beginning to grow on me. How long

do you think it would take us to get friendly enough to—"

"I'm not going to answer that," she interrupted, feeling pressured. "I told you I don't sleep around—now you want me to tell you how long it would take to break my word?"

"Okay, so I was pushing it. You want to keep things friendly. No sex—lovemaking," he amended at the look on her face.

"I don't believe I'm having this conversation," she murmured. "This is ludicrous."

"Can you honestly rule it out?"

Could she? Could she continue seeing him and not succumb to his allure? Adventure might be difficult to resist, but she'd best remember the story about the lady and the tiger—she might have been the smug one as they set off into the jungle, but it was the tiger who came back licking his chops.

By the hungry look on Wyatt's face, he wasn't going to be satisfied until he had the answer he wanted. She eyed him warily. "I . . . don't know . . . what can I say?"

"Well," he grinned, pleased with himself, "how about this? Let's spend time together, and see where things go."

Liss was defensive, yet something prodded her to declare, "You're suggesting we spend time together just to see how long it will take you to seduce me."

Wyatt hesitated, then spoke persuasively. "That sounds damned cold-blooded. I'd like to think you thought better of me."

At the doubtful look she gave him, he opened his hands in a peace-making gesture. "Look, I'm not going to deny that I hope something physical might happen between us, but tell you what. Maybe you'll let me help you with the floor, maybe a couple of other things around here. We could have dinner, talk, go out—just get to know each other."

"Why me?"

He heard the confusion in her voice. Why her? If he was desperate for feminine companionship, for the warmth of a body next to him in bed, he knew he could find what he sought elsewhere without much trouble.

He'd done it before, discreetly, but the thought of that now left him cold. In fact, he realized, the idea filled him with distaste.

What did Liss Thayer have that made the memory of other women fade away? If he had any brains left after that kiss last night, he should be running out the door without so much as an "I'll call you." Why ask for complications when the job he had to do here demanded all his attention? The job. Damn. Thinking about the job gave him more than answer enough.

Yet, he couldn't walk away from her. Hoping he wasn't making the mistake of all time, he tried to make her understand. "Liss, you're the only nice thing that's happened since I came to Oakmont. Quite apart from the fact that you're a beautiful woman and I'm attracted to you, I need a friend. Someone who'll let me be me—not just the sea-gull."

"The *what*?"

Wyatt chuckled at the look on her face. "It's the guy who flies in, eats all your food, sh—messes all over you, and takes off."

Liss smiled, understanding the unspoken meaning. "And that's what you do for Intratec?"

He shrugged. "Sometimes it seems like it with all the traveling I do. It can get pretty lonely."

She narrowed her eyes. "Aren't you over-playing the poor-little-me bit?"

"Uh uh. If I really wanted to make you feel sorry for me, I'd tell you about eating alone, waking up and not being sure where I am, not having any friends, being the bearer of bad news—"

"It's that bad?" she asked, feeling sympathy rise. What kind of life was that for anyone? It was so different from her own newly or-dered life in which she'd deliberately chosen solitude.

Wyatt grinned again. "It's not always that way. Sometimes it's worse."

"Oh, you!" she laughed, amusement overcoming a momentary flash of irritation that he'd been pulling her leg. "You were teasing me."

"Maybe a little."

Her good humor faded. "There's still one thing that doesn't change. You're here to do something I can't agree with. If you close the plant, put a whole lot of people out of work, how can I shut my eyes and pretend that I don't care? Some of those people are my friends and customers. I can't stand by and see them hurt."

"It has nothing to do with you."

She bristled. "Maybe not, but that doesn't mean I can close my eyes to it. I don't like what you're here to do."

"You know I can't talk about it, Liss."

"Whether you admit it or not, Wyatt, you and I both know what's happening."

"Why does it have to have anything to do with us?"

"Didn't you hear what I just said? I don't like what you're doing here. I don't like what you're going to do to people I know."

"If—and I'm not saying it's the case—if you were right, you couldn't change a thing. So why let it get in the way?"

"Listen to yourself! How can you expect me to do nothing while you hurt my friends, my town?"

Wyatt paused and went for broke. "Because, damnit, I think that what you and I have—could have—together, is more important than all those other things put together."

"That's impossible!"

"Is it? Look at us. You can't deny that since we met the other day, there's been something between us."

She looked away. "I don't know what to say," she murmured.

"Don't say anything. All you have to do is see me, be with me. Will you do that?"

"Can we see each other without . . . without?"

"Falling into bed? You're the boss. You call the shots."

They exchanged a tentative smile.

"I'm making a mistake, I know I am," she said.

"No, Liss. Live a little. Take a chance with me. Please."

"Friends only?"

"If that's the way you want it."

Liss admired his candid answers, his humor, thinking it took a special type of man to be so honest and forthright about his intentions. She'd enjoyed their day yesterday

164

more than anything she'd done in a long time. They'd talked and laughed together like old friends. And if things had gotten a little out of hand last night, when she'd responded so hungrily to his kisses, well, now she knew better.

"That's the way it has to be," she said.

Wyatt's blue eyes darkened momentarily, but he kept his voice even. "Friends to start. Who knows what next? Okay with you?"

She firmed her shoulders, absently catching the strap before it slid down her upper arm. "Okay. Friends only. We'll give it a try."

"Great." Wyatt's smile convinced her she'd made the right decision. "So, pal, you gonna let me help you with this floor, or what?"

"Don't you think you'd better get out of those clothes?"

His startled look disappeared quickly, replaced with a smile that made Liss catch her breath. He pulled his black knit shirt free from the waistband of his chinos. "Just give me a couple of minutes."

At the sight of his bare abdomen, Liss clamped her jaw shut and looked quickly away. *Friends only, remember? Friends don't ogle each other.*

Wyatt went out whistling, leaving her propped for support against the sander, wondering if she'd made a mistake. Wondering how she'd be able to keep her hands to herself.

He reappeared in a short time, wearing an old pair of jeans and a faded blue T-shirt. Liss flicked her eyes over him, then allowed her gaze to linger on his shoulders and pectorals. Forget the young men in the television commercials. Wyatt's body was what T-shirts were made for.

His shoulders were broader, more muscular and well developed than any youngster who had to pump iron to develop that same physique. The indentation at his abdomen that made his waistband stand out from his body tantalized her. There had to be at least a finger's, maybe two finger's, width between him and his jeans.

She grinned, sure that getting soaked in the sprinklers would do much more for him than it had for her.

He grinned back, as if he hadn't been aware of her looking him over. "Okay, what do you want to do next?"

Reluctantly, she turned her mind back to the job at hand. They finished sanding the old oak floor, and when they both judged it smooth enough, they cleaned and vacuumed until no more dust clung to the corners.

Liss wound up the cord to her vacuum cleaner. "That's it for tonight. I'm beat."

Wyatt stared at her face, the sawdust clinging to her temples and delicately flushed cheekbones. She'd smeared her glasses and looked like an urchin again; he had to reach for the memory of her in conservative business clothes. Oddly enough, he thought, he preferred this side of her. "Hungry? Shall we change and go out?"

"The only thing I'm going to change into is my nightie . . ." her voice trailed off as she heard herself issuing what could be construed as a blatant invitation.

Wyatt bit his lip, holding back the response he wanted to give.

She raised uncertain eyes to his.

"Well, since you don't feel like going out, shall we order in?"

She exhaled in grateful recognition that he'd deliberately defused any possible tension. "I'm afraid Oakmont doesn't run to delivery places. Pizza, maybe." At his grimace, she added, "if you'd like to stay, I can fix something for us here."

"You don't mind?"

"Of course not. It won't be fancy, but—"

"I'd love another home-cooked meal," Wyatt said honestly.

"Fine. If you want to wash up while I investigate the fridge, the bathroom's at the top of the stairs."

Wyatt began to say he'd go next door to clean up, but the thought of seeing more of Liss's home, the private part, was too appealing. "Thanks. I won't be long."

He took the stairs two at a time. On the landing, he looked down a short hall with several closed doors. Taking a guess, he opened the first one on the left, and stood in the doorway, staring. Intrigued and lured by the pastel florals, by the soft pillows trimmed with lace that lay strewn against the white wicker headboard of her large old-fashioned bed, Wyatt felt rooted, unable to retreat or move forward into her extravagantly feminine bedroom.

She'd left a satin and lace slip across the arm of a wicker chair. It tempted him, but he resisted the urge to run the exquisite ivory fabric through his fingers. He knew it would be delicate, silky and a pleasure to touch. Like her skin? He let himself imagine what it would be like. Much as he liked her slightly disheveled and mussed, he could imagine her in that bit of nothing. He closed his eyes and let the idea seep through him.

After a moment, taking a long look to last him through the night, Wyatt turned and softly closed the bedroom door behind him.

The next door he opened led to the bathroom. A deep claw-footed tub sat under a skylight, raspberry enamel glowing in the diminishing evening sun. Wyatt sucked in his breath, suddenly seeing her bathing there, porcelain complexion contrasting against the rich shade of the tub. If the thought of her in nothing but her slip was enough to spin him around, the fantasy of her in the tub was enough to knock him off balance.

Without any difficulty, he imagined her blotting the moisture from rosy-tipped breasts and the downy juncture of her thighs. He smelled the fragrant bath powder she lavishly used on her silky-soft skin.

Taking another deep breath, he closed his mind to those erotic thoughts and picked up a translucent bar of soap. He ran the water, lathered, and then raised his hand to his nose. "Damnit, Liss, now you've got me smelling like a petunia."

After he'd dried with a soft cotton finger towel, wondering if she'd used it, too, he lifted the stopper from a large flagon of bath crystals. He inhaled deeply, enjoying the fragrance, feeling himself transported to a sweet-scented meadow.

Shaking his head at the contrast between the dusty urchin downstairs and the sexy, seductive woman she must be upstairs, he left the bathroom. He was curious about the other closed doors, but started down the wide wooden stairs and met Liss coming up.

"There you are. I just put some chicken on the barbecue—is that all right?"

"Sounds great. Is there anything I can do to help?"

They passed on the steps, then Liss stopped. Standing on the step above him, she turned just as he did. Their eyes met, almost at the same level. Feeling suddenly exposed to him, as if he knew a secret she wasn't ready to divulge, she looked quickly away from his knowing look. "Would you mind watching the chicken while I have a quick shower?"

"Fine."

"There's wine or beer in the fridge. Maybe you'd like to wait in the gazebo? I set a table out there."

"Fine."

Liss wondered at his abruptness, but shrugged and went on upstairs.

Wyatt went into her white, airy kitchen, helped himself to a beer, and walked out on her verandah, where he took several deep breaths.

He paced, did deep knee bends, stretched to relieve tension, and then walked down the flagged path to the gazebo and stared at the white wicker table which she'd set with floral placemats and napkins. The pattern reminded him of her flower-strewn bedroom and sensuous bathroom.

He held the cold beer can to his temples, trying not to imagine her in that raspberry tub, moving the hand-held shower over her body, stretching and flexing the womanly curves that were driving him crazy.

"Friends, Harrow. Remember, just friends," he spoke aloud, reminding himself that friends didn't entertain such libidinous thoughts about each other.

The odor of mesquite drifted on the air. Wyatt lifted the lid to the barbecue and used the tongs Liss had left on a nearby table to check the cooking chicken. Relieved that he hadn't let it burn while his mind was otherwise occupied, he turned the meat and lowered the lid.

Stretching out in a deck chair, he let his long legs sprawl, while he closed his eyes and imagined all the wonderfully erotic things he'd do to her, and with her, when she finally recognized the passion growing between them.

Not just passion, but something more he was afraid to label.

He'd been with her only a short time, yet he saw in her a stability and a steadfastness that made him curious about a lifestyle he'd never even remotely considered before. His rootless way of life was hard for any woman to accept, but now he began to wonder what it would be like to settle down, to live in one place.

"Some cook you are! I hope you're not letting our dinner burn?"

Wyatt got to his feet and grinned sheepishly His grin changed under the impact of her powder-blue jumpsuit with a shirred elasticized waistline that emphasized her slenderness. He wondered if the big white buttons on her shoulder were decorative or functional. If he slipped them free, would that scooped neck fall clear of her breasts?

She'd left her hair loose. He went to her, intending to sink his fingers into the ash blonde waves on her nape, but at the last moment, at a guarded look from her, he contented himself with a small tug on the loose sleeve. "I like this."

She moved her arm, pulling the fabric free. She placed a chilled bottle of wine on the table. "Thanks. I left some more stuff in the kitchen. Would you mind bringing it out?"

Obediently, he fetched tossed salad, warm rolls, and a crock of fresh, sweet butter. He set them down on the glass-topped table just as she brought the chicken over. "It looks delicious, Liss."

"Not very elegant, but it'll do. Would you like some wine?"

He pulled the cork, and poured. "Good year." He gestured at the food on the table. "This is more than I expected."

She took a small sip and smiled. "I'm all out of microwave dinners."

Wyatt grinned and sank his teeth into some chicken breast. He moaned theatrically. "Mmm, manna from heaven."

She laughed. "You've earned it. It would have taken me another night of sanding to finish that floor."

He buttered a roll. "How come you work so hard on your house?"

Thoughtfully, she let her gaze sweep the expanse of the back yard, then the large white house beginning to fade in the dusk. Sometimes, at times like this, she could almost imagine the generations that had lived here before her.

She could see the men, in their high starched collars, their stiff manner easing as they came up the walkway and crossed the verandah to enter their castle. She could hear the rustle of heavy skirts as their wives lifted faces for a husbandly kiss while small children in short pants or ruffled dresses with big sashes clustered around them.

It was fanciful, she knew, but it helped to know that even if her life wasn't all it might be, her family before her had lived and prospered in this big house. If she couldn't look forward to her descendants, she could at least look backward.

A little wistfully, she answered, "The easy answer is that it's the family home and if I don't take care of it, who will?"

"What's the other answer?"

She let the silence build while she searched for the right words. "I guess it satisfies some need in me to nurture things."

His voice was very gentle. "Why didn't you fill this house with children?"

She was glad the deepening twilight shadows obscured her face. Hid the pain she knew she couldn't hide on her own. "It just didn't happen."

"Should I say I'm sorry?"

"No . . ." she managed to get out before she had to clear her throat. "I guess it wasn't meant to be."

"Why haven't you re-married?"

"Guess no one wants me," she said as lightly as she could.

"Are all the men in Oakmont blind, or what?"

Embarrassed, she could barely speak. "Must be—"

He leaned forward and touched a match to the citronella candle on the table between them. In the flickering light, he studied her face, still hidden mostly in the shadows. Every now and then, as she moved her head, her glasses reflected the glow of the candle. He found himself waiting for that brief glimmer. "Are you telling me that you've never considered marrying again?"

"Briefly. Things didn't work out."

"What happened?" he probed, disregarding his mixed feelings. Disbelief that some man hadn't snatched her up the minute her divorce was final, relief that no one had, and curiosity about the things she obviously didn't want to discuss. He didn't want to acknowledge the jolt of jealousy he felt that she'd consider, even briefly, another man.

"I don't think that's any of your business, is it?"

"Probably not, but you've got me too curious to be polite."

"Try," she suggested.

He chuckled. "C'mon, Liss. Tell me. Why hasn't some guy snapped you up, given you a bunch of babies to fill this house?"

"I'm too old to have children," she admitted, forcing the words out.

"That's silly. Lots of women your age are having kids."

"My age?"

"Uh, forties?" he guessed, feeling trapped. He was no good at this guessing game, and no matter what he said, she'd be upset with him.

She laughed, but he sensed it wasn't humor. It took a minute or so, but she answered, "I should be flattered that you think I'm still capable, but no, no children."

He considered her words, trying to make sense of them. He detected surface acceptance, but underneath, he sensed there was pain.

Sharp, bitter pain. He should let it alone, but everything about Liss concerned him.

Knowing he had no right to ask, he did so anyway. "Why not?"

"Wyatt, I'm fifty-one."

"What?" he could feel his jaw actually drop at her simple explanation. "You sure as hell don't look it. I thought you were maybe forty-two, forty-four, tops."

"Thanks, I think." Her lips quirked in something that wasn't quite a smile, but it touched Wyatt all the way down deep. "Now that we're getting so personal about me, how old are you?"

He considered lying, but knew that with a woman like Liss, you laid all your cards out on the table. Honesty was not only the best policy with her, it was the only policy. "Uh, I'm forty-five."

"Oh . . ."

"The hair, right? You thought I was older?"

He knew she was uncomfortable with the difference in their ages. He could tell by the way she moved back in her chair, away from the dim candlelight, that she was withdrawing from him. He didn't like it. Not one bit. "Six years isn't much, Liss. Don't let it worry you."

"Maybe it's not much to you, but—"

"But what? We're adults. What the hell does it matter?"

"Enough for you to make an issue of it, evidently."

"Don't turn this around on me," he said, provoked now by her attitude.

"Well, you're the one pushing this!"

"Can't we just ignore it?"

Nine

She moved restlessly, her hand smoothing the arm of the chair. "It hardly seems necessary. After all, there's no point to this discussion."

He felt his jaw flex at her polite way of telling him to stick his questions in his ear. "If you say so," he replied.

What made her think of herself as old? She was young in both spirit and body. Studying her through narrowed eyes, he took in her casual hairstyle, blonde tendrils tucked carelessly behind her small ears, exposing her throat.

Wanting to kiss the pulse at the base of her smooth neck, he let his gaze linger on the upturned thrust of her breasts under that blue outfit that kept him wondering what would happen if he unbuttoned those big white buttons.

Closing down his imagination wasn't easy, but he managed to say, "What are we going to do tomorrow?"

She blinked. "Tomorrow?"

"Sure. I should be done at the plant by six. Want to start with the varnish, then?"

"Wait a minute. Who said anything about—"

"I thought we'd agreed I could help out, do some of the things around here for you?"

"We did no such thing.

"C'mon, Liss. What are friends for?"

"But you didn't come to Oakmont to do odd jobs—"

Wyatt sighed. "I know why I'm here, and I'd appreciate a break."

Put that way, how could she refuse? Afraid of the anticipation that rose inside her, Liss picked up their plates and began carrying things back inside. Wyatt picked up an armload and followed her, not speaking, giving her time to think. Together, in silence, they loaded the dishwasher and made coffee.

When they'd settled on the tall stools at her counter, he couldn't wait any longer. He lifted an eyebrow. "Well?"

She relented. "If you're sure you want to."

He gave her that slow smile that made her insides tremble. "Oh, I want to. I want to do lots of things with you."

"Now, Wyatt—"

His smile deepened. "Varnish your floor, watch television, talk. Move the furniture back into the morning room. I really need a friend, Liss."

Liss flushed, sure she hadn't misinterpreted his intentions. Her eyes narrowed with suspicion and she studied his face, searching out double meanings.

Wyatt bit his lip. Liss had picked up very quickly on his wordplay and he'd only squeaked by with some fancy footwork. "And now, friend, I'd better say good night. I have an early meeting."

"It's not going well, is it, Wyatt?"

Surprised by her sympathetic tone, he took his time to answer. "No. It's not. I'm trying to do the best thing for both the company and the people involved, but sometimes good intentions just aren't enough."

"It's so sad—all those people out of work. Isn't there any compromise solution?"

"I wish there were. Will you walk me to the door?"

"Ah . . . sure."

At the door, he took her hand and turned it over, looking carefully at her palm. "No calluses."

"Gloves and lots of lotion," she said, and managed a smile despite the sensations shooting up her arm.

He bent and pressed a gentle kiss in her palm. "Night, friend."

Wanting much more than a simple peck, Liss kissed his cheek. "Night."

"See you tomorrow."

After seeing Wyatt out, Liss made her nightly rounds, securing her house. She checked the doors, locking the side door she'd opened earlier, and walked from room to room turning off lights. Pausing for a moment to study the new look to the morning room, she had to smile. Who would have thought that Mr. Hotshot VP would get such a kick out of sanding a floor?

Catching her thoughts before they could dwell on the memory of him on hands and knees, smiling up at her, she flipped off the light and went on to lock the front door. The routine, homey tasks weren't enough to distract her from her growing obsession with Wyatt; she remembered him in every room they'd been in together.

Even in those they hadn't occupied simultaneously, she thought, and recalled how she'd felt while showering. His presence had been so strong that at one point she'd whisked back the curtain, expecting to see him, and was surprised when she found herself alone.

She opened her bedroom door, smelling again the faintest whiff of his after-shave, and smiled. Earlier, she'd known immediately that he'd been in her room. Rather than say anything, she'd hugged the knowledge to herself, imagining his reaction to her frankly feminine Laura Ashley bedroom ensemble.

If it was juvenile of her to lose her heart to some lavishly flounced and colorful flowered sheets after all the years of careful, understated decor, then so be it. She loved her new bedroom, where not a stick of furniture reminded her of her old bedroom set.

This was hers, all hers, and if it made her imagination soar, who would know? All through dinner, she'd found herself drifting off, losing the thread of their conversation, while she visualized Wyatt reclining on her bed.

Her traitorous hormones kicked in, reminding her that her decision not to become intimate with Wyatt Harrow was purely mental, and had nothing to do with the warmth pooling in her belly every time she thought of him.

Even if she could get over her abhorrence of affairs, there was now her knowledge of the age difference between them. She'd always looked down her nose at older women parading a younger man around as though he were a trophy. While she'd never make the mistake of thinking Wyatt some kind of gigolo, the idea of his being younger still made her uncomfortable.

She undressed slowly, preparing herself for bed without really thinking of what she was doing, only what Wyatt would think if he ever saw her doing it. David had hated to watch her clean and cream her face. She could only imagine what Wyatt would say if he saw her performing that nightly ritual.

While she took good care of herself and was proud of her healthy, fit body, there was just no way she could compete with a younger woman. Wyatt had a point about their ages not making a difference, but that was rational, not emotional. And what she was feeling right now had nothing to do with rational thought. She was a fool to even consider it!

For the second night in a row, she slept poorly, awakening cranky and feeling every one of her fifty-one years and a few extra besides. By the time she arrived at the library, she was loaded for bear. During Joe's regular Tuesday morning progress meeting, it was all she could do not to snap at the others present.

Joe grew curious. "Are you feeling all right, Liss?"

"I'm fine. Can we get on with this?"

Joe looked away, distancing himself from her. His attitude annoyed Liss, but she controlled her anger and bit back a sharp comment.

When the meeting was over, Joe ushered them out of his office and firmly closed the door.

Dani waited until the other staff members were out of hearing. "What's the matter with you, Liss?"

"Sorry. Just stress. Let's get to work."

"Okay. I want to get out of here early at lunch. Jack's coming by."

"Is there any news?"

"Jack's worried. He called me earlier, on his break, and he told me that there are a lot of hush-hush meetings going on. The big brass have faces down to here," Dani indicated her belly button, "and Jack's pretty sure they're gonna announce layoffs soon."

"That bad?" Liss frowned.

Dani started to answer, then interrupted herself to answer the phone. "Oakmont Public Library. May I help you?"

She listened, then grinned widely. "Just a moment, please." To Liss she mouthed, "It's him."

"Who?"

"Him—that guy! He said, 'Wyatt Harrow for Ms. Thayer.' " Suddenly, her face fell. "Harrow? That's the big boss from Sunnyvale."

"I'll take it over there." Liss picked up the

receiver on the reference desk, then tensed at the sound of his voice.

"Good morning, Liss. Busy?"

She swallowed and tried twice before her voice sounded normal. "Morning. How did you know to call me here?"

"Called your shop, and got your recording. You're closed on Tuesdays and Wednesdays."

"So we are. Did you want something?"

"I just thought I'd take a chance, see if you were at the library—"

"Wyatt, what do you want?"

He picked up the tension in her voice. "Something wrong?"

"No, not really. I just got up on the wrong side of the bed this morn . . ." Oh, Lord, why did she have to mention that word? Flooded with images, fleeting and fantastic, from her dreams, Liss clenched the receiver and willed Wyatt to ignore her reference.

"Didn't sleep well? Neither did I."

"Oh?" she asked, barely breathing.

His voice lowered, grew more intimate. "I kept thinking of you, Liss. I'm looking forward to seeing you again. Can we have lunch together?"

"N . . . No."

"Too busy?"

She agreed instantly, although at that moment she had no idea what her schedule was like for the rest of the day.

"Guess I'll just have to wait until later. I'll bring dinner over. Are we going to varnish tonight?"

It took her a moment to catch up with his change of subject. "Uh, yes."

"I'll be home as soon after six as I can get away. Work clothes again, huh? You gonna wear that same little number?"

She fell silent, ignoring his comment about her falling-apart overalls, wondering if he'd heard himself say *home*. The thought filled her with apprehension, yet tantalized her with possibilities.

"Liss? You still there?"

"Oh, yes, of course. What did you say?"

"Never mind. Listen, I have to go. I've got a meeting waiting for me."

"You don't sound thrilled."

His laugh was short. "No, that I am definitely not."

"Well, good luck."

"Thanks. I need it. Uh, Liss—I'm giving you fair warning, pal. Tonight, I want—"

Liss thought fast. "Oh, sorry, Wyatt, someone's here."

"Coward," he chuckled. "See ya."

Seeing Liss hang up, Dani came over. "That was the guy from Intratec, wasn't it?"

Liss studied the girl's worried face. "Yes, it was."

"That's the guy that's gonna fire Jack."

"We don't know that for sure, Dani," Liss said gently.

"Oh, right," Dani retorted. "We can all pretend, until Jack's laid off and we can't afford to get married."

"Married," Liss echoed in surprise. "You're engaged? This is a surprise. Congratulations! When did this happen?"

Dani preened. "Last night. We're gonna pick out the ring this weekend, but if Jack hasn't got a job, we—"

"Married?" another clerk chimed in.

"Yeah, isn't it great?" Dani burbled. "Say, Liss. Do you think you can talk to this Harrow guy and get him to ease up?"

Liss was stunned. "Whatever makes you think I'd have any influence with Wyatt?"

An older woman, the acquisitions clerk, allowed herself a little smile. "Maybe Dani's referring to the difference in your mood before and after that call?"

Liss flushed. "I don't know what you're talking about,"

"Tsk, tsk. A Thayer fibbing?"

Liss had to smile at her gentle teasing. "Even Thayers know better than to incriminate themselves publicly."

Dani crowed. "I knew it! I knew the minute he called. Look, Liss, you gotta stop him before he fires everybody and closes down the plant."

"Oh, Dani, I can't interfere. There's no reason why he should listen to me. He might not like it, but it's his job."

Dani spoke quickly, "You mean he's unhappy with the idea of closing the plant? Maybe he'll change his mind?"

Wondering why she'd defended Wyatt when last night she was upset with him for the same thing, Liss hesitated. She hated to burst Dani's bubble of optimism. "Don't count on that. Wyatt will do what he has to." She spoke slowly, hoping that he would be able to find some way to save jobs.

"Well, this is all very interesting," Joe drawled from his office door, "but we still have a job to do here."

For the rest of the day, although Liss tried to concentrate on the Oakmont Collection, her mind was on Wyatt. Was he telling the truth when he said he wanted to do the best thing for both the company and the employees? Or was that all hype, said just to impress her?

Across town, in the modern steel and glass complex that housed Intratec's assembly operations, Wyatt pinched and rubbed the skin between his eyebrows. The meeting was getting steadily out of hand, yet he waited before stepping in to exert his authority. He preferred to let the department managers have their say, bitter and openly antagonistic as they were, until they'd gotten all their feelings out of the way and could get down to the core issue.

"Damnit, Harrow. I just moved my family down here. You know what it's gonna cost me to move back to the Bay Area? And what my wife's gonna say? I'll tell you, she said she'd kill me if we had to move again."

"The company will relocate you, Jim."

"That doesn't cover the difference in the cost of living, and you know it."

Two more chimed in to add their grievances. The quality control manager groused, "My wife likes it here, too. The kids can play in the yard. All we had before was a condo."

"I don't see why we have to foot the bill on this," a young engineer complained. "I've been talking to Sunnyvale for months. No one listens. It's like we're nothing more than a bunch of local dummies out here."

"Yeah," another added. "We're so hamstrung by company policies we can't do anything. That's what's been causing the delays in production schedules. Every time we need something, we have to talk to Sunnyvale first. We can't even wipe our noses without having to ask for permission. Why don't they fix that instead of closing us down?"

Wyatt had heard enough. Though he agreed in principle with a lot of the comments the Intratec staff were making, this wasn't the time or place. "Okay. Nobody likes it, but that's the way it is." He paused to make sure he had everyone's attention. "I want detailed operating scenarios from each of your departments. Headcount, expenses, overhead, inventory."

One of the managers asked, "When do you want all that?"

"Eight o'clock tomorrow morning," Wyatt replied, and walked out of the conference room, leaving stunned looks behind him. He almost ran down the secretary who had her hand up to knock on the conference room door.

"Oh! Mr. Harrow, I have a—"

"I thought I told you to call me Wyatt," he snapped.

"Oh, yes, of course," she faltered. "I have a caller on hold, she said she's your daughter, but I wasn't sure I should disturb you—"

"Toby? What's the problem?"

"She said it was personal," the secretary said to Wyatt's retreating back.

He strode quickly to his borrowed office, jerked up the phone and said, "Toby?" He released the hold button and repeated her name. "What's the matter?"

"Hi, Dad. I got this number from your office in Sunnyvale. Angie said it would be okay. Hope you don't mind."

"Of course I don't mind. Are you in Dallas?"

"Yeah. I'm calling you on company time," she confessed.

"Is there a problem?"

She seemed to hesitate. "Does there have to be one to call you?"

"No," he said and let out the breath he didn't realize he'd been holding. "Sorry, kid. I guess I just assumed that something was wrong."

"I'm fine. Work's fine. No problems here. How about there?"

He laughed, a short harsh laugh that held absolutely no humor. "Looking pretty bad."

"Dad, are the rumors I hear true? We're closing the Oakmont facility?"

"Don't know where you get your scuttlebutt, kid."

"Why deny it? It's all over the place. Even here."

"Well, if you've heard it in Dallas, it must be true."

He heard her start to speak, hesitate, then start again. "Dad, I've got a few days off coming up. How about I come visit you?"

He knew she'd been about to say something else. She must have changed her mind and come up with this idea as a way of cheering him up. That she'd offer made him feel better without her even having to make the trip. Why waste her vacation days on her old man?

Smiling, he said gently, "I'd like to see you, Toby, but the timing's off. I don't know how long I'll be stuck here."

"So? I could spend a day or two, at least. I've never seen the assembly operations there. It would be good experience for me."

He had to chuckle. "Nice try, kid. Fact is, I'm too busy. I wouldn't be able to spend much time with you. If any."

"Oh, oh. As bad as all that?" She laughed. "I could come bust you out. We could go over to the beach, soak up some rays and eat seafood."

"Sounds tempting. Another time, okay?"

"Sure, Dad." They spoke for another few minutes until at last Toby blew him a kiss and hung up. Though he'd enjoyed talking to her, and the conversation had taken his mind off the last several hours, in the end he still had a problem on his hands.

He sank behind the desk he'd borrowed,

liking his job less every moment. He hadn't managed that meeting well. Too many things on his mind, and the one becoming most important to him wasn't the electronic assembly plant but one small, slender woman.

Damn, what was Liss doing to him? Before he came to Oakmont, closing down the plant was just another assignment. Since he'd seen the small town through her eyes, and understood how much the Intratec employees liked living here, it was almost impossible to keep her reactions from interfering with his decisions.

He kept hearing her soft voice ask if there weren't some compromise. He remembered her dismay when she thought of people out of work. The thought of causing her further misery hurt him, too.

He began to understand her feelings. He felt the pull of this little town and empathized with the employees who didn't want to move back to Silicon Valley. He could almost see himself here, with Liss, part of the community.

Damnit, Liss, will you get the hell out of my mind and let me get back to work?

Ten

Liss opened her front door to Wyatt and smiled hesitantly.

He wore an expectant look and a grin as he shifted the brown grocery sack from one arm to the other and tugged at the screen. "Hi. You going to let me in?"

Uncertainly, Liss unlatched the outer door. "You didn't have to do that—bring groceries, I mean."

"I warned you earlier that I wanted food—*lots* of food."

"You did?"

"Sure, you remember," he paused, recalling how she'd cut him off before he finished his sentence. Another thought occurred to him. "You thought I meant something else?"

His grin grew into a laugh that brought deeper color to her cheeks. Liss turned and moved away from the door, scolding herself for letting Wyatt get to her.

Last night she'd finally convinced herself that she could accept a relationship with him based on friendship only, and had resigned herself to enjoying what companionship he'd offer her while he was in Oakmont, but here she was—heart going pitty-pat just at the sight of him.

Still grinning, he followed her through the house to the kitchen. He plunked the groceries down on her counter, then pulled huge steaks, fresh corn, a loaf of sourdough bread and Texas-sized potatoes out of the bag like a magician experimenting with rabbits.

"Are you planning to feed an army?"

He seized her, planted a noisy, hard kiss on her mouth, and released her before she could rebuff him. "Nope. I'm planning to work up an appetite tonight."

She felt her eyes widen. "Oh?"

"Physical labor always makes me hungry. Tonight, we're going to varnish that floor and make some plans for the rest of the week."

He put the perishables in the refrigerator. With his back turned partially away from her, Liss took a deep breath, pulling herself together. He'd been in her house only a few minutes and already she was ready to tear that yellow T-shirt right off his back and—

"How come you're not wearing those snazzy overalls?" Wyatt turned back and scanned every inch of her loose jeans and blue chambray blouse, her sleeves turned modestly back at mid forearm.

Liss raised her eyes from his pectorals. "What?"

"I liked that little red thing you were wearing last night."

Without thinking, she answered, "That bandeau? The elastic's about shot. It doesn't stay up . . ." Hearing herself, she stopped short, but the damage was done.

Wyatt's blue eyes subtly darkened.

She felt his interest as though it were her own. How could she deny that she'd wondered what it would be like to make love with this man? One kiss like the one they'd shared the other night was enough to set her imagination running vividly.

She had to keep a closer guard on what she said. Telling herself she'd be all right if she took no notice of him, she walked to the door of the morning room. "Shall we get started?"

They got to work. It was as if they hadn't come close to fighting last night. It seemed as if Wyatt was determined to keep things light and friendly. With good humor, he checked the surface of the floor and then the brushes and varnish.

Liss couldn't believe how much fun it was to squabble companionably about the best method of applying the varnish. By the time they were done, he had it smeared across his pants legs and his Nikes would never be the same. Liss had somehow escaped unvarnished.

He complained loudly.

She slanted a mischievous look at him. "Well, if you'd moved your tush when I told you—"

"Whose tush?" He reached for her.

She skipped aside. He stalked her. She danced down the hall and into her parlor. He followed.

"No, you can't come in here!" she commanded, as lighthearted and flirtatious as a teenager.

He stopped in the doorway. "Why not?"

"This parlor is for genteel goings-on. I can tell that you don't have refined conversation on your mind."

"Is that so?" he challenged. "What *do* I have on my mind?"

"You know," she gestured, feeling flustered and yet exhilarated by the game they played. It was dangerous, she knew, yet all the sweeter for the risks.

He stood his ground. "You're a mind reader, too?"

She smiled mysteriously. "Maybe."

"Oh? What am I thinking now?"

Her smile faded. His expression mirrored the need she felt building within herself. Unable to look away, she felt him studying her, as though he could look deep inside her and clearly see the way her body clamored for closeness.

"Liss?" he whispered.

"I forgot," she apologized. "It wasn't fair of me to . . . I forgot all about being friends."

"Is that so bad?"

She exhaled. "Maybe we should think about dinner?"

Feeling overwhelmed, he stared at her for a moment, then moved back a step. "Okay. I'll start the barbecue, then go clean up. I'll be back in twenty minutes."

"You're leaving?"

It was his turn to breathe heavily. He didn't want to leave, but he needed a cold shower. Needed it badly if he wasn't going to turn into a caveman and bodily cart Liss up to her lush lair. "I want to get this varnish off. I'll be back after I change."

Liss nodded stiffly "I'll get the other things started, then."

Following a restrained dinner during which neither felt comfortable, even though the steaks were grilled just right and the corn was especially succulent, they perched on the kitchen stools and drank coffee. The flirtatious game they'd shared before dinner had changed the rules.

She didn't know how to get back on a safer footing, wasn't even sure she wanted to, even though every bit of common sense in her shouted for her to retreat while she still could.

He set the cup down and leaned back. "Now that's what I call dinner."

"You look like you're going to pat your stomach at any moment."

"Maybe. I sure as hell feel a lot better than I did earlier."

"Oh?" She wanted to ask why, but she was learning that when it came to Intratec or his reason for being in Oakmont, it was better to let Wyatt bring the subject up himself.

"I had a rough meeting this afternoon. But, hey, Toby called."

"Your daughter? Is something wrong?"

"That's the first thing I asked," he grinned. "But apparently everything is fine."

"I'm glad. Did you have a good talk?"

"Yeah," he started, then stopped. "Come to think of it, she never did say why she was calling. Said there wasn't a problem, but now, I think maybe there was something she wanted to say and didn't."

"Oh? About what?"

"Now how would I know that?"

"Well, she might have dropped a hint."

"Nope. Funny thing is, we've always been able to talk. Today, though, it sounded like she was uneasy about something."

"Maybe it was a problem at work and she felt uneasy coming to you about it because of your position?" Liss suggested.

"I don't think so. I keep my nose out of her job area. She's in development, not manufacturing, like I am, so there's nothing to prevent her from talking over a problem with me."

"I'm not sure I understand how she can work at the same company and not have people wonder about nepotism."

Wyatt nodded. "It can be a problem. But Intratec has close to thirty thousand employees, scattered across the country. Just to keep things clean, when she joined the company, right after she got her masters, I made sure that she wouldn't be placed in one of my areas. Even when I was in Dallas, I rarely saw her."

"You didn't live together?"

"Hell, no."

"Why not?"

"She moved out when she went to college. It would be hard to move back home after she'd started living on her own."

Liss nodded. She herself hadn't had much choice, but she knew how hard it was to go home and live with parental rules after being independent.

But then, she'd never wanted to live anywhere but here, at home, in Oakmont.

"But you sound like you're still pretty close."

He nodded. "I admit I keep track of her at work, see how she's doing, if she's keeping her nose clean, that sort of thing. But I don't get involved."

"Maybe she'll call back," Liss suggested as his worried look returned.

"Yeah. Maybe," he frowned. "Maybe I should call her. Do you mind if I use your phone?"

"Of course not. Use the one in the parlor if you'd like."

He got up and went to her kitchen phone. "This one's fine." He punched a series of numbers, listened, then replaced the receiver. "Not home."

"Well, you can try later," she offered, then caught his brooding look. He seemed to be staring right through her, and she was sure his mind was far away. Probably on Toby.

What kind of father was he? It was hard to imagine him with an adult daughter. Or with a child. He and his wife were so young when they married. If Toby was twenty-six, then she was born when Wyatt was only nineteen.

So young to be a father! Had he had time for her then, when he was up to his ears with school and, later on, a new job?

Liss tried but couldn't see him playing with Toby, or teaching her to ride a bike or any of the things fathers did. Would he listen if Toby did want to talk to him? She found herself wondering what kind of relationship he had with his daughter. Did he enjoy her company? Were they close? He seemed proud of her success at Intratec, but what were his real feelings for her?

By the way he fussed over the telephone call of this afternoon, she thought he must love his daughter very much, but was he able to show it?

This was a new side to him. She watched him, feeling safe to do so since he wasn't paying her any attention, very likely wasn't even aware she was there. It didn't help, though. His mind might be on other matters, but he was right here. Right in her kitchen, threatening her peace of mind.

Feeling much too aware of him, she got up to clear the dishes away.

Wyatt seemed to shake himself free of whatever thought had held him. Over her protests, he helped her, rinsing the steak platters and stacking them in the dishwasher.

She turned from putting the butter in the refrigerator to see him shoving steak bones into the disposal and flipping the switch. "No, wait!"

Through the grumbling roar of the disposal, Wyatt asked, "What?"

"You can't put those steak bones in there," she yelled over the din.

Abruptly, the noise died.

"Oh, oh," Wyatt looked at the sink and then at her.

"It's an old disposal. Temperamental."

"I'll fix it," he offered.

She wasn't too sure he had the skills, but she'd learned the hard way that when a man got that tight-lipped look and said he'd fix something, she'd better let him get on with it. Without a word, she went into the utility room, got her toolbox, and brought it to him.

Raising an eyebrow at her, he turned his attention to the sink. He fished the remains of their dinner out of the disposal.

Several minutes later, he gave up trying to fix it at sink level and crawled into the cabinet. She perched nearby, ready to hand him a tool when he needed it.

"You know, Liss, I never thought I'd be doing this."

She looked at Wyatt, lying flat on his back with his head under her kitchen sink. Drawn by the sight of his muscular body, she peeked at him once, twice, and then made herself look away. "What? Fixing my garbage disposal?"

"Nope. Enjoying it."

"I wouldn't put it on my list of fun things to do."

He grunted and then offered, "Neither would I, but don't knock it until you've tried it."

"Right," she said, amused.

Moving closer, she leaned against the dishwasher and realized he wouldn't know it if she did ogle him. She looked her fill. His belly sank behind his belt, creating a most intriguing hollow, while his narrow hips poked hillocks into the faded jeans. One long, masculine leg extended halfway to forever, and the other was bent at the knee, pulling the denim fabric into fascinating patterns.

Though she tried to keep her gaze from the rounded mass at the junction of his jeans legs, it was as effective as telling the Mona Lisa not to smile.

Liss tried, unsuccessfully, to lift her eyes—and her thoughts—upward. When the silence grew too long, she said, "I'm sorry you got stuck with this."

He grunted. "Hand me a wrench, will you?"

Bending from the waist, she passed him one and stayed to eye the muscles working under his yellow shirt. The need to touch, to caress rose within her; resolutely, she pushed it away, but her treacherous body did just as it pleased and whispered enticements.

"Ummph! Got it." Moments later, he slid out from under her sink. "You really need a newer model. Did this come off the Ark?"

"I can't afford a new one just now."

He got to his feet. "Why don't you let me replace it for you?"

"Absolutely not."

"Why not? After all, I broke it."

She tried the switch again. The old machine groaned, but worked.

Accepting that the subject of a new disposal was closed, Wyatt replaced the tools and washed his hands.

She handed him a towel. "Thanks for fixing it."

He smiled and nuzzled the tip of her nose, then pressed a light kiss against her mouth. Instinctively, she closed her eyes and breathed in his scent, hoping he'd take the kiss deeper. When he didn't, Liss opened her eyes, wondering who'd sandbagged her when she wasn't looking.

When she got her balance back, she smiled tentatively. "More coffee?"

When he nodded, she asked, "You want to sit in here, or—"

He eyed the bright kitchen, and hesitated. He'd prefer the wicker armchair in her bedroom, but that was out of the question. For now. Wyatt leaned against the counter. "This is fine."

While she ground the coffee beans, Wyatt turned his thoughts away from her bedroom and contemplated her back yard. He was used to an urban silhouette, towers and rooftops cutting into the sky. This was different.

Even though he could see the lights on in the second story of a house down the block, he didn't feel any neighbors pressing in on him. Absorbing the tranquillity, he couldn't explain why he found the dark outline of branches against the moon so appealing; he merely accepted the easing of tension within him.

Turning to him, Liss saw the fatigue in his face and felt compelled to give comfort, she wasn't sure what kind, but somehow she wanted to ease his weariness. Something bothered him, and he didn't want to talk about it, but if she could help, shouldn't she offer?

If she did, however, would he take it to mean more than she meant it to be?

Before she could say anything, he looked back at her. "How was your day?"

"Busy," she answered with a quick smile, grateful that he'd bridged the conversational gap. Bringing him a cup of coffee, she placed it on the counter near him. "We're so close to the move that things are getting awfully hectic at the library, but we're all excited. Everyone is wondering whether the governor will show up."

"The governor. Oakmont must rate."

"Well, I don't know about that, but we've been getting a lot of good press."

"The library or the Collection?"

"Both." She colored faintly. "Actually, the Collection. Someone on the governor's staff is a history buff. He's been here several times. It'll be good to talk to him again."

"Must be nice to have something to look forward to."

"Sounds like you had a rough day," she suggested, noticing the downcast look around his mouth.

"Nothing I didn't expect. Nothing I can't handle." In a flash, the morose Wyatt was replaced by the hard-edged corporate executive.

Liss stared, fascinated by the way his face changed and became more sharply defined. She was struck by the way he drew in on himself, sealing all the cracks against invasion.

His eyes seemed to glint with a power she'd only guessed at before. She took an involuntary step backward, putting space between them.

Suddenly, as if it had never been there, the ruthless side of him vanished. Wyatt smiled, a warm, attractive smile that Liss couldn't resist.

She didn't try. Putting her hand on top of his, she asked, "Do you want to talk about it?"

He turned his hand and captured her fingers. He held them gently, all too aware of the delicate bones in his grasp.

His thumb moved slowly over her knuckles as he drew her closer to him. "No. I just like being here with you. I don't want to think about the mess at Intratec."

She felt the warmth of his breath on her temple. "Okay."

"Do you know what I thought about this afternoon?"

She shook her head. "What?"

"I could hardly wait to leave, to come here to be with you."

Nervous again, she tried to pull her hand away.

He tightened his grip. "No, don't be scared. I'm not coming on to you. This is something new—I've never felt this way before. I like coming home and puttering—"

"But surely," she interrupted, raising her eyes to his, "when you were married, you—"

"No," he said abruptly, then continued more slowly, holding her gaze. "It wasn't like this, like it is with you. My ex-wife liked to socialize. At first, it was with other students, then later, with the people I met at work."

"And then?" she prompted when he fell silent.

"Most evenings we were out. A lot of it was connected with her job, with making her look good. I got damned tired of being polite to strangers."

"What about Toby?"

"Babysitters. I didn't like it. We didn't see much of her during the day, and then at night, it was worse."

"Your wife didn't stay home with the baby?"

"Sure she did—at first. Then she went crazy, climbing the walls at home. She went back to work as soon as Toby was toilet trained."

"Oh." Liss knew it was old-fashioned, but she couldn't imagine a mother leaving her child with strangers.

"That's why I like coming here like this,"

Wyatt said, stretching contentedly. "It's something I never had."

"Maybe you just like the newness of it. It's a game to you, like playing house. Believe me, it'll wear off."

"Maybe, maybe not. But now, I like the . . . domesticity, I guess. It's not something I would have thought would hold any meaning for me. I sure as hell didn't like being tied down to a house before. Elaine—you mind if I talk about her? I should have asked sooner."

"I don't mind," Liss said, and was surprised to find she meant it. If she could learn more about him by listening to him talk about his ex-wife and his marriage, she'd be glad to listen. She wanted to know all she could about him.

"All I know is, all afternoon, I could barely wait to get home to you. The thought of you kept me going."

"Don't say that!" She tugged her hand back and moved away from him, away from the thought that he called her house "home." "We agreed, friends only."

"Friends can't miss each other?" He reached for her again, but she evaded him. "It's true."

She poured herself some coffee and raised it to her mouth, then set it down without drinking. All this talk of his ex-wife and daughter made her restless, made her see the futility of pretending that they were anything more than strangers. "This is absurd, you know that?"

He looked at her for more explanation.

"I don't need this." She turned away from him. Picking up a damp sponge, she scrubbed the already clean countertop. "This isn't going to work."

"What?"

"This pretense of being friends. You come waltzing into my life, tell me how things are going to be, and . . ."

"And?"

"You don't understand. I don't like the way you make me feel—"

He crossed the kitchen to stand behind her. "Do I make you ache as much as I ache? Can I kiss it and make it better, Liss?"

His words seared her already sensitized emotional nerve-endings. His breath, damp and moist on the back of her neck, made her shiver. "Stop that!" she demanded, not sure if she pleaded with him or with her own needs.

"Stop trying to seduce me!" She felt, lost, threatened, exhilarated—and determined to be honest with him. "You make me feel things I've never felt before. You're using my weakness against me. I don't want you to use those feelings against me. I don't want to feel them!"

His voice roughened as he took her shoulders to turn her to face him. "What feelings, Liss? Tell me."

"No," she said, dropping her eyes to study the toes of their shoes, which were almost touching. "It's too late for me—for all this."

"Are we back to the age thing again? If we are, you can just forget it," he snapped. "I don't care if there's six or sixteen years between us."

Deliberately, he paused to take her chin and gently turn it up until she looked him in the eye. "What we have is too good to lose because you have some stupid hang-up about being a few years older."

"It's not a stupid hang-up. It's a fact," she protested, not sure if she was trying to convince him or herself.

"Screw the facts," he said crudely. "The way I see it, you're hiding behind this age thing. Have you looked at yourself recently, Liss? You're a healthy, beautiful, sexy woman, and to tell you the truth, I'm tired of hearing you put yourself down."

"I don't do that."

"The hell you don't. Every time you open your mouth to tell me to get lost, out comes this garbage about you not being what you think you should be."

She opened her mouth to protest, but he spoke first. "Don't bother trying to deny it. Accept yourself for what you are. Are you going to ignore the way we feel?"

"I don't know what to do! I've never felt like this before . . ." she admitted, and then stopped when she realized what she'd said. No one had ever talked to her the way Wyatt did. No one challenged her feelings about herself like he did. It made her uncomfortable to have him know so much about her. She felt stripped bare, naked under his dissecting glare.

His anger disappeared in an instant, the moment he understood. He traced a thumb across her cheek. "Ah, Liss. I'm sorry. Talk to me."

"You make me feel like you know things about me that I don't," she blurted, unable to resist being so close to him. "How can you do that? Get under my skin like that? You make me hungry to touch you—"

His smile turned triumphant the moment he realized what she'd just confessed. He swept her into his arms and buried his face in her neck, reveling in the sweet floral fragrance of her skin. "Oh, God, Liss. That's just the way I feel. I want you so much I hurt."

"But I don't want to feel this way," she cried, at odds with her emotions and the way her body melted into his.

"Why not?"

She wrenched herself free of him and moved several steps away. "I won't have an affair with you! I don't sleep around."

"I don't, either. No one can afford to any more—"

"It's not just that."

He spoke gently. "Then what's the problem? I want you. You just admitted you want me, too. The lovemaking will be wonderful between us."

"There, that's it! You said lovemaking, but it's not. We don't love each other. Without love, without commitment, it's only sex."

He recoiled as if struck. "Only sex? What I'm feeling is more—damnit, Liss, I'm talking about more than hopping into the sack."

"Don't be vulgar."

"Vulgar be damned. Liss, believe me. Since the morning we met, you've become more important to me every day. I can't deny that I've wondered what it would be like to take you to bed. You're an attractive, sexy woman and you appeal to me in a way no other woman has ever done. I—"

"Stop it, Wyatt! That just makes it worse. You're going to leave Oakmont soon and I don't want to be the one left kicking myself for getting involved."

"We're already involved."

"No!" she cried, desperation tingeing her voice. She couldn't take any more of this . . . this whatever it was that urged her to forget what she'd said earlier. Trying to keep herself strong, ignoring the sudden urge to weep, she shook her head. "Forget it."

"Liss, we have to talk."

"No, we don't. I can't take any more—you'd better leave."

"Don't throw me out now."

Eleven

"Good night, Wyatt."

Frustrated, he spoke harshly. "All right. I'll go. But when you lie awake tonight in that big wicker bed, ask yourself if you wouldn't rather be sharing it with me."

She gulped back hot, angry tears. "That's not fair."

Wyatt left, slamming the front door behind him. What a way to end the evening. He'd come on to her like a jerk, after he'd promised himself that he'd use restraint, woo her with friendship until her inhibitions melted away.

Now look what he'd done.

Cursing his impatience, he jogged to the sidewalk, then turned up the driveway of the Greenley house. He heard the phone ringing a few paces away from the guest quarters and picked up speed, hoping it was Liss. "Hello?"

"Harrow, where the hell have you been? I've been calling for the last hour!"

Disappointed, Wyatt bit back an expletive and tried to place the frantic voice. "Who is this?"

"It's Pete. Pete Dodge. We've got trouble, Wyatt. Trouble at the plant."

All business now, Wyatt snapped, "What is it?"

Pete's words tumbled out. "Some of the hourly employees have barricaded themselves into the cafeteria. Others are on the main assembly line. They refuse to work until you guarantee them their jobs are safe."

"Not likely," Wyatt snorted. "How bad is it, Pete?"

"I've got the local police on their way."

"I wish you hadn't done that—not yet, anyway. Are the security guards on duty?"

"Of course, but things are getting out of hand. One of the guards got roughed up."

"What happened?"

"She—she was knocked down. Stomped on, I think. Her arm's broken."

Wyatt's voice betrayed his concern. "I'm on my way. Don't do anything more until I get there. Keep things as calm as you can."

Liss heard Wyatt's car squeal out of the driveway and accelerate rapidly down the street. Where could he be going in such a

217

hurry? Was his speed due to his anger with her? Pretending that it was an evening like any other, she locked up her house and went to bed.

When Wyatt made the turn into the Intratec parking lot, he had to thread his way between police vehicles parked at odd angles. Swearing at the news van blocking his way, he braked sharply in front of the main lobby and jumped out of the Legend.

Pete saw him coming and gestured to a security guard to unlock the big glass doors.

A television reporter saw Wyatt's approach and hastened over to him, exclaiming, "You're Wyatt Harrow?"

Wyatt nodded but didn't stop.

Keeping up with Wyatt, the reporter motioned for his cameraman to start filming. "Mr. Harrow, what's going on inside?"

"That's what I'm here to find out. Excuse me." He blinked against the bright camera light and pushed open the glass doors to the darkened lobby. The news team followed right behind him, the reporter still shouting questions.

Wyatt beckoned to the guard, who moved into the doorway to prevent them from entering.

The reporter tried to shove his way past.

The guard forced him back.

Wyatt noticed the resulting scuffle. He paused and caught the reporter's eye. When the man stopped pushing, Wyatt said firmly, "I'll have a statement for you later. Now—leave the building."

"Is it true you're here to shut down the plant and lay off all the employees?" the reporter shouted before the guard managed to eject the news team and lock the doors behind them.

Wyatt squared his shoulders. "All right. Let's get on with this."

Pete walked Wyatt down a long corridor. "Sorry about that. Don't know how word got out that we've got a mess on our hands. I talked to the guys out on the floor, well I tried to, but their ringleader refused to talk to me. He's waiting for you."

"Who is he?"

"Technician named Jack Brody. He's sharp, a firebrand. He's got them quite worked up."

"How many others involved?"

"All the hourlies on shift."

"Damnit! How'd this get started?"

"Don't know for sure, but I hear Brody started belly-aching at the dinner break and got everybody organized."

"What does he want?"

"Like I told you. He doesn't want to be fired. They want guarantees."

"I can't do that."

"What can we do?"

Wyatt flashed Pete an approving look, glad that the older man had said "we." "I'll talk to them, see what I think, then we'll go from there."

Pete nodded and stopped before wide double doors with wire-meshed windows. "Here we are. They've got this door blocked from the inside."

"Hell of a fire risk."

"That's the least of their worries right now."

"How many other exits?"

"Fire escape, emergency exit at the other end. They've got the kitchen doors locked, too."

"We have to get them opened. Have you got the fire department on stand-by?"

"Yeah."

"Good. Let's see what we can do here." Wyatt knocked on the door. "This is Harrow. I understand you want to talk to me?"

A dark-haired man peered through the window. He looked from Wyatt to Pete and back again. "Just Harrow. Nobody else."

"Fine with me," Wyatt said, keeping his voice relaxed. "Pete, take a break while I talk things out here."

Pete's eyes widened, but at Wyatt's gesture, he agreed and moved a few paces away.

The door opened slowly. The man stuck his nose out and scanned the hall. "Come in."

"You Jack Brody?" Wyatt asked, studying the young man in jeans, a black T-shirt with a Harley logo, and black hightops. He didn't look much older than twenty-five, but his dark eyes blazed with conviction.

Wyatt sighed. The kid could be anybody. Firebrands didn't wear a uniform.

"Yeah."

Wyatt extended his hand. "Pleasure to meet you, Jack."

The younger man looked puzzled, but he shook Wyatt's hand.

Wyatt smiled amiably. "Where can we talk?"

"Uh, the foreman's office."

"Okay. Lead the way."

In the small, Spartan office, Wyatt deliberately chose the plastic visitor's armchair, leaving the foreman's desk free. He sat and crossed one ankle over the other knee.

Leaning back into the chair, shoulders slouched, he presented a relaxed, receptive stance. "Okay, what can I do for you?"

Jack folded his arms over his chest and remained standing by the door.

Reading the other man's rigid body language, Wyatt sat up straight, then leaned forward, placing his forearms on his knees. "Want to talk about this before the situation gets worse?"

Jack advanced a few paces into the room. "Look, man, don't try to snow me."

"Wouldn't dream of it, Jack. Something's eating at you, and if it's important enough to you to stage all this, you'd better talk to me about it. Let's get it out in the open."

Jack bit his lip and moved closer. "You mean straight?"

"Straight up."

"Okay." Jack planted his fists on his hips. "You're gonna shut down the plant, throw us all out of work. We don't wanna lose our jobs."

Wyatt didn't stop a slight smile. "You think this demonstration is going to make a difference?"

Jack bridled. "Hey, man, we got rights, too."

"Sure you do, but there's a better way of handling things."

"Yeah? Like what?"

Ignoring the challenge in Jack's voice, Wyatt kept his own calm. "Did you know what you're doing is against company policy? That you could get fired for this?"

"So what? Get fired tonight for speaking

up for our rights or get fired next week like a sitting duck? Same difference, man."

"Not necessarily. For sure you could get fired for staging this show, but getting laid off isn't a done deal. You're jumping to conclusions, Brody."

Jack scoffed. "Oh, sure. It's all over the plant, all over town. Everybody knows you're gonna boot us all out!"

"Really? Somebody knows more than I do."

"This isn't a joke, man!"

"Do I look like I'm laughing, Brody? You're putting yourself in one hell of a risky situation here. I could fire you right now on the spot, but what would that prove? We have a product that has to get out. This plant is losing money. You think this stunt is going to improve our deliveries? Keep the plant open?"

Jack looked confused.

Wyatt pressed harder. "You want to keep the plant open, you'd better make sure it's worth our while."

"You're full of it, Harrow. All you want is to get me to call this off, so you can lay people off without a squawk from us."

"That's where you're wrong, Jack." Wyatt's voice changed, becoming hard and assertive. "I want you to call this off. What's more, I'll tell you this: I don't give in to pressure. I won't make you any promises that I don't intend to keep. Whatever I decide, it'll be the best I can do. Nothing like this demonstration or any other damned-fool stunt, will make me decide one way or the other. Not you nor anybody else will influence me. Is that clear?"

"That gives us nothing."

"On the contrary, it gives you a helluva lot more than you had before I walked in here."

"Let me get this straight. You're saying you won't fire me, or anybody else? Nobody in here," Jack waved at the assembly operation outside the foreman's office, "or the cafeteria?"

Wyatt nodded.

"What do we have to give away?" Jack asked, eyes narrowing with suspicion.

Wyatt laughed harshly. "You aren't giving anything away. I am, and you're taking it, if you know what's good for you."

He paused to let that sink in. Then, watching Jack carefully, he asked, "Instead of working against me, why don't you work with me?"

"Huh?"

Wyatt nodded as if Jack's exclamation had been agreement. "I meant what I said. Work with me. I have to find an answer to the problems in the plant. Why don't you get involved in finding the solution instead of adding to the problem?"

"That's the usual line we get around here." Jack sneered as he quoted, "If you're not part of the solution, you're part of the problem."

Wyatt said nothing. Leaning back, he watched Jack Brody pace. At last, he stopped by the desk. Without looking at Wyatt, he stated, "You're putting me on."

"I'm dead serious. Get together with your buddies out there, talk it out. You guys know what's happening around here. You know what has to be done to improve production. See what you can come up with. Then we'll see."

"That's a load of—what can *we* do?" Jack whirled around and stared at Wyatt. "We're just the grunts. It's you guys who want to make more money by giving our jobs away—"

"Prove us wrong," Wyatt challenged.

Jack looked stunned. His mouth dropped open, but when he found his voice, it was sarcastic. "Yeah, right. Who's gonna listen to anything we say?"

"Say something worthwhile, and I'll listen."

"You mean it?"

Wyatt softened his tone at the look of hope in the other man's face. "I mean it, Jack. But I also mean this: any more stunts, and you're out the door so fast your butt will burn. Got that?"

"Got it." Jack nodded, then his face fell. "Uh, what about that guard? We didn't mean—"

"What happened?"

A muscle worked in Brody's jaw. "The guards pushed in here. We didn't want them, so we pushed them right out. One of them was a woman. She, uh, she . . . got trampled."

Wyatt blew his cheeks out. "That's bad. I won't kid you. I'll see what I can do, but if she wants to press charges, it'll be up to her."

Jack glanced away, then looked back to meet Wyatt's eyes. "It's my fault. If she's going to press charges, then she should charge me."

In that moment, Wyatt's impression of Jack Brody changed. He had to admire the younger man's willingness to accept responsibility. Brody had to know that if the guard pressed charges and he was found guilty, he could be looking at jail time.

He studied the determination in the younger man's eyes. Maybe they could actually work something out together.

He stood and moved to the door. "Here's what we'll do. I'll talk to security, to Pete Dodge, and see what we can come up with. In the meantime, you get things back to normal around here. Deal?"

Jack met Wyatt's extended hand with his own. "Deal, and uh, Mr. Harrow—thanks."

"It's Wyatt, Jack, since we're working together. But one last thing."

Jack looked wary.

Wyatt spoke, his voice flat and even. "There'll be no more publicity out of this. If there's going to be a statement to the press, I'll make it. You keep your mouth shut. No more grandstanding. Got it?"

Jack looked like he wanted to protest, but didn't. Lips pressed tightly together, he nodded.

"Good. I'll talk to you tomorrow."

By the time Wyatt had cleared things with the security guard captain, assured himself that the injured guard had received appropriate medical care, and settled things with Pete Dodge, it was almost three in the morning.

Exhausted, he gave a carefully-worded statement to the press and drove back to his place.

Maybe his tactics with Jack Brody would prove effective. If nothing else, they bought him a little time, but he hoped his favorable reaction to the younger man was justified. If he hadn't won Brody over, or persuaded him to think twice before he did any more rabble-rousing, Wyatt felt sure that, at the very least, he'd planted a few seeds in his mind.

There was much more that needed doing, so much that could make the plant really productive, but now wasn't the time. He didn't like to think that if he closed the plant down, there'd be no time at all. No time to explore his burgeoning feelings for Liss.

Much as he wanted her, he had to solve the problems at the plant before he could turn his attention to her. He shook his head, feeling the weight of the burdens on his shoulders.

Mulling over possible plans of action, Wyatt drove through the serene streets of nighttime Oakmont. His was the only car around. He reflected that even at this late hour, there'd be traffic in Sunnyvale. He remembered the serenity he'd felt when he stood in Liss's kitchen and looked out over her back yard.

He needed some of that peacefulness now.

Wishing he could talk with Liss, he glanced at her house, expecting to see it darkened. Instead, he saw a light behind an upstairs window—she was awake.

He sucked in his breath, regretting the words he'd flung at her earlier. He knew how it hurt to lie awake at night hoping for something he couldn't have. He was ashamed of himself for wishing that on her.

Debating whether he should call her, he showered and climbed naked into bed. He tossed for several minutes, then got up and went into the living room, heading for the phone. On the way, he detoured past the side window to look at her house.

Her bedroom light was out. He couldn't call her now. Damn, he'd have to wait until morning to eat crow. Knowing he had to get some sleep, he stood by the window and stared at her house, trying to come to terms with the things that had happened to him since he'd come to Oakmont.

In her own bed, Liss quivered with her need to find out where Wyatt had gone, and why he was back so late. She'd given up trying to sleep much earlier, and rather than stare at the ceiling, she'd turned on the light and picked up a novel.

She'd heard his car purr down the street, had heard him close his car door, and even imagined she'd heard his door key in the lock. She knew he could see her light, if he just looked up, and she waited, hoping he'd call her.

When he didn't, she rolled over and turned off her bedside lamp, missing the comfort and sanctuary her room usually gave her. For once, her pleasure in her bedroom failed her. And it was all because of Wyatt Harrow.

Damn him, why did he have to make her feel this way?

* * *

Wyatt woke early, stiff and still tired, but after a few minutes he acknowledged he wasn't going to get any more sleep. He heaved himself from bed, stretching to work out the kinks. He went out for his run, wishing he could free his mind as easily as his body limbered under exercise. He ran down his driveway, up past Liss's front yard, and along a route he'd picked out several days earlier.

As he ran, he reviewed what he'd promised Jack Brody and wondered why problems at work never seemed to take as much solving as his personal problems did.

He returned the same way, retracing his steps, slowing down to look up at the darkened second story windows of Liss's house. It was too early for her to be up, yet he wanted to apologize before any more time went by. He showered and dressed, absently putting on his clothes, knotting his tie by rote, wondering how soon he could call her.

Across the oleander hedge, Liss rubbed sleep from her bleary eyes and reluctantly faced the new day. She dragged herself through her routine, and went out to snip her morning bouquet, taking the scenic route to retrieve the newspaper from the front verandah.

She took her time, hoping she'd see him, but after she'd dawdled as long as she could, she sat down with her coffee and unfolded the paper.

Wyatt's face stared up at her from the front page. Eyes widening, she put on her glasses for a better look and studied his image, grainy and harshly lit by the camera light. He looked tired and worried. Her heart softened with sympathy when she recognized Intratec's logo on the glass door behind him.

She scanned the article, reading about the trouble at the plant the night before, and then flipped on the television, sampling channels, looking for news of him.

She had to speak to him, right away.

Casting aside the ingrained reluctance, her fingers fumbled with the telephone. She pulled off her earring with a jerky motion and held the receiver to her ear, listening to the phone ring unanswered.

Her doorbell rang. She dropped the phone, and raced through the house. Yanking the front door open, seeing him, her heartrate went into overdrive. "Wyatt! Are you all right? I just saw the paper."

He came in and stopped just inside the hall. "I'm fine. Look, Liss, I'm sorry. I said things last night that I regretted as soon as they were out of my mouth—"

"Oh, Wyatt. I'm sorry, too—"

"Are we still friends?"

Liss hesitated. "We'll talk about it, but first, what happened at Intratec?"

In terse phrases, wanting to be done with it and get on to more personal explanations, he described the situation. "That's it. The press made more of it than necessary. Once Brody and I came to an agreement, it was all over."

"Brody? Jack Brody?"

"You know him?"

She nodded, her face paling.

"What's the matter?"

"Jack's engaged to Susan's daughter, Dani. Oh, my—"

Wyatt smiled. "So that's your source?"

It took her a minute to make the connection. She'd teased him the other day about having an inside scoop on Intratec's doings. Nodding, she reached out to touch his arm. The fine worsted of his suit felt soft and luxurious to the touch, and unaware that she did so, she rubbed a bit of fabric between her fingers. "They've been so worried that he'll lose his job and they won't be able to get married."

Wyatt laughed. The sound of it was so

warming, so comforting, that without a second thought, Liss moved closer.

He opened his arms and she walked right into them as though she belonged there. He snuggled her closer and laid his jaw against her temple.

She breathed in the subtle scent of his after-shave and had the sudden thought that if she never had to move again, she'd be just fine. "I'm sorry we fought last night," she murmured.

"No sorrier than I. It ate at me all night long."

"You were too busy to think of me."

"Hardly. I wanted to call you when I got home—"

"I wanted you to call."

He lifted her chin. "You did?"

She nodded. "When you didn't, I felt awful."

"Why didn't you call me?"

"I couldn't do that. It's not proper."

He smiled, pleased with her old-fashioned standards. "You can call me any time you want."

"Mmm," she stalled, more interested in the way his voice had deepened.

"I mean it. Promise?"

"Promise," she whispered, an instant before his mouth took hers.

233

He increased the pressure, feeling her softness, drawing in her quickened breath, tasting her sweetness. When she parted her lips, he thrust his tongue inside to explore, more leisurely, the hidden pleasures of her mouth. He lifted his face long enough to slide her glasses off and hold them safely out of the way before he lowered his mouth again.

Liss heard herself making little noises of invitation. Feeling her body liquefy and lean against his for support, she absorbed his strength. His mouth moved against hers, deepening their kiss for several glorious, dizzying moments. Reluctantly, he gentled his touch, brushing his lips against hers before finally releasing them. "I have to go. It's going to be a busy day."

"Mmm," she replied, still dreamy.

He replaced her glasses on her upturned face. "Liss?"

"What?"

"I'll call you. We'll make dinner plans."

She tasted the word like a rare delicacy. "Dinner."

Wyatt let himself out, smiling. Let Liss try *now* to convince him that there wasn't something special between them!

Twelve

By mid-morning, Wyatt had conferred with the president of Intratec, Dick Fields, and then with the plant managers, before issuing another statement to the press. He'd managed to downplay the trouble at the plant last night and maybe, just maybe, if he'd handled it right, he'd defused a grim situation. He didn't need any more press like the story in this morning's news.

Now, sitting back in his borrowed office with his feet on the desk, he inspected a small scuff on the side of one of his loafers, feeling like he'd just lost a decathlon and been run over by a garbage truck all at once. He had back-to-back meetings scheduled for the rest of the day, yet he couldn't summon up enough energy to lift a coffee cup to his mouth.

Exhausted and confused by his uncharacteristic inability to concentrate, he could only think of seeing Liss again. The telephone sat on the corner of the desk. He stared at it, seduced by the thought that all he had to do to hear her voice again was pick up the receiver and punch a few buttons.

He dialed.

"Thayer's. May I help you?"

He recognized her voice immediately. He made his as deep as possible, disguising it. "Do you have any recommendations for men who can't think straight because all they can remember is a good-morning kiss?"

"Mmm. Would that morning be Eastern Standard Time or Pacific?"

He heard recognition and humor in her question. Abandoning the pretense, he drawled, "Definitely Pacific."

"Oh, that makes all the difference, you know."

Suppressing laughter, he asked, "Does it?"

"Oh yes," she said, her own voice warm and throaty. "You see, it's only ten-thirty. There hasn't been time for the . . . stimulus in question to wear off."

"How am I going to make it until tonight?"

"Well, I have heard that abstinence—"

"You don't sound very sympathetic, Ms. Thayer."

"Should I be?" she teased.

"Considering you're the cause, I expect a whole lot of TLC."

"Oh, my. I don't know if that's appropriate during business hours."

"And after?" he asked, no longer teasing. He wanted to know, had to know, where he stood with her. After last night and this morning, he felt like a whirlwind had run through him, leaving him disoriented and confused. He couldn't afford to feel like this, if for no other reason than that he needed to be sharp and focused to handle the situation at Intratec. As delightful a distraction as she was, he couldn't let Liss knock him any further off-balance. He needed some answers. One way or the other, he had to get his perspective back again.

Losing the humor, he said, "I had intended asking you out to dinner, but would you mind eating at home again? We have to talk."

"You're right," she said, "We do."

"Would you like me to bring dinner?"

"Would you mind if we go out after all?"

He considered that. "So we'd be on neutral territory?"

Her answer was slow in coming, but he expected it. "I guess you could call it that."

"Seven thirty?" he asked, keeping his voice brisk.

"Fine."

Uneasy, Wyatt hung up, swiveled in his chair, and looked out over the peach orchard that adjoined the complex. Rubbing a hand over his jaw, he thought about Liss, about the sound of her voice and the things she wanted to say to him. He was no genius, but it didn't take one to know that she was still extremely wary of getting involved with him. Maybe he should just give up any hope of forming a relationship with her. He needed to clear his mind of all distractions and get this business with the plant taken care of. He needed to get his butt back to the Bay Area where he belonged.

He sighed heavily. Maybe Liss had been right all along. Maybe he shouldn't even wait for tonight. He could pick up the phone, call her again. He'd close his heart to the sound of her voice, low and throaty and feminine, and make himself say all the appropriate things. It was fun while it lasted, but she was right. They had no future. Yeah, right. With any other woman, he'd do that without a second thought. He'd walk away without so much as a backward glance. But the idea of leaving Liss got him deep in the gut.

What was there about this place that had him acting like he'd never acted before? Maybe something in the water, some chemical that they used on the surrounding fields and orchards which also turned outsider's brains to mush. The sight of the peach trees, heavy with fruit not yet ripe, contrasted sharply with the view out his window in the Sunnyvale facility. There he looked out over a parking lot, the Intratec manufacturing complex and the rooftops of another semiconductor facility. He'd heard that Intratec, like a lot of the other semiconductor facilities, was built on what had once been acres of orchards. Apricot, cherries, peaches . . . peaches. No doubt Silicon Valley had once looked like this.

Staring at the peaches, he slowly became aware of his own mixed emotions. The sight of the ripening fruit trees seemed to calm him down and yet he resented being here, needing to be calmed down. He couldn't imagine himself doing anything like this in Sunnyvale. How different it was here! He began to reflect on the community as Liss had shown it to him, analyzing what it was about Oakmont that inspired such strong feelings.

Not one of his senior staff wanted to return to the Bay Area: in fact, several had said they'd quit rather than return. Others had protested laying off the local employees, saying that if they, as the imported employees, got to keep their jobs while the locals were let go, feelings in town would turn ugly and make living here a hassle.

And if workers like Jack Brody were willing to risk their jobs to keep the plant open, how was he supposed to find a solution that would make them all happy? And protect the bottom line? He was no Solomon, for crying out loud! Yet, the longer he sat and watched the peaches ripen, the more he knew he had to do something. There had to be a way to keep operations here in Oakmont and make a profit at the same time. But how?

Liss heard the heavy footsteps approaching her office and looked up. "Well, Howard. This is a surprise," she said, forcing herself to sound brisk and businesslike. "Didn't expect to see you in an antique shop. Planning to change the decor in your office?"

Mayor Upjohn smiled, lowered his bulk into an armchair, and smoothed a palm over his vested paunch. "Why would I need a reason to come see my best girl?"

Liss cringed inwardly. "Howard, I am not your best girl. I'm not your girl in any way, shape, or form."

"You could be. All you have to do is say yes."

"Not again, please. I am not going to marry you."

"Why are you playing so hard to get? What

could be better? You with all your background, and me—hell, with my connections, we could go all the way to Sacramento. Maybe even the governor's mansion. Whaddaya say?"

Not bothering to hide her revulsion, Liss snapped, "I say *no.*"

"Don't be so fast there. Liss, I'm telling you—"

Liss stood up and leaned over her desk, fingertips resting against the polished wooden surface. "Howard, if you say one more word on that topic, I am going to throw something at you."

Laughing as though she'd just cracked a joke, he held his hands up, palms out. "No need to get so excited. I can wait."

"Don't hold your breath," she muttered.

He ran a finger under his shirt collar. "Matter of fact, I'm here because I need your help."

She took her glasses off to rub the bridge of her nose. "Really?" she said, her tone wary. "What for?"

"Ever since your great granddaddy took his horsewhip to my predecessor unlucky enough to get caught with his pants down, your family's been a mainstay—"

Liss sighed with exasperation. "Not again, Howard." She really didn't have time for him in one of his folksy, reminiscent moods, particularly not if the subject was the Thayer family's past inability to keep their collective noses out of Oakmont politics.

The mayor ignored her sigh and went right on. "Your family's always been there, right in the midst of things, looking out for the welfare of our community."

"What is it, Howard? I've already contributed to United Way and every other charitable organization in town."

He allowed himself an appreciative smile. "Oh, no, nothing like that! You do a great deal already, but I'm here to ask you to do more."

Suspicious, Liss lifted an eyebrow and said nothing. Howard when he was bent on courting was enough of a steamroller, but when he had his political boss hat on, she kept her mouth shut. If she said one word at all, Howard would take it for acquiescence to whatever he was after.

"Now I know you're a busy lady but I haveta ask you to take on a little extra for the town. This isn't for me, so you can stop glaring at me like that. This is for Oakmont. Everyone needs you."

Ignoring the blarney, Liss cut straight to the point. "Just what is this *little extra*?"

Upjohn studied her for such a long time that Liss wondered if she'd smeared mascara on the end of her nose. Knowing that Howard was rehearsing the words to convince her to do whatever chore he had in mind for her, and knowing also that his definition of a little job wouldn't match hers, she waited, giving him no help.

Finally, he spoke. "It's come to my ears that you and Mr. Harrow have become . . . uh, friendly."

So that's it, she thought. He wants an inside scoop, as if I know what Wyatt intends to do. She kept her face impassive while she waited for Howard to continue.

"Dash it, Liss! You know what I'm asking."

"No, Howard, I don't. Suppose you tell me, straight out."

"Well now, Lissie, you gonna deny he's been over to your house at night, staying who knows how late—"

She inhaled sharply. She didn't know whether she was angrier at his use of that detested nickname or at his insinuations about Wyatt. Her voice colder than permafrost, she said, "Wyatt doesn't confide in me. I don't know where you got that idea."

His eyes glistened. "Not even a little pillow talk?"

"Goodbye, Mayor. Don't come back."

Howard leaned back in his chair and spread his hands over his knees. "Now, Liss, don't get upset. I just want you to use your influence with Mr. Harrow to get him to forget about closing down that plant of his—"

"What?" Liss exploded. "I can't do that! I resent your thinking that I can."

"Whoa, whoa. I didn't mean anything by that. Don't get so mad."

"Listen, Howard, and get this straight. If Wyatt and I are friends, and I said *if,* then it's nobody's business but our own and I will not play some kind of Mata Hari for you."

"Now, Liss, who said anything like that?"

Anger not at all abated, she continued, "If you want Intratec to stay in town, why aren't *you* doing something about it?"

"I am. I'm having a special town meeting tomorrow night over at the Auditorium, and I've invited Mr. Harrow to attend to spell out his plans. After that set-to at the plant last night folks are getting concerned."

"Wyatt handled that very well. Jack Brody can be a troublemaker, and you know it, but Wyatt turned that situation around so that they can both get what they want."

"Well, then, let him explain it to the rest of the voters."

"I don't think that's a good idea, Howard."

"Can you come up with something better, Liss?"

She said nothing.

Howard lowered his voice. "You're not forgetting what you have at stake here, are you?"

"If you're referring to anything personal between Wyatt and me, I'm warning you, Howard—"

"Oh, no, nothing like that! I'm just reminding you that a lot of your customers work at the plant. Who's gonna buy your fancy gimcracks if they close down? And more than that, Intratec's been very generous with Oakmont. They've funded part of the new hospital wing, the new football field . . ."

Liss knew what was coming as Howard went smoothly on, "Then there's the grant to the library, and so on. What's going to happen to your special project in the new library if there are no funds to keep the library open?"

Liss slumped back in her chair. She'd been trying so hard to keep finances, her own and the library's, out of her relationship with Wyatt, and here Howard had just tossed them back in her lap. She doubted Wyatt even knew about the grant. She didn't want him to find out. "That money is already committed, Howard," she refuted. "It's too late to retract it."

"What about next year, and the year after that?"

"Why are you asking me? Joe's the one you should be talking to—"

"Oh, I've talked to Joe. He's just as worried

as I am. In fact, he agrees that you're the one who could make a difference with Harrow."

"All right, Howard," Liss said wearily. "You've made your point. I don't have any influence with Wy—with Mr. Harrow, and I am not going to say one word to him about this. Just forget it. Don't you have any big important mayor-type things to be doing?"

His eyes hardened. "I'm only asking what your folks woulda done without any prompting at all."

Liss began heatedly, "I have to work for my living, Howard. I don't have time for—"

Howard put up a hand, palm outward. "Just listen for a moment. I'm not asking you to do anything against your principles, not at all. I just want you to make sure your Mr. Harrow comes to the meeting tomorrow night. He has to understand what it will mean to our little town if we lose so many jobs at one time."

She ignored his reference to a personal relationship with Wyatt. "I'm sure he understands all that, Howard, and I will remind him about the meeting, but I can't guarantee that he'll be there."

"Sometimes the personal touch is all it takes. Don't you agree?"

"There's no need to keep beating a dead horse."

Howard Upjohn laughed out loud. "Sometimes you sound just like your daddy, Liss."

"I'm not sure that's a compliment."

"You can consider it one. Your grandparents and your parents, all your family, made Oakmont what it is today. We all owe them."

"Goodbye, Mayor."

It seemed to Liss that she'd no sooner settled back to work than Susan popped her head through her door. "Hey, did you hear about Jack and Wyatt? What he did for Jack?"

"What?" Liss asked, curious about Jack's reaction.

"Wyatt could have fired him right there on the spot, but instead he told Jack to help him find a solution. It could have been a lot of hot air, but Jack was really impressed."

"Do you think Jack can come up with anything?"

"I don't know. He's got a head on his shoulders, despite that tough act he puts on. I think he's got a future. Otherwise I wouldn't feel right about Dani's being engaged to him."

"How does Dani feel about this?"

"She's all for it. Anything's better than sitting around waiting to be laid off, isn't it?"

Liss nodded just as the front bell tinkled, announcing a customer.

"Oops, back to work." Susan left, as Liss pondered whether perhaps Wyatt had done more harm than good by inflating Jack's hopes. In a moment, Susan was back. "Someone to see you."

Liss stood and followed Susan into the shop, almost bumping into a slight figure who carried herself as though she wore a steel spine. "Aggie! Is something wrong?"

"I just wanted to see how you're doing."

Liss smiled. Of all the members of the city council, she liked and admired Aggie Fairchild the best. Remembering how awed she'd been of her as a girl, she also recalled that it was thanks to Aggie that she'd gotten involved with antiques in the first place.

In the days after her mother's death, when Liss had needed a substitute grandmother, Aggie had been there for her. Remembering all the things the elderly woman had done for her, she lightened her tone to counter her rising emotions. "Checking up on me, huh?"

Aggie smoothed a stray white tendril back into an untidy bun. Looking at her thin, gnarled hand, Liss realized once more that the older woman must be at least eighty, yet she was still vitally interested in Oakmont affairs. Not much happened that Aggie wasn't involved in up to her lively black eyes.

Aggie gave her an assessing look. "This is a big step you're taking, Liss. I don't want you to get hurt."

Astonished, Liss asked, "Get hurt? What do you mean?"

"You're putting an awful lot of yourself into something that's not even yours."

Bewildered, Liss crinkled her eyes. "What are you talking about Aggie?"

"Your involvement with the library. You're a generous, well-meaning woman, donating so much of your time and your family's belongings to the library—"

"The Collection belongs where people can see it and learn from it," Liss demurred, surprised that Aggie, with her way of finding out secrets, apparently didn't know about her gift of money to the library fund.

"I know you feel that way, Liss, but be careful. You've got too much of yourself wrapped up in it."

Surprised by the older woman's caution, Liss knew there had to be a reason for it. "What's going on?"

Aggie's old lips thinned. "Something funny. I don't know what—not yet, anyway—but Don Simpson is acting strange."

Liss laughed it off. "Don's always strange."

"You listen to me, girl. You can joke about it, or you can keep your eyes and ears open. I tell you, Don's up to something, and he's acting mighty close-mouthed. He's got the library board all stirred up and the city council's listening to him. You mind your fanny, now."

"Thanks, Aggie, but I think you're over-reacting. Everything's just fine."

"You remember what I said. What's this I hear about you and . . . that man?"

"Oh, Aggie," Liss blinked in surprise to the rapid change of subject. "You should know better than to listen to gossip."

"At my age, it's all the enjoyment I get."

"Right. If I'm as active and involved at your age as you are, I'll be doing great."

Aggie chuckled. "How nice of you to say so. Now stop stalling and listen to an old lady. You know what you're doing with that man?"

"No," Liss confessed, seeing the elderly woman's eyes narrow with speculation.

"You gonna let him hurt you like that miserable excuse for a husband of yours?"

"Ex-husband, Aggie. Wyatt's not like that."

"Wyatt, hah? Hope you're right, girl. You could use some happiness."

Her throat closing, Liss patted Aggie's wrinkled hand.

"Enough of that," Aggie muttered. "Walk me out to my car."

Liss moved her hand under Aggie's elbow and steered her through the shop. When she'd tucked her behind the wheel of the big aqua Chrysler with the flaring tail fins that

Aggie still drove in defiant disregard of her deteriorating eyesight, Liss asked, "Want to tell me what's really worrying you?"

"Maybe I'm seeing gremlins under the bed, dear, but I haven't lived this long not to know when someone's trying to pull a fast one. Don's just like his father, you couldn't trust him either."

Liss smiled. "Maybe you're just upset that we're moving out of the City building. Didn't your father build it?"

Diverted for the moment, Aggie shook her head, dislodging several wisps of white hair. "No, my father-in-law. It's still a good old building."

"It is, Aggie. It'll be put to good use for a lot of years, yet." Liss leaned in to press a warm kiss on Aggie's wrinkled cheek.

Aggie patted her hand and set the car in gear. Just before she drove off, she called, "Remember what I said."

Several hours later, Liss stopped in at the old library. Dani sagged against the check-out desk. "One more day, and then the next patron we see will be in the new library!"

Joe looked up from the soon-to-be-replaced card catalog. "Can't happen any too soon for me."

Liss lingered, storing up memories. Despite Aggie's concern, she knew she'd done a good job with the Oakmont Collection and was fully prepared for anything that could happen between now and moving day. Musing over the older woman's warnings, as formless as they were, she walked through the library, wondering why Aggie had seemed so upset. It was more than leaving this old building, more than the feud that had existed between Aggie and the Simpsons since before she was born. She didn't know the reasons for their enmity, but they'd enlivened many a public function with their caustic comments.

Shrugging off Aggie's concern as something to think about later, Liss headed for the exit. On her way out, she met Wendy Franklin, Joe's very pregnant wife, entering the library. Involuntarily, her gaze centered on Wendy's abdomen. A dull ache spread through her, a painful awareness that she'd never have children. Everywhere she went she seemed surrounded by fertility. It felt like a slap in the face, a bitter reminder of her loss.

Wendy moved to edge around her. "Hi, Liss."

"Wendy, oh, I'm sorry. Here I am blocking your way!"

"You looked lost in thought. Are you all right?"

"Heavens yes," Liss answered, making her

voice light and pleasant. "I should be asking you that. It won't be long now, will it?"

Wendy grimaced. "Can't be a moment too soon, but I'm not due for another three weeks. I feel like a bloated elephant."

Liss looked at her face, splotched around the eyes with pregnancy discolorations, and thought she looked beautiful nonetheless. "You must be very excited, you and Joe."

"Oh, I am. Sometimes I think all Joe can think about is his library. I'm sure he dreams about it at night. I'll be glad when the dedication's over."

"Me, too."

Wendy looked away, then back at Liss. "Joe said you two weren't getting along."

"It's nothing serious, I'm sure. When everything settles down, we'll get back to normal."

"I hope so. Oh, there's Joe—I'd better go. He's taking me to my doctor's appointment."

"Good luck to you both."

Wendy hesitated. "Same to you, Liss."

With Wendy on her mind, Liss drove slowly to the grocery store. No matter where she went, she was bound to be surrounded by young mothers and their children. This cycle of the baby boom had hit Oakmont with such enthusiasm that even her store had profited. She couldn't seem to keep baby furniture on the floor for longer than a day.

She had to get over this thing about babies. She dawdled in the market's refrigerated air, remembering how she'd fled at the sight of David's new wife and their baby. If she ran into them again, she'd stand her ground. It was silly to let them ruin her life. Oakmont wasn't all that big, and she couldn't hide out all the time. She would have to get used to seeing them occasionally. She didn't want any part of David, not any more, so why should she care if she saw his new family? From now on, if she saw them, she'd treat them as she would anybody else.

Feeling better about herself, she drove home and parked under the old porte-cochere. Thoughts of the Collection, Aggie, and everybody else in town vanished as she wondered if Wyatt would also be late. She'd managed to keep thoughts of their upcoming talk at bay most of the afternoon, but soon she'd have to be honest and fair with him.

Not sure she was prepared for Wyatt's response, she put away the groceries and went upstairs to change. At the last moment, she detoured into the bathroom for a lazy soak. Propping her feet up on the edge of her raspberry tub, she thought about the things Aggie would only hint about. That made her think of Howard's vile insinuations. She hoped Wyatt wouldn't hear any of them. With everything else on his mind, he didn't need to be bothered with that.

When the water turned cool, she dried and dressed, pulling on a lavender silk jumpsuit. She brushed out her hair, refreshed her makeup, and went downstairs in bare feet.

On her way to the kitchen, a movement in the gazebo caught her eye; Wyatt stood silhouetted in the arch. The evening light was soft on his silvered hair, giving it a cool sheen that belied the warmth of his expression when he turned and saw her through the window.

Liss watched him approach, knowing that if he took her in his arms, if he made the slightest move toward her, she'd have no resistance left. She unlocked the back door for him. He came up onto the verandah, his footsteps even and steady on each of the risers, crossing the old planks to the doorway where she waited for him. "Hi," she murmured.

Nodding, he stepped past her, not touching her, but the warmth of his body enveloped her, the muted woodsy tones of his after-shave floating in the air behind him.

He turned to her, letting his gaze roam up from pink-tipped toes past slender thighs to the enticing curves of hip and breast. "For God's sake, Liss, couldn't you at least wear a gunny sack?"

Thirteen

She looked down at herself, then up at him, bewilderment plain on her face. "Should I have worn a dress?"

"No." He shook his head as if he were in pain. "How am I supposed to keep my hands off you when you look like that?"

"Like what?"

"Do you need a demonstration?" he asked, one brow lifting as he reached out for her.

She smiled at him, understanding at last. With a woman's self-satisfied smile, she asked, "Would you prefer I change?"

"The damage's done now. Come here."

She hung back, enjoying the moment and his admiration, just for milliseconds, but it was too long for Wyatt. He reached out and hungrily drew her close. "All day I've been driving myself crazy thinking of you . . ."

His words stopped when his mouth met

hers. Passionately, he opened her mouth and touched her tongue with the tip of his. Forgetting all her intentions to stay away from him, she responded avidly, reaching out to draw his tongue deeper into her mouth. Groaning, he took full possession of her, pulling her close, fitting her body to his.

For long moments, she was aware of nothing but the delectable sensations Wyatt drew forth from her. She felt his hand moving from her nape down her spine, following its path with sensory delight. His hand stopped for a moment on the flare of her hip, then reached to cup her bottom.

He groaned. "You feel so good."

"Wyatt," she whimpered into his mouth.

He raised his head and looked at her with glazed eyes. "What?"

"Wyatt," she repeated, pressing tiny little kisses into his collarbone, before forcing herself to move away.

He sensed her withdrawal before she actually drew back. "Oh, God, you're going to refuse me—"

"I don't want to," she whispered, unable to lie to him.

"Then why?"

She pulled herself out of his arms. Going to the refrigerator, she pulled out a bottle of white zinfandel and unsteadily poured them each a glass. "Let's sit outside."

His body aching with suppressed hunger, Wyatt accepted the glass and followed her out to the verandah. He sat beside her on the porch swing, wordlessly following her pace when she set the old, comfortably cushioned swing in motion.

Taking a deep breath, she gathered her wits. "I'm sorry, Wyatt. It's not fair, but I just don't have any control when you kiss me."

He moved closer, halting when she made a brief gesture. Puzzled by her uncertain expression, he paused, debating whether to push the issue and take her into his arms, knowing he could make her want him as he wanted her.

His body taut with restrained desire, he rose up from the swing in one swift motion. He paced from one end of the verandah to the other, then came back to stand behind her. "I don't understand, Liss. We're both adults, not committed to other people—why are you so hesitant?"

She grimaced and looked out over her garden.

Turning the swing so that she had to face him, he asked, "Can we talk about this?"

"There's nothing to talk about."

He pulled the swing toward him, so that

their knees touched. "What's going on that you can't even look me in the eye?"

"I am looking at you," she protested, and looked up to meet his gaze squarely. "There's just nothing to talk about."

"I think there is." He let go the swing, and hunkered down in front of her. With his hands on the arm rests, he brought her forward again so that they were breath to breath. "What are you scared of, Liss? Is it me?"

Her throat closed. She wanted to close her eyes, look away, do anything but gaze into his. The fine lines around his eyes appeared pale against the tan of his cheeks. She could count each individual eyelash and the variations of color around the cornea. This close, it was impossible to ignore the tender expression, or the integrity she saw shining there. Sighing, she admitted, "Yes."

He closed his eyes briefly, then opened them to spear her with a look. "You think I'll hurt you?"

She nodded.

"Like someone else did? Your husband?"

She nodded again, unable to look away.

"Will you believe me if I tell you I won't hurt you?"

Hesitating, she bit her lip and then shook her head. "No."

"Well, that's plain enough." He released

the swing abruptly, letting her swing free, and went to clamp his hands on the verandah railing. "Maybe you'd better tell me about him."

"No."

His lips thinned. "Help me out here, Liss."

"What's the point, Wyatt?"

He heard the pain in her voice and went back to sit beside her. "If you don't tell me what you're afraid of, how can we get beyond this?" Taking her hand in his, he asked, "What happens to us?"

She let her hand stay within his, but she didn't return his grip. "You're assuming too much."

"I'm assuming nothing," he spoke harshly. "I'm not playing games with you, Liss. What's happening here between us may not be something either of us expected, but it's here. I don't deny that I want to take you to bed and keep you there until neither of us can walk again—"

He stopped at her quick intake of air. "Sometimes I forget how prissy you are."

She turned to him, her eyes widening. "Prissy?"

He had to chuckle. "If you could see yourself. I didn't insult you, Liss. Maybe I should have said innocent."

"Innocent," she echoed. "How on earth . . .

I'm fifty-one years old, married for thirty of those years . . . how can you call me innocent?''

His chuckle deepened. ''Tell me about those years. Tell me how you got so *experienced*.''

Where she could deny his concern, his demand for more intimate knowledge about her, she couldn't withstand his laugh or the sparkle in his eyes. ''You are very hard to resist, you know that?''

He relaxed and eased back. With his head against the cushions, he rolled it to look at her. ''So stop holding out on me.''

''All right.'' She picked her words, stepping carefully through the tension hidden under the laughter. ''I grew up in this house, as you know. The Greenleys lived next door. Right there,'' she said, pointing toward the big house that dwarfed his guest quarters. ''Their son, David, is two months older than I. We were inseparable . . . in fact, our fathers finally put a gate through the oleanders after we broke the branches using it as a shortcut.

''We were together all through high school. He was the only one who could comfort me when my father died during my sophomore year. We went steady. We always knew one day we'd marry.''

''Was that your idea, or your parent's? An arranged marriage?''

She hesitated. "You know, I never thought of it like that. Our parents were pleased, they encouraged us, so I guess you could call it arranged."

"But you wanted it?" he probed, eager to understand.

"I thought we'd have a bunch of kids, settle down here, and live happily ever after."

He squeezed her fingers, offering his understanding at her bitterness. His voice sounded rusty. "I get the picture. What happened?"

"I never dated any one else, not even in college. We went to Cal Poly, and took as many classes as we could together."

"And?" he prompted when she fell silent, knowing it was important to Liss that he understand. He clenched his jaw, silently promising her his support.

She exhaled. "When my mother got sick and needed me at home, David stayed there. I thought I was taking time off, that I'd go back when Mom got better. David and I both thought it was only temporary. But she didn't get better, and I stayed on."

"What did you do with yourself?"

Liss paused, recognizing his ploy to sidetrack the conversation, giving her time to change her mind. She smiled faintly in acknowledgment. "A friend of the family, Aggie Fairchild, nagged me to get out of the house, to make time for myself, even if it was for only a few hours a day—"

"You didn't go back to college?"

"No. Things happened . . ."

Abruptly he interrupted her. "What about David?"

She looked out over the rosebushes, condensing her emotions. "We were married six months after he graduated."

"And?"

"Since my mother was still so ill, we moved in here. I looked after her while David got a job. We . . . we decided to put off having children until . . . until . . ."

"David was working and you had too much to do looking after your mother."

"Yes," she said, grateful for his understanding. What she didn't add was that living with her mother, and being right next door to his parents, made her feel that they were being watched all the time. Chaperoned, somehow. She bit her lip, remembering how inhibited she'd felt about making love with David with the thought that her mother would know what they were doing. "After my mother died, David went back to school to get his masters in engineering."

"Did you?"

"No. We could barely afford his tuition. I went to work to help out."

"I see," Wyatt said flatly. "And you were going to get your turn after that, right?"

She looked at him, puzzled at the tone of derision in his voice. "That's right."

"Did it happen that way?"

Avoiding the knowing look in his eyes, she answered, "No."

"So what did happen?"

"David got his degree. We lived in Sacramento for a while, then we came back here when David got a job at the other plant." She named one of Intratec's competitors.

Wyatt waited for a moment while she gathered her thoughts. "And then?"

Liss still hesitated, recalling the hurt and confusion of those days when she learned of David's first fling with a secretary. "Oh, nothing much. We had a lot to do here in the house. I got into gardening then."

"Still no children?"

"No." How could she explain that she'd hated the thought of making love with David while the touch of that other woman was still fresh on his body. She looked down at her hands, surprised to see how tightly she'd clenched her fingers. Making herself relax them, she heard herself say, "We were having some problems. In fact, we separated for a while . . ."

"You got your divorce, then?"

She gazed at him with an expression he didn't understand. Why should she look so vulnerable, so humiliated? Quelling the notion to take her in his arms and replace her pain with passion, he asked, "You didn't?"

"David came back after a few months, wanting to take up where we'd left off."

He stared hard at her. "You didn't take him back?"

She blushed.

"You did?"

She bristled at the displeasure in his voice. "He said he was sorry. I wanted my marriage to work!"

"So you let yourself get suckered into patching things up."

"It wasn't like that. We both wanted to make things work."

"And did they?" Wyatt asked harshly. "How much did you have to give in, to forget, in order to make it work?"

"That's none of your business!"

He clamped his lips together to stop the words she wasn't ready to hear. When he was in control again, he asked, "That's why you didn't have children? Because your marriage had problems?"

"Partly. But, even though I wanted them, it didn't seem to happen."

Wyatt thought he knew why. You had to

make love to your wife to have children with her. If the jerk was out screwing around on her, no wonder they'd had no children. Maybe it was all for the better. Now she had no reason not to put him out of her life completely. *And make room for me,* he caught himself thinking, and turned his focus back to Liss. "How much longer after that did you divorce him?"

She said nothing, face pale except for the bright blights of shame on her cheekbones.

"Son of a bitch! He divorced *you?*"

She turned away, trying to hide the residual anguish of rejection from Wyatt.

"When was this?"

"Last year."

His eyebrows rose. "You stayed with him all this time? Why in hell would you do that?"

"We . . . we had so much in common. The family . . . we tried, we really did, until . . ."

He saw her shoulders move convulsively, and eased her around to face him. "Why? After all that time, why did he want out?"

"He got one of the girls at work pregnant. He had to marry her."

"Had to?" Wyatt asked incredulously.

Nodding, she flicked a glance at him, then looked quickly away again. "Her parents threatened a paternity suit. It would have ruined his career."

"Her parents?" he asked, his brow creasing. "How old is this girl?"

"She was nineteen then."

"Good God!" he exploded. For a moment, he could say nothing else.

"It's just as well. There was nothing left for us by then."

"I should hope not. You've been hurting for that b—for him ever since?"

Snuffling, she shook her head. "No, I'm over that, except . . . once in a while I see him and his new family, and—"

Wyatt swore, long and fluently. "And it eats you alive. That's why you hide out here?"

"I'm not hiding out! At least, not any more," she confessed. "I like my life."

"Yeah?" he challenged. "You like it so much that you're still single? How come you haven't gotten involved with anybody else? Damn, what am I saying? I don't want you involved with anybody but me." He stopped abruptly

Fascinated, Liss watched the expressions run across his face.

"That's it, isn't it? He hurt you and now you're scared of getting hurt again? That's why you don't trust me?"

She licked her lips, afraid to answer, confounded by his anger.

"You think I'm going to hurt you? You can be damned sure I'm not."

"That's the most ridiculous thing I've ever heard," she burst out, emotions frayed to the quick by the last half hour. "How can you say that—you came to town only to close down the plant. You'll be leaving as soon as that's done."

"Don't lump me in with that bastard," he said, his voice low and dangerous.

Liss heard, but didn't pay attention to the warning. Focusing only on her own anger, she snapped, "Why not? You're divorced, aren't you? You couldn't stay married, either. What makes you think I'd believe you'd stay with me?"

Wyatt erupted out of the swing so fast the backwash almost ejected Liss. "There's one thing about me you'd better learn, Alice Louisa, and learn it damned quick. I'm not a sweet talker. If I say something, you better believe it."

Glaring at him, she hung on to the armrest until the jerky movements eased. "Why? You haven't shown me one thing to prove what you say."

He thumped his palms down hard on the verandah railing. A potted pelargonium quivered and fell into the flower bed below. Wyatt jumped off the verandah and retrieved it, using the time to calm himself. He moved up the stairs, replaced the plant, and said, very quietly, "Liss, I am not going to argue with you about my trustworthiness. You'll have to find out for yourself."

"And just how am I supposed to do that, Wyatt, when you don't tell me what you're doing at the plant?"

He bent over her, trapping her in her corner of the swing. "You know I can't tell you about the plant, but you're just using that as an excuse. That's not what this is all about, is it?"

Liss stared up at his eyes, so close to hers that she could see every tense line radiating from them. Her gaze didn't falter under his hard-edged stare. "It is," she insisted.

Wyatt sighed, blowing tiny blonde tendrils off her forehead. "All right. Have it your way. Do you trust me to make the right decision for the company?"

She was silent, remembering all the favorable comments she'd heard about him today. Even the press, avid for conflict, reported that he'd handled a potentially dangerous situation with skill and grace. After a moment, she nodded.

"Good. Come to that dog and pony show the Mayor's putting on tomorrow night and hear for yourself."

"All right. I'll be there, but . . ."

Wyatt straightened. "But what?"

She looked out at the gazebo, glimmering in the dusk, then back at his dark blue eyes heating up the space between them. Willing herself to be strong, she said, "I think we shouldn't see each other any more."

"No way!"

"Yes. You want things from me I can't give you. What I need, you can't give me. There's no reason for us to go on."

"Oh? Those kisses we shared doesn't give you a reason?"

"That's just sex."

Angered by her dismissal of something that he knew was far from being "just" anything, Wyatt searched for a way to convince her. "Look, I'm not throwing my experience against yours, but believe me, I know that what we feel when we're together isn't something we can dismiss lightly—"

"I don't want to talk about it."

"Liss, don't hide from me. Talk to me, give me good, valid reasons why you don't want to see me again."

"I told you. We want different things."

"Like what? Tell me what you want."

She waved her hand, loosely encompassing her house and yard. "This is my home, my life. It's small town, routine, knowing your neighbors and your history. I need that continuity in my life.

"You're restless, Wyatt. No place is home to you. You told me so yourself. That's one of the reasons for your divorce. I can't see getting involved with you just while you're in town. I don't want a temporary romance, a fling. That's not good enough for me, no matter how attracted I am to you."

Stung by her words, Wyatt moved away from her. "You've got it all figured out, haven't you?"

"What's to figure out? That's the way it is."

"I don't buy that. You're throwing up roadblocks. Stonewalling me. It's too soon to know what will happen with us, but I'm not going to be put off by your fears. We've got something good here, and I intend to see it through."

"No."

"Yes," he said forcefully. "I'm very sorry that you got hurt before. I'd be a fool to promise that you'll never be hurt again, but I'm not going to back off. I'm here, and I'm going to stay."

"For how long, Wyatt?" she cried. "How long does it take to shut down a plant and break my heart?"

In an instant, she was in his arms. He pressed flurries of kisses against her brows,

271

her temples, her ears, and down the curve of her cheek to her mouth. Long, achingly tender kisses later, he muttered, "I'm not going to break your heart, sweetheart. No one is, ever again."

Two hours later, Liss pushed her plate away. "I can't eat another bite. It's a shame to waste that," she murmured, eyeing her half-eaten prime rib. "We should have stayed in."

Wyatt grinned. "Then I wouldn't have enjoyed seeing you smear horseradish on your chin."

"Don't remind me!" Laughing, she dabbed at her face again. "All gone?"

"Yeah." Sighing, he stretched back in his chair. "I'm glad we did this, Liss. We needed a break."

She agreed. The emotional outburst they'd gone through earlier had left them both exhausted. It was good to sit back and let someone else take care of the dinner details. "I'm sorry I dumped all that on you."

"Don't be," he said, and leaned forward to take her hand. "Look at it as moving forward."

Leaning toward him, her eyes on his, she murmured, "You always get your way, don't you, Wyatt?"

"Not always. But you can be damned sure that if I want something, I'll fight for it."

"I'm finding that out for myself. Look, at me, here with you when not too long ago I wasn't going to see you again."

He squeezed her fingers. "Are you sorry you're here with me?"

"No-o. I—oh oh. Do you know these people?" She gestured as an older couple approached their table.

Wyatt looked up, frowning, then smiled. "Sure. Hi, Pete."

"Thought this was you, Wyatt. Heard you'd been seeing Liss. Have you met the missus? Grace?"

Amused that the rumor mill got as far as the Dodges, Wyatt stood and took the other woman's hand. "A pleasure. Would you two like to join us?"

Grace and Liss shared a look. Liss smiled. "Please do. How are you both? Haven't seen you in a while."

Pete chuckled as they sat down. "Not since Grace finished redoing the house with all those doodads from your store."

"Doodads?" Grace groused, with a private loving smile for her husband. Turning back to Liss, she said, "Men. Who can expect them to know the difference between Chippendale and Louis XIV?"

"Louie Katorze? Sounds like a linebacker for the Forty-Niners," Wyatt said. "Or maybe a pool hall sharpie."

Over Pete's booming laugh, Grace and Liss rolled their eyes in unison. Wyatt grinned, pleased that Liss shared his liking for the Dodges. When Pete's laughter subsided, he asked, "You two out for an evening on the town?"

"Just sent the grand-kids home. Had them for a week, you know, while the kids had a little vacation—"

Grace broke in, "Now *we* need a vacation. You can't imagine, what a mess seven and nine year old boys can make!"

Wyatt caught Liss's involuntary wince. No, he couldn't imagine and neither could Liss. "So, Pete, you bought one of those old-fashioned houses when you moved out here?"

"Yeah. We wanted something where those little hellions could come visit and we wouldn't have to worry about the neighbors calling 911."

Liss smiled. "I'm sure it can't be as bad as all that."

"Worse," Grace confided. "Do you know if I can get my dining room table re-finished?"

"How bad is it?"

"Why don't you come over and see it when

274

you have time? Maybe you can tell me what I should do about it."

"I'll be glad to. Later this week?"

Pete stood. "Good. Anyone knows how to take care of it, Liss does. You seen the Collection out at the library yet, Wyatt?"

"Not yet. I'm looking forward to it." Turning to Liss, he said, "Maybe you'll give me another guided tour?"

She shook her head. "It's all packed up for the move. You'll have to wait till after . . ." She caught herself, knowing he wouldn't be in town that long. Hiding her disappointment, she turned to Grace and Pete. "Will you two be at the dedication? It's supposed to be quite a show."

"We'll be there," Grace said, with a curious look at the expression on Wyatt's face as he stared at Liss. "I'm eager to see how you're going to display the Collection in the new library."

Liss began to explain, while Wyatt asked Pete, "How's it going? Anything new at the plant?"

"Nope. All quiet when I left. Don't know if the guys will have all that info you wanted ready for the morning, but they're working on it."

Wyatt nodded. "We don't have any time to spare on this."

"Yeah. Better be going, Grace, let these two finish their dinner."

As the other two left, Wyatt smiled at Liss. "So much for a quiet dinner."

"Part of living in a small town. People have been watching us all evening. I can just hear them now."

"Damned small towns. Nothing better to do than talk about other people!"

"It happens everywhere. Don't you ever run into people you know?"

"Well, sure," he began, then stopped at the smile on her face, "Did I remember to tell you how exceptionally gorgeous you are to-night?"

"Something about a gunny sack, I believe."

He grinned. "Maybe I should rephrase it." He took her hand and traced a finger over the pulse at her wrist. "You are one beautiful woman, Ms. Thayer."

"Thank you," she murmured, giving him a soft smile. He watched the smile fade as her attention was drawn to something over his left shoulder.

Turning to see for himself, he cursed. "Don't we rate any privacy around here?"

"Well, well, look who's here. If it isn't Mr. Harrow. Enjoying yourself, sir?"

Liss tugged her hand free.

Wyatt stood. "Evening, Mayor."

"You having an evening out with my best girl?"

Wyatt flicked a look at Liss, then back at Howard. "Best girl?"

"Sure," the Mayor said expansively. "It's just a matter of time until Liss here becomes Mrs. Upjohn."

"What?" Liss gasped. "Howard, that's not—"

Wyatt's eyebrows shot up over eyes glinting with hard-edged anger. "Well, isn't that a nice surprise. Liss, how come you didn't let me in on your happy news?"

"Because there is no news!" She turned away from him to glare at the other man. "Howard, how could you say such a stupid thing?"

Howard spread his hands. "Now, Lissie, don't get your dander up. You know how I feel about you." He turned to Wyatt. "She keeps protesting, but you know women. They say no all the time when they mean yes."

"Is that so?" Wyatt looked at Liss as he spoke.

"Howard, this is absolutely ridiculous. You know my answer," she snapped, anger rising and overcoming her embarrassment. "But just in case you've forgotten, let me repeat it one last time. The answer is no, Howard. Now and forever."

She grabbed her purse, stood, and headed

for the door. Wyatt looked around for a waiter and when he didn't spot one, tossed several bills on the table and hurried after Liss.

He caught up with her in the parking lot. "Hold on there!" He took her elbow and swung her around to face him. "You and I have some talking to do."

She yanked her elbow away from him. "What could you possibly have to say to me?"

"Is Howard right? Are you going to marry him?"

"Didn't you hear what I told him?"

"I heard. I also heard what you told me. Are you having trouble keeping your stories straight, Lissie?"

She recoiled from the contempt in his voice. "You asked me to trust you. Without any explanations. Just accept your word for things. Well, I see that doesn't work both ways. I'm supposed to accept anything you say, but you don't hear what I say. Well, fine," she said hoarsely. "I see there's nothing more to say. Good night."

"Where are you going?"

"Home."

She was several paces down the sidewalk before Wyatt reacted. "I brought you here. I'll take you home."

"Don't bother."

"I said I'll take you home," he said through

gritted teeth. "Or do you want to cause another scene for all those people watching us?"

Liss stopped and peered over his shoulder at Howard and a group of his cronies. They stood in the restaurant doorway, eyes bright with curiosity. Lips narrowing, Liss silently walked over to Wyatt's car, waited for him to unlock the doors, and got in without a word.

Wyatt turned out of the parking lot, ignoring Howard and the others who watched them go. A few blocks from the Thayer house, he slowed to take a corner and asked quietly, "Why didn't you tell me about this, Liss?"

She shot him a look. "I don't owe you any explanations about anything, Wyatt."

"Oh? That fat slob's going around telling people he's going to marry you and you think I wouldn't be interested?"

"There's not a word of truth to that!"

"Right," he snorted. "When's the wedding?"

"I'll tell you this one last time. There will never be a wedding."

"Just what did you expect to get from me, pulling a stunt like this?"

Liss felt her mouth drop open. What on earth was he talking about? "What stunt?"

"Letting me go on, falling for you. What did you think you'd get out of me?"

Too incensed to answer, Liss sank back into

279

her seat and counted to herself until they reached her house. As soon as he pulled up in her driveway, she had the door open and was out of the car.

She headed for her verandah, then paused and looked back at him. "Thank you for dinner, Mr. Harrow. Now I am going inside, and with any luck I won't see you again before you leave Oakmont."

Fourteen

Soon after nine on Thursday morning, Pete's secretary popped her head through the doorway to Wyatt's temporary office. "Jack Brody's waiting to see you."

Swiveling his chair away from the window overlooking the peach orchards, Wyatt put the image of Liss, angry as she'd been the night before, out of his mind. He couldn't let her interfere any more than she already had, even though she couldn't have known that she was distracting him.

Pulling his focus back to Intratec business, he replaced the coffee cup on his desk and mentally geared up for work. "Send him in," he instructed the secretary.

Waving Jack to a seat, he studied the younger man, noting his nervousness, seeing only a trace of the earlier aggressiveness.

Jack sat, rubbing his palms on his jeans.

"Uh, morning, Mr. H—Wyatt. I've been thinking about what you said."

"That's good. Come to any conclusions?"

Jack studied his kneecaps. "Uh, yes, but first, uh . . . I'd like to thank you for stepping in for me with the security guard. I hear she wanted to hang me out to dry."

"Thank her, Jack. She's the one who decided not to press charges after all."

"Yeah, but . . . anyway, I've been doing some thinking. I don't suppose you know, but I'm going to school, part-time."

"That's good," Wyatt commented when the younger man paused. "What are you studying?"

"I'm going for my degree in electronics. With a minor in Business Ad."

Wyatt was surprised. "Hey, how about that? Going to take over my job, huh?"

Jack almost smiled. "Yeah. One day."

"So before you boot me out, let me ask: What brings you in here?"

Jack's fingers tensed on his thighs. "I read all the technical papers and magazines, and I've been wondering . . ."

"Wondering what?"

"Why can't we buy the plant and run it ourselves?" Jack blurted.

Surprised again, Wyatt leaned back in his

chair and crossed an ankle over the other knee. "Tell me what you're thinking."

Once Jack began to speak, his words came fast and clipped. Wyatt listened, hearing nothing new but impressed by Jack's research and analysis. "So, you think by employee ownership we can justify keeping it open?"

"Yeah, man, if we own it ourselves, we have a stake in what's going on. I mean, we're not going to waste our own money! We improve our quality program, we wind up putting more product out the door. What can we lose?"

"Have you talked to anyone else about this?"

Jack nodded. "The guys out on the floor. They're all willing to invest. If the brass will go along, we could swing it with some financing from the local banks. Hell, we're even willing to take a cut in pay just to keep the plant open."

Wyatt concealed a grin. Faced with this much enthusiasm, it was hard not to get a little excited, too. "Look, Jack, making no promises, I'll check it out."

"That's it?"

Wyatt held up a hand. "I know you're disappointed, but that's all I can do for now. It's a good idea, a very good idea, and I'm pleased you brought it to me, but conversion to employee ownership is risky. It's a big capital expense—lots of money. You buy into it, you'll be putting your ass on the line. I can't guarantee anything, but I'll look into it."

Jack got up, a sullen pinch to his mouth. Halfway to the door, he turned. "Look, we got to do something, man. You can't let the whole thing go down the tubes."

Wyatt stood, too, stretching to ease the kinks left in his back by lack of sleep. He came around the desk and clapped Jack on the shoulder. "You did the right thing coming to me with this. It's a damned good idea. Maybe it's just what we need, but I can't jump in half-cocked. I'll think about it, sound out the brass in Sunnyvale, then we'll talk some more."

Appeased, Jack grinned. "Later, man."

Wyatt grinned back.

Several hours later, Wyatt looked up from the reports the department heads had given him and shook his head. He wished they displayed as much optimism as Jack did. Just the thought of Jack's proposal made him grin—the kid had something there.

The more he dug into the problems at Intratec, the worse the situation looked. It would take a massive infusion of capital to revamp and revitalize operations, and even then, success wasn't assured.

By mid-afternoon, enduring another frustrating meeting with uncooperative managers, he was ready to bang heads together.

Keeping his face impassive, Wyatt tuned out their discussion and let his mind wander. Inevitably, it circled and settled on Liss. At least he had the evening to look forward to—she would be at the town meeting. He wasn't sure yet what he would say to Oakmont's voters, but right now, he was more worried about Liss.

Even if they'd parted in anger last night, he was confident that they could get together, talk things over, and iron out their differences.

God, they had to!

How could he have been so stupid, to accuse her of coming on to him for ulterior motives? He had no reason to think that of her, no reason to blame her, yet in his jealous fury he'd done just that.

Would she forgive him? Would she even listen to him long enough for him to apologize?

Was she still mad at him? Frustrated that he didn't know enough about her yet to know how she handled her anger, he debated. Should he send her flowers? Let her temper run its course and burn itself out? Could she be talked into making up?

Letting his imagination run wild with the different ways he could love her into forgetting her indignation, his mind roved back over the images of her last night.

She'd been radiantly lovely in the muted light of the restaurant, quick to laugh and relax in the aftermath of their argument earlier. He winced, remembering how he'd made her tell him about her marriage. He'd seen how it hurt her, and yet he'd forced her on, so sure he could fix anything that troubled her.

Jerk. He'd only caused her more pain. No wonder she didn't want anything to do with him. He'd been insensitive, a boor.

And then, how sweetly she'd burrowed into his chest and let him comfort her. He was sure she hadn't harbored any resentment toward him after that, no matter that he'd put her through a hellish time. Their dinner had been companionable, and yet more, they were more than friends. Not lovers, not yet, but close to it. And then that son of a bitch Upjohn had come along.

On reflection, it seemed that he'd delighted in provoking both Liss and Wyatt. Eyes narrowed in concentration, Wyatt went over every word and gesture of the mayor's. Damn, but he'd done it deliberately! He'd seen them having a quiet dinner together and had purposefully ruined it. Why?

Perplexed about the other man's motives, but very clear about his intentions, Wyatt came to a decision. One way or the other, he'd find out why that pompous old fool had willfully embarrassed Liss and caused her discomfort. Then he'd make him pay for it.

No one was going to hurt Liss and walk away unscathed.

Not while he was around.

How had she burrowed under his skin so quickly? He wished he could protect her from whatever pain she'd experienced. He wondered how to convince her that while he didn't know where their relationship was headed, he felt something for her that he'd known with no other woman.

He wanted to be with her, to take care of her, to show her that his passion was only part of his feelings for her.

He didn't dare put a name to those emotions just yet. For now, he wanted to let them develop, let them grow until neither one could deny them. He wanted her to put away her fears and explore the possibilities, admit she felt the same passion as he—surely she *had* to feel the extraordinary power of their attraction, even though she protested that they had no future.

The thought of her, warm and openly receptive to him as she had been earlier, had kept him awake most of the night. He'd dragged himself from bed, lethargic and slow with the weight of her pain like a monkey on his back. He had to do something soon, but what? He suppressed a yawn, realizing that if he didn't get some sleep soon, he'd be crawling.

Noticing a sidelong look from one of the managers, he tore himself away from thoughts of Liss.

He swallowed the dregs of his cold coffee and made an effort to follow the conversation. At the first opportunity, he jumped in. "All right. Let's table this discussion for now. We'll pick it up tomorrow morning when we're fresh."

The participants streamed out of the conference room like kids on the last day of school. Wyatt shrugged and watched them go. "Just a minute, Pete," he said, gesturing to the plant manager to stay.

Pete resumed his seat.

Wyatt toyed with a pen, then set it down in the middle of his notepad. "Jack Brody came to see me this morning with an interesting suggestion."

"Burn us all at the stake?"

Wyatt laughed mirthlessly. "Maybe we'll

wish it was as simple as that. He suggested the employees buy the plant and run it themselves."

Pete whistled in astonishment. "I'm surprised he knows what that means. That's a damned good idea, come to think of it. Wish I'd thought of it myself."

"Don't sell him short. Not only does he understand it, but he has a good grasp of what we'd need to do to implement it here."

"Well, I'll be—"

"Listen, I want you to get together a study team—your best minds. Make sure Brody's on it, maybe another hourly employee, and a couple of forward-thinking engineers. Some smart money guys. Check out the local banks—but discreetly. We don't have much time, but I'll arrange to be here for a while longer. I don't want a whitewashing committee, Pete, I want real effort here. Tell me what it would take to convert the plant to self-ownership, and tell me fast. Authorize overtime, whatever, but get me some working figures."

"You're serious?"

"Keep this quiet," Wyatt ordered, ignoring Pete's question. "I don't want it all over the plant, and I sure as hell don't want the press asking questions."

"Anybody else?"

"You head up the team. Appoint whomever you need, but keep it small."

"Hmm." Pete's brow furrowed, then smoothed. "I'll check with the hourly supervisors, but for the engineers, it's Atkinson and Greenley."

"Who?" Wyatt asked sharply.

"Atkinson and Greenley. They're both hungry, ambitious. They'll work like dogs to—"

"Is that David Greenley?"

"Yeah. You know him?"

"Not yet," Wyatt muttered, thinking of Liss. Maybe he'd better not meet him. If his gut spasmed like this now, sight unseen, how would he feel coming face to face with the guy? "How long has he worked here?"

"Two, three years. Is there a problem?"

"Is there anyone else you could put on this?" Wyatt asked, hoping he could avoid any contact with the bastard who had hurt Liss so much.

"Nope," Pete said without hesitation. "You want the best, you get Greenley."

"Damn."

Pete's wrinkled brow furrowed further. "Is this due to your involvement with Liss Greenley?"

"Liss Thayer," Wyatt said fiercely.

"Gotcha," Pete nodded. "Kinda strange,

all the years David and Liss were married. Everyone knew they weren't happy."

Hating himself for asking, but desperate to know, Wyatt stumbled over the words. "What do you know about them?"

"Always liked her," Pete answered. "A real lady, you know? Now him, he can be a real jerk. He was the one who fouled things up between them. Made a real mess of things."

"How?"

"Played around. Couldn't keep his hands off other women. The younger, the better. Everybody knew what he was doing. It was only a matter of time till he got burned."

Wyatt cursed fluently.

"You heard about it, huh? The man was a fool, throwing a fine woman over. Way I hear it, he regrets it already."

Wyatt ground his teeth.

"You okay, Wyatt? Now, I don't listen to talk, but there's a lot of it going around. Some of it's pretty low down. After seeing you two together last night, I figure you should know that."

"Talk about Liss?"

"And you," Pete confirmed.

Wyatt shook off the overwhelming anger that threatened to swamp him. He didn't have time now to dissect his feelings, but soon he'd have to explain to himself why this need to protect and comfort Liss was taking precedence over every other priority in his life. He brought his attention back to Pete. "I'll take care of it. Now—how soon can you get started with the feasibility study?"

Pete stood. "I'll get right on it."

Wyatt nodded. "Fine. Let's get some ideas together by the end of the week. If it looks good, I'll have one helluva job selling it to the brass."

Pete whistled. "That's not much time."

"Do the best you can."

Dismissed, Pete left the conference room, shaking his head.

Alone again, Wyatt tried to concentrate on work, but all he saw was Liss's pale face, lips trembling, as she asked him how long it would take him to break her heart. Break her heart? If she thought he had the power to do that, it must mean she cared. *Damnit, Liss, what am I going to do about you?*

Liss placed another carefully wrapped edition from the collection of early Californian works into the moving box, then turned to wrap another. She'd chosen this job herself primarily for the solitude it offered, although no one had questioned her right to it.

With a clerk manning the front desk, Joe

at the reference desk, and Dani supervising the last children's hour in this building, she was safe from the curious scrutiny they'd been giving her ever since she'd walked in late this morning. After a sleepless night, herbal tea and another long, hot bath had relaxed her physically, but her mind still reeled with the emotions Wyatt had forced to the surface. Try as she might, she couldn't forget the stunned look he'd given her when she told him she wouldn't see him again.

It's better this way. I did the right thing. Better to end it before it goes any further.

But her words hadn't convinced her body. Lonesome last night in the house where her solitude had never before been a burden, Liss had walked through the empty rooms, turning on lights as she went, until the entire house was emblazoned with her desolation. In the morning room she paused, remembering Wyatt on his knees applying varnish and teasing her. She fled into the parlor, where she collapsed on an antique horsehair loveseat and finally cried herself into an exhausted sleep some time near dawn.

She'd awakened cramped and sore this morning. Still groggy, she'd turned off lights and stumbled up the stairs, despairing at the cold lump which had gown during the night to replace her heart.

For once, she hadn't taken the time to snip a morning bouquet. Susan had noticed immediately and had teased her about it until she stomped into her office, leaving Susan with her mouth agape. Sorry now for the way she'd snapped at her long-time friend, Liss rehearsed the apology she'd deliver as soon as she could face people again.

Now, she moved an errant tendril of hair off her forehead, leaving a smear of dust behind, and moved on to the next item, precisely and with great concentration, trying to keep every niche of her mind occupied. The routine of identifying, wrapping, and labeling calmed her, and by the time she had finished with the Collection it was almost two and time to get back to the shop.

Driving through the familiar streets to the plaza, she remembered the day she'd given Wyatt a tour of Oakmont and the laughter they'd shared. Even after she'd parked in the lot behind the store she remained at the wheel, unable to put him out of her mind.

Covering her face with her hands she leaned forward, wondering how she could have let herself get so far off center.

"Liss? Are you sick?" Susan's voice was warm with concern.

Startled that she hadn't even heard her best friend approach, Liss shook her head. She was sick all right, but it was nothing that time wouldn't cure. Her heart had been broken once before, and it had healed. It was scarred, and perhaps not as strong or as trusting, but it had mended. It would do so again, if she could just survive until then.

"What are you doing sitting out here? Come on in out of the heat."

With an effort, Liss pushed the car door open and followed Susan inside to her office, where she collapsed into her desk chair.

Susan reached forward and tipped up Liss's chin. Gazing thoughtfully at the pallid face before her, she turned it one way and then the other. "Dani's right. You do look like death warmed up. What's the matter?"

Liss tried to smile. "Nothing."

"Cow doo. Tell me."

Liss gazed up into Susan's brown eyes. "I feel so stupid . . ."

"Why?"

"It's Wyatt," Liss confessed. "I've gotten in too deep with him, and now it's over."

"What do you mean, it's over? What's happening?"

"Oh, Susan, I don't know if I can explain. We've been having such a good time. It's been so much fun, having him over, working with me on the house. And now . . ."

Susan said nothing, waiting for Liss to continue at her own pace.

"He wanted an affair—"

"Fast worker, isn't he?" Susan's mouth pursed. "My, my."

Liss smiled weakly. "I'd like to put all the blame on him, but I can't."

"The feeling's mutual?"

Liss could feel her cheeks blooming with pink. "Was mutual. It's over, now."

"So you keep saying, but it sure doesn't look like it from here."

"Believe me, it is. You wouldn't believe what happened last night. We were having dinner, and Howard—" At Susan's groan, Liss continued to tell her everything that had happened.

"Howard really said that? Out loud? In public?"

"He did. I was so mortified. I denied it, but I could tell Wyatt believed him."

"He didn't believe you? Your hunk believed that idiot, Howard?"

Liss nodded emphatically. "Not only didn't he believe me, but he accused me of leading him on for some . . . some nefarious purpose of my own."

"Oh, my. What did you do?"

"What else? I told him I didn't want to see him again."

"You think he'll accept that?"

"He'd better!" Liss bit out, then seemed to collapse into herself. "Who am I kidding? Part of me is hoping he'll walk through that door and the other part is afraid that if he does, I'll fall into bed with him."

"So, what's the problem? You're both grown-ups."

Liss turned bright red. "Susan!"

Susan chuckled, a comforting earth mother sound that reduced Liss's embarrassment to no more than a faint wash of color against her porcelain complexion. "Still dithering whether it's proper?"

"Nothing like that," Liss admitted, not up to Susan's teasing about her old-fashioned values. "I want him," she continued in little more than a whisper, "but I know he'll be gone in a few days and—"

"And you think that'll be the end of it?"

Liss nodded.

"I can't tell you what to do, Liss. You have to follow your inner voice on this one, but let me ask you—what will you do when Wyatt leaves if you haven't given yourselves a chance to find out what you mean to each other?"

Liss raised stricken eyes, acknowledging without words the depth of her feelings.

"I think you already know, don't you?"

The sympathy in Susan's voice tore at Liss. "I can't feel any worse than I already do."

"Want to bet? We're no spring chicks any more, old pal. Here's your chance for happiness. Grab it."

"I told him about David."

"Wow. You must be having some serious thoughts about him, to dredge all that up. What did he say?"

"At first he was angry. I thought it was at me, for being such a dunce about David, but then I realized that he was mad at David."

"Good. Shows he has his priorities straight. What else?"

"He said he was sorry I'd been hurt, that he couldn't promise I wouldn't get hurt again."

"He's honest."

"He is. Oh, Suze, I'm afraid I'm falling in love with him!"

"Is that so bad?"

Liss swallowed. Her throat throbbed with unshed tears. "It's awful. I can't sleep. All I do is think of him, but last night I told him to go away."

"For a smart woman, sometimes you sure do some dumb things."

"If we make up, and we have an affair, he'll leave and I'll feel bad. If we don't, I'll still feel bad."

"Out of that garbled syntax, I gather you're going to feel bad no matter what happens, so why not grab a little happiness along the way?"

Astonished, Liss could only stare. Susan looked back blandly.

Liss lowered her eyes and fiddled with the edge of the desk blotter. "Wyatt's going to be at the town meeting tonight. I told Howard I'd go, before he pulled that stunt. I don't want to be alone. Can I sit with you and Tom?"

"Well, of course, but we're not hiding you. You're going to have to face Wyatt on your own."

Halfway through his hastily prepared presentation, Wyatt looked up from his notes and saw Liss slipping into a seat halfway down the auditorium. He noted her light gray suit and white blouse. Wondering if she'd taken refuge in her conservative clothes to hide her emotions, he stumbled over a word, then gathered himself and continued.

Liss heard his hesitation and knew that he'd seen her. She smoothed the summer-weight skirt over her shaking knees and tried to concentrate on what Wyatt said, listening for the meaning, and not just the sound of his voice as it swirled through her like fine aged brandy.

Almost dizzy from her conflicting feelings, her mind commanded her to get up and walk out, to take this last glimpse of Wyatt home with her and store it up for the desolate days ahead. Her body urged her to stay, to talk with him, to make things right between them and take whatever risks she had to in order for them to be together.

Wavering, she listened to the interminable questions and answers, admiring Wyatt's manner. He handled himself well, not allowing himself to be sidetracked by hecklers.

A man stood, and having caught Wyatt's attention, he asked, "I hear you're thinking of finding another way to keep the plant open. Any truth to that?"

Only long experience of dealing with explosive situations allowed Wyatt to keep his face impassive. "I'm sure we'll consider all our options. Any other questions?"

Another man yelled from the back of the room. "Are you sleeping with Liss Greenley to get her to use her influence with the mayor?"

Wyatt's jaw muscles flexed. That and his thinned lips were the only signs that he was raging inside. "My personal life is no one's business but my own. You malign a special woman with that comment. You owe her an apology."

Several people shouted at once, demanding he apologize. Lifting her eyes first to Wyatt, who stared at her intently, then to the heckler, Liss bit down her embarrassment. She looked steadily at the man until he did apologize. She nodded, then returned her gaze to the front.

She met Wyatt's questioning look. When their eyes locked, she noted the instantaneous flare-up in his dark blue eyes, then saw how he disciplined his reaction, waiting for her to make her decision.

She could feel the heat rising up from her breasts, up her throat, to flood her cheeks with color. She wanted to look away, to stare at anything but Wyatt's eyes pinning hers, but she made herself hold his gaze.

Oh, Lord, what was she doing here?

At last, questions and answers over, Wyatt escaped the crowd around him and made his way to her. She waited, biting her lip, feeling the hot swell of anticipation rise in her and crush her lungs until she could barely breathe. She stood when he reached her, then grabbed the seat in front of her when her knees mutinied.

"Hello, Liss."

"Wyatt," she whispered, loving the way his

silver hair gleamed under the lights. She couldn't take her eyes off him.

Susan nudged her.

Wyatt saw the motion and grinned.

Liss belatedly joined in. "You remember my friend Susan, don't you? This is her husband Tom."

While he shook hands with them, Wyatt shot Liss an affectionate glance.

Liss felt the warmth, and her nervousness eased.

Susan took her husband's arm. "Nice to see you again, Wyatt. You gave an interesting talk. We really have to be going."

Tom looked startled, but at his wife's insistence, moved away with her. Watching them leave, Liss saw Susan speaking rapidly, then Tom's look of understanding. Turning to Wyatt, she saw comprehension on his face as well.

"I like your friend. She's got a great sense of timing."

Grateful for Susan's tact, Liss could only nod.

He said simply, "Only a day and I missed you like hell."

"Me, too. I'm sorry about last night."

"Come on, let's get out of here. I have things to tell you."

"Wyatt—"

"Tell me later."

She picked up her purse and moved into the aisle with Wyatt, where they joined the others headed toward the rear exit. The press of the crowd jostled her a few feet away from Wyatt.

Suddenly, an arm came down around her shoulders, turning her around.

"Liss, I thought it was you."

Liss tensed, turning brittle. She jerked her shoulders, dislodging the arm. "David," she hissed. "What are you doing?"

"I'm here alone. Let's go have some coffee or a drink and talk."

"She has nothing to say to you, Greenley. Leave her alone."

Hearing Wyatt's cold voice, Liss turned to him in amazement.

With eyes glittering like chipped ice, Wyatt stared at David Greenley, not at all surprised to find that the other man was tall, broad-shouldered, and handsome. Fist clenched at his side, it was all he could do to stop himself from centering it neatly in the middle of Greenley's nose.

Looking from Liss to Wyatt, then down Wyatt's arm past the elegantly cuffed shirt, David shrugged. "I get the scene." He placed his hands in the air, palms out. "Just a friendly word with my wife, that's all."

"Your *ex*-wife doesn't want to talk to you—"

"Looks to me like you're the one butting in where you're not wanted."

"Greenley, don't take me on. I'm warning you—"

David's dark eyes glittered. "You may be the head honcho at Intratec, Harrow, but I don't have to listen to you here."

Wyatt smiled, the tight-lipped smile that he used when he closed in for a corporate kill. "Listen to Liss, then."

Standing between the two men, both tall and well-built, both capable of provoking deep emotions within her, Liss looked from one to the other. They waited for her to speak, David with a smug look, sure of her, while Wyatt gazed steadily at her ex-husband.

Stunned that they'd openly paw the ground, preparing to prove dominance, she reeled under a surging mass of emotions. Along with her obvious embarrassment at a public scene, Liss recognized and then quickly suppressed the flicker of feminine satisfaction that they would fight over her.

She was dimly aware that somewhere deep inside her, she'd just reached a decision and had made it without a backward glance.

With regret that she'd wasted so many years deluding herself that she and David ever had a chance of making their marriage work, she now knew irrevocably that he was no longer part of her life. She looked again from David's dark good looks to Wyatt's handsome strength. She didn't know whether her future would include Wyatt, but no matter what happened, she was free of David.

Immediately, she felt lighter for having fully and completely discarded the burden of her pain.

Sensing Wyatt's hand held out to her without looking, she took it firmly. She heard him exhale as his fingers surrounded hers, giving her his strength and support. Gripping Wyatt's hand, Liss looked at David, wondering how the man she'd once loved had turned into this stranger. "I have nothing to say to you, David, now or ever again."

Without a backward look at David, she turned and left the auditorium with Wyatt. He kept her hand tightly in his and didn't release it until they were in the parking lot. "Where's your car?"

She gestured beyond his shoulder, wondering at his terse manner. He turned and walked her to her car. "Get in. I'll follow you home."

On the short drive to her house, with her mind on automatic pilot, she relived the emotional turmoil she'd just been through, knowing instinctively that the greater tumult was yet to come. Even if she denied him yet again, by taking his hand when he'd offered it, and by publicly accepting his presence in her life, she'd made a promise to Wyatt.

There was no doubt at all in her mind that he'd expect her to honor that pledge.

And she would.

Whatever she had to lose, she'd risk it all, for the joy of their being together. Despite her earlier refusal to have a short-lived affair, she knew now that she'd willingly brave anything for the chance to love him.

Suddenly calm and resolute, she parked in her driveway and went quickly inside to wait in the darkened foyer. She heard a car door slam, then his quick steps as he jogged to her house. She opened the door for him, impatient as he ran up the stairs and across the verandah.

Immediately, his hot and demanding mouth took hers, claiming her as his even as she yielded. She turned her submission into urgent demands of her own. Pulling her closer, he lifted his head only to murmur against her open mouth, "Liss, oh God, I need you. Please say you forgive me for saying those terrible things to you. I didn't mean them, sweetheart. I haven't thought of anything but you—"

"Wyatt," she whispered, closing the gap between their lips. His mouth was hard and demanding until hers softened, then his became tender and ardent. He moaned before he broke loose and stepped away from her.

"Wyatt?" she asked in confusion.

"What am I doing?" he muttered. "I want you so much I can't see straight, but we have to talk."

"Not now," she protested, and reached out for him once more.

His voice came harsh through his shallow breathing. "Hear me, Alice Louisa. If I make love with you, I'm moving into your life and everything else be damned. You got that?"

Fifteen

She dared to look into his eyes, so intense they reminded her of a summer heat storm. Barely breathing, she felt his passion rising, swirling around her, sweeping her from her careful routine, awing her and thrilling her in the same delirious moment. Her fears gone, her inhibitions about their age difference washed away by the need in his eyes, she whispered, "Yes."

"Oh, God, Liss."

His response was everything and more than she could have wanted. She watched his eyes close while he absorbed the import of what was happening. Tension etched his face with sharply defined lines. He inhaled deeply.

She sensed the energy spreading through him, the triumphant surge of his arousal. His eyes snapped open and he smiled, a lazy, sensually possessive smile that erased the lines and made her mouth go dry.

"Will you let me stay tonight?"

"Yes."

Wyatt wrapped her in his arms. Leisurely at first, softly, gently, taking all the time in the world now that they both knew what was to come, his lips covered hers. Keeping his touch light, he fiercely controlled his long-repressed need.

His mouth was warm against her own, unhurried, exploring anew the softness of her. She moved against him, returning the pressure of his kiss, wanting whatever he wanted, craving more. He awoke sensations in her that she'd never experienced before, not ever, and had never dreamed she could feel. Eager to experience more, to learn more, she leaned into him. Her lips opened hungrily as he teased her with the tip of his tongue, flickering in and out, thrusting, retreating, outlining the contours of her lips.

He lifted his head, his breathing ragged, and looked at her closely in the dim light of the foyer. Her eyes were half closed, her head thrown back, her sweet mouth still open from his kiss. He muttered deep in his throat and lowered his head again, hungrily claiming her mouth, forgetting his intention to move slowly.

She responded, greedily demanding more, folding her arms around his neck as he lifted her against him. He grasped her securely by the waist and hips, the touch of his body hardening her nipples, creating a hunger so intense that she moaned in protest when his mouth left hers.

He covered her face with kisses, at first light and barely-felt kisses, and then kisses so searing she thought he'd brand her skin. She felt them on her eyes, her temple, her throat, before his mouth moved steadily downward, leaving her breathless, helpless against the blaze that engulfed her.

"Your bedroom?"

She couldn't speak, could barely nod.

Swiftly, he carried her up the stairs and into her room. Inhaling the fragrance that meant Liss, he set her down gently, sliding her body down the length of his, never taking his hands from her. She raised her arms to him, starved for his kisses, for the feel of his body next to hers. He complied, kissed her thoroughly, deeply, so fervently that she broke away, gasping.

He ran his arms down her shoulders and arms, leaving a trail of seared nerve endings, feeling her quiver under his touch. He moved one hand over her shoulder, caressed with the very tips of his fingers the hollow of her throat before he put his lips on that vulnerable spot where her pulse raced madly under his mouth. His hand moved gently down the contours of her breast, cupping and caressing the fullness of it, and on down past the slenderness of her waist.

With his hands cupping the rounded flesh of her bottom, he muttered, "Damn this suit. Why aren't you wearing that one piece thing?"

Her throat tight, Liss reached for his hand. She brought it up to her mouth and pressed her lips to the palm, as he had done once to her.

She stood entranced under his touch, gazing at him in rapture, following every move of his hands as he removed her clothing. First the fitted jacket, then the pencil-slim skirt, using his palms to draw the material down over her hips and thighs. Her stomach contracted at his touch. In the back of her mind, she had an instinctive need to cover herself, to hide her less than perfect body from him, but his words, soft and encouraging, prevented her.

Where once she'd have demurred at the idea of any man undressing her, making her vulnerable to him, now she stood straight and proud. Glad that she hadn't let herself go, that she worked hard in her house and garden and kept herself fit and lithe, she stepped out of her skirt.

His dark eyes smoldered at the sight of her in silken blouse and lace-edged slip.

She undid the pearl buttons on her blouse one by one.

He waited, restraining the need to yank her clothing off and take her where they stood. When the fabric of her blouse parted, he eased two fingers in under the material, caressing the upper slope of her breast, then edged the blouse off her shoulders. She stood absolutely still, eyes half closed, while he undid her bra and let it drop to the floor.

"You wear the flimsiest things," he whispered hoarsely.

Impatient now, she lifted her arms around his neck and stretched on tiptoe, straining to reach his lips. He bent to meet her. His mouth became fierce, his tongue reaching deep into her sweetness.

Taking her cue from him, she let the need of the moment urge her. "Take off your clothes."

"You do it."

She inhaled, then undressed him as sensuously as he had removed her clothing. Jacket, tie, and shirt she handled quickly, murmuring her appreciation of his hard, finely sculpted body. She molded her body against his naked torso, seeing close up the chest and shoulders she'd admired from the first moment she'd seen him. Hard workouts and running pay off, she murmured to herself as she ran her hands over his muscled contours.

He eased her down onto the big bed, saying, "I've wanted you so much. I've lain awake at night, dreaming how it would be for us."

"Me, too," she breathed, and placed a string of moist kisses along his collarbone, tasting the salty heat of him.

"I've waited for this, but now I'm afraid it'll be over too fast." Groaning, he straightened to remove the rest of his clothing, and his swollen manhood sprang free.

Her eyes widened at further proof of his hard, masculine body. Her yearning grew fierce and swift. She pulled him down to her, trusting him implicitly. His laugh was low and supremely masculine. Liss heard possession in its undertones and didn't care. His mouth teased hers, leaving a trace of molten kisses from her lips to her breasts. He captured a swollen nipple gently in his teeth, holding it easily while his tongue flicked across the rosy tip.

Fascinated by the aching warmth that grew and expanded from the center of her being until it enveloped her completely, Liss gave herself up to it completely. Nothing had ever been like this. She felt as though she were a new woman. Her breathing quickened to match his.

He stretched out beside her, on his side, his body alive against hers. Mesmerized by the movement of his hand as it caressed the swell of her hip and eased in to feel the petal softness of her inner thighs, she felt every nerve-ending electrify. He slid a finger in under the lacy edge of her panties, tantalizing her. Impatient with his sensuous teasing, she sat up and slid them off with one swift movement.

"In a hurry, honey?" He laughed out loud, then lowered his mouth to her belly. "Is this what you want?" he whispered against her, as he ran his lips over the sleek skin until she whimpered with passion. He circled her navel with his tongue, dipping into it as though it were manna.

"I want *you!*" she moaned, the ache between her legs demanding relief.

He paused for a moment, breathing heavily, reaching for control, but oh, God, he couldn't stand much more of this delectable torture. He eased into her, hoping to satisfy her insistent demand with only a fraction of himself, to let her get used to him, but Liss arched up, taking him fully inside.

She gasped at the wonderful feel of him, inside her at last, stretching her intimately. A moment's reflexive recoil of muscles long unused disappeared under the dazzling sensations of being one with him.

"Are you all right?" he groaned, feeling her stiffen. Barely able to restrain the need to plunge into her again, he pulled back, prepared to wait until she could accept him.

"It's been so long . . . don't stop, not now."

"I don't want to hurt you."

"You won't. Please," she whispered arching against him.

He groaned and gave in, plunging again and again, filling her deeply, moving freely into a passion-filled paradise where only Liss and he existed. The tempo of his thrusts increased as her hips worked rhythmically with his.

"Now?" he moaned, unable to tear his mouth from hers.

"Yes, yes, love me!"

He let go his control and his body moved faster and deeper into her womanhood. His breath came harshly as he plunged into the voluptuous pleasure of her ecstatic climax and he allowed himself respite at last.

Liss woke in the middle of the night, drowsily aware of warmth and slow, even breathing. *Wyatt.*

Recalling the pleasure he'd given her, she felt amazed that she could feel such passion.

She'd never dreamed such depths existed, never ever imagined that she'd experience such oneness, such exaltation. To find out that this existed after so many years!

She curled deeper into his arms, wearing a contented, sated smile.

Wyatt felt her mouth move against his chest, and even half-asleep he knew the motion for a smile. His hand tightened on her breast; he felt the nipple harden before she drifted back into sleep.

Her alarm went off as usual, but after that, nothing was routine. She turned over in bed to see Wyatt watching her.

"Morning, beautiful."

Running her fingers through her disheveled hair, Liss doubted his assessment.

Wyatt grinned and reached for her.

She backed away. "I need to shower."

"Later."

She scooted further away. "I have to go to work."

"So do I. Later." He wanted her right now, just as they were, love-stained and sleepy, heat rising from their bodies like early-morning steam.

Something in his expression made Liss slow her hasty exit from the bed. She glanced around, at the comforter tumbled on the floor, the lace-trimmed pillows scattered wherever they'd been thrown, then down at the sheets, still perfumed by their lovemaking. Her cheeks warm, she peeked at him from under her lashes.

He gave her a look so tender and heartwarming that her world shifted. No longer embarrassed or uneasy, she went willingly into his waiting arms, laying her head on his chest.

"That's better. Thank you."

She raised curious eyes to his, lifting her head to do so.

He pressed her back in place. "Thank you for trusting me, for coming back."

She murmured something he didn't catch, but in the next moment, he felt her tongue tickling his nipple through the hair on his chest. Then he felt her small hand coast down the planes of his ribs, circle the hollows of his belly, and float over his growing tumescence. He held his breath until her fingers stilled, then gently grasped him, beginning a motion that stiffened every muscle in his body. Rolling over, he pinned her beneath him, arousing her quickly and creatively, until both were swept up in a maelstrom of passionate emotions.

Much later, Wyatt opened his eyes "Oh, no. Liss," he moaned, shaking her shoulder. "Liss, wake up. We're late."

Groaning, she rolled over and looked at her clock. "Nine o'clock!" She jumped out of bed, looking around wildly at the mess in her bedroom, then back at Wyatt, sitting up and smiling at her from the middle of her rumpled sheets.

She grabbed a robe and threw it on.

In a flash, he was on his feet and struggling into his pants, hopping from one foot to another. Grinning at her ferociously, he promised, "Tomorrow we can sleep late. Or early."

She handed him his shirt. "Oh?"

"You'll see. Now let's see if I can't get over to my place without scandalizing your neighbors."

She waved her hand airily. "No problem."

They went down the stairs, arm in arm. He headed for the front door. Turning him, Liss led him through her kitchen, scooping up her clippers on the way, and into her back yard. A quizzical look on his face, Wyatt let himself be guided past her gazebo to her rose garden. Time was forgotten as he enjoyed the feeling of the morning sun on his face, the freshness of the air scented delicately with the fragrance of blooming flowers.

Inhaling deeply, he savored the new day.

She stopped at her rosebushes, clipped three white buds and one deep red rose, so dark it was almost black. She handed it to him.

Touched, he lifted it to his nose, enjoying the fragrance, then smiling, he skimmed it across her lips. "This reminds me of the day we met. You were cutting roses then."

"Yes. I saw you, and even without my glasses I liked what I saw."

He grinned, remembering her in her wet T-shirt, scampering across the lawn. "I liked what I saw, too."

At the sight of her lifted eyebrow, he confessed. "I watched you through the window. Couldn't see much through that hedge, but it was enough to make me very interested, even then."

She looked away, seeing herself as she'd been that day. "I was a mess.

"You were fantastic." Sliding his hand under the edge of her robe, he cupped her breast. At her quick gasp, he circled her nipple with his thumb. "I want to stay with you."

Suppressing a moan, she said, "I wish we could . . . but I have to go to work. Saturdays are always busy."

She stepped back, dislodging his hand. "Look behind you. There's a gate in the hedge. If you use that, no one will see you."

His smile froze when he realized that this was the shortcut gate placed there by her father and David's. He didn't like the reminder that David had had a place in her life for so many years.

She saw his expression. "It was a long time ago."

He relaxed and pulled her into his arms. "Jealousy isn't much fun. I'm sorry."

She hugged him. "Don't worry about it."

He released her and went to the gate. The oleanders had grown up around it, and the lock was rusty, but Wyatt wrestled it open. The hinges squeaked.

He grinned. "I'll put some oil on those later."

She grinned back, enjoying the sense of naughtiness that flavored their actions. "Wouldn't want the neighbors complaining."

He stopped halfway through the gate and kissed her thoroughly. "If I don't get going, they'll send the search teams out after us. We're both going be later than hell."

He kissed her again and pulled her tight against his body. "How come other people get Saturday off and we're running like crazy? I'll call you."

She kissed him, delicately running her tongue over his. "Okay. What would you like for dinner?"

He groaned. "Stop that. Let's plan on dinner out. Think of someplace you'd like to go."

She pressed closer, feeling something rise between them, and chuckled. She liked this new side of herself. Being wanton and unashamed of her sexuality felt good.

She liked it a lot.

He squeezed her harder. "Don't even think of it, or we'll never get to work."

Wyatt spent the day at the plant, going over the shut-down plan and hoping that Pete and his team could pull something together to present to Dick Fields and the board of directors. During a lengthy call to Dick he explained the situation, knowing he placed his rear on the line.

Dick's voice expressed his reserve. "I'm not sure I approve of this change in plan, Wyatt, but it's your show. I'll give you three extra days, that's all. I'll expect something concrete by mid-week."

Wyatt fought a losing battle with his temper. "Hell, Dick, what do you expect me to do in three days?"

"What you're there to do. What's the problem?"

"Like I told you. I think we may be able to turn the plant around. Make it productive."

"You have a magic wand up your sleeve, Wyatt?"

"Sure as hell wish I did."

"What's going on that you're not telling me? Nothing's stopped you from doing what has to be done before. What's holding you back now?"

"I'll get the job done." Wyatt hung up, gritting his teeth and wishing he'd never heard of Oakmont. But then, he'd never have met Liss. The muscle in his jaw relaxed and he reached for the phone again, needing to hear the calm, peaceful cadence of her voice.

He called her several times during the day. During one call she accepted his dinner invitation. During the next call, they discussed timing.

At last he said, "All right. See you at seven-thirty."

Still smiling, Liss hung up the phone.

"Well, I guess you and the hunk have made up?"

Liss looked over at Susan, who was tidying up an arrangement of cranberry glass. "We're having dinner tonight."

"Ah. And by that smile and the glow in your eyes, I'd guess you saw him last night, too."

Had she ever seen him! Hiding a smile, Liss nodded.

"I'm glad," Susan said simply. "It's time things go right for you."

The words struck a chord within Liss. Things weren't really going well. Since Wyatt had come to Oakmont, more than her personal life was changing. "I don't know that I'd go so far as to say that. You heard what those people said last night."

Susan's face creased with concern. "Don't pay any attention to those jerks."

"It's more than that, Suze. Look at these . . ." Liss broke off when the bell over the door jangled, announcing a customer.

Susan moved to greet the woman, whom Liss recognized as the wife of an Intratec engineer. They'd come to Oakmont last year, bought a large old farmhouse outside the town limits, and spent a small fortune remodeling it. Liss had supplied a lot of the furnishings.

Seeing the unease on the customer's face, Liss put down the sales slips she'd been holding and made her way over to her. "Good morning."

"Oh, hi. Listen, Liss, about those things I bought last week?"

"They'll be back from the refinishers in a week. When would you like them delivered?"

The woman bit her lip. "Well, that's what I'm here about. I'm afraid I'll have to cancel." She hesitated, then rushed on. "I hate to do this, but my husband doesn't want to spend

323

any money, that is any more than we absolutely have to, until we learn if he's going to keep his job."

"I understand," Liss said. She understood, all right. It wasn't the first time this had happened. The sales slips she'd been about to show Susan were definite proof that if Intratec pulled out of Oakmont, a lot of people were going to be left hurting. Including her, and in more ways than one. "Why don't we just put a hold on those things? You can let me know what you decide."

Gratitude warmed the other woman's face. "Oh, thank you. I hoped you'd understand. After all, you and the guy from Sunnyvale . . . oh, oh. I shouldn't have said anything."

Liss said nothing. Susan drew the customer away and soon had her out the door.

"Are you all right?" Susan asked, coming up behind Liss.

Liss turned. "I guess we'd better get used to that."

"She was only repeating what she'd heard."

"I know. And I can't blame her for not wanting to spend anything else right now. I can just imagine how hard it is for all those people at Intratec, waiting for the ax to fall."

"Does Wyatt ever talk about it?"

"No. I've asked him over and over what he's going to do, but he just gets that boss look on his face and says he can't discuss Intratec business."

"Men!"

Liss nodded.

"Doesn't he give you any clue at all?"

"He asked me to trust him to make the right decision."

"Can you do that?"

Liss hesitated. She'd agreed to do that, but that was before she got to know him as well as she did now. But then, how well did she really know him? He'd pried all her secrets from her, making her relive the hateful days of the past. He'd accused her of lying to him, but he hadn't told her much about himself.

All she had to go on, until she forced him to be as open with her as he'd made her be with him, was the little she knew of him from their interactions.

She knew his passion, his need. She knew his body, his quick temper, his sense of humor, and she'd seen his integrity and compassion. But was that enough to trust him? To trust him not just with herself, with her body, her heart and her life, but with Oakmont? It was a big decision.

Hesitantly, she told Susan, "I said I would."

"Sounds like you're having second thoughts?"

"Maybe I am," Liss admitted.

"Why? I thought you two were working things out."

"We are. It's just . . ." she paused to gather her thoughts. "It's different now. Before, I could separate what was happening with Wyatt and his work at Intratec."

"And now?"

"You heard what happened last night! You heard that lady just now. Everybody seems to know that Wyatt and I are involved. They're expecting me to help them!"

"Can you?"

"I can't!" she cried, then lowered her voice. "I have no control over Wyatt. He'll do what he has to, no matter what I say."

"I wouldn't be too sure of that. I saw the way he was with you last night."

"What way?" Liss asked, afraid to hear that others had observed the passion flaring between them

"Good grief, Liss. He all but had his brand stamped on your fanny! Come to think of it, I haven't seen you sit down today."

Liss felt her face flame, then despite herself, had to laugh. "He is a little possessive."

Susan rolled her eyes. "I thought he was going to deck David last night."

A little smugly, Liss agreed. "That would have given everybody something to talk about, all right. As if they aren't doing a lot of it already."

"Can you blame them? Intratec is big stuff in town. Everybody's worried. If they pull out, it's going to be hard on everybody."

Liss glanced at the pile of return receipts on her desk. "Don't I know it."

On her way to the library a short time later, Liss stopped when a woman with two small children hailed her from the front door of the toy store.

"Hi, Carol," she asked, pausing to chat. "What's new?"

"I heard what happened last night. Bob came home and told me all about it."

"News sure gets around."

"Is there any truth to what they're saying? Can you get that man to change his mind?"

Liss moved to avoid a sticky hand being placed on her skirt. "I wish I could."

"Bob said some hecklers gave you guys a hard time."

"Wyatt handled them."

"I heard that you're more interested in him than in us."

Shocked, Liss stared. "What does that mean?"

"That you don't care if people lose their jobs. That you're more interested in what you can get out of the situation."

Confused and hurt, Liss faltered, "But there's nothing in this for me."

"That's not what people are saying, Liss. I heard that if Intratec pulls out, Oakmont will lose a lot of funding. Everyone knows you were involved with that."

"That's true," she admitted, wondering how much of anything was private business any more. "But you know I don't have any say in how the money is allocated."

"I know some of that fund goes to the library," Carol said, her voice questioning. "What I hear is that you're looking out for yourself in this."

"That's not true," Liss gasped. "I don't have anything to say about the way the library budgets its money!"

"Maybe not," Carol lifted her shoulders. "That doesn't stop people from wondering. Look, I'm sorry to be the one to tell you this, but I figured you'd better know about it."

"I suppose . . ."

"I'm here to buy a birthday present for a party the boys are going to this afternoon. I'd better get it while I can still afford it."

Liss watched Carol re-enter the store, and in a daze, forgot about going to the library. Retracing her steps, she went back to her shop. For once, the elegant shopfront with her surname on the window gave her no pleasure. If people in Oakmont thought that a Thayer would sell them out, what were things coming to?

"Liss? What happened?" Seeing her expression, Susan came rushing to her.

In short sentences, Liss told her about the unexpected meeting.

"Oh, Lord. This is getting ugly. What are you going to do?"

"I don't know. Would you hold down the fort out here? I don't feel like seeing anyone."

"Of course," Susan said, and gave her a brief hug. "Close the door and just put all of this out of your mind."

It sounded like good advice, but could she follow it? Liss sat down at her desk, cleared it of everything she needed to do that afternoon, and stared at the three white rosebuds she'd cut this morning.

With Wyatt.

The rose fragrance teased her senses as vividly as the memories of the lovemaking they'd shared. He'd awakened in her a part of herself she'd thought long dormant, breathing life and warmth into her again. She was grateful—more than grateful—she corrected herself as she recalled the sensations, the pleasure, the sense of rightness, of oneness, that he'd given her.

Was it a mistake to have given herself to

him? Their new intimacy couldn't help but influence her thinking, her reactions, in fact her every response to him from now on. Every time she so much as heard his name, would her body throb as it had today? Would those feelings wear off?

Could she trust her judgment any more?

If she felt this susceptible to him now, what would happen if they continued as lovers? She swallowed. She should call it quits right here. She should learn her lesson, thank him from the bottom of her heart for what he'd done for her, and then tell him goodbye.

That's what she should do, all right.

Common sense told her that if she wanted to stay on in Oakmont, to be as respected as she had been before Wyatt moved into the carriage house next door, she had to disassociate herself from him as quickly as she could.

Reason told her that she'd gotten in too deep and that she'd suffer all the more for having accepted him into her life. Not just into her life, but into her house, her body, and her heart.

Reason had its point, but her heart won the battle. She'd already given in. As long as Wyatt remained in Oakmont, as long as she could see him, be with him, there wasn't anything else she would do.

As long as it lasted, she was going to enjoy her affair with Wyatt.

Wyatt heard feminine voices outside his office and thought nothing of it. Even though it was Saturday, he had a full crew in at work. Weekends off were for people who knew their jobs were secure, and no one at Intratec wanted to risk complaining about the overtime. Pity. He was sure they all had things they'd rather be doing, just like he did. Wondering what Liss was doing just then, he speculated for a few moments on their up coming evening.

He could feel himself smiling.

Would she let him stay with her again tonight? Maybe he could even talk her into letting him move in with her for as long as he was here. He could feel the heat pooling low in his groin. Turning his attention back to the draft plan he had before him on his desk, he tuned those thoughts out.

"Wyatt? Someone here to see you."

"If you're busy, Dad, I'll wait."

Raising his head, he looked from his temporary secretary to his daughter. "Toby? What on earth—what's the matter?"

The secretary gave him a confused look and left, shutting the door behind him. The sound of the latch clicking galvanized Wyatt. Standing quickly, he went around the desk to greet his daughter.

Hugging her hard, he pressed a kiss to her temple. "What's wrong, kiddo?"

"Nothing, Dad. I just thought I'd come see you after all."

He shifted her in order to look down into her eyes. Damn, she looked like Elaine, her soft blue eyes gazing up at him, with only the faint circles under them giving her away. "How did you know to come to the plant?"

"Well, I called the number where you're staying, and when I got no answer, I knew you had to be here."

"Yeah?" He hid a grin, thinking how he might have been with Liss.

"Sure. Where else would a workaholic like you be?"

He grinned. "Think you know your old man, huh. Maybe one of these days I'll fool you. Now, you want to tell me why you tracked me down?"

"Does a girl need a reason to want to see her Dad?"

It didn't take him long to figure out that despite her words, something troubled her. "I'm glad to see you, Toby, but I have to tell you this isn't the best of times."

She moved out of his embrace and went to

stand by the window. "Different here, isn't it? Not like Dallas or Sunnyvale."

She echoed his thoughts exactly. It worried him. "You didn't come all the way out here to talk about the view from my window."

"Do you like it?"

Puzzled, he allowed her the lead. "It grows on you. Why are you here, Toby?"

"Listen, Dad," she asked, without turning away from the window. "Have you ever had to make a decision that you know, either way, is going to change your life forever?"

"What's this all about?"

"I . . . uh . . . have to think something out, and if you're not too busy, I could use some help."

"Whatever you want, Toby. You want to tell me about it now?"

Toby opened her mouth then abruptly shut it. "Not yet. Okay? I have some more thinking to do. Could we talk later?"

"You want to talk after work?" he asked.

She turned back to him. "Look, Dad, I'll get out of your way. Why don't I wait for you at your hotel, and then you can take your favorite daughter out to dinner."

Damn! He hesitated. At his lack of response, Toby questioned, "Bad idea?"

"I'm not staying at a hotel. I've rented the guest quarters behind an old house." He reached for a memo pad and drew a rough map of Oakmont. "You have a car?"

"Sure. I rented some wheels in San Jose."

He handed her the map. "Here. Go on over there, and I'll see you later. We'll arrange dinner."

"Am I interrupting something, Dad?"

He felt his ears burn.

"I am. Oh, Dad, I'm sorry! Look, I'll just leave and you can pretend I never showed up here."

"Don't be stupid. I have a dinner date, but we can work that out."

Toby flicked a curious look at him. "What's she like, your new friend?"

"You can stop that right now, young lady."

She reached out to run a finger over the rose in his lapel. "Never seen you wear one of these before."

He brushed her hand away. "Could be things aren't the same as before."

Toby's eyes widened. "M'mm, this sounds interesting. Do I get to meet her?"

"Why?"

"C'mon, Dad. I can tell this one is different. Right?"

"Yeah." Wyatt couldn't help the smile he felt spreading across his face. "All right. If she says it's okay, you can come to dinner with us. But you'll have to disappear early."

Her eyes widened. "Gotcha. Can I nose around the plant for a while?"

"You have your badge with you?"

She dug through her purse and came up with a laminated rectangle that bore her photo and employee number. She snapped it to her lapel and waved at him from the door. "See you later."

He watched her bounce out of his office, her pale blonde hair a shoulder-length swirl. Whatever had bothered her when she first came didn't seem to be a problem any more. He grimaced. Maybe the idea of messing around with his life had cheered her up.

Damn. What was he going to tell Liss?

He reached for the phone and dialed.

"Thayer's. Can I help you?"

It wasn't Liss. The voice was warm and cheerful, but not the low and throaty one he'd hoped for. "Susan? This is Wyatt Harrow. May I speak to Liss?"

"Oh, you just missed her. She's gone over to the library, but she'll be back here to close up. Do you want to leave a message?"

Wyatt thought. "No. Just tell her I called."

"Sure."

Wyatt could almost feel the warmth of Susan's smile.

"Uh, Wyatt. Be careful of her. She's been through a lot."

When Wyatt didn't answer right away, Susan apologized. "It's just that we've been friends a long time and I don't want her hurt anymore."

"I understand. You're a good friend."

"Wyatt?"

"You don't have to worry about me, Susan."

Sixteen

Liss detoured through Oakmont's most sophisticated boutique on her way back to her shop from the library. Open less than a year, the boutique was popular with young wives and the women who'd moved here along with Intratec.

Although she'd heard Dani raving about it, Liss hadn't been in it before now, and as she crossed the threshold, she stopped in amazement.

The air was scented with a fragrance that promised sensual intrigue. Hanging from hooks and tossed over chairs as if they'd just been removed by an impatient lover, brief, lacy garments left nothing to Liss's imagination. Though she loved and wore fragile, lacy underthings, nothing she owned was anything like the frankly explicit, sexy lingerie she saw here in such lush profusion.

Dazed, fascinated, and not sure she should be in here, Liss took several cautious steps forward.

"Can I help you find something?"

Liss turned to the young sales clerk. "I'm not sure. I thought maybe something new . . ."

"I'm sure we can help you. Are you looking for yourself? Lingerie? A chemise and wrap? Maybe a teddy?"

She had no idea what the clerk was talking about. Even though she'd seen pictures of scanty underwear in her mail order catalogs, nothing connected with what she saw in here. "Could you show me?"

"Sure." Looking Liss up and down, she pursed her lips. "I'd say a medium would do." Beckoning Liss over, she went to a rack and held up one item after another. "For a first time buyer, I'd recommend something like this," she said, holding up something which took Liss's breath away.

"This is a camisole and tap pant set. Loose, lovely, and very enticing. It's silk charmeuse, easy care."

Liss reached out to stroke the fabric. "O-oh, that's nice. I like that blue—no, make it that emerald green! What else do you have?"

The clerk picked up a sheer mesh lace bra and bikini set. "This little number is very popular."

"My goodness!" Liss stared at the tiny embroidered flowers on the black lace. "At my age?"

"Why not? You have the figure for it."

Flattered, Liss reached out to touch the bikini and then drew her hand back. "I don't think I'm quite ready for that."

Giggling, the clerk showed her more. From rack to rack, Liss chose one luscious underthing after another.

Finally the younger woman held up a barely nothing garter belt. "A lot of our customers like these."

Liss swallowed. "Those aren't anything like the garters I used to wear!"

The clerk laughed. "Maybe not." Leaning closer, she whispered, "But they're a lot of fun!"

Liss wanted that. She wanted all the fun, happy, laughter-filled hours with Wyatt that they could manage. She took an armful of scanty silks into the dressing room, and once she got over the shocking image of herself in rose lace cut down to there, she began to smile, a smile she'd never even known she owned.

Dressed again, she gathered up the frothies, determined to wear one tonight for her dinner with Wyatt. Pulling out her credit card, she heaped all her treasures on the counter.

As the clerk began to ring up the sale, her eye wandered over the rest of the shop. If he liked these things, she'd come back and buy more.

Maybe even that black lace set!

With each passing hour it was more difficult for Wyatt to concentrate on Intratec business. He wondered where Toby was, what she was doing here in the plant, and what was so important that she had to come all the way out here to talk to him. On his way to a meeting with Pete and the department heads, he caught a glimpse of her fair head bent over a schematic as she studied it with another Intratec engineer.

His vice presidential response was satisfaction that a bright engineer, even though she was his daughter, would take time out of her day off to pore over a working design.

His fatherly response was to frown at the way the male engineer couldn't keep his eyes off her. He couldn't remember meeting him, but maybe he'd remedy that after this meeting with Pete.

However, Toby was the last thing on his mind during the long discussion with Pete and the other managers. Everything said about the plant reminded him of the arguments he'd had with Liss, and he had trouble keeping his mind focused away from thoughts of her. His hand kept straying, as though he had no control over it, to his lapel, to the red rosebud she'd given him that morning.

Cursing at himself for his inability to stop thinking of her while he listened to their preliminary plans for keeping the plant open, he jotted down notes, and a few minutes later found he couldn't read his own handwriting. By four-thirty, he was as hard as a man could be without ossifying.

Making his excuses, he stuffed his briefcase with papers to review later when he had his head on straight. First he had to talk to Toby. He dismissed the other men and strode back to his office. Sinking into his desk chair, he swiveled to stare at the peach orchard.

Who would have ever thought that he, Wyatt Harrow, ambitious and experienced climber of the corporate ladder, would risk blowing it all because he couldn't keep his mind on the bottom line?

While he waited for Toby, he tried calling Liss again. She'd evidently heard from Susan that he'd called, because she'd called and left him a message. Getting no answer from the shop or from her home, he stretched his shoulders to ease the tension building at the base of his neck.

He'd just have to talk to her when he got home.

He was still smiling at the thought of Liss and home when Toby walked in with the young engineer he'd seen her with earlier. "Hi, Dad. Do you know Bill Connors?"

The younger man advanced, his hand outstretched. "How do you do, sir?"

"Sir makes me feel ancient. Wyatt will do," he said, noting the slight tremble in the other man's hand. "What department are you in?"

As the two talked shop, Toby listened, her gaze going from one to the other. Finally, she interrupted, "Listen, Dad, Bill and I are going to catch some pizza, so you don't have to worry about me horning in on your dinner date."

Wyatt had difficulty controlling his relief. Toby grinned. "I thought you'd like that."

"You still want to talk?"

Her grin slipped away. "Yeah. Maybe tomorrow, okay?"

"Sure."

Ignoring the curious and sometimes hostile looks he got from Intratec employees as he walked out with Bill and Toby, Wyatt strode out of the plant and toward his Acura Legend with nothing on his mind but getting home to Liss.

342

He was at her back door on the dot of seven. She opened it, dressed and ready.

They laughed, speaking simultaneously, "I couldn't wait!"

He kissed her long and hard. Dimly, he realized that he either had to let her go or make love to her right there in her kitchen. Reluctantly, he stood back.

She looked up at his set face. "Rough day? You look tired."

He kept a hand on her bare shoulder. "Yeah, but I don't want to talk about work. Just us." He made a production out of ogling her. "You're looking especially beautiful tonight, Liss. I like this dress."

She did a little turn for him, letting the full skirt of her new white dress swirl around her hips. After the boutique, she'd made a mad dash through the dress shop and had been rewarded with this fabulous find. With a horizontally pleated bodice and thin straps, the dress complimented her slight tan and made her eyes sparkle.

She felt pretty and just a tad wanton knowing she was also wearing her new lingerie.

"C'mon, we'd better go while we still can," Wyatt muttered. "Damn. I nearly forgot. Toby showed up today. She's next door, but I told her I was having dinner with you."

Liss felt her eyes widen, then the slow heat

spread across her cheekbones. "Oh, does she know about . . ."

"Us?" he supplied. "Sort of."

"Don't you want to ask her to have dinner with us?"

"Not on your life," he retorted.

"Wyatt," she chided. "After she came to see you? It's mean to leave her on her own."

"She's got an engineer from the plant taking her out for pizza. She works fast," he added with a frown.

"Like father, like daughter?" she couldn't help teasing. "Do you suppose I could meet her while she's here?"

"I don't think you could prevent it," he muttered. "I'm surprised she isn't over here right now, checking you out."

Liss laughed. "We have time before dinner. Why don't you ask her over? I think there's still some wine."

Grousing, Wyatt called the guest quarters, and a few minutes later answered a knock at the back door.

Toby greeted him with an impish grin. "Hey, Dad, did you know about that nifty gate back there in the bushes? A guy could come and go that way and no one would know. Want me to show you where it is—or do you already know?"

"Keep it up, smart mouth, and see what happens. Behave yourself."

Liss came forward into view.

Toby's mouth dropped open. "She looks like Mom," she said in an aside to Wyatt. "I can't believe it."

Frowning, Wyatt whispered. "Quiet. Once you meet her, you won't notice the resemblance any more."

"Yeah, right," Toby said skeptically.

Wyatt made the introductions.

"Come in," Liss smiled and welcomed them into her home. "Once Wyatt said you were here, I could barely wait to meet you."

"Uh, me, too. Don't let us keep you. Dad said you're on your way out to dinner."

"Why don't you join us? I'm sure you and your Dad have a lot to talk about."

Toby threw Wyatt a quick glance. He shook his head, telling her without words that he'd said nothing to Liss, and furthermore, she was not to accept the invitation.

"Thanks, but you two are all dressed up. We'll just grab a pizza, right, Bill?"

Bill nodded, his eyes going from one woman to another. Wyatt followed his glance and saw how much his daughter also looked like Liss. They could almost be mother and daughter. Though Toby was taller and sturdier than Liss, they both shared the same fine bone structure, delicate blue eyes, and pale blonde hair.

Wyatt smiled, as though he'd had something to do with it.

"Well, listen, we don't have to stand around in the kitchen! Come in." Liss led the way into the parlor, while her guests followed, Toby bringing up the rear, her face showing her awe of Liss's home.

"My goodness," she breathed. "I've never seen anything more beautiful. I love it!"

Liss turned to see Toby run her hand appreciatively over the surface of a Hepplewhite table with eagle inlays. "Your father helped me redo this room," she gestured at the floor of the morning room. "He sanded and did most of the varnishing himself," she added, with a private smile for Wyatt which recalled the laughter they'd shared.

Toby flicked an amazed look at Wyatt. "You did? Wish I'd seen that."

Wyatt's eyebrows rose, but Liss beckoned Toby into the room and told her all that she and Wyatt had done.

Toby listened intently, her gaze tracking every move Liss made through the room. "I love your house, Liss. I wish we had one like this, don't you, Dad?"

Wyatt started to deny it, but checked himself. Every moment he spent here with Liss made him more and more aware of the hold her house had on him. It wasn't just the house or the fine furnishings, but the spirit that lived within it.

It was tradition, generations of it, richly layered and satisfying.

It was Liss.

He stood back and watched the two women—his women, he amended with a possessive smile—as they wandered through the house. Bill trailed behind, silent and puzzled as Toby forgot his existence.

Wyatt caught his eye and motioned to the kitchen. Opening the refrigerator, he plucked out two beers and tossed one to Bill. "Might as well get comfortable. Once Liss gets going on her house, she's gone."

"What's so great about all this old stuff?"

"Beats me, but they like it." What he didn't say was that if it made Liss happy, he was all for it. What surprised him was Toby's interest. By the way she looked at Liss, with something close to hero worship, he figured there had to be something more going on than reverence for this great old house.

"So, Bill, how long have you been in Oakmont?"

"Almost a year," the younger man answered, standing stiffly as though expecting a reprimand.

"You like it here?"

"Yeah, sure. Well, not at first," he amended.

"How come?"

"You kidding? They roll the sidewalks up at dusk here."

Wyatt understood his attitude, having felt the same way himself not so very long ago. How much had changed in a matter of days. "So, what changed your mind?"

"What's not to like?" Bill leaned back against the counter, his manner more relaxed now that they were on a safer topic. "The Sierras are a coupla hours away. I go backpacking, skiing in the winter without fighting the traffic. I keep a ski boat over at the lake. You should see her go! My buddy and I had her out last weekend, and zoom—"

"I get the idea," Wyatt grinned. "What's it like, living in town?"

"Dead, unless you've got a girl." He shrugged. "I work a lot."

"I thought you and Toby . . . ?" Wyatt probed.

"Nah. I haven't seen her in over a year, not since we both worked on that project in Orem." He flicked a glance at the door, then said, "Any chance of getting her transferred to Oakmont?"

"You'd have to talk to her about that."

"What I mean is, are we going to be open long enough for her to put in for a transfer?"

"You know I can't discuss that with you, Connors."

Bill's face fell even as his shoulders stiffened. "It's true, then. Guess I'd better start making plans to move."

"Don't pack your suitcases until—" Wyatt broke off as he heard Liss's voice in the hallway.

Toby spoke as they entered the kitchen. "Could I come see your shop, too?"

"Of course. Come whenever you like."

"You sure you don't mind?"

Liss smiled. "Never."

After a few minutes, Toby and Bill left, Toby promising to come back and see Liss tomorrow.

Wyatt waited until the door was shut behind them before he reached out and snagged Liss. "I thought they'd never leave. What were you two gabbing about?"

"Just girl stuff."

Wyatt moaned. "Do I have any secrets left untold?"

"Who said we were talking about you?" Liss smiled. "We had something much more interesting to discuss . . ." At his admonishing look, she added, ". . . the best way of refinishing a chest of drawers she has. You gave it to her when she went away to college."

"I did? Oh, yeah. It was something my mother gave me years ago—just junk."

"Fat lot you know. It may be a bachelor's chest."

Wyatt's brow creased. "Come to think of it, that's what Mom called it. I thought she was teasing me."

Liss rolled her eyes.

Wyatt slanted an appraising look at her from head to toe. "Look, do we have to talk about kids and furniture? Come here and kiss me."

She did just that, to Wyatt's great enjoyment.

At last he released her and looked down into her shining eyes. "Do you want to skip dinner?"

"After I bought a new dress? And . . ." she broke off, wanting to show, not tell, him about her new lingerie. "Sorry, I'm afraid you'll have to honor your promise."

"Damn. You're a hard woman, Ms. Thayer. Okay. How about I make you another promise?"

"What?"

"We go to dinner," he said as he kissed her nose. "We come back," he continued, nuzzling her neck, "and then we go upstairs and . . ." he whispered into her ear, his breath warm against her bare skin.

Shivering, she arched her neck to give him more room to maneuver. "I guess we could eat later."

"No. I keep my promises."

During dinner, Liss was aware of two very different selves. One laughed and flirted, happy with her new, easier relationship with Wyatt. Her second self sat back, storing every sensation, every laugh and sensual half-lidded look, folding them carefully into her mind's memory book, keeping them safe against the day she would be alone and would need to pull them out, one by one, to savor and remember.

"I like your daughter. She's a lot like you, but there's something I can't quite put my finger on."

"She likes you, too. Or maybe it's just your house she's crazy about."

Liss smiled. "I enjoyed showing it to her. It was fun." Her expression turned somber. "Wyatt, is Toby worried about something?"

"What?"

"I'm not prying, but it seemed to me that she was distracted by something."

"She said she wants to talk, but I don't

know what it's about. We haven't had a chance to say much of anything yet."

"You should be with her tonight! She needs you."

"*I* need *you*. Toby will still be here tomorrow. And longer, if Bill can talk her into transferring."

Liss's eyes lit up. "She can do that? The plant won't close?"

"I didn't say that. Look, can we talk about something else? Like you and me?"

"You and I?" she probed.

"Like how I'm going to keep my other promise to you," he challenged.

"Ah, I hate to bring this up, but maybe you should know what's going on," she said, reluctant to speak of unpleasant topics but afraid if she didn't change the subject, she'd fall drooling with anticipation onto the carpet.

"What?" Mentally, he shook himself. "Sorry. My brain's fried."

She lifted an eyebrow.

Immediately, Wyatt remembered the sweet fragrance of her skin and wanted her more than ever. "Don't do that unless you want to be embarrassed in public."

She smiled, deliberately enticing, then remembered how she'd felt at the meeting last night. "I was embarrassed last night," she admitted. "That's part of what we need to talk about."

He sipped iced water. "If you're talking about that jerk ex-husband of yours—I don't normally go around offering to punch someone's lights out. I'm sorry if I upset you."

"Two men threatening to fight over me. That's more than enough to keep Oakmont in stories for a month."

"That wasn't my intention, believe me. It's just that when Greenley put his hand on you, I saw red."

"I'm touched."

"I'd like to touch you right now," he muttered.

Her smile was pure feminine seduction. She teased, she provoked, she tantalized, accepting every lascivious suggestion Wyatt whispered over his wine glass, and adding her own until the sweat glistened on his brow.

He forgot how to breathe. His groin tightened, turning the screw on his torture rack up another notch. Grimly, he fought to control the overwhelming need to sweep the table clean and lay Liss across it. He could imagine her intimate muscles tightening around him and feel her explosive release.

He retaliated by slipping a hand under the table cloth and gathering the folds of her skirt until he'd pulled it high on her thigh. He ran a finger down the top of her leg, grinning at the stunned look on her face.

When she inhaled sharply, he chuckled. "I know one thing. You're wearing garters."

"Stop that!" she bleated when he snaked his finger down her inner thigh. It was one thing to fantasize about his reaction to her new sexy underthings, but another to have him find them in a public place!

He plucked the elastic and let it snap gently against her leg. "I feel lace here. Is it like this all the way up?"

"Wyatt . . ."

He ran his hand into the soft heat between her naked thighs. She closed them tightly against him, but the damage was done. She shut her eyes to keep the sensations at bay.

"Stop! Someone will see!"

"Who?" With his hand still under the table cloth, he looked around. When he saw several people looking their way, even though he knew they could have no idea what he was doing, he removed his hand, but only after he made little circles along the quivering nerve endings of her upper thigh.

She opened her eyes. "That's not fair."

"Who said anything about fair?"

Seventeen

Wyatt's look made her long for privacy.

With his voice low, rough, a little dangerous, he warned, "If you play the game, you have to pay the price." Then he smiled, his voice coaxing. "Besides, you can get even later."

The waiter brought their entrees, putting a temporary halt to their titillation. She concentrated on her dinner for a few minutes, until she put down her wine glass and saw him staring at the swell of her breasts. She felt her nipples harden against the twin barriers of lace bra and dress.

Wyatt licked his lips. "Maybe we'd better think about something else. So, Ms. Thayer, how did your day go?"

She took a deep breath, searching for equilibrium. At her age, to be playing naughty games in a public place. It felt wonderful! "Oh, not bad. I did a little shopping."

"Did I just discover something new?"

Nodding, she allowed herself one more little smile. "And a few other things, too."

"Lord. Talk about something else."

"A couple of things happened today. I wasn't going to say anything, but . . ." she hesitated and make an uneasy gesture.

"Tell me."

She sensed he'd lost their light-hearted sensual mood, just as she had. So she told him, leaving nothing out.

He closed his eyes. "Small towns. Save me."

His attitude annoyed her. She shouldn't have told him, but now that they'd started this, she had something she wanted to say. "Maybe you can't see it when you're insulated from the people you're directly hurting, Wyatt, but gossip and resentment happen everywhere. Even in big cities."

His eyes popped open, then narrowed. "Aren't you over-reacting here?"

"I don't think so. What do you think is going to happen when people don't have jobs at Intratec anymore? People like me are going to get hurt, too."

At his look, she explained, "The small businesses, Wyatt, like the toy store, where Carol won't be able to afford to buy toys for her kids if her husband is laid off. My sales are down, too. And it's not just us. I'm sure this is happening all over town. We lose business, maybe we go out of business. This is bad for the town. Tax money is lost, so city improvements are delayed or put off. What happens if we can't afford a police or fire department any more? How about the schools?"

"I hadn't thought of that," he admitted.

"Well, think of it now. I may be painting too grim a picture, but who do you think gets hurt in the long run? We all do, Wyatt, everybody living here."

"I thought you didn't get involved in stuff like this."

"Maybe I never had a reason to before."

"And you expect me to do something about this?"

"I don't know what I expect anymore, Wyatt," she admitted honestly. "I know I can't sit back and do nothing."

"I don't want to argue about this."

"Neither do I. But we can discuss it, can't we?"

"Until I make my decision, there's nothing to discuss."

She sat back in her chair, shoulders slumping at the cold tone of his voice.

"Let me ask you this, though. While you were elaborating on all the terrible things that will happen to Oakmont if I close down the plant, how come you didn't mention your own involvement? How much you have riding on this?"

Liss showed her confusion. "But I did. Thayer's is losing money already. I told you that."

"Why didn't you tell me Intratec was heavily into funding the library?"

"Wha-at?"

"How come I had to find out the hard way?"

"I don't understand."

"Imagine how surprised I felt when I was looking over the plant's expenditures over the past two years." He raised an eyebrow at her while his dark blue eyes took on a steely glint. "Don't you think a quarter of a million dollars to the library is a little too much to forget?"

Taken aback by his attack, she faltered, "But that's the library money. What does it have to do with me?"

"Where's the money coming from for your Collection? Seems to me that if the library can't afford it, your hard work goes down the tubes. Sounds like a pretty good reason for working on me to keep the plant in business."

"I never even thought of that."

"No?"

"No. I wondered why you didn't say anything. It never occurred to me that you didn't know."

"That's the truth?"

Her lips thinned. "I don't like being questioned like this, Wyatt. You want my trust, but you don't seem to realize it works both ways."

He raised his water glass to his lips and took a sip, his expression closed. Liss watched him, saying nothing while he worked on things in his own mind.

"How much of that money goes to the Collection?" he asked abruptly.

"Why?"

"Because if I'm going to get hit with conflict of interest charges, I want to know how much truth there is to them."

"I don't understand."

"Don't you?" he said, his expression softening. "If everyone knows I'm crazy about the Collection's curator, don't you think someone will think to ask how much I'm willing to do to keep her happy?"

"Oh," she murmured, feeling a blush steal across her cheeks. "I don't know about the money. You'd have to talk to Joe. Or maybe Don Simpson."

"Who are they?"

"Joe's the head librarian. Don's on the city council. He chairs the library board committee and handles the finances."

"All right. I'll find out."

She nodded, then studied the weave in the tablecloth. "I don't want your dealings with me . . . our relationship to influence your decision."

His smile came quick and genuine. "You are one fantastic woman."

Her return smile raised his internal thermostat past the comfort level. The feelings for her, fueled by passion and desire, put on hold during their brief argument, flared up again. He felt like he was on the rack again, tormented by his need for her. The rack revolved another half turn. He drained his ice water, keeping his eyes on her.

"I found something out last night, while you and David were toe to toe."

"Don't remind me," he groaned. "I have to work with him on a project that—never mind."

"That what?"

"Nothing. I shouldn't have said anything. What were you saying?"

She refused to let his secrecy ruin their evening. "Okay. I'll tell you my secret, but one day, you'll have to do the same."

He reached for her hand and kneaded the delicate flesh between her fingers. "For you—anything."

Appeased, she began again. "I realized last night that David is past history."

The look that grew and took over his face was worth every risk she'd ever take.

Thrilled by his response, she said softly, "There's just you, Wyatt."

"Oh, God, Liss, let's get out of here." Impatient, he looked around and signaled for the waiter. At last they left the restaurant, walking sedately, a discreet foot apart. He tucked her into the passenger seat of his car and fastened her seat belt, using the opportunity to slide his palm across her breasts and finger an already peaked nipple.

She shivered.

He laughed, a low, deep masculine sound of satisfaction. "Just so you don't forget."

"You're awfully proud of yourself, aren't you?"

He went around the car and seated himself gingerly behind the wheel, unobtrusively easing the tightness of his pants. If he didn't try for a lighter mood, he'd zoom the car into the nearest alley and take her on the spot. "I'm suffering, and you're—"

"Suffering?" she quirked an eyebrow, making his ache score deeper.

"All during dinner, you knew what you were doing, and yet you kept right on. Then that last comment. That calls for retribution."

"Mmm, I can hardly wait."

He was still listing all the things he would do to her when he pulled up into her driveway. Rather than getting out, he undid his seat belt and pushed the seat back.

Liss watched him curiously.

He caught her eye and smiled. In the dim light, his eyes were dark blue, almost hidden in the shadows of his face, but Liss knew the power and heat they revealed.

"In a minute," he said casually, "I'm going to take you to your front door, give you a sedate goodnight kiss, then go home."

"What? What about your promise?"

He grinned at the befuddled disappointment on her face. "Then, I'm going to use the shortcut and come back. Do you have any objections?"

Her face lost its confusion as understanding swept through her. "Thank you for worrying about my reputation, Wyatt."

"You're welcome."

"Ah, about Toby?"

Wyatt smiled. "I warned her not to expect me back. She can have the place to herself."

Liss couldn't help frowning. "That seems a little too open, even for her generation."

It took Wyatt a minute, but at last he understood. "I don't for one minute expect Toby

362

will be using those guest quarters for anything more than sleeping."

"Oh," Liss could feel her cheeks burning. "But she'll know that we . . ."

"And she'll be discreet about it. She's an adult now, too."

"I guess," Liss said, still a little doubtful and embarrassed that Wyatt's daughter would know that they slept together.

"It'll be all right. Now, I don't want to talk about anything except us. Come over here, Prissy, let me kiss you goodnight."

He played his role perfectly, opening the car door for her, assisting her up the stairs, and lingering for only a few moments before giving her little more than a perfunctory kiss. "See you in a few minutes," he whispered when a curtain twitched across the street.

She laughed, feeling young and mischievous as she opened her door and went inside. She left the foyer dark and went immediately back to the kitchen. Rooting through the pantry, she spotted a bottle of brandy.

Anticipation at fever peak, she rinsed the dust off the bottle, then washed and polished two snifters. Setting bottle and glasses on a tray, she waited for Wyatt. Moments passed. He still didn't come.

She paced the kitchen, anticipation fading until she heard a sound on the verandah. She ran to unlock the door. "I thought you'd changed your mind," she blurted.

Wyatt swept her into his arms. "Never. Just had to return a phone call."

"On Saturday night?"

"I've got some people at the plant working overtime. They wanted to check something out before they went any further."

"And?" she questioned, noting the excitement in his voice.

"And I told them to go ahead."

"Sounds interesting." She arched an eyebrow in query.

"Stop fishing for information," he said lightly, then his voice changed, becoming deep and husky. "Oh, God, Liss, I've waited for this all day."

"Me, too."

He twirled her, watching how her skirt flared. Abruptly, he set her down and smiled. "Be right back."

Confused, she watched him walk quickly down the hall. In a moment, the first strains of Strauss's *Emperor Waltz* accompanied him back to the kitchen door.

He bowed. "May I have this dance?"

Enthralled, she moved to join him.

He offered her his arm, and placing her hand in the crook of his elbow he escorted her to the empty morning room. "Shall we break in our floor?"

She smiled, delighted with this side of him, and moved into his arms. Following his lead, she glided gracefully into a slow, perfect waltz. "M'mm, where did you learn to dance like this?"

"Corporate charm school." He grinned at her startled look. "Where else do rough, tough engineering types learn how to handle social situations?"

"Dancing lessons?" she asked, stifling a smile.

"Other things, too. Ask me which fork to use first."

That did it. The smile became a laugh. "I don't believe it. All this—you learned at men's finishing school?"

"Women's, too. But there's one thing I learned on my own."

"What's that?" she asked.

"This." He dipped her over his arm, holding her securely, and ran his mouth down her throat and into the valley of her breasts. His tongue laved the silky slopes while she grasped his shoulders and hung on.

He took one last nibble and lifted her to her feet, never losing the beat, then swept her around the room in a series of twirling, swirling circles that left her breathless. "Oh, Wyatt, what you do to me!"

Abruptly, he stopped. The music continued, another waltz now, but all he heard was the deep inhalation she took to steady herself. He could feel the pulsing of her heart through his clothes and the thin dress she wore.

Glancing down at her breasts rising and falling in excitement and anticipation, he could hardly contain himself.

"Liss, I want to make love to you."

She looked up at him. "I want to make love to you, too."

His smile said it all.

She took his hand and led him up the stairs. In her darkened bedroom, he took her in his arms for a long, drugging kiss that sapped every bit of strength from her knees.

He traced her neck with kisses, then nudged the thin straps of her dress to one side. He pulled the straps down slowly, then slid down the bodice. Burying his face between her breasts, he licked and suckled until her nipples hardened in his mouth.

She groaned and grabbed his hair. In the dim light, it shone like silk. She traced the shape of his earlobe, then the line of his brow. When he pulled hard on her breast, she inhaled deeply. Her hands fell away.

He raised his head again. She stood, her

neck arched, her head thrown back. The pulse at the base of her neck fluttered. He put his mouth to it. His body throbbed and hardened in response. He wanted her right now. He wanted to be so deep inside her that there'd never be any doubt again that they belonged together.

"God, Liss, I wanted to go slow this time, but it's happening too fast."

She reached for his zipper. "Now, Wyatt, now."

They fell together onto her bed. The floral fragrance of her sheets enveloped them as he stripped the clothes from their bodies. She helped. They needed no further preliminaries. With a muffled shout, Wyatt embedded himself in her.

"So hot, so tight." He set a deep, wild rhythm that had her convulsing beneath him within minutes.

"Wyatt!" she cried as pleasure beyond belief overtook her.

He lifted her long slender legs around him. "Hold on," he muttered, and shuddered and thrust his way to his own culmination. He collapsed on her, breathing heavily, sated and content.

She lowered her legs to his side, cradling him still within the embrace of her body. She breathed in the mingled scents of their lovemaking, the sweat-sheened flavor of his skin, and loved him.

"I'm too heavy for you," he mumbled, and rolled to his side.

Liss clutched at him. "Don't go."

He hugged her close to him. "I'm right here. Sleep now."

They both slept. In the morning, he roused her with intimate kisses and slipped into her while she was still half-asleep. She opened her eyes to stare into his. They lay on their sides, her leg lifted over his.

She traced the curve of his torso past his waist, over his narrow hip and down into the softness of his belly, to the place where he was hard and buried in her. She caressed him.

He stiffened. "Do that again and it'll all be over."

She smiled sleepily. "This is a nice way to wake up. M'mmm, do that some more."

He repeated the thrust.

Their lovemaking was slow, idyllic. Give and take, thrust and counter-thrust. Long tender kisses, one after another. Liss closed her eyes and let her body drift until at last, she could drift no longer but experienced a release so perfect she cried.

Wyatt climaxed moments after she did. He stayed where he was and tenderly brushed the teardrops away. "Liss, you are the most perfect thing that's ever happened to me."

They slept again. Hours later, with effort, he released Liss and climbed out of bed. "I need to go into the plant for a few hours this morning."

"Wyatt," she protested, her voice not much more than a whisper

"Go back to sleep. I'll see you later. Can we spend the day together?" he asked with a sudden grin that teased her heart.

She responded to his grin with a heartwarming smile that made him hungrier than ever.

Liss pushed herself up against the pillows. "What are you going to do at the plant?"

"I'd like to tell you, Liss, but I can't. I'll be back as soon as I can." He tucked his shirt into his pants. "What are your plans?"

She pushed her hands through her disheveled hair and made herself think. "Normal weekend things—shopping and laundry, errands. That sort of thing."

"No work?"

"Nope. We're closed on Sunday." Her eyes widened as she remembered. "Wyatt, I forgot about church! If you get back before, do you mind waiting until—"

"I don't want to interfere with your traditions, Liss. I want to share your life, not dis-

369

rupt it. Maybe we can go together next Sunday?"

She looked up at him with narrowed eyes. "Attending church services together in this town is tantamount to an announcement in the papers. You sure you want to do that?"

"We have an understanding, don't we?" he asked.

She cocked her head. "Understanding about what?"

He sat on the bed beside her, his face serious. "I told you that if we made love, I was moving into your life. I asked if you understood. Do you remember that?"

Her face equally serious, she nodded. "Yes."

"We made love, Liss. I am in your life now."

"And am I part of your life?"

Wyatt took her into his arms. "You're becoming the biggest part, Liss."

She quivered in his embrace. That statement sounded very much like commitment, but it couldn't be. Wyatt was leaving in a few days.

How much a part of her life could he be with her in Oakmont and him in Sunnyvale?

"So, do we go to church next Sunday?"

"Will you be here then?"

"I plan to be," he said evenly.

Her eyes sparkled. "Can you believe it? Next Sunday is the dedication."

She glowed with excited expectation, with anticipation. Wyatt felt her elation as his and leaned over to kiss her.

"Oh Wyatt, it's going to be marvelous!" she exclaimed when he released her mouth. "We'll have such a good time."

Wyatt wanted to share it with her. Clearing his throat, he suggested, "We'll make plans for that later. Liss—I forgot about Toby. I'll have to make time for her today. Okay?"

"Maybe we'd better forget about making plans," she suggested. "You should spend the time with Toby while she's here."

"I'll see what she wants to talk about, then you and I are on our own."

"She could join us, if you like."

He raised an eyebrow at her. "Not on your life, Liss. A father has to draw the line someplace."

"Oh. Well, I wouldn't want to cast aspersions on your parenting skills," she murmured while she hid a smile.

"Are you laughing at me?"

"At us. I've never had to arrange my life around children."

Wyatt grinned. "That's why parents have to take a lot of naps. Think you'll be tired enough for a long one later?"

When she nodded, wondering a little at herself that she'd been able to joke about children, he asked, "Could I be selfish and ask you to do your errands while I'm gone, so we can have the rest of the day to ourselves?"

Her skin warmed under the tone of his voice. "All right. But you might wind up helping me with the yard work."

"If you wear something as skimpy as you did before, I can't guarantee we'll get any work done."

Liss smiled. "Promises, promises."

He kissed her again, deep and hot. When he lifted his head, they were both breathing heavily. "Remember where we left off."

After church, Liss shopped, and back at home, raced through her weekend chores. She fed the dryer another load and then leaned back against the machine, allowing herself at last to think about the subject she'd been pushing to the back of her mind since last night.

Wyatt. He was everything she could ever want in a man, humorous, virile and self-confident. He was inquisitive, sensitive, persuasive, attractive, empathetic and too sexy by half. Caring, creative in his lovemaking, gentle and powerful, he made her heart smile. He was satisfyingly possessive.

He'd already demonstrated his willingness

to fight for her. She shivered at the memory, thrilled but a little scared by her perception of the lengths he'd go to for her, no matter that she was older. The six years didn't seem to exist for him. And because he ignored them, she found it increasingly easy to do the same.

In fact, she thought with an amazed smile, he made her feel years younger, like a young girl just discovering her womanhood.

If the age difference didn't matter to him, then she wasn't going to let it matter to her.

Wyatt found her on her knees in the flower beds surrounding the gazebo. A pile of weeds at her side, she wielded a hand trowel with precision. He stood behind her for a few minutes, admiring the neat curves of her hips and bottom.

When she moved forward, coming up off her haunches to reach for a weed, he swallowed hard at the sight of her cutoff jeans revealing tender, untanned skin.

He grinned with anticipation. "Well, good afternoon."

Startled, she sat back and turned her face to him. "I was beginning to think you were a figment of my imagination."

He sank to his knees beside her and buried

his face in her neck. "Oh, I'm no figment. Want me to prove it?"

She tried to push him away. "I'm all dirty and sweaty."

He resisted her shove and kissed her soft throat. "I like you sweaty."

Giving in, she arched her neck for him. "That feels good. Do it some more. After I clean up."

He nibbled her earlobe. "I love the taste of you. I can't get enough."

"If you don't stop, I won't be responsible for my actions," she warned.

He sat back, looking delighted. "My, my. Am I going to be ravished right here in your petunias?"

She laughed. "These are carnations. And I was referring to bopping you one with my trowel."

"Whatever." Wyatt lay back in the grass. "I'm easy."

Liss raised her trowel as if she were going to carry through on her threat. The sight of Wyatt's prone body, shirt stretched taut against his chest, made her change her mind. She dropped the trowel.

Casually, she stripped off her gardening gloves. "Easy, huh? Well, if that's the case, I'm going to go have a quick shower and then ravish you to my heart's content."

Wyatt's eyes narrowed. Liss saw his eyelids flicker, then wondered at the wide smile that acted like a love potion on her insides. "Wanna play in the sprinklers with me?"

"What?"

"That first time I saw you, you were playing in the sprinklers—"

"I wasn't playing," she began to explain.

"I thought then that I'd like to join you. Play some games of our own."

She gasped, then laughed. Her cheeks felt hot. She didn't care. "That water is co-old."

He stood and nonchalantly started for her house. "Okay. You convinced me. I'll shower inside. Want to join me?"

"Join you?" Liss snorted inelegantly. "That's my shower, and there's not enough room for two."

"Well," he drawled, "maybe we can improvise."

Eighteen

"Improvise, huh?" She laughed up at him. "I do love a resourceful engineering type."

"Better make sure that's only one engineer. Me."

She saw the shadow crossing his dark blue eyes, and smiled. "You're the only one I'll let into my bathroom."

"Be sure you keep it that way."

He grabbed her and carried her up the stairs. "Put me down," she said in protest. "I'm too heavy."

He stopped halfway up to kiss her. "This is my show."

He marched into the bathroom and set her down, letting her slide all the way down his body.

She stared at him. "You're not even breathing hard. How can you do that?"

"Hormones." He wiggled his eyebrows and stripped off his shirt.

She watched wide-eyed as his torso was bared to her. "You must work out a lot."

"Enough. I haven't since I came here, but then, I'm getting a lot of other exercise."

She colored.

"Sanding floors, carrying you up and down stairs—"

"Not down," she protested.

"An oversight. I'll take care of that later, if I'm still capable. Let's shower."

She trailed a finger down the soft thatch on his chest. "Are you serious about this?"

"Very serious. C'mon."

A little nervous, a lot expectant, she bent to unlace her tennis shoes.

"Let me, Liss."

At first she held back, but she lost all her reticence when he kissed her kneecap. He removed one shoe, shaking a small clump of dirt out onto the floor, then the other. "Messy, messy," he chided her as he caressed her instep.

He ran the palm of his hand up her calf to her thigh, loving the way her flesh quivered under his touch. Reaching up, he unzipped her cut-offs and then smoothed them over her hips and down her legs.

She stood in front of him, shorts puddled

at her ankles, while he stared at her bikini. With his fingertips, he traced the narrow fabric over her hips, then down to the minuscule patch of fabric at her mound. "Is this standard uniform for gardeners?"

Swaying on her feet, Liss felt she had a choice: either remain silent and use her last bit of control to stay upright, or answer and fall in a heap.

She chose silence.

He slipped her bikini down. Obediently she raised one foot, then the other, as he whisked her jeans and panties off.

She shivered and grasped his shoulders for support. "I thought we were going to take a shower?"

He thrilled to her barely-there voice. "All in good time, Alice Louisa. Here, let me help you with that thing you're wearing."

He reached around and undid her pink halter, letting her breasts fall free into his waiting hands. "Oh, that's nice," he breathed, "even better than I imagined the first time I saw you in this little number."

Instinctively, she covered her body with her hands. To make love was one thing, but to be looked at like this was too much. Embarrassed that he'd see the marks of her years, she moved away.

Grasping her hips with his large hands, he

held her still. "Don't you go getting all prissy on me now. Be still."

He went to the tub and turned the water on. When it was the right temperature, he reached down and firmly put the old rubber plug in the drain. "H'mm, maybe a bath after all."

"But—"

"Patience," he counseled, and smiled the seductive grin that weakened her spine. "Didn't you say that once to me?"

Quickly he stripped, then reached for a jar of honey bath gel.

"Are we going to have a bubble bath? I wouldn't have thought you'd like—"

"Oh, there are a lot of things I like. Come here," he coaxed.

"I'm too old for all this."

His lips thinned. "I do not want to hear another damned word about how old you are or how much younger I am. Got it?"

She swallowed a hasty retort. Wasn't it just hours ago that she'd told herself she'd ignore their age difference? She took a step forward, but before she could take another, Wyatt hugged her.

She allowed herself to be persuaded by a kiss. While the tub slowly filled, Wyatt scooped up a handful of gel and began smoothing it into her shoulders.

She raised startled eyes to his and jerked back.

He soothed her with another kiss. "Let me. I won't hurt you."

He massaged the gel into every inch of her skin, taking his time to work the tension out of each muscle, softly soothing her intimate folds and creases until she moaned under his hands.

He used long strokes down her flanks and short ones along the delicate bones of her ribs. "I can feel your heart beating," he murmured, and put his ear against her chest.

She laid her palm on his head and pressed his head closer.

He drew back and gently stroked her breasts. She moaned once more under his touch.

He lifted her and placed her in the steaming tub.

The gel foamed instantly, covering the surface of the water with sweet-smelling suds which mounded up to Liss's breasts. Wyatt stepped over the lip of the raspberry tub and sank into the water, moving her feet into his lap as he did so.

He worked his magic on one foot and then the other, massaging her toes and ankles, kneading the soles of her feet until she whimpered. He put her little toe in his mouth and sucked. When she murmured her pleasure, he repeated the gesture with the other toes. "Open your eyes, Liss. Look at us."

Lazily, her eyelids lifted. She tried to focus dazed eyes on him.

"Yeah," he whispered in encouragement. "Look at us in this big tub. We're covered with suds, we smell like honey, and I'm going to make love to you until we drop."

With an effort, she murmured again, "Promises, promises."

His laugh whooped through the fragrant bathroom. "I mean it. I'm going to make love to you in places you never dreamed of."

Much later, lying back in the diminished suds, Wyatt grinned at her. "I'm hungry. What have we got to eat?"

"I swear, ever since you got here, if I'm not feeding you, I'm . . ."

"Yeah? Go on," he challenged her. "What are you doing?"

"Never mind." She stood up and stepped out of the tub, moving as gracefully as she could with his hand running up from ankle to buttocks. "I'm going to fix dinner."

She dried herself, then tossed him a towel. While he used it, she made no bones about studying every inch of him. "It's easy to see how Toby got her good looks. She has you for a father."

He slanted her a curious glance. "She doesn't look much like me."

"Not in physique, of course," she cocked her head to study him better. "But she has your carriage. Strong, upright. She carries herself proudly, just as you do. You must be very proud of her."

"I am."

"Did you have a good time with her today?"

"Didn't see her."

"But I thought—"

"So did I. She and Bill are out somewhere."

"Oh? You sound disappointed."

"I guess I am. I made time for her and she took off."

Liss touched his arm. "She still wants to talk to you. Maybe she thought she was being discreet."

"Maybe," he nodded. "But whatever she wants to talk about can't be all that important if she can keep putting it off."

"Give her time."

Over an impromptu supper in the bedroom, Wyatt leaned back on one elbow. "I feel drunk."

"On two glasses of champagne?"

"On your love. You do love me, don't you?" His voice had suddenly turned serious and doubting.

Liss watched him, her own face sober. How could she reassure him when she had her own questions? Even though they were beginning to talk more, there was still an ocean of unknown things between them. She'd been burned badly by David and thought all her capacity for loving had died.

Wyatt had proved over and over again that her ability to experience passion, passion stronger and more uplifting than anything she'd experienced, was not dead. To be able to feel like this after so many years of feeling lifeless was intoxicating.

More than that, it was enlightening. She felt rejuvenated, made brand new, better and more alive than she'd ever felt before. Wyatt had given her the gift of laughter. To be able to laugh at silly jokes, tease him, and make private gags, was something she'd never appreciated.

How could she?

She'd never experienced this kind of fun. She loved every moment they spent together, for freeing her from the humorless existence she'd known before he came to Oakmont.

She loved it when he made her laugh helplessly at their banter. She thrilled at the humor they shared, even while they were making love. This must be one of the greatest things two lovers can share, she thought. To be able to truly enjoy each other, in and out of bed. To want to spend time together for the sheer delight in the other's company.

She loved him for bringing to life this side of her.

Suddenly, the truth became very clear to her.

The time for foolishness was over. Speaking softly, feeling her way through her tangled emotions, she said, "I am completely and totally in love with you."

She held up a hand to stop his surge toward her. "I don't know how it happened so fast, or what will happen next. I do know that what I feel for you I'll never experience with anyone else."

He wouldn't be held back any longer. Holding her close to his pounding heart, wanting to shout, he whispered in her ear, "Oh, God, Liss, I love you with everything that's in me. You make me feel like I can do anything. I can't even imagine being away from you—"

He stopped abruptly

Liss spoke, her voice tremulous. "What is it, Wyatt?"

He groaned. "I have to go back to Sunny-vale on Thursday."

She didn't utter a sound, but he felt her resignation. He dropped kisses on her temples and cheeks. "I don't want to go, but there's a board meeting. It's something I can't miss."

"I'll miss you."

"I'll be back in a day or two."

"Don't make promises to me, Wyatt," she said flatly. "We both knew that you'd have to go back to Sunnyvale."

He kissed her quickly and hard. "I *am* coming back, Liss."

When she didn't respond, he leaned back to see her face. Reading her passive acceptance of what she thought was his departure, he felt her pain. Indignation pulsed within him. "Such a martyr!"

Her mouth dropped open.

"Look at you, ready to kiss us off, just like that! I thought you loved me. But here you are, all but waving goodbye. So much for trust."

She inhaled deeply, ready to defend herself, but he gave her no chance. Standing abruptly, he pulled the sheets and blanket with him. He leaned over her, nose to nose. "Well, listen up, Alice Louisa, I'm not ready to be bounced out on my rear. You got that?"

She blinked. The suave corporate negotiator was gone, replaced by pure outraged male. Speechless now after her earlier inclination to explain, she could only stare.

His voice lowered dangerously. "I thought we had an agreement?"

She found her voice. "You're deliberately misunderstanding—"

He interrupted, silky smooth. "Oh? What should I think, then?"

"You want trust and love, how about my needs, Wyatt?"

"I told you I'd be back—"

"I'm—"

He interrupted her. "I will be back, just as soon as I wind up some business in Sunnyvale."

"Oh," she said, looking up into his eyes.

He watched understanding change her expression.

"I'm sorry," she murmured. "I jumped to conclusions."

"I apologize, too." He sat beside her, his hip nudging her thigh aside to make room for him. He ran his finger tenderly down her forearm. "I guess we're both learning which buttons to push—"

She shivered and leaned into his chest. "I don't know what to say. I've never been this emotional—" Her voice turned into a throaty purr. "You're a wild man when you get mad. I didn't know whether to run or call animal control."

She felt the laughter burbling in his chest, felt his efforts to control it, felt him lose the battle. "Alice Louisa, I love you."

"I'm sorry," she whispered. "I don't know why I lashed out at you. I don't like fighting."

"Sometimes it clears the air."

"Couldn't we just talk things out?"

"We can try, Liss, but we're alike in some ways. We're controlled on the surface because that's what is expected of us. In my position, I can't let off steam when I'd really like to, so that anger gets shoved down. Sometimes, when I'm stressed, it explodes and the wrong people get it in the neck."

"I know what you mean," she said slowly, sifting through her thoughts. "I've always thought it wasn't right to lose my temper, to let people see me angry"

"Oh?"

"I never yelled or screamed at David when he was . . . when I should have. Maybe if I'd let him know how angry I was, it wouldn't have been so easy for him to walk all over me."

"Are you saying you would have stayed with him?"

"No. He dumped me, remember? Maybe I

would have felt better about myself if I'd told him how I really felt about him instead of bottling it all up," she said ruefully. "It's not easy being a lady all the time."

He laughed and then pulled her close. "You can be anything you want to be with me."

She looked up into his eyes again, needing to believe him, still afraid to.

"I mean it. If you're angry with me, let me have it. You share your joy so easily, why not your other emotions?"

"It's not ladylike to yell and scream."

"Alice Louisa, you're a lady through and through. If you're mad, let it out. If something bothers you, let me have it."

"What if you get mad at me?"

"So I get mad. I'll stomp around and swear." Wyatt grinned suddenly. "I'll yell a lot until you get fed up and put me in my place."

"Me?"

He looked down at her, so delicate next to his bulk, and nodded. "You're the only one who can do it, Liss."

She shook her head in disbelief.

"I mean it. One look from you is all it takes—I'd sit on my nose before I'd hurt you."

Her eyes widened at the absurdity, then she realized the true meaning of what he was saying. She put her arms around him, loving the firm muscles under his skin. Pressing a kiss just below his breast-bone, she whispered, "I don't want to hurt you either."

He lifted her chin and kissed her properly, a long, satisfying kiss that eased strife and sparked other emotions. They wound up stretched flat, Liss underneath him. "Shall we kiss and make up?"

Breathless, she reminded him. "Didn't we just do that?"

"Not properly. After all," he said, breaking into a sensuous smile. "It stands to reason. This was our first fight, and we didn't do too badly at that. No doubt we'll have lots of opportunity to get better." His smile widened and grew naughty. "Now we have to practice the making-up part."

"Ah," she nodded sagely. "You may have a point there."

She felt him growing against her and then felt the heat in her cheeks.

"I love it when you blush like that."

Much later, he rolled over, sated and tired, but unable to sleep. He listened to Liss breathing softly and wished a lot of things were different. When sleep evaded him, he got up and went to stand by the window.

Liss felt the mattress move. She opened an eye. "What's the matter?"

"Nothing. Go back to sleep."

She sat up and turned on the light. Blinking in the sudden glare, she pulled the sheet up to her waist. "Are you worrying about the plant?"

Wyatt kept his gaze on the garden. "I should be," he sighed.

"Then what?"

He turned his head halfway to her. "I've been thinking about us."

"Are you having second thoughts?"

He heard the wariness in her voice and faced her fully. "Oh, no. That's not it."

She relaxed against the pillows. "Then what?"

He studied her, her body pale and silky soft against the floral background. Her fragrance floated in the air around him. Soft, feminine and seductive, yet tinged with the scent of their lovemaking. It felt so good to be here with her.

"I've been thinking about me," he admitted. "And you, too, of course, but mainly about some things going on inside me."

"Like what?" she prompted gently.

He shrugged a shoulder. "I was thinking about earlier, our argument."

"I thought we settled that."

"We did, but I was thinking about me. Why I flew off the handle so fast. I finally figured out it's because of you."

She sat up a little straighter. "I already apologized—"

"Not that," he responded quickly. Coming to join her on the bed, he took her in his arms and rolled her over so they faced each other. He continued softly, "It's the way I react to you. When we first met, I figured with your age and your looks, being divorced, you'd be as experienced as the next woman."

Seeing her brow furrow, he kissed the wrinkle away. "Maybe I came on a little strong. But as I got to know you better, I realized that under the surface, you're not like other women. You challenge me," he caught her hand as she waved a disclaimer.

"You do. You make me re-think a lot of opinions I've taken for granted. You make me hungry for things I've never wanted or had time for before. Your life is so different from mine—you've opened my eyes to possibilities I'd have laughed at just last month." He pressed a gentle kiss in the palm of her hand. "Don't you see, Liss? You're changing me. It's damned uncomfortable—sometimes my reactions are going to be off-base."

"You're changing me, too."

"Am I? How?"

"Well," she began hesitantly. "Before we met, I'd never have believed that I could . . . I mean, that I would want to . . ."

"Do what, Liss?" he asked softly.

She waved a hand. "Oh, lots of things."

"Like what?"

"You know."

"Liss, if I knew, do you think I'd be dragging it out of you like this, one word at a time?"

She lifted one shoulder. "I've never had this much fun before."

He grinned. "Me, either. Who would have thought?"

Just before she fell asleep Liss remembered how Wyatt had kept all of his promises. He'd made love to her repeatedly, in her bedroom, in the gazebo, and in the grass under the full moon while the scent of night filled the air.

She was exhausted, sated and boneless, yet in her innermost self, she exulted. Fifty-one years old and she felt twenty—no, thirty—years younger.

And it was all due to Wyatt.

When the phone rang the next afternoon, Liss knew immediately who would be on the other end. The sound of Wyatt's voice, deep and resonant, did things to her insides that no proper Thayer woman would ever admit recognizing, but Liss was done with being prim and prissy.

Reveling in warm anticipation, she pitched her voice low. "Hello, Wyatt."

"Hey, sexy lady. Toby's here at the plant and I thought I'd take her to dinner, give us time to talk. Do you mind if I come over later?"

She bit down disappointment that they wouldn't be able to share their dinner, and then chided herself. She had no right to expect him to spend every moment with her. He had to spend time with his daughter. Especially when she'd come all this way to see him. "Of course not. Want to bring her for dessert?"

"I thought you'd be dessert," he said, his voice lowering.

Alone in her office, she could feel the heat rising up from her breasts. "Wyatt!"

"Let's see what happens, okay? She and Bill may have made plans. He's mooning over her like he's never seen a woman before."

Liss chuckled. "And how does Papa feel about that?"

"Hell. It's not easy to look at your daughter and realize she's the object of some guy's lust. I feel like rearranging his front teeth."

"Sooner or later she'll find someone she

wants to spend her life with. Are you going to punch him out, too?"

"If I feel like it."

She had to laugh. "Wouldn't be many marriages if fathers gave in to that urge."

"Guess not," he grumbled, then brightened. "Doesn't look like she's encouraging him any. Every time he gets too close, she brushes him off."

"Well, are his teeth safe then?"

Wyatt laughed. "You're good for me, Liss. See you tonight."

"Tonight," she echoed, hanging on to the receiver long after the dial tone buzzed in her ear.

It seemed the phone rang as soon as she replaced the receiver. Still wound up in her conversation with Wyatt, it took Liss a minute to recognize Don Simpson's voice. "What can I do for you, Don?" She kept her tone cordial, while remnants of the warnings Aggie Fairchild had given her about the chairman of the library board floated through her memory.

"Liss, I need to talk with you."

"Sure, what's up?"

The long pause tipped her off. Don had something serious to discuss. She asked, "It's not bad news about the new library, is it? Some hitch?"

"Not with the new library, no."

"Whew," she relaxed audibly. "You had me worried."

"Can you come by my office later?"

"Don, I'm swamped. Can we talk now?"

"Not on the phone," he said firmly. "You name a time."

Curiosity aroused, she quickly scanned her desk calendar. "How about Wednesday afternoon? After four? Can you come by the shop?"

"I guess that will be all right." He hung up abruptly.

Liss jotted the appointment down on her calendar, wondering what on earth Don could want with her. Probably last minute details for the move to the new library, although she had the Collection well in hand. Or maybe it was the Collection itself. Had Joe been complaining again?

Let him, she thought. She'd use this time to clear the air with Don, to let him know how uncooperative Joe was being. She hated to do it, but if Joe's attitude didn't improve, she might have to consider moving the Collection out of the library.

She didn't want to do that. In her mind, the new library and her Collection were linked. She'd given so much of herself to each that while she knew she shouldn't, she couldn't help feeling a distinct sense of ownership.

She was perfectly willing to be reasonable, but if she had to, she'd move the Collection someplace else. The Oakmont Museum had been disappointed when she'd chosen to display the Collection in the library. No doubt they'd be glad of the opportunity to house it.

Feeling more positive now that she'd mapped out her options, she exchanged a few words with Susan and then set off to walk the few blocks to the library. Knowing she was running late, she still took the time to savor the walk. She wouldn't be able to do it much longer.

Once the new library was open, she'd have to schedule her time much better, so that her work with the Collection didn't take too much time away from her business. But then, she thought, if she didn't have any business, she'd have a lot more time to devote to the Collection.

Late as she was, the music coming from the high school drew her. Detouring a few blocks to walk past the football field, she stopped to watch. All their practice for the dedication was paying off. The band marched past, jauntily in step, the music blaring. She listened for a few minutes, tapping her foot and feeling like marching right along with them. Still humming along, she retraced her steps and headed for the library.

Howard Upjohn was halfway up the stairs, headed for his office but at the sight of her, he turned around and waylaid her just as she pushed the library door open.

"Liss, got a moment? I need to talk to you."

Her lighthearted mood disappeared instantly "I haven't got anything to say to you, Mayor."

"C'mon Lissie, don't be like that. Let me apologize."

Gritting her teeth at the hated nickname, she didn't stop. "No need."

"There is. I shouldn'ta said those things in front of Harrow."

"No, you shouldn't have," she agreed coolly.

"He called me earlier. Too busy to come into town, but he had some questions, so Don and I met with him out at the plant."

"You and Don? He's had a busy day. He just called me."

"What did Don say?" the Mayor asked quickly, his eyes intent on Liss's face.

"We didn't have time to talk. We set up an appointment for later in the week." Without missing a beat, she asked, "What did Wyatt want to talk about?"

"Quite a set-up they have there, if you like all that computer stuff."

She didn't pay any attention to his comments about the plant or his attempt to milk her curiosity. She wanted to know about the meeting. "What did you talk about?"

"You know that money Intratec donated?" he asked abruptly.

"I know about it. They've been very generous with Oakmont. Football and everything else," she mentioned, deliberately calling Howard's attention to their earlier conversation. "In fact, I just came from the high school. The band is practicing for Sunday on the new football field. It's looking good."

He ignored that. "Seems Harrow was concerned that the library would get short-changed if they close the plant. Won't be able to make another donation."

"I guess not."

"He wanted some assurance that if they did pull out, the money they gave to the library would stay there. That the Collection wouldn't be *impacted.*" He looked at her slyly as he quoted Wyatt's word, then continued, " 'Course, I couldn't promise that. The money came to the city, and we'd have to decide how we should use it."

"I wouldn't have expected anything else from you, Howard."

"Have to think of all the good citizens of Oakmont, of course, not just the one or two Harrow happens to know *personally.*"

She felt slimy, thinking ahead to the next mayoral race. One way or the other, she'd make sure Howard Upjohn was not re-elected, even if it meant she'd have to forget her intentions to stay out of local politics. "Why are you telling me this?"

"Why?" He raised his eyebrows in mock confusion. "Why, Lissie, I know you're worried about the library. You won't have to worry for much longer."

"Is that so?"

Howard smiled. "Well, gotta take care of business. Just wanted to let you know that your friend is looking out for you. Wouldn't it be nice if he felt the same way about all those people working out at the plant? Maybe you should talk to him about that?"

"Wyatt will make his own decisions."

"Howard?" A very familiar voice caught her attention. Looking up to the head of the stairs, she saw David waiting.

"What's he doing here?" she asked Howard without taking her eyes off her ex-husband.

"Now, Liss, you don't have to worry about David."

"What's he doing here?" she repeated, her voice louder.

"Business, just business." Howard started up the stairs, then paused. "See ya around, Lissie." He continued upward, leaving Liss with a feeling of uneasiness. She'd swear he had a satisfied smugness about him.

What was that all about? She'd have to ask Wyatt.

She entered the library, catching the interested stares of patrons and staff alike. Refusing to acknowledge the knowing glances, she walked directly to the small cubbyhole she'd call her office for a few days yet, and settled down to work.

Before she knew it, Dani popped her head through the door. "How's it going?"

"Hi, Dani," she smiled, and relaxed against the back of her chair. At last, a friendly face. "How are the wedding plans?"

"Well, not so good." Dani advanced into the small room and propped a black leather-clad hip on Liss's crowded desk. "Mom and Dad want us to have a big wedding, the church, the whole nine yards, you know—"

Liss stifled a smile at the thought of Dani in a black leather wedding dress, her hair in spikes and three earrings on one ear. "What do you want?"

"Well, Jack's working real hard on a special project at work, and—"

"He is?" Liss interrupted, intrigued by this second mention of a special project at Intratec. "What is it?"

"Dunno. Jack won't say. He's working with a couple of the engineers and the big honcho himself."

"With Wyatt?" More curious than ever, she probed, "Doesn't Jack tell you anything about it?"

"Nah. Just that maybe he won't lose his job. But just in case he does, he figures we should have a small wedding, and let my folks give us the cash they would have spent on a big wedding."

"Your mom will be disappointed," Liss warned. "She's been talking nothing but wedding ever since you announced your engagement. At last count, she had an even dozen in your bridal party. Oh, and the ring-bearer of course."

Dani groaned. "I know. Ever since I was a little girl, she's had these plans for me. White dress with a train back to there, a big fancy reception, all the trimmings." She hopped off the desk to gesture, arms spread wide. "It doesn't make sense, you know, to spend that much money when Jack might not have a job."

"You'll have to do what you think is best," Liss said, and then returned to the subject at hand. "What does Jack think about his job? Does he have any guesses?"

Dani frowned. "You'd know better than me, Liss. What with your ex and the big honcho working together. Ask them."

"David and Wyatt?" Liss echoed faintly.

Wyatt hadn't said a thing! Half the people in Oakmont could be in on this little secret but Wyatt hadn't said anything to her. If Howard knew about it, then who knew how many other people did?

Was that why David was upstairs?

She wondered if Wyatt knew that David was over here talking to Howard during business hours. Rats. She should have gotten to the bottom of it instead of letting Howard escape up the stairs. Him and his "I've got a secret" smugness. No wonder.

He probably knew everything that was going on in the plant.

Fine thing when Wyatt wouldn't confide in her, and yet by now half of Oakmont probably knew he was working on something secret. Perturbed that he'd repeatedly ask her to trust him when he didn't trust her enough to tell her what he was working on, she recalled their conversations. In each one, he'd said he wished he could tell her, but asked her for patience.

Well, she was out of patience. Now she wanted to talk.

Real talk, with real answers.

"Well, gotta go. See you tomorrow."

Liss looked up at Susan's daughter. "What?"

Dani laughed. "You can stay if you want to, but Jack's waiting at home."

Liss smiled at Dani's enthusiasm. Then she remembered. She had somebody to go home to as well.

Home. Home to Wyatt. She could barely wait to see him, to tell him about her day and hear about his. No matter that she was angry with him, she wanted to see him, to be with him, to touch and be touched.

She wanted to share things with him, but more than anything else, she wanted him to do the same with her.

She needed to know that he trusted her enough to confide his plans to her safe-keeping.

This time, he was going to have to give her some answers.

Nineteen

Wyatt was unusually quiet when he arrived at her back door later that evening. He kissed her, his mouth hard and demanding. When at last he lifted his head, he smiled down at her. "Hi."

"Hello yourself. You've had a hard day."

"It shows?"

She nodded. "How did your dinner with Toby go?"

"I can't believe it," he ground out. "That girl hasn't stopped yakking since the day she was born, but you think I could get two words out of her tonight? Beats the hell out of me why she came here wanting to talk if she won't say anything. When I tried to push her, she just clammed up and wouldn't say a word."

"I don't know anything about daughters, but even I can tell you're forcing her to talk before she's ready—"

"Oh, now you're on her side?"

"Don't be silly, Wyatt. It's not a matter of choosing sides."

"Hell. What's the matter with her? She came all the way here from Dallas when I told her not to, and now she won't say why."

Liss heard his frustration and studied him more closely. Wyatt looked tired, the stress of his responsibilities with Intratec was taking its toll on him.

She sensed his anxiety over Toby. His brow was furrowed more deeply than usual, his eyes were red-rimmed, and he'd run his hands through his hair more than once.

She longed to smooth the silver lock back off his forehead. "Why did you tell her not to come?"

He gave her a puzzled look. "You know why. I didn't want any more distractions—"

"But now that she's here, it's all right, isn't it? You're not angry with her?"

"No. Just confused."

He looked so weary she longed to comfort him. "Can I get you anything? Coffee?"

"No. I'm too jumpy for more caffeine. I need to do something."

"What?"

"Dunno. Is there anything you want to do tonight?"

She shook her head. There was something

she'd wanted tonight. She needed answers to the questions Dani's careless confidences had aroused, but she didn't want to ask those questions.

Not now. Now that she had the opportunity, her determination dwindled. She couldn't add any more to Wyatt's stress level.

"Let's finish that room, then," he suggested.

"The morning room?"

"Yeah. I'd like to see what that floor looks like when it's all done."

"Some of that stuff's pretty heavy."

"How did you manage to get it out?"

"Jack moved it."

"The ubiquitous Jack." An eyebrow rose as he asked, "Think this old man can't do what that young stud can?"

Liss looked him over carefully. He'd changed before coming over, putting on a well-worn T-shirt and jeans that left nothing to her imagination.

Old man indeed. She couldn't imagine how she'd once thought him older than she. His silver hair was beautiful and she loved to touch it, to caress it, but it certainly wasn't an indication of his age. Even as tired as he was this evening, he was still fit and healthy. He could give a much younger man a run for his money. In her book, he was many times sexier than any other man she'd ever met.

"Well, you understand I can't speak for everything Jack does," she stated, hiding her pleasure that Wyatt's mood seemed to be changing for the better. "But I imagine you can shift a few pieces of furniture. Just don't strain yourself."

"Guess I'll have to show you, then." Wyatt caught her eyeing him and grinned. "What will you give me if you like the way I work out?"

Pursing her lips, she gave him a blatant up and down scrutiny, delighted that the sparkle had returned to his eyes. This was the man she preferred being with, alive and filled with the joy of living. "Going rate, maybe."

He caught her up to him and planted a hearty kiss on her half-open mouth. "Make that premium."

"You drive a hard bargain."

He looked startled for a moment, then broke into hearty laughter. "What I could do with that line."

She rolled her eyes at him. "Never mind. You wanted to work off some of that restless energy, get busy."

He laughed harder. "Yes, Ms Thayer. Anything you say, Ms Thayer."

As before, Liss couldn't believe what fun it

was to work with Wyatt. He took the brunt of the labor, rolling out the beautiful old oriental carpet over the floor they'd so carefully refinished. "Seems a shame to cover up that wood again."

"Enough will show around the edges."

"But not enough to dance on."

Her breath quickened as she recalled their impromptu waltz and the impassioned love-making that followed it. She'd never forget those moments with him. Lost in the memories, she stood motionless while he brought in the furniture she'd stored in another room.

He hefted a table, lifting it by one spindly leg. "Where do you want this?"

"Careful, careful!" she gasped when she saw what he held so nonchalantly. "That's a cherrywood tilt-top piecrust!"

"A what?" he asked, looking down at the scalloped edging.

She eased it from him and set it down. "Look, the top comes up, like this. See, now it's a table. You can put your teacup on it."

He repressed a smile. "Whatever you say."

Catching his expression, she smiled. "Plebeian."

"Prissy," he smiled back, insulting her with equal glee.

"That's enough break time," she said. "There's more to move."

A short time later, he glanced from her satisfied, smiling face to the room crowded with small tables, uncomfortable-looking chairs, and too many little doodads just waiting for him to accidentally smash. He scowled again at the carpet all but obscuring the floor. Their floor.

"What's the matter?" Liss asked. "Don't you like it?"

"You can barely see the floor under all this junk."

"Junk?" Eyes widening at the real insult, she threw her arms wide. "These are antiques. Some of them are priceless."

"You really love this old stuff, don't you?"

"Yes, I do." She tried to make him understand. "It means a lot to me, to see these things, to use them like my family did before me."

"How you can feel so strongly about people you never even met?"

She looked surprised. "My mother used this room, and I can remember sitting with my grandmother while she wrote thank you notes at that lady's desk."

"Oh. You plan to use this room, too?"

"Maybe. Not for the same things, though. I like it, just having it, because it makes me feel part of them."

"You miss being part of a family, don't you, honey?"

He'd called her that before, that and other endearments, but this time it made her throat catch. Pleasure seeped through her, making her feel contented and cared for. "I do. I just wish there was someone I could leave all this to."

"Why?"

"Well, because I'd like to know that someone would take care of and love these things as much as I do."

"They're just possessions, Liss."

"Maybe so," she said fiercely, "but they're mine. They're all I have left. Someone has to care about family traditions."

"Why is that so important to you? Lots of people get along just fine without them."

She sensed he meant himself, and she sympathized for the lack. She looked for the words to explain. "Every time I walk through the parlor and see Arthur and Louisa Alice, I'm reminded that everything in this house, our place in this town and the things we've got, come from them. It's hard not to feel the continuity, Wyatt. They may be dead, but they're as much a part of my life as . . . as you are."

"Am I as important?"

She flung her arms around his neck and

hugged him tight. "More. More than you know."

Envy mollified, he hugged her back and buried his face in her sweet-scented hair. "Could we go upstairs now? I've got a hankering for white wicker and those sexy petunia sheets."

"Why is everything a petunia to you?"

"It's the only flower name I can remember," he admitted.

"Oh my. We'll have to do something about that, won't we? There are roses and carnations and dahlias and . . ."

He stopped her words with a kiss. "I'd rather learn about you, now. Not furniture or plants."

Snuggling into him, she pressed a kiss to his neck. Loving the way his pulse leaped under her touch, she murmured, "Who needs flowers and antiques at a time like this?"

Laughing together, they barely heard the peal of the door bell. Liss noticed it and, still chuckling, she pulled herself from Wyatt's arms.

"Whoever it is, get rid of them. Fast," he instructed.

She went down the hallway and came back with Toby and Bill.

Toby spoke first. "Hi, Dad. Whatcha doing?"

Liss saw the way Wyatt's jaw tensed, and spoke for them both. "We're putting this room back together."

"Looks great. Need some help?"

Liss flicked a glance at Wyatt, leaving it up to him.

"What are you doing here?"

"Dad, you said Liss invited—"

His eyes widened as he turned to Liss. "Hell. I forgot. We decided to take you up on your dessert offer after all."

"Oh oh. I'd planned to pick something up . . ."

"No problem. We'll send the kids for it."

Toby's eyebrow rose in perfect imitation of Wyatt's. "Better still, we'll send the guys."

"Hey," Bill protested, clearly uncomfortable at the thought of more time with his boss's boss.

"Go on. I want to see more of Liss's house . . . that is, if you'll show me."

"Sure." Smiling, Liss turned to Wyatt and Bill. "You guys are elected. Bring us back something good."

Wyatt grumbled but he dug out his car keys and left, Bill trailing behind as though going to his own execution.

Liss watched them leave. "Okay. What do you want to see?"

"Actually, Liss, that was just an excuse. Um,

do you think I could talk to you about something? I tried to talk to my Dad, but . . ." her shoulders lifted in an expressive gesture.

"Why me, Toby? I mean, I'd be glad to listen, but you hardly know me."

Toby flicked a glance around the room and then looked back at Liss. "My Dad likes you. If he trusts you, why wouldn't I?"

"How do you know that?"

"He said so."

Liss didn't know what to say. A fierce surge of joy cascaded through her at the thought that Wyatt had praised her to his daughter. Then she calmed herself. This was Toby's time, and there wasn't much of it before Wyatt and Bill returned. There'd be time later to savor her delight. She opened the conversation. "Your father said you didn't talk much at dinner. Is there a problem?"

Toby nodded. "I need to talk to him about it but I just can't get started."

"Maybe you should try again? He's a little baffled that you didn't say much."

"I've tried several times, Liss, really I have. I try to tell him, but nothing comes out. Please, couldn't I talk with you first, maybe as a rehearsal?"

"This sounds serious. Is it?"

Toby nodded again.

"I'm not sure I'm the one you should be

talking to," Liss protested. It was one thing to get involved with Wyatt, to have to steel herself to deal with the pain of losing him when he left Oakmont, but to counsel Toby, that was asking a lot of her.

If she did this, wouldn't that create a tie to Wyatt's daughter that would make it doubly painful when she lost them both?

She swallowed. "Maybe you should talk to your mother?"

"No. Not now. She'd never understand."

"What makes you think I will?"

"Do you know you look alike? You and my mother, I mean?"

Liss felt her stomach drop. Was that why Wyatt was so interested? Did he still harbor tender feelings for his ex-wife? Did he see her as a substitute?

"At first, it's really obvious," Toby went on. "You have the same color hair and eyes, but after a while, you don't even notice it."

"Oh," Liss murmured.

"In fact, now that I know you better, I look at you and see only you. Not my Mom. She couldn't care less about antiques, or keeping the family traditions—not unless they were connected to money."

"Is this what you wanted to talk about?" Liss asked, absurdly pleased that she wasn't like the ex-Mrs. Harrow.

Toby bit her lip. "No. I guess I was putting it off." She took a deep breath. "Look, Liss, something happened, and I need to figure out what to do about it. I suppose there are several choices and if I could just talk to you, maybe it will be easier to make a decision."

Reluctantly, Liss agreed. "I'm not sure I should do this. Why do you need a rehearsal?"

"Oh, Liss, I'm pregnant!"

"What?"

"I said I'm pregnant!" Toby wailed.

"I heard you. I just don't know what to say." Liss felt faint, as though Toby were her own daughter. What did parents do at times like this? "I think we'd better sit down."

Collapsing into the nearest chair, Liss motioned for Toby to join her. Toby sank to the oriental carpet in a boneless heap.

"I'm not sure what to do," Liss confessed.

Toby managed a smile. "Me either. That's why I need your help, Liss."

"Are you asking for advice, Toby? Or help?" Liss asked hesitantly. "What is it you want from me?"

"Could I maybe just talk for a bit?"

Liss reached out and gently squeezed her shoulder. "Of course. You understand that I may not be any good at this—I've never had a conversation like this before."

"That's okay," Toby smiled faintly. "Neither have I."

Reassured, Liss ventured, "Have you told anyone else? How about the father?"

"No! And I'm not going to. That's one thing I already decided."

"Oh," Liss murmured, shocked to her core.

"Don't look at me like that, Liss! See, I met A—I met this guy and we hit it off, but I don't love him. I don't want him to know, to think I'm asking him for anything."

"But doesn't he have a right to know, Toby? After all, this is his child, too."

"I can't. He can't." Toby raised her legs and wrapped her arms around her knees. Lowering her forehead to rest against them, she wouldn't look at Liss. "He's already married."

"Oh, Toby," Liss moaned. She didn't have the words to express herself or the experience to deal with this. Her heart went out to Wyatt's daughter. Wanting to wrap her arms around Toby, she held back, afraid of intruding. "I thought maybe Bill . . ."

"Bill? He's not the father! I've never even kissed him."

"Then what—"

"Why is he hanging around? I'm not sure," Toby shrugged, "but it's been good to have a friend here."

"Let me be sure I understand. You had a . . . a relationship with a man and now you don't want him to know that you're pregnant. Right?"

Toby nodded. "Right. This has nothing to do with him."

Privately, Liss disagreed. It had everything to do with him. What kind of man would sleep with a woman not his wife and impregnate her? Over the lump in her throat, she knew exactly what kind. Putting David out of her mind, she studied Toby's bent head.

"I don't know what I'm going to do." Toby lifted her head for a quick glance at Liss and then went back to studying the bare oak floor. "At first, I thought it would be easy to go to one of those clinics, you know, and—"

"Oh, Toby, no." Liss could barely speak past the constriction in her throat. It wasn't fair! She had no right to compare herself to Toby, but how could anyone not want a baby? "Oh, no, don't do that."

Toby looked up to meet her gaze. "I won't. I changed my mind."

"That's good." Liss carefully wiped a tear from Toby's cheek.

"I have to make some decisions. That's what I wanted to talk to Dad about. How do you think he'll react when I tell him he's going to be a grandfather?"

"I don't know," Liss said automatically. She knew how she'd react to being a grandmother. Nothing could be more wonderful, but then, she wasn't Wyatt. It wouldn't be right or fair to project her own wishful thinking on him. "You'll have to find out for yourself. Does this mean you're thinking of keeping the baby?"

"Maybe."

"I imagine it would be difficult caring for a baby all by yourself."

"A lot of women do."

"But you're young, just getting started in your career." Liss felt she had to point out the negatives, to make sure Toby considered them before she made her decisions. "Wyatt's so proud of you. Are you willing to give all that up, or at least put it on hold while you care for a baby?"

Toby's head sank back onto her clasped arms. "I don't know. I've been thinking and thinking, going around in circles, until I just don't know what to do."

Liss heard a car door slam, then footsteps on the verandah. "I don't know what to tell you, Toby," she said quickly. "But I can say this, you've got to talk to Wyatt."

"All right, you two," Wyatt's voice preceded him down the hall. "We've got the goodies, where are you?"

Toby dried her eyes on her sleeve. "I must look horrible!"

"Quick, go up the back stairs. Use what you need out of my bathroom."

Toby bounded out of the morning room an instant before Wyatt popped his head in. "Where's Toby?"

"Upstairs," Liss said as calmly as she could, though her head was spinning. How was she going to keep her emotions in line until everybody left? Pasting on a bright smile, she gestured to Wyatt's hands, hidden behind his back. "What did you bring us?"

He brought his hands around to the front.

Liss glanced at the Dairy Queen bag, then up at Wyatt's pleased face.

"Bill said it was the best place in town for dessert."

Eyeing the gooey sundae Wyatt drew out of the bag like a magician, Liss had to smile. She remembered their first day together, how they'd ended up at the drive-in and how he'd flirted with her. It was obvious Wyatt remembered too, the way his eyes glimmered with suppressed humor.

"It is. Take that into the kitchen."

He followed her instructions, with Bill once again at his heels. A few minutes later, Toby came down. Her face was carefully made up, yet Liss detected the traces of fresh tears.

Toby's red-rimmed eyes grew larger. "Wow, is that double chocolate fudge?"

"Is that good for you?" Liss asked without thinking.

Toby's face fell, then grew wary when Wyatt asked, "Are you sick?"

"No, Dad," Toby tried a smile. "It's my . . . complexion. Girl talk, you know," she added with a hopeful look at Liss.

Feeling guilty for having almost betrayed Toby's confidence, Liss pasted on another bright smile for her. She felt as though her face would crack under the strain. "I don't think one sundae will hurt, do you?"

In response, Toby grabbed up her plastic spoon and scooped out a large bite. "M'mm."

Bill did the same. Wyatt, his eyes narrowed, motioned Liss to one side. "What's going on here? Toby looks like she's been crying."

"Ssh." Liss led him toward the verandah. "Come out here for a moment."

He followed her, his eyes still questioning. "What did you say to her to make her cry?"

"It's what she said to me, what she's been trying to say to you."

"I don't follow," he said, his accusatory tone softening. "She talked to you about whatever is troubling her? Why?"

"She called it a rehearsal," Liss confided. "She's nervous about talking to you."

"She's never been this way before. We've always been able to talk about anything."

"I suggested she talk to her mother."

"What did she say to that?" he asked, his gaze probing in the dim light.

"She didn't want to. Wyatt, why didn't you tell me I look like your ex-wife?"

"Hell. Did Toby tell you that? She must have."

"Why didn't you?" she persisted. She hadn't meant to bring up the resemblance between them, but now that she had, she wanted an explanation.

"It's not a big thing."

"No? I'm not so sure. I've seen the way you and Toby look at me. I don't like being compared, coming out second best."

"Oh, honey, never that. Look, let me explain. Yes, there's a definite similarity. Your hair, eyes," he paused, wondering how to explain that his instinctive reaction to aristocratic blue-eyed ash blondes with delicate features and satin skin had become more, much more than he'd ever felt for his ex-wife. "Elaine's looks are all on the surface. You have warmth, tenderness. You're a lady, through and through."

"You're not interested in . . . spending time with me because I remind you of her?"

"If I ever was, that's gone now. I want to

be with you because you're you, Liss. Nobody else."

Warmth spread through her as she accepted Wyatt's explanation. "I'm glad," she said, tenderness in her voice. "Toby said something like that, but I . . ."

"Worried?" he supplied. "Don't do that. Toby was right. We know a good thing when we see one."

"Oh, Wyatt I was forgetting Toby! You need to talk to her—"

"What's this all about?"

"I can't tell you." She saw the question forming and answered it before he could speak. "No, she didn't swear me to secrecy, but this has to come from her."

"Why doesn't she just say it, then?"

"You'll have to talk with her, Wyatt. I can't tell you."

"Hell." He sighed heavily. "Guess I'd better go take care of this. Can I come back later?"

"I don't think you'll want to."

"You're being damned mysterious, Liss."

"Talk with Toby. Then see how you feel."

"Yeah. Right." He studied Liss for a moment, then abruptly turned to the door. "Let's get this over with."

Inside the kitchen, he said to the younger man, "Bill, haven't you got work to do?"

Summarily dismissed, Bill looked at Toby.

When she said nothing, he shrugged. "See you tomorrow?"

"I'll let you know."

The silence hung awkwardly for a few minutes after Bill's departure. Liss busied herself wiping a sticky ice cream smear off the counter. Wyatt looked from her to Toby before his gaze settled on his daughter. "I think we have some talking to do."

Toby bit her lip but met his eye. Wyatt dropped a kiss on Liss's cheek. "I'll call you later."

Liss watched them go, father and daughter, so much alike. They were tall, fit and lean, sharing the same proud stance. Her heart went out to both of them. Would the next few minutes bring them closer together or drive a wedge between them?

She wanted to be there for them, to console if necessary, to help plan, to look forward with joy to a baby in the family.

A baby.

Wyatt's grandchild. He seemed too young to be the father of an adult daughter and yet . . . In that moment, she envied him bitterly. She'd wanted children so desperately and had never been granted that privilege. Toby, so young, on the brink of wonderful things, had a child coming who would inevitably alter her life. Wyatt's life, too.

It wasn't fair!

Blinking back tears, wondering what they were saying, if Wyatt was managing to hold on to his temper, she returned to the morning room and finished arranging the furniture to her satisfaction. "There," she said to herself. "Now. This is what it must have looked like before."

Her triumph faded with the realization that it wasn't as much fun to do this alone. Having experienced the joy of working with Wyatt, doing it by herself left her feeling incomplete. When the phone rang, she darted to answer it.

"You're right. I won't be back tonight."

"How are you? And Toby? Did she tell you?"

"Yeah. Hell."

"What is she going to do?"

"I don't know. We're still talking. Look, Liss, I'd better go. I'll see you tomorrow."

"All right. Wyatt, be gentle with her."

Twenty

Liss glanced up from her morning coffee to see Toby trudging across her back lawn. She went to the back door to let her in. "How are you this morning?"

Toby gave her a fragile smile. "Okay. Daddy and I talked for a long time."

"Did you settle things?"

"I guess so." Her face brightened. "I'm going to keep the baby. I'm going to raise it myself."

Liss felt a weight lift from her shoulders. "I'm glad, Toby, I really am."

"Can we talk for a few minutes?"

"Of course. Have you had breakfast?"

Toby's face paled. "No."

"Oh, I should have known. Morning sickness?"

"It's not as bad as it has been."

"How far along are you?"

"Almost four months."

Liss couldn't help studying Toby. "You don't look like it."

Toby giggled. "I'll probably get bigger than a house."

"Do you have a doctor?"

"In Dallas. I'll probably stay with her."

"That means you'll stay there to have the baby?"

"I guess so," Toby said slowly. "I really haven't thought much beyond just making this decision. You know—one step at a time."

"And are you happy with this decision? Or is that too personal a question for me to ask?"

"Of course not. After all, if you hadn't let me talk to you first, I might have gone back without saying anything to Dad."

Liss felt her throat constrict at the thought of what Toby might have done. "I'm glad you were able to talk to Wy—your father. What does he say?"

"He wasn't very happy with me. But he seems to accept it now." A smile spread across Toby's face, lighting her from within. "He wants to help me with the baby. Can't you just see my Dad changing diapers?"

The trouble was that Liss saw him doing that all too clearly.

The birth of Toby's baby would make him into a different person. How could it not?

He'd told Toby he'd help her with the baby, and knowing Wyatt's habit of getting right into the midst of things, she had to believe that he would do just that. He wouldn't be happy merely providing financial assistance and perhaps some baby-sitting now and then. No, he'd be a hands-on grandfather. While she felt pleased that he and Toby had come to an agreement, at the same time she felt left out.

She hated the feeling. She'd known it for years, first as she'd watched other young mothers play with their children in the park; later as she watched the teenagers in the library, and now, full circle again, she felt jealous of a baby.

Scolding herself didn't take away the sting of regret.

Seeing Liss look over her shoulder toward the back gate, Toby said, "Dad's already gone to the plant. I'm leaving this morning, so I came over to say goodbye."

Liss swallowed. "So soon?"

"I have to get back to work. I need to save as much as I can before the baby comes."

"I see. Toby, have you thought any more about telling the baby's father?"

Toby's mouth thinned. "You and Dad. He wanted to talk about that, too. What's so important about a few minutes in bed?"

"Oh, Toby, it's so much more than that! It's life, it's creation. It's passing yourself, all the things that make you unique, down to the next generation. Even if you don't want this man to have any say in the way you raise the baby—"

"I don't!" Toby interrupted, her mouth still set.

"You still ought to tell him he's fathered a child!" Liss said, her voice rising.

"Why? I don't want to break up his marriage, do anything more than I've already done. I was sorry the minute it was over, and I don't want anything more to do with him! If I tell him about the baby," Toby laid her hand protectively over her abdomen, "he might think he has to do something. And I don't want anything from him! Not ever again!"

"Couldn't you explain that to him?"

"Liss, just drop it, okay? I don't want to argue about this any more."

Liss nodded, a little tight-lipped herself. She just didn't understand how Toby could refuse the child's father that knowledge. Straightening her shoulders, she asked, "So you're going back to Dallas today?"

"Yes." Toby hesitated, then blurted, "Liss, would you mind if I look at your house some more?"

"Why?"

"Dunno. Something about it just makes me feel good. Does that sound stupid?"

"Of course not. I feel that way about it myself. Come on." Wondering about the change in Toby's manner, she led her through the parlor, the ornate dining room, and then up the stairs.

When she opened the door to one of the guest rooms, furnished for a young girl, Toby gasped. "Oh, this is perfect! I wish I'd had something like this when I was growing up."

"I thought you'd like it. Maybe you can do something like this for your baby—when she's a little older, of course."

"She?" Toby questioned, and then grinned. "Yeah, I hope it is a girl. I love that bed! Can I sit on it?"

At Liss's nod, Toby sat gingerly on the edge of the mattress. "I've never seen anything like this. What is it?"

"It's called a sleigh bed. See, the ends come up and back like an old-fashioned sleigh."

"I feel like Santa Claus!" Stretching her arms out to see if she could reach from end to end, Toby gave Liss a radiant smile. "Liss, you have the most perfect house. I could live here forever and never get bored with admiring all your things."

"You're welcome to come stay with me any

time, Toby." Liss said the words automatically, but she meant them from the bottom of her heart. "Maybe you'd bring the baby with you. There's some baby furniture up in the attic I could restore . . ."

"Could I? You'd do that for me even after . . ."

At Liss's nod, Toby bounced up and threw her arms around her. "I can't thank you enough."

"Well, you're welcome. All you have to do is let me know when you want to come—"

"Thanks for the invitation, Liss, but more than anything, you really helped me with Dad."

"All you needed was to rehearse," Liss demurred.

"No, really. Dad lost it for a while last night, but when I told him how understanding you were, I could see him—I mean, here he was biting his tongue, controlling his temper, all because you'd kept your cool. It was something, all right. I've never seen him do that."

Liss frowned, but before she could speak, Toby rushed on. "No, it's true. He even said you'd told him to go easy with me. Thanks, Liss! Whatever you have going with Dad, I'm all for it."

Feeling the heat rise up her neck, Liss

tucked the good feeling close to her heart to take out and examine later when she had the time to linger, to savor Toby's words.

The young woman hugged Liss again. "I have to go or I'll miss my flight out of San Jose. Don't want to get docked a day's pay when I'll have another mouth to feed."

They walked downstairs arm in arm. Liss hated to see her go, hated to wave goodbye as Toby drove off down the street, hated to face an empty house made suddenly emptier by the absence of a young woman with a lot to look forward to.

"Liss, my God, it feels so good to hold you again."

"You make it sound like it was weeks ago."

"It feels that way." Wyatt rubbed his hand across the bristle on his chin. "Guess I'd better shave. With Toby hogging the bathroom this morning, I didn't have time for more than a quick shower."

"Are things all right between you now?"

He looked at her thoughtfully.

"I don't mean to pry," she said quickly. "It's just that when Toby came to say goodbye this morning, she mentioned that you'd worked things out, and . . ."

He pulled her to him again. "I can't say I was

happy to hear about this baby. She wouldn't tell me who the father is.''

"She said she doesn't want him to know. Wyatt, how can she do that?''

"Honey, I don't know. It's different now, kids don't seem to think the same way we did.''

Liss snuggled closer. "I hate to think of her raising that baby all alone, no one to share the burden with.''

"It won't be that bad. I'm trying to get her to transfer out here so I can help. She'll have me.''

Reassured in one sense, Liss still fretted. A baby needed more.

"Let's not worry about it anymore tonight, okay? I've missed you, honey. Can we think just about ourselves for a while?''

"I'd like that. Are you ready to go up?''

"Do you have to ask?'' he grinned with the familiar sparkle back in his eye.

They walked around her house, securing it for the night together. It was a good, homey feeling and Liss enjoyed every moment of it until Wyatt paused at the foot of the steps and hefted a suitcase.

Frowning, she glanced from the bag to him. "That's more than you usually bring over for the night.''

He studied her worried face. "I was going to tell you in the morning, but—"

"It's about work." She stiffened.

"I'm driving to Sunnyvale early tomorrow—I know I said Thursday, but something's come up."

"Is this the secret project you've been working on?"

His mouth dropped open. "Where did you hear that?"

"I have my sources," she said, protecting Jack and Dani from the hard expression frosting Wyatt's eyes.

His brow furrowed. "Jack. Dammit. That guy gets around. What did he do, whisper secrets to his girlfriend? She tell everybody in town?"

"Of course not!"

"Well, then how did you find out?"

"C'mon, Wyatt. Be reasonable. They're young and in love. They want to get married, but they're worried about their future. Jack's excited about whatever he's working on with you—it means the difference between being able to get married or not. You can understand that."

He relented at her soft pleading. "I guess. Damn kid's big mouth is going to get him in trouble yet."

"Will they be able to get married?"

"How should I know?"

"Well then, tell me what you're working on."

"You know I can't do that."

"Evidently, it's okay for everybody else in Oakmont to know about this but me."

"Why do you say that?"

"Wyatt, David was at the mayor's office yesterday. He and Howard were having some sort of meeting. "Business," Howard called it. He mentioned some project you were working on."

Instantaneously, the corporate persona was back. Wyatt's eyes narrowed, his mouth firmed, and his whole face took on a cold, impersonal look. "Damn. I should have expected something like this."

"Wyatt, what is going on here? Howard told me some story about you calling him out to the plant. Something about the library? Why did you do that?"

He put out a hand to stop her questions. "Forget that for a moment. If my plans would let me stay in Oakmont, what would you say?"

"How could you stay? I couldn't ask you to give up your job."

"Don't intend to." He took her hand in his free one and urged her up the stairs. "What would you say?" he repeated after they'd reached the bedroom.

"I don't know," she answered without looking his way. *Calm down, Alice Louisa. Don't get your hopes up.* It did no good to scold herself. She was already so deeply involved with him on all levels, it did no good. He was deeply entrenched in her heart. She slanted a quick glance at him. "I've never considered the possibility."

"Would you think about it?"

She fought very hard to control the urge to beg him to stay with her forever. She said softly, "Yes."

"I'll be back, Liss, Friday night, early Saturday at the latest—"

She closed her eyes. "It's okay. I'll expect you when I see you."

"I'll be back for the dedication. We'll go together."

Needing him with her, she asked, "Why do you have to go? Couldn't you send someone else?"

He sighed. "I wish I could, Liss, I really do. I've got a wild idea about something, and until I check it out personally, I can't say anything."

Excitement built within her. "You've thought of a way to keep the plant open!"

He inhaled sharply.

She pounced. "I'm right, aren't I?"

"You're right, and too damned smart for

me. But, Liss, you can't tell anyone. I don't want to raise false hopes."

"I won't say a word." She hugged him happily. "I promise." She kissed him again and again. "I hope you can do it, though."

His lips against her cheek, he asked, "Would it be okay if I stayed in Oakmont with you?"

"Oh, Wyatt, it'd be more than okay. I love you."

"I love you, too. Can I show you how much?"

In her best gracious lady voice, she lifted her mouth to his. "You certainly may."

An endless kiss later, he growled, "If I don't make love to you in the next thirty seconds, I'm going to explode."

Her laugh was soft and seductive. She arched closer into his body, aligning every inch of her length against his. "Make love *with* me, Wyatt."

Much later, passion spent and bodies satiated, they lay a-tumble across her wide bed. He opened one eye and noticed his sock hanging from the white wicker headboard. Grinning, he lifted his head from her breast and looked around with satisfaction. How they'd managed to get their clothes off with Liss still in his arms remained a mystery. Comforted and contented, he lowered his head again, hearing her heartfelt sigh.

He wasn't going to let her go.

Not now, not ever.

In the coolness before dawn, she heard his car door slam. Barefoot, she raced downstairs, out the door, and flagged him down.

He stopped and jumped out, leaving the engine running and the lights blazing. "What are you doing out here?"

She threw her arms around his neck. "I couldn't let you go without one more kiss."

He kissed her. Long and hard and so tenderly she thought she'd weep. He put his hands on her shoulders to move away. She clung to him.

He chuckled. "What would all your neighbors say if they saw you out here in your nightie?"

"Let them talk," she whispered. "Kiss me again."

Late that night, Wyatt called. "The preliminary meetings are going well. By the time I meet with the full board of directors on Friday, I should be able to convince them."

"Convince them of what?" Liss coaxed.

"Oh no, you don't. You're just going to have to wait to find out."

"Rats. Well, I'll keep my fingers crossed for you, anyway."

He laughed shortly. "Better throw in a couple of toes, too."

"Whatever you say."

Lowering his voice, he murmured, "I wish I were there, holding you. Kissing those sweet little toes of yours."

"M'mm, me too."

His voice turned husky. "What are you wearing?"

Liss glanced down at the outsized Forty Niner T-shirt she had on. She smiled. "Oh, nothing much. Just a little satin and lace thing . . ." Deliberately, she lowered her voice seductively.

He growled. "Know what I'd like to do?"

Softly, breathlessly, she asked, "What?"

Later, after replacing the receiver back in its cradle, Liss fell asleep with Wyatt's lovewords still floating deliciously through her mind.

Liss lifted her head at the knock on her door and went to unlock it. "Come in, Don."

Don Simpson stood looking around the quiet showroom. "Why are you still working when the store's closed?"

Liss stretched the kinks out of her neck. "You should know that paperwork never ends."

"You've put a lot of effort into your store. It shows."

"Why, thanks, Don. It's been a good investment."

"You like doing this, then? It keeps you busy?"

"Usually. Lately I've been putting in a lot of work at the library, getting the Collection ready to move."

Don nodded and looked down at his feet. "You've been a very dedicated volunteer. You've done a fine job with the Collection, better than anyone expected. It's a wonder, since you have no formal training."

She caught his uneasiness and wondered again why he wanted to see her. It had to be more than to compliment her on her shop. "Come on back to the office."

"Everything still set for the dedication?" he asked as he followed her.

She waved him to a chair big enough to hold his bulk. "Yes, it is. You could have asked me all this over the phone."

He sat heavily. "Well, actually, Liss, that's not what I came to say. Shoot. There's no easy way to do this." He gestured at her desk. "Sit down, Liss, you're not going to like this."

She stiffened her spine and sat.

"Uh, Liss, like I said, you've done a fine job, and no one's finding fault with you." He glanced around her office, avoiding her eye. "But it's time to let an experienced person take over."

"There's nobody here more qualified than I," Liss gasped in shock. Of all the reasons for meeting with Don, losing the Collection had never crossed her mind. She'd thought he wanted to talk last minute details.

What on earth did he mean—her Collection needed someone else?

"Maybe the word is certified." He met her stunned gaze briefly, then straightened his tie. "With all the publicity over the Collection, Joe got a federal grant for the library. One of the stipulations is professional management—for all the areas in the library. Joe's a degreed librarian, so he's okay. The weak spot is the Collection. We'll lose the grant if we don't have a curator." He waited a beat. "You're a volunteer, Liss, not a professional. You'll have to step down."

"You're telling me that for a grant we didn't need in the first place, for money," she heard her voice rise and made an effort to control it. "You want to kick me out over money?"

He ran a finger under his collar. "That's about the size of it."

"I don't believe this." She leaned toward him. "Don, ordinarily I don't toot my own horn, but the only reason there's a new Oakmont Public Library is because of me. Who got the funding for the city? Donated the land?" She swallowed and lowered her voice. "After all that, you're telling me I'm not good enough to run the Collection I created? After I donated ninety percent of the contents of the Collection?"

"No one's saying that—"

"No? You're saying I'm not competent enough to do what I've already been doing—"

"No one's questioning your competence. We're going to catch a lot of public attention. We need this grant, Liss, to put Oakmont on the map."

"I've heard that before," she broke in bitterly. "That's the nonsense Joe's been spouting. I should have realized he had something going on."

"He's only saying what the rest of us think."

"The rest of you meaning who?"

"The city council, naturally."

Liss blew out her breath, but Don ignored her. "This is a good thing for Oakmont You're not going to stand in the way, are you?"

"I can't believe that the only way Oakmont has of getting ahead is to trample on me."

"Don't think about it like that. Think what you can do for your home town. What Thayers have always done."

"I can't believe this."

"I'm sorry that's the way it has to be. We need this grant."

Slumping back in her chair, she felt boneless, defeated. She understood the requirements, but understanding didn't ease her feelings of rejection.

"We'd be glad to have you stay on. In fact, we'd like you to—"

"Don't say you want me to train someone to take my place!"

He ran his finger under his collar. "Oh, that won't be necessary—"

Liss felt like he'd just punched her in the stomach, and dazed by pain, she searched for explanations. "You'd better tell me what you do mean."

"Maybe you'd consider being one of the docents?"

"*One* of the docents? How kind of you."

"Now, Liss—"

"Don't *now Liss* me!" She took a deep breath. "How can you come in here just a few days before the dedication and tell me I'm not needed any more?"

Simpson crossed his arms over his paunch. "Well, you see, we think it'd be more appropriate if you step down and let your replacement take over the opening. There'll be a lot

442

of press there, public officials—we should start off on the right foot."

She stood and walked to her window. Staring unseeingly at the old oak trees in the parking lot, she asked tightly, "And just who is my replacement?"

"Joe Franklin hired somebody from San Francisco."

She whirled around. "I knew it! That explains why Joe's been so uncooperative and sullen lately—he was just waiting. Why did you do this, Don?"

He shifted in his chair. "Like I said, the Collection needs a certified professional. The grant—"

"Let me ask you this, Don. How come this is the first time I'm hearing about this grant?"

Don's head snapped up. "What the hell are you talking about, Liss?"

She narrowed her eyes. "I'm telling you that I never heard of the grant before. Since it involves the Oakmont Collection, don't you think I should have been consulted? At the very least?" She paused for control. "So who wrote this grant, Don?"

He blustered, "I thought you knew."

"Not good enough. You and I both know who wrote it. Who wants me out of the library so bad he'll resort to something like this?"

Don Simpson colored and said nothing.

Liss kept her voice even and reasonable. "Don, no matter who wrote the grant, I can understand that it's a good thing for the library."

Don's eyebrows shot up.

"But the Collection doesn't have anything to do with the library. Grant or no grant, I'm perfectly capable of overseeing the Collection," Liss averred.

He looked confused and mumbled, "That's not the way I hear it."

She grimaced. "Why aren't I surprised? Don, the Collection is mine. I'm not giving it up."

"Now, Liss, don't get so worked up. What's done is done. The City appreciates your work here, of course. But you don't have any say in things anymore."

Liss slapped the desk with the flat of her hand. The noise echoed through her small office. "You're out of your mind. Even if he got this grant or six more, Joe's not the one to take over the Collection. He doesn't care about Oakmont the way I do."

"Well, we've talked about that. If you agree to assist Joe with the transition, maybe you can have some say in how they do things—"

"Let me get this straight," Liss hissed. "You're not only replacing me as curator, but you want me to help? Hand me the knife and expect me to cut my own heart out?"

Simpson waffled. "It's just a reshuffling of responsibilities, Joe said."

"Joe said, Joe said," she shouted. "What else did he say to undermine me with the library board? Besides going behind my back with this thing?"

"Don't get huffy, Liss—"

"*Huffy!*" she exclaimed. Fighting the rage that welled up from deep within her, she snapped, "I can't accept this."

"Don't do something you're going to regret."

"I'll do what I think is right, Don." She took a deep breath. "When you called the other day, I thought our meeting would be a good time to tell you about Joe's attitude. I was going to tell you how uncooperative he was about the Collection."

Don started to speak but she held up a hand to silence him. "That's not necessary now. I had decided to move the Collection out of the library if Joe's attitude didn't improve, but now I'll go ahead and do it. I'm sure the museum will be glad to house the Collection."

Don shook his head. "Sorry. It stays with the library"

"What do you mean? That's my Collection, and I'll do what I want with it!"

"You gave that Collection to the library. That means you no longer own it. It belongs to the City of Oakmont now."

Liss could barely breathe. She knew he was right, but oh, sweet heavens, how hard it was to accept. She sank back against her seat and closed her eyes, trying to stave off pain.

"I'm sorry to be the one to tell you this, Liss."

She waved that away. "If you're ready to leave, I've got work to do"

"I want you to help Joe right away, Liss. Give him everything he and the new curator need to be ready for Sunday."

Her eyes snapped open. "Forget it."

"Suit yourself." Don Simpson heaved himself out of the chair. "It's not the way I like to do things, but it has to be." He moved to the door. "Maybe you'll enjoy having more time for your shop. You've made a success of it."

"Don't expect me to thank you."

He was almost at the front door when she stopped him. "Don, answer me one question. Does the city council go along with this?"

He turned back to face her but his eyes shifted away. "There was some discussion. Not everybody agreed."

"Who?" she asked quickly. Could she get Aggie Fairchild's help in reversing the council's decision? The library board answered to the city council. If Aggie spoke up for her, maybe they'd tell Don Simpson to un-hire that curator.

He gave a little jerk to one shoulder as he walked out the door. As if he knew what she was thinking, he turned back and stuck his head through the opening. "Won't do you any good."

Liss felt totally drained. All the emotions that had welled up in her during Don's visit had ebbed, leaving her limp. For long moments, she stared listlessly at the floor. Feeling weak and helpless, she longed for Wyatt. She wanted to talk to him.

She wanted him, period.

But that wasn't going to solve this problem. Gradually, the numbness began to recede. She stood, firmed her shoulders, and after locking her shop, strode down the street and into the library.

She walked straight into Joe's office.

He looked up and shifted restlessly in his chair. "You heard?"

"Oh, yes, I've heard all the reasons why the library needs a certified curator for the Collection." She spoke calmly, enjoying the sight of Joe squirming. "What I don't understand is why you thought we needed a grant in the first place."

"Aw, Liss, I can explain."

"There's no need. You're ambitious. The Collection is getting a lot of publicity. We've got researchers parading through here all the time. It's been written up in the genealogy journals." She paused for breath. "It's a feather in Oakmont's cap to have the Collection. I understand your wanting to horn in on the publicity. What stinks is your underhanded methods. You got me dumped to make yourself look better. You might have succeeded, temporarily, but you haven't won."

Bristling at her remarks, Joe snapped, "It's out of your hands now. Face it, Liss. If you don't want egg on your face with a public announcement that you couldn't handle the job, you'd better back off." He leaned back and put his feet on the desk. "You can let people think it's your idea, if you want. Save face."

She stared at his dirty athletic shoes in disgust. "You think I'd stoop to your level?"

"You're behind the times, Liss. Oakmont is growing. It needs more than you can deliver."

Her chin went up. "We'll see about that, Joe."

Twenty-one

Too upset to go back to Thayer's, Liss picked up the phone at the check-out desk and dialed Aggie's number with shaking fingers.

Aggie's answering machine kicked on. "Damn! Sorry, Aggie, this is Liss and I have to talk to you. It's urgent. Please call me at home as soon as you can."

Frustrated, Liss drove home quickly. Reverting to her tried and true way of handling emotions, she dug out her cleaning equipment and attacked the dust she'd ignored for the last few days. She was polishing the dining room table when the phone rang. She dropped the cloth and ran to answer.

"Liss, it's Aggie."

"Oh, Aggie, do you know what Don did today?" Liss blurted without greeting the older woman.

"I do," Aggie answered shortly. "I told the

449

old fool he was making a mistake, but the pig-headed man wouldn't listen."

"I don't want to lose the Collection, Aggie. You know how much it means to me."

There was a long pause before Aggie spoke. "I can't help you with this, Liss."

Her voice sounded frail. At once, Liss remembered Aggie's age. "Listen to me, going on as though I were the only one with problems. Aggie, are you all right?" she asked.

"No, I'm not, but I'm not dead yet. No need to apologize. I'm just tired of fighting those idiot Simpsons every time they get a crazy idea in those pea brains of theirs."

"What happened, Aggie? Can you tell me?"

Aggie sighed. "You know how Don runs off at the mouth. For months now he's been shouting the praises of that young toady until he's convinced everyone on the library board that Franklin walks on water. They've got some idea that the Collection will put Oakmont on the map and they'll wind up rich and famous. Famous anyway, 'cause if they get a nickel out of this I'm taking them to court."

"I'll be right there with you," Liss promised. "I don't understand, though, how they got this whole thing past the council."

Aggie sighed. "I didn't catch on soon enough. By the time I did, it was too late. I couldn't get the council to listen to me."

Aggie prided herself for her role in deciding Oakmont affairs, Liss knew. It must be hard for her to admit she'd failed. Despite her own stressful day, she could still empathize with how Aggie must be feeling. "That's a first for you. I know you did your best."

"No one wants to listen to an old woman anymore. I told them all they were looking at the wrong person, but they believed Joe and Don. I'm sorry, Liss, but I just couldn't influence the vote. Now they'll have to live with that idiot."

"You did what you could," Liss murmured, more concerned with Aggie's hurt feelings than her own.

"Not enough. Time was, I'd whisper and people in this town would fall all over themselves. Now, I can't even get the time of day."

"You tried to warn me, didn't you?" Liss twirled the phone cord through her fingers as she spoke. "When you came to see me, even though you didn't come right out and say it, you told me Don was up to no good."

"It was just mutterings. Nothing definite. When the grant came in, it was too late."

"Goodness, they can work fast when they want to. It's only been a couple of days. For Joe to have interviewed and hired somebody, he must have known about this months ago."

"No doubt."

"Why didn't they tell me about the grant?"

"Tell you what? The terms were plain as day."

"I didn't know anything about them until today."

"You mean no one said anything to you at all?" Aggie asked incredulously.

"Not a word. Joe did the whole thing without so much as asking my opinion." Liss paused. "I feel so dumb that I didn't catch on when he was pumping me for information."

Aggie sounded impatient. "Didn't you even suspect that jerk?"

"No, Aggie, I didn't. I don't know how he managed to do it—"

Aggie's frail voice still managed a sturdy Anglo-Saxon expletive.

"I really feel stupid, Aggie," Liss repeated, her voice laced with pain. "How could all this go on under my nose and I didn't see any of it?"

"You weren't looking for it. I'll tell you something. It's all well and good to mind your own business, but sometimes, when you don't watch where you're walking, you're likely to fall in the mud."

Liss had to chuckle. "I think I found that out for myself. Now the question is, what do I do about it?"

"Are you asking me for advice?"

"Yes . . . no. Oh, Aggie, I don't know. You've been involved in everything for so long. What should I do?"

Aggie didn't reply immediately. When she did, her voice seemed far way. "I can't tell you what to do. This one you'll have to figure out for yourself. I will tell you this, though. I'll be behind you whatever you decide."

Liss felt better at once. "Thank you for trying to help."

"Didn't do you any good, did it?" Aggie retorted. "I couldn't change a thing."

Liss spoke from her heart. "It's enough to know I still have a friend on the council."

"No, you don't," Aggie promptly denied.

"Aggie," Liss chided. "Are you telling me you're not my friend any more?"

"Not any less, either, but I'm not on the council. I resigned."

Liss felt like one more brick had been added to her load. She sagged and sat heavily. "Oh, no, why?"

"I'm too old to fight windmills anymore. I've lost my influence," Aggie mourned. "Better some young person come along and take over for me."

"Oh, Aggie," Liss came back at once, almost in tears. "You're not old. You're just feeling down because you didn't win this one. Next time you'll feel better."

"Not going to be a next time."

"Oakmont can't get along without you, Aggie." Liss comforted her old friend. "Who's going to make us all keep our noses clean?"

"From what I hear, your ex-husband thinks he's just the one to do it."

"David?"

"How many ex-husbands do you have?"

"It's not that," Liss answered, reacting to the asperity in Aggie's voice. "I just never thought David had any more interest in politics than I do."

"Seems to have developed some lately."

Liss considered that. He had been at Howard's office. "I don't think David's the one to replace you on the council."

"Likely not. How about you?"

"Me?" Liss asked, her voice rising in surprise. "Thanks, but no thanks. You know I have no interest in politics."

"So, grow one. No time like the present to stand up for what you believe in."

"But I've never—I wouldn't know what to do."

"So you can learn, can't you?"

Before she could gather her thoughts, Aggie spoke again. "What are you going to do about those hacks?"

"I'm going to fight them."

"You'll lose." Aggie sighed. "When money talks, no one has any common sense. Start thinking of some alternatives."

Liss closed her eyes to ward off the pain. "I have to try, Aggie. You just said I should stand up for what I believe in."

"I know I did, but you'd better be prepared . . ." Aggie's voice brightened. "What about your young man?"

"What about him?" Liss asked suspiciously, not bothering to deny what everyone in Oakmont already knew. She wondered if Aggie somehow also knew that she was older than Wyatt.

"Is it serious between you? Maybe it's time to forget about the past and start building your own future." Aggie's voice gained strength as she continued enthusiastically. "You're the last of the Thayers, Liss."

"Well, Aggie, really," Liss protested, almost spluttering.

"Now listen up here. It's not enough to memorialize all your ancestors. You should be carrying on the family traditions."

"It's a little late for that."

"Nonsense. You're not getting any younger, you know. Can't wait around forever. Marry him and let him take care of things"

Liss had to laugh at the notion. "Wyatt and

I are not talking marriage. You know he's here only because of the plant. As soon as that's settled, he'll—"

Aggie cut in, "But you'd marry him if he asked you?"

"I don't think this is any of your business, Aggie," Liss said gently.

"I'm making it my business."

"It won't come to that, Aggie," Liss said, forcing herself to ignore the quick hope deep inside her. Wyatt had asked her how she felt about his staying on in Oakmont, but that was a far cry from commitment. "Listen, I have to go. Thanks for everything."

"What are you going to do, Liss?"

"Right now, I'm going to call Howard and see what he has to say."

"Good luck, dear, but don't get your hopes up." Aggie hung up without saying goodbye.

Liss placed the call to Howard uneasily. After a number of rings, a recording announced the business hours for the City of Oakmont. Frustrated, Liss didn't know what to do next. Tomorrow morning, she'd be in Howard's office on the dot of nine, but what was she going to do to fill the hollow hours of the night?

She'd quickly gotten used to Wyatt being here with her, having dinner with her every night. Dinner. She smiled at how easy it was to say dinner now, instead of supper. Amusement fading, she walked through the morning room, missing him with every pore.

If she missed him this much now, how would she manage without him? He'd changed her life so much since the day he'd moved into Leona's guest quarters.

She smiled, remembering the ludicrous way they'd met, and the way he'd made her laugh more since then than she'd ever laughed before.

Sinking down into a chair he favored, she propped her chin on a fist and began to tally all the differences he'd made in her life.

Some were good. She felt her breasts begin to warm as she remembered how she felt when she'd first made love with him. Immensely surprised to find that she could experience passion as she'd never known it, she was also grateful beyond measure that it was Wyatt who had taught her.

And that it was with Wyatt that she was learning to plumb the depths of that passion. Their sex life was varied and always thrilling.

So many new things she'd experienced since Wyatt entered her life. Satisfaction waned as she recalled some of the other new things Wyatt had brought along with him.

And the things that had happened to her since Wyatt came to Oakmont. Just days ago, she'd been happy and excited about the opening of the new library. Feeling so much of herself in it, she felt great satisfaction in being able to help with her anonymous gift to the city. It had enabled Oakmont to build the new library on land she'd all but given to the city.

It was gratifying to know that through the pain and suffering of her humiliating divorce she'd been able to create some good. The library would be a lasting and worthwhile reminder that out of ugliness and despair, good things can grow.

She'd looked forward to working there every day, to tending the Collection, seeing it grow and become ever more useful to scholars and lovers of history like herself. She bit her lip. Now when she went to the library, unless she could get the Collection back, she'd be no different than any other patron.

The thought crushed her. For years, she'd been David's wife. Oh, to be sure, she was the last of the Thayers, and that still held a great deal of importance to a number of people in Oakmont, but to the people in David's world, the up and comers, she was merely an extension of him.

After the divorce, she'd fallen into that depression from which she'd seen no end, until one day, polishing her grandmother's escritoire, she'd gotten the idea for the antique store. From there, like dominoes falling one after the other, had come her involvement with the library and, ultimately, the Oakmont Collection.

She'd created her own success. She'd done it on her own, with help from friends, of course, but the final decisions were hers. Sink or swim, she'd done it by herself. So many of her feelings of self worth, or personal importance, were intricately linked with the Collection. If that was gone, where would she be? She couldn't bear the thought of losing the Collection.

She *wouldn't* lose it!

Wyatt stretched out and propped his feet on the coffee table before he dialed Liss's number. All day he'd looked forward to the sound of her voice, soft and melodious. He'd held out the thought of talking to her as the carrot to keep him moving forward when the discussions bogged down.

And then, just when he thought he'd lost his gamble, several of the hold-outs wavered. He'd zeroed in on them to convince them of the benefits of employee ownership. He stressed personal involvement and motivation, increased quality, profitability and return on investment. At least, they now agreed to consider his proposals seriously before the vote on Friday.

Flushed with the prospect of victory, Wyatt had raced back to his apartment to share his news with Liss. While he waited for her to pick up the receiver, he noticed how boring his rented furnishings were compared to the warmth and charm of Liss's home. It amused him to think that for someone who'd never wanted to be tied down, he was now eager to adopt all her family traditions and create new ones of their own.

He could barely wait to tell her about his change of heart.

"Hello?"

He smiled, rewarded at last. "Liss? Did I catch you at a bad time?"

He heard her intake of breath. "No."

He spoke gently. "I miss you. I've been busy, but the day drags without you to come home to."

"I miss you, too."

He paused. Her voice wasn't low and throaty, as it usually was when she spoke with him. It wasn't the voice which provoked images of candlelit rooms and Liss in her sexy, delicate underthings. No, her voice sounded strained. "What's wrong, honey?"

"Nothing," she said after a pause. "How are you doing?"

"Forget about me. I want to know what's the matter with you. Are you mad at me?" The silence over the phone line made him nervous. "Liss? Talk to me. Please."

Finally, she spoke. "I'm not angry with you. It's something else."

"Damnit, what? Talk to me, Liss!"

"Not over the phone. How are you?"

"You can ask that after you drop a bomb in my lap and won't tell me if it's armed?"

"Look, Wyatt. I can't talk now. Leave it until you get back."

He heard her unspoken "if you do" and kept his voice firm and positive. "It's looking good here. Unless something drastic comes up, I'm leaving right after work on Friday. I'll see you about nine."

"Fine."

Wyatt realized she'd hung up without saying goodbye. Worried and hurt, he dissected their conversation. He couldn't find any reason for her reserve. He'd known that she wasn't pleased that he'd returned to Sunnyvale a day early, but she wasn't petty enough to let a small annoyance grow into a major grievance.

Come to think of it, she hadn't sounded so much angry as hurt.

Eyes narrowing, he wondered if there was more gossip going the rounds. She'd tried not to show it, but he'd seen how distressed she'd been to be the subject of malicious scuttle-butt. Who had said what to hurt her now?

He didn't like this, not one damned bit, and when he got back to Oakmont, he was going to put a stop to it. Liss was too fine a woman to be flayed by flapping tongues.

How am I going to make it to Friday without seeing her?

Liss regretted her actions the minute she set the receiver down. She'd picked up the phone thrilled to hear his voice, yet none of her pleasure came through. Instead, she'd been short with him. *You've blown it now, Alice Louisa. Why should he want to come back to you? You'd better find something else to do with your life, because for sure, Wyatt Harrow won't be in it.*

She lay stiffly in bed, steeling herself to sleep. For hours she stared at the ceiling while her thoughts reeled from Wyatt to the loss of her Collection. Although he hadn't said anything specific, she hadn't been able to stop thinking about a life with him.

Aggie's questions only clarified her own desires. What would it be like to be married to Wyatt, the one man who saw below her surface composure and tapped the wellspring of her passion?

Missing him, angry with herself for being

rude to him, she made herself face the fact that her dreams were only wishful thinking.

Though she loved him deeply, she had no reason to believe he intended to stay with her.

He'd made no commitments.

It was a very long time before she slept.

Liss strode down the hallway to Howard's office, her heels clicking against the old black and white marble squares. She hadn't called him, afraid that if she tried to make an appointment he'd make some excuse not to see her.

She walked right past his secretary and had his office door partly open by the time the woman reacted. "Liss, wait! You can't go in there!"

"I'm already in, Betty." Shutting the door firmly behind her, she advanced to see Howard getting awkwardly to his feet. Staring only at him, noting the color that crept up his neck, she knew she'd been right to march right in.

"Did you hear I got fired?"

"Liss, what are you doing here? I don't have time for you."

"You'd better make time, Howard, because I have a few things to settle with you."

"Now, Liss, you weren't fired. You just need

to step down and let trained people do their jobs."

"Trained people?" she echoed, her voice rising. "Are you referring to Joe Franklin?"

"That's not very professional of you, is it, to get so emotional?" Howard admonished. "You're too wrapped up in—"

Stung by that undeserved barb, Liss lowered her voice. No way would she let Howard get the upper hand. "You're getting even because I wouldn't agree to use my influence with Wyatt Harrow."

"Now that you mention it, seems to me you've let your social life interfere with—"

She sucked in her breath. "That's despicable, Howard. You know very well that Joe had to start this grant thing long before Wyatt came to Oakmont—"

"Makes no nevermind. We need someone who knows where his duty lies. You shoulda been looking out for Oakmont instead of—"

"All right, Howard, you've made your point. I refused to get involved with your political deals, and now I'm paying the price." She paused, then confronted him. "You're not going to help me, are you?"

"Afraid I'm much too busy with Intratec business to look into your little problem, Liss. Maybe when all this is over . . ."

"Goodbye, Mayor."

She swung on her heel and marched out of his office, feeling lonelier than she'd ever felt before. Old allies were unable or unwilling to help her now. She didn't know where else to turn. Blinking back tears, she stood at the top of the stairs, barely able to see the big mahogany doors opening into the library.

Could Howard possibly be right? If she hadn't been so besotted with Wyatt, would she have seen this coming? Since he'd come to town, she'd lost her clarity of thought. Her stomach roiled with the thought that she might be responsible for her own downfall.

What have I done?

Keeping her back straight, Liss went down to the library, and without speaking to anyone, into her small office. There she worked like an automaton, checking the progress of their move and ticking off the items from her "to-do" list.

When the movers carted out the last box just before noon, the staff took an early lunch hour. Once they were gone, Liss wandered around the rooms, empty now and shabby. Sunshine caught the dust motes hovering over the scarred floor. She had longed for this day, yet now she dreaded leaving. So much of her life was bound up in this building, but now she faced a different path ahead.

Holding her arms protectively across her

stomach, she paced in and out of the bands of sunlight, sniffling and suppressing tears. No matter that she'd determined to go on with her life, she still ached with her losses.

If only she didn't have to face losing both her Collection and Wyatt at the same time.

The phone rang several times before she automatically picked it up. "Oakmont Public Library. May I help you?"

"Uh, may I speak to Liss? Liss Thayer?"

"This is she," she said stiffly, aware that this would be the last call she ever took at the library.

"Oh, Liss, thank goodness! This is Toby. I called your shop and someone said you were at the lib—"

"Toby! Is anything wrong?"

"No, no. I wanted to tell you I took your advice."

"You did? About what?"

"Well, first I talked to my mother—"

"That's good."

"It wasn't good," Toby's voice lowered. "She's upset with me."

"Surely that's just temporary," Liss soothed. "When she gets used to the idea, she'll—"

"You don't understand. She wants me to get rid of the baby!" Toby wailed.

"Oh, no," Liss barely whispered. "Are you going to do that?"

"No. I'm going to do just what Dad and I decided," Toby said, calming down. "I've already put in for a transfer to Sunnyvale."

"That's good. Do you think it will go through?"

"I think so. After all, I've got connections!"

"Toby," Liss scolded.

"I don't make a big thing of Daddy being a VP, Liss, honest I don't. But if he can make this happen for me, why shouldn't he?"

"Well, maybe under the special circumstances . . ."

"Hey, guess what!"

Accepting the change in subject, Liss dutifully said, "What?"

"I took your advice. I told the father."

"You did? Toby, I'm proud of you."

Toby snorted. "Huh. You should have heard what he said. What he yelled! He called me irresponsible for getting pregnant, as if I did it all alone! Then he went on to say he wanted no part of me or the baby."

"Oh, Toby . . ."

"No, it's okay. I'm glad he feels that way He signed a legal agreement, giving up all rights to the baby. He'll have no responsibility at all, not for anything." She giggled. "He couldn't sign it fast enough!"

"You got what you wanted, didn't you?"

"Yeah. You know what? I'm excited about moving to California."

"That's good, Toby," Liss said, and meant it. She was truly glad that Toby had talked with both Elaine and the baby's father. It couldn't have been easy for her, but she'd done it. She wasn't Wyatt's daughter for nothing. Smiling at that thought, she added, "I'll look forward to seeing you once in a while."

"Me, too. Oops, better go. Can I call you again?"

"Any time you like."

Later, feeling much better for having talked to Toby, for knowing that she was getting her life in order, Liss parked at the new library, got out of her car, and stood for a few minutes. She gazed out over the lush green fields surrounding the building, storing up courage to go in and do what had to be done.

She entered the library briskly, only to stop and gawk at Susan, Dani and the Friends of the Library volunteers who stooped, gathered a handful of books from the packing cartons, stretched, shelved, and bent again. The frantic pace had them sweating, but they worked in silence.

Dani looked up. "Here she is!"

Everybody stopped. Liss thought they looked like that childhood game when everybody froze, like a statue, on command. Susan's arm was extended over her head; Dani crouched over a partially empty box, only her face raised, staring at Liss. The others waited in total silence.

Susan placed the book on the shelf. Dani put down her books and stood. The Friends chairperson put her palms together and clapped.

The applause spread. Overwhelmed, Liss could only stand, rooted in the foyer, mouth open. She felt herself blush, felt the sting of tears and blinked hard.

Swallowing, she advanced.

Susan came forward and hugged her. "Don't look so surprised."

Liss wiped away a stubborn tear and hugged her back. "Who's minding the store?"

"It won't hurt us to miss a few minutes."

Liss looked around, peering into the stacks.

Dani noticed. "If you're looking for Joe, he was here a while ago and then disappeared. He knows he's not wanted."

"Listen, don't you do something silly, on my behalf," Liss counseled. "You've still got to work here, you know."

"No, I don't know," Dani retorted. "If Jack keeps his job, I just might quit."

At the sight of the large sheet cake, with the words "Liss—We'll miss you!" in red icing, Liss choked back the laugh-turned-sob that caught in her throat. Finding it hard to breathe, she blinked hard several times until she could force a smile.

Wyatt faced the Intratec Board of Directors. Standing at the podium with a pointer in his hand, he spoke confidently, masking his uneasiness.

"So as you can see, by making the initial investment into the employee ownership plan, loaning the funds to the employees to buy Intratec out, over a period of time our return on investment will be heightened by the increased production in the Oakmont facility. Historically, employee ownership leads to pride, increased quality, and lower overhead costs. That in turn will benefit us. In addition, the shortened manufacturing times will position us well within the industry to counter any foreign interests."

The comptroller looked up from his notes. "Run that by me again, Harrow. How do you figure we'll come out ahead here?"

"We, Intratec, sell the Oakmont plant to the employees. They in turn become an Intratec subsidiary. We buy the product. If they can't produce, we go elsewhere. We don't have to cover the costs of running the plant."

The comptroller jotted down a few figures, his lips pursed.

One of the manufacturing directors leaned back in his chair, staring hard at Wyatt. "You're asking us to put up with slack time?"

Wyatt responded affably, "Yes. Initially, we'll experience some down-time while the new owners ramp up, but we'd have expected that, especially if we relocated the assembly operations offshore. I foresee that we'll be up and running again sooner than we would have been by moving abroad."

"What about personnel, Harrow?" one of the vice presidents asked. "We'll be losing a hefty number of good people."

"That's true. But after talking to a number of employees, most of whom said they'd rather give up their jobs than have to move back to Silicon Valley, it'll be a wash. We'd have to replace those employees anyway. This way, they get what they want, which will make fewer problems for us in the long run. Those that are willing to transfer back here should be welcome to do so, of course."

"I'm still not convinced some inexperienced employees are going to do a better job than we could," groused the operations manager.

Wyatt's anger flared before he suppressed it. "Who knows? They've got more at stake—

their jobs, their community—it's important to them. How many of us here in this room would walk off the job before we'd take that kind of risk?"

At the sound of embarrassed laughter, Wyatt relaxed slightly. He hadn't won yet, but he was hopeful. Soon now, he could call Liss.

Hours later, when he finally had a chance to dial, he leaned back exhausted and listened to her phone ring repeatedly. Just as he was about to hang up in disappointment, she answered.

Relief washed through him. "Hi, Liss. You sound like you've been running."

"I just got in—I heard the phone before I got the door unlocked."

"Where've you been? A movie?"

"Don't I wish! I've been unpacking boxes and getting things ready for the dedication."

"You work too hard."

She heard the tired slur in his voice and smiled. "I'm not the only one. How did your meetings go today?"

"Better."

"You sound happier about them."

"Are you fishing for information again?"

"Couldn't you give me just the teeniest little hint?"

"Nope. How have you been?"

Wyatt gave her the perfect opening to tell

him about losing the Collection but somehow it was still too fresh. Too raw. She couldn't get the words out. "Not too good, but one nice thing happened. Toby called."

"Yeah? There's a message on my machine from her, but it's too late to call back. What did she say? Is she okay?"

"She's fine. She said she'd put in for her transfer, and was looking forward to moving out here."

"That'll be great. What else?"

"Ah, maybe she'd better tell you the rest."

"Why?"

"It's personal."

"We don't seem to have any secrets from you, Liss. What did she say?"

"You're going to have to hear it from her. It's not my place to—"

"Wait a minute! Back up there. What are you talking about, honey? What's this non-sense about your place?"

Liss sighed. "Don't get so upset. It's nothing bad," she stretched the truth, wondering how Toby's mother could be so unsupportive. "Toby can tell you herself, and that's final."

"Final, huh?" he chuckled. "If you say so. I guess I can wait until I talk to her."

"Fine." She paused, hesitating, then said softly, "I miss you."

He yawned hugely. "Sorry, honey. I miss

you, too. I've been waiting to talk to you all day and now I can barely keep my eyes open."

"Wyatt, hang up and go to sleep."

"Mmm, in a moment. I don't want to let you go just yet."

"You're falling asleep. Hang up."

"Kiss me good night first."

She blew him a kiss. "There. Sleep well. Oh, wait—Wyatt?"

"I'm here," he mumbled.

"I'm sorry about last night . . ."

"What?"

She smiled and blew him another tender kiss. "Tell you tomorrow. Go to sleep now."

"Yeah," he rumbled through another yawn. "See you tomorrow—it might be late."

"I'll be here."

Late Friday night, dozing over a novel, Liss roused when she heard a car park in the Greenley driveway. *Wyatt's back!* She got up, fumbled with her robe, then dropped it when she couldn't make the sleeves work.

She raced down the stairs in her bare feet with only one thought in mind. Wyatt. She had to see Wyatt to tell him how much she loved him.

She yanked the back door open, heading for the shortcut to the property next door, when she heard his footsteps on the walk. Breathless, she stopped and waited.

He came out of the shadows into the moonlight. Dressed still in a dark suit, with only a glimmer of white visible at his chest, he was silver and black velvet.

"Wyatt! Oh, Wyatt—"

He bounded up the steps and caught her up into his arms. The loose folds of her nightgown swirled around them as he lifted her up to meet his descending mouth.

He ended the deep kiss only long enough to mutter against her lips, "Liss. God, I missed you."

"Wyatt, I'm so sorry—"

He interrupted her with another kiss. Liss felt his hunger and gave him everything he demanded. After a moment, his lips gentled their voracious clamor.

She drew back a little, just enough to murmur, "I missed you, too, Wyatt. I'm sorry I was such a witch . . ." Suddenly, her eyes widened. "Wyatt? How did it go?"

He gave her a wide, triumphant smile. "Okay, I guess. I won a little, gave a little."

"What? Tell me!"

"Do you suppose I could get something to eat? I can't remember when I ate last."

Her blue eyes concentrated on him, reflecting both her anticipation and her concern. "Why not?"

His stomach rumbled. He grimaced. "I was too nervous before the board meeting, and in too much of a damned hurry to get home to you after."

She ushered him into the kitchen. "Sit down, I'll bring you something." Wyatt sank onto a stool and propped his elbows on the counter to watch her work. He thought about the things he was going to tell her, anticipating her reaction to his news. Maybe she'd blush with her pleasure, or merely smile at him with that soft, feminine enchantment that filled him with wonder.

She brought him sandwiches, fruit, and coffee.

"Thanks. All for me?"

"I'll share your coffee. Tell me what happened."

He heard the change in her voice. He put down the coffee cup. She watched him with such hope that he determined that no matter what it took, he'd make sure she was never hurt or disappointed again.

He took her hand in his and lifted it to his cheek. "You know I went to make a proposal to the board, but what you don't know is that I put my butt on the line for this."

She cupped her palm against his jaw. Her eyes darkened with concern.

Quickly, he said, "I didn't mention that to worry you, but just to tell you how much I had riding on this. How much I believe in this plan."

She nodded. "I know how hard you worked."

He grunted as he lifted the coffee to his lips. "Not just me. I had Pete Dodge and the study team do most of the work. I only had to sell it."

"Wyatt, tell me," she begged.

"The details aren't fully worked out yet, but the Oakmont plant stays open."

She threw her arms around him, knocking the cup right out of his hand, and hugged him hard. "Oh, Wyatt, thank you, thank you!"

He ignored the damage to his suit. He hugged her back, feeling her tears as she pressed grateful kisses on his cheek, his throat, his chin and finally his mouth. He kissed her deeply, then lifted his lips when her tears ran salty in his mouth. "Hey, take it easy—"

She withdrew a small distance. "You did it, Wyatt!"

He smoothed the tears away from her cheek. "There's more."

"What?"

He smiled. "If I tell you, will you cry all over me again?"

She firmed her chin and blinked hard, trying very hard to look like the portrait of old Arthur in the parlor. "A Thayer can take anything."

Even as she said it, the contrast between his good news and her bad news hit her like a fist to the heart. She'd thought she'd be able to wait until later, much later, to tell Wyatt of her ouster, but she'd misjudged herself.

Her face paled as she doubled over in anguish.

Wyatt shoved the dishes out of the way and leaned over her. "Liss! What is it, honey?"

Twenty-two

Liss got her breathing under control and whispered, "I'm all right."

She reached out to brush a worry wrinkle away from his set mouth. "Something happened and I suddenly remembered it and over-reacted, I guess."

"Over-reacted? To what?" He watched the color return to her face, but he didn't like the pinched look to her mouth or the dark circles under her eyes. "Alice Louisa, what the hell is going on here?"

He watched her bite her lip, as if chewing over a particularly complex problem. "Can I tell you about it later? You had the floor."

He hesitated. Whatever was bothering her was bad. Very bad. He wanted to know right away.

Whatever hurt her, he wanted to fix it, to

make the pain go away, to make her smile and laugh for him again.

"Please?" she asked softly.

He pulled her into his arms, paying no attention to the wet stains on his suit. "All right—against my better judgment. But you will tell me every single thing, you hear?"

"Everything," she promised.

"Okay." He began, then stopped to peer into her eyes. "You sure you're all right?"

She nodded.

He was unable to keep the deep note of satisfaction from his voice. "You can't tell anyone yet, but the employees are buying the plant. They're going to run it themselves."

Understanding brightened her face. "Own it and run it?"

He reveled in it, in the admiration and satisfaction he knew he'd put there. It felt good to know that he'd proved himself to her. Still, he had to warn her. "There are some conditions—"

"Oh, Wyatt, you did it" she exclaimed. "You said you'd do the right thing—I'm so proud of you. Oakmont has so much to thank you for."

"Hold on, honey. Don't make me out to be the hero here." He picked up her hand and squeezed gently. "There'll be problems. No matter how I feel personally, this is still a business decision. The plant will be on it's own. If it goes down the tubes, Intratec won't put any more money into it. If the plant doesn't show it can handle our needs in a reasonable turn-around time, Intratec will have to pull out."

Her face sobered. "I didn't realize that. There's still some risk, then?"

"Honey, there's always a risk."

"What will happen to the employees there now?"

"Those that want to buy in will stay. The others can stay or leave."

"And Jack Brody?"

Wyatt smiled. "That's one young man on the move. He doesn't have to worry. Did you know he's the one who suggested the buy-out program? If he can control his grandstanding, he'll go far."

"Oh, I'm glad. Dani's been so worried that he'd lose his job, and with her threatening to quit hers, they thought they wouldn't be able to get married."

"Well, they can." He tightened his grip on her fingers. "Hold it right there. Why would Dani want to quit the library?" His eyes narrowed as he studied her. "Does that have anything to do with what you're going to tell me?"

From the look on her face, Wyatt knew the answer.

He waited until she'd found just the right words.

She looked down at their hands. "I was fired."

"*What?* How can you be fired? You're a volunteer."

"Well, maybe fired isn't the right word," she admitted. "It feels that way, though. They told me they no longer needed me."

"Who said so?" he demanded.

"Don Simpson told me that they've hired a degreed curator for the Collection—"

"He can't do that," Wyatt said in a low voice that didn't conceal his anger.

Liss shook her head. "He already has—the whole board voted for it. I'm not qualified to . . . they said I could stay on and help Joe, but—"

"That's the most ridiculous thing I ever heard. Who says so?"

Liss explained.

Wyatt listened, growing increasingly angry. His eyes narrowed and his jaw clenched shut while he absorbed the facts. "They really did this? They went out and applied for an unnecessary grant . . . hell, isn't the money Intratec is feeding into the city enough for them?"

"It's not just the money. They want the prestige and the reputation of the Collection."

"I spoke to those two jerks down at the mayor's just last week. They sat there with smug looks on their faces, smiling all the while. Damnit, they knew then that this was in the works. They had to know what it would do to you." He paused, feeling the blood surge through him. "Liss, do you want me to take them apart for you?"

She almost smiled. "It wouldn't do any good. What's done is done."

Cursing, he saw the truth in her eyes, mixed with the rejection and humiliation lingering in her expression. He hurt for her.

"Come here, honey."

She went willingly into his arms and laid her head on his shoulder. He spoke gently, controlling his need to go out and bang some heads together. "What do you want to do about this?"

"I tried to fight it," she explained, telling him what she'd done. "The grant specifies professional management. That lets me out."

"Not necessarily. How much is the grant?"

She told him.

He sucked in his breath at the amount. "I'll talk to Simpson tomorrow. You won't need that grant. I'll see that Intratec doubles the amount, but only if you stay on."

Liss raised her head from his shoulder and stared at his clear blue eyes, now frozen in anger. A muscle jumped in his jaw. She felt the blood drain from her face. For one heart-stopping moment, she was tempted.

How easy it would be to let Wyatt fight her battles. How safe he made her feel, cosseted and protected by the strength of his feelings.

He was so good at it, so masterful, so used to winning.

Why not let him?

She continued to stare at him, unaware that all her thoughts raced clearly across her face.

Wyatt saw her temptation, saw her struggle with it, saw her decision. He frowned, waiting for her words.

Liss lifted her chin and looked squarely at him. "No. You can't do that."

"Why not?" Wyatt asked, his bewilderment wrestling with his desire to protect her.

"I can't let you do that. How could I hold up my head in this town if I let you buy me?"

"Buy you?" he asked harshly. "What does that mean?"

"It's very simple, Wyatt. If I let you storm Howard's office, make him reverse Don's decision, you know what will happen. Everyone in town will know. That's all they'll talk about—how you used Intratec to save my Collection. Because we're sleeping together," she stumbled over the last few words, then righted herself. "If I can't have it legally, morally, then I'll have to do without it."

"Is that what this is all about? Your pride?"

She straightened her shoulders. "It's all I have left." Her voice resonated with dignity.

"You have me," he said fiercely, and lowered his mouth to hers to kiss her possessively. He knew he must be hurting her, yet apart from a small moan as she opened her mouth to him, she made no sign. She kissed him just as ravenously. At last he lifted his head and brushed his tongue lightly against her swollen lips, soothing the hurt he'd inflicted. "Why won't you let me help you? It tears me up inside to see you like this. Damnit, that Collection is yours."

"Not anymore. This is something I have to do myself." She paused and searched for the right words. "I've done a lot of thinking while you were away."

"About what?"

What hadn't she thought about? In the long hours of the night, when she couldn't sleep, when she thought of all the changes in her life since Wyatt had come to Oakmont. It seemed as if he was the catalyst for more than she'd ever dreamed of. He'd shaken her out of her cozy little shell, demanded more from her than she'd had to give, and rewarded her for the giving. He'd also given her a brand new awareness of life, of the potency of desire and the passion they shared. Of love.

If his presence pointed out all the things she'd never have, such as family and children and continuity, he also had taught her more about herself as a woman. She pondered the price of that knowledge. Was it worth it to at last become a woman in every sense of the word, if by doing so she opened herself up to further pain and loss?

Seeing his patient expression, she began with some of the decisions she'd made. Easy ones first. "Well, over the last few years, I've gotten some recognition in early Californiana. I don't have to stay here where everything would remind me of the Collection." Eagerly now, she explained, "I could go to San Francisco, get some more training, and—"

"What about me?" he interrupted sharply. "Where do I fit into all these plans?"

She stopped short. "What do you mean?"

"You made all these plans without including me, didn't you?"

Puzzled, she nodded. He was partly right. Although she hadn't discussed them with him, he was the center of each of them.

Wyatt's burst of laughter was short and humorless. "That's great! I come racing back to Oakmont to tell you I'm transferring here, and you've decided to leave." Unable to restrain the bitterness that welled up in him at the way she'd done all this herself without even thinking of him, he snapped, "Some future that leaves us."

"I thought you'd be in Sunnyvale. I thought that if I moved to the Bay Area, we could still see each other . . ."

"How about that?" he said roughly. "To get the employee ownership deal okayed, I had to agree to quit Intratec and take on the job here as plant manager. I'm replacing Pete Dodge."

"Wyatt! Quit Intratec?" Then his words penetrated. With her mouth opening in surprise, she gasped, "You'd really move here?"

"Isn't that something? I agreed to those conditions willingly, because I want to live here with you. Some joke."

"Wyatt, I didn't know . . ."

He closed his eyes, mentally counted to ten, then to twenty, and opened them slowly. "Alice Louisa, why didn't you discuss any of this with me?"

"Why should I? We never spoke of a future together. You have no rights in any decision I make."

He took a slow, calming breath, then another. Ignoring that last ridiculous statement, he asked as calmly as he could, "Did it ever occur to you to wonder how we're going to live if I'm here and you're somewhere else?"

She shook her head, confused. Why did he keep harping on living arrangements? Could he mean he wanted a commitment from her?

"Obviously not," he paused, looking for control. Then as if speaking to himself, he muttered, "It's been a very long day. You're upset. I'm wiped out. Why should I expect a logical discussion?"

Her temper flared when instead of voicing his intentions, he spoke so sarcastically. "Well, how am I supposed to know what you're planning? You never said a word—kept it all a secret!"

"You know how I feel about you—that's no secret! The whole damned town knows."

"That's right!" she interrupted. "The whole damned town knows that you had some hush-hush plan going, but did you ever take me into your confidence? Oh, no! Not me. Not the woman you spent practically all your free time with. Not the woman you took to bed and . . ."

He put his hand over her mouth to quiet her. Over her muffled mutterings, he asked conversationally, "Alice Louisa, how the hell are we going to have any kind of married life if you sell the house out from under us when I've agreed to stay here for at least the next two years and you're someplace else?" He ran out of breath.

Only one word penetrated. "Married?" she squeaked against his palm.

"Yes, married." He removed his hand and dropped it to her shoulder. He gave her a little shake. "What did you think I meant by all this? Why else would I work my butt off to get this plan going and agree to move? To say nothing of sinking a lot of my own money into the new plan."

"I didn't ask you to do any of that," she defended herself automatically.

He blew out his breath explosively. "I thought it would make you happy."

"You did it for me?"

"Well, not all of it," he answered honestly. "I'd never be able to swing the deal if it didn't make financial sense, but I wouldn't have taken the transfer here, either."

"Marriage," she said, subdued, unable to deal with the emotions which galloped through her, trampling common sense and leaping to impossible heights. "Oh, Wyatt . . ."

His gaze fixed on her. "Honey, why didn't you talk to me first?"

"I can ask you the same question. Why didn't you talk to me first?"

"If you remember, you agreed to trust me

to do the right thing. Or have you forgotten that?"

Her retort died on her lips. She had done that. "I wanted to talk to you," she admitted. "Listen, Wyatt, I wanted to talk to you, but I had to figure some things out in my own mind."

"Have you done that?"

"I think so. At least, I thought so. Now I have to sort them out all over again."

He pulled her into the curve of his shoulder. "Okay, so let's work this out together. Forget about Intratec for a moment. Let's talk about you first. Do you want to keep your ties to the library?"

She took her time answering, making sure she was absolutely clear in her own mind. "No. I've given so much of my life to it that I don't want to cut all ties, but I don't see how I can continue to work there."

"All right," Wyatt said, all business now. "How about the Collection?"

She had to consider before she could answer him. "That's not so easy. I gave the contents to the library, and as both Don and Howard have reminded me, they don't belong to me but to Oakmont. I don't have any rights there."

His look said it all. Feeling defensive, she said, "Well, how was I to know Joe would pull a fast one like this? I thought I'd grow old being old lady Thayer with her growing Collection . . ."

He grinned. "How about growing old being Mrs. Harrow?"

"A much nicer choice." She tried to return his grin but failed. Instead she pressed a kiss against his neck, loving the feel of him against her tongue, the scent of him that filled her senses.

"Don't distract me now," he said with a fleeting smile. "We're on a roll here. This Collection means a lot to you, honey. Do you want to fight for it? I don't know that you'd have a hope in hell of winning, but if you want to, that's what we'll do."

She slowly shook her head. "The Collection belongs to Oakmont. I'll have to be content with visiting it from time to time."

"You could do as Simpson suggested—be a docent?"

"No. Better to walk away than have to work with it under somebody else."

"That seems a little drastic."

"Maybe so, but that's how I feel."

"If you change your mind?"

"I doubt that will happen. I intend to be very busy with other things."

"Like what?"

"You, for starters."

He kissed her. "Right answer. Now for my next point. About the house. Can we live here together?"

Her breath was warm against his throat as she considered his words. He forced himself to relax, and in doing so, felt her soft and fragile against his body. Tenderness washed through him. He was doing this all wrong. This wasn't exactly the scenario he'd visualized, but he'd improvise.

Before she could answer, he asked tenderly, "Alice Louisa, will you marry me?"

She stared up at him, her eyes very wide. A blush bloomed on her cheeks. "Didn't you just ask me that?"

"You didn't answer me," he reminded her. "Let's get married as soon as we can arrange it."

"I don't know."

"You need more time?"

"No. I mean I don't know if we should get married."

Disbelieving and disappointed, he moved her away to stare at her face. "You don't know?" he repeated hoarsely. "What kind of answer is that?"

"It's the only kind I can give you right now, Wyatt."

He persisted. "Marry me and let me take care of things for you."

"I may be old-fashioned about a lot of things, but no way am I ever going to let you or anyone else take care of me."

Her answer threw him. "I didn't mean it quite like that," he said, staring at her stubborn expression. "One of the reasons I love you so much is because you are your own woman—I don't want you to change. But when I see you hurting, I want to take away the pain."

Mollified, she cuddled closer. "Okay. I can live with that."

"So you'll marry me?"

"Wyatt," she sighed. "I wish I could say yes, right this minute, but I've got a lot to work out."

"Like what?"

His affronted tone only served to stiffen her resolve. She moved away from him and looked him straight in the eye. "Private things. I love you, Wyatt, but there are some things I have to do for myself."

"Does Toby have anything to do with your reluctance to say yes?"

"Toby? Why do you ask that?"

"Well, you're not just getting me," he warned her. "You're also getting a built-in daughter and a baby on the way. It won't be easy. Do you think you can handle being a grandmother?"

Her heart soared at the thought. A grandchild! As though her every wish for children and continuity would be granted, her inner-most being thrilled to the idea. Yes, yes! She could handle being a grandmother. There wouldn't be a child who would be loved more. Though she wanted to run and jump, exulting with joy, she made herself speak calmly, "I could handle that."

Wyatt smiled as if he knew what she held back, what she kept tucked safely inside. "Toby will be happy you said that. She thinks you're the greatest."

"I think pretty highly of her, too."

"So what's the problem, Liss?"

"Please, just give me a little time. I need to work some things out."

"What can I do to help?"

She put her hand against his cheek. When he turned his face to press a kiss into her palm, she said tenderly, "You already have."

She spent a long day Saturday at the library, setting up the retrospective display for the Collection in the foyer. As her last official act, she placed each item carefully to maximize its visual impact, changing and re-arranging until everything was perfect. This was her farewell.

She wanted it to say all the things she could not.

Dani and the other clerks had left her strictly alone, realizing she needed the time by herself. Joe closeted himself in his new office, until at last he emerged and walked over to her. Liss looked up and watched him approach, thinking he appeared as impossibly angelic as ever.

Joe studied the exhibit for long moments. "You were right, Liss. This display of Oakmont history is just what we need to tie the old and new together."

Liss shot him a disbelieving look.

"No, I mean it. Look, Liss, I know you're mad at me, and I just want you to know there's nothing personal—"

Liss said nothing and re-settled a portrait of her great-great-grandparents next to the display of early Oakmont street maps.

"Uh, Liss. Don tells me you won't stay."

"That's right."

"You're not going to help us?"

Liss laughed for the first time that day. She could be gloating at the dismayed look on his face. It clearly showed her how much he had counted on her expertise and good nature to help him over the rough spots. Instead, she felt a new freedom, like a breeze blowing fresh air through a stale room. "No, I am not staying. You'll be able to figure it all out by yourself. You and your new curator. So long as you both keep the library board happy, you'll be fine."

"What are you going to do?"

"Joe, when my plans are ready, no doubt someone will tell you."

"You sound awfully bitter."

Abruptly, her good humor deserted her. "Should I be all sweetness and light, Joe? Your underhanded tactics got you what you wanted. What more do you expect?"

Joe's ears turned red. "Your boyfriend's making noises at the city council. You think he'll pull their funding out?"

"If you're referring to Wyatt Harrow, I don't speak for him. If you're worried, talk to him yourself."

"You've changed, Liss."

"I've had to." She turned away from Joe, effectively ending their conversation. Angry at herself for letting him disturb her newly-found balance, she put away the items she hadn't used in the display. She paid no attention to Joe's scowls until he turned on his heel and left. A few minutes later, upset that she'd allowed him to disturb her private goodbyes, she went to gather up her things.

Dani caught up with her by the check-out desk. "See you tomorrow at the dedication?"

Liss nodded. "I'll be there."

Late that night, after tossing restlessly for what seemed hours, Liss rolled over and bumped her nose against Wyatt's chest. At his muffled grunt, she asked, "Are you awake?"

"Hard to sleep with you bouncing all over the bed."

She caressed his shoulder. "You're a grump."

"A sleepy grump," he agreed, but nevertheless he pulled her closer.

"Too sleepy to answer a question?"

"If I do, will you shut up and go to sleep?"

"Wyatt, if I wanted to do something, would you be upset if I made the decision without discussing it with you first?"

"Huh. Haven't we already had this argument?"

"That's why I'm asking. Would you mind—really mind?"

He propped himself upright against the pillows and leaned over to snap on the bedside lamp. Squinting against the light, he studied her face. She was worried about this, he knew, seeing the faint shadows under her eyes and the tightness around her mouth.

He dropped a kiss on her lips, hating to see her worry about anything. He knew he shouldn't feel so protective of her, that she was an adult who had lived the major portion of her life before he'd blundered into it, but now that she was his, whether or not she accepted that, he didn't want anything or anybody to upset her ever again.

"Would this theoretical something take you away from me?" he asked.

She shook her head. Her already tousled hair floated around her temples in blonde tendrils. "No. It might keep me busy, but you'd always be my first priority."

"Then go for it, honey."

Her smile began slowly, no more than a brief relaxing of her mouth, then grew until it took over her face. Like a child, she surrendered to sleep. Wyatt watched her for a moment, confused by her, but absolutely sure she meant what she said.

He flicked off the lamp, settled down, and drew her into his arms. In her sleep, she snuggled closer and Wyatt relaxed.

Sunday morning dawned crisp and clear. Liss awoke filled with a sense of purpose. Before she opened her eyes, she felt Wyatt's absence and knew that once again, he'd left her bed in the pre-dawn hour to slip across the back garden and through the gate in the oleanders to the Greenley guest quarters. It probably wasn't necessary now. She doubted that anyone in Oakmont didn't know that they were together. It didn't matter anymore.

During the long hours of the night she had thought, re-thought, and finally resolved her indecision.

Wyatt's trust meant everything to her.

She knew exactly what she wanted and how she was going to achieve her dreams, starting today.

Today was the day on which her whole life would change.

Feeling calm in the aftermath of a sleepless night, she took her time making coffee and squeezing oranges into juice. She searched out the most perfect rose and placed it in a vase. A long, leisurely shower later, she carefully applied makeup and dressed. Walking back downstairs, she stopped in the kitchen doorway.

Wyatt strode across the back lawn in a summer-weight suit.

He slowed when he spotted her, but said nothing until he'd climbed the five wide steps to the verandah and kissed her thoroughly. He studied her pale yellow suit. "You're more beautiful every day."

She bloomed under his gaze. "You're not so bad yourself."

His shoulders squared. "Yeah? You're actually going through with this ceremony thing?"

She ushered him in and poured them both

coffee. "Yes. I worked hard for it, and I want to see that the dedication goes well."

"I don't want you upset."

She held out a cup to him, then picked up her own. She took a sip, then another before she answered him. "I hope I've talked myself out of that. But if it happens," she shrugged, "It happens."

"You're one hell of a woman."

She blew him a kiss. "I think you're pretty special, too. Not many people would have gone to the trouble you did."

"What trouble?"

"Did you forget about Intratec?"

He shrugged that away. "I'd rather concentrate on us right now. Did I tell you I love you, Alice Louisa?"

"Once or twice," she murmured, and slanted him a gratified look. "I love you, too."

"Ready for church?"

"You're going with me?" she asked, unable to hide her pleasure.

"We're together, aren't we?"

She smiled happily.

He played with the buttons on her fitted suit jacket and toyed with the froth of a silk flower in her lapel. "When are you going to accept my proposal, Alice Louisa?"

She captured his fingers with hers. "Don't muss me. I need to make a statement today."

He took his fingers back and used them to lift her chin to his steady regard. "What kind of statement? To the press?"

"You'll see."

"Oh? Have you made up your mind?"

She gazed up at him and nodded.

"You going to tell me what you've decided?"

"Soon," she promised with a lilt in her voice.

At the dedication ceremony, they stood close together, fingers linked, as they had earlier during the religious services. The endless speeches droned on. Liss found herself near tears several times, but each time, she remembered what she had to be thankful for and squeezed Wyatt's hand.

The return pressure was warm and steady, giving her the sense of security and well-being she'd craved all her life. Standing tall next to the man she loved, she let her gaze roam over the crowd.

The parking lot of the new library had been set up as a temporary reception area. Once the speeches were finished, Mayor Howard Upjohn was scheduled to cut the ribbon and escort the crowd into the new facility. The governor had sent his regrets, but their state senator stood by looking important as the high school marching band played a rousing Souza march.

A tug at her sleeve caught Liss's attention. A bridge crony of Aggie Fairchild's pitched her voice to carry over the tuba's *oom pah pa,* "Made me mad to hear that you'd been dumped."

Liss touched her gnarled hand in gratitude. "Don't let that stop you from using the library."

"Heard that Aggie resigned. Seems strange to think of her out of politics, she's been running things for so long."

Liss's smile widened. "Maybe she'll have a good replacement."

The woman looked her up and down and smiled back. "I don't see why not."

Wyatt bent his head and asked softly, "What was that all about?"

"Wait a few minutes," the older woman murmured mysteriously. "You'll see."

Wyatt watched the elderly woman move through the crowd. From the vantage point of his height, he saw her stop to speak with this person, then that one, saw the nods of approval before she moved on.

His brow furrowed. "What's going on?"

Liss turned away from the person she was speaking to. "What?"

Wyatt pointed.

Liss looked mystified. "I have no idea."

When the older woman reached another equally old woman, they talked for a long time, then shared similar conspiratorial smiles.

Looking on, Liss caught Aggie's eye, then glanced up quickly at Wyatt to see if he'd caught the by-play.

His eyes were on Aggie's slow steps to the podium.

Mayor Upjohn interrupted his speech to hear her few words. Wyatt watched the mayor shake his head. His interest caught, Wyatt saw her speak more forcefully and wondered what she said to make the mayor scowl and then reluctantly nod his head in agreement.

Fascinated by the scene developing in front of him, Wyatt realized that Liss couldn't see over the heads in front of her. He whispered, "Something's definitely going on. That little old lady in black just said something to Upjohn that he didn't want to hear."

"That's Aggie. Remember, I told you about her?"

Suspicions forming, Wyatt clasped her elbow. "Let's move up a little closer."

They edged their way through the crowd just as the mayor deviated from his prepared remarks. Liss halted at his words.

"Next," Howard said as if it were all his idea, "I'd like to give public thanks to the woman who was the moving force for the new library. She not only sold the land to the city for a dollar an acre, she also contributed substantially to the library fund. Oakmont owes her a mighty big thank you." He made a big production out of searching her out of the crowd. "Liss, c'mon up here a moment."

Blushing, Liss made her way up to the podium. Wyatt watched her, bright and radiant in her yellow suit. His love for her welled up.

"Now, Liss, a few words?" Howard Upjohn prompted as though this was all his own idea and as if he wasn't hating every moment of it.

Liss nodded. Looking out at the crowd, she took several deep breaths to calm herself. She saw Susan and Tom standing with Dani and Jack Brody. They watched her with great interest and when Susan caught her eye, her smile of encouragement warmed Liss down to her toes. Behind them she saw some of her customers, and off to one side, Pete and Grace Dodge. Grace gave her a thumbs-up and Pete grinned as he wiped the perspiration from his balding head.

She'd decided what she wanted to say. "Thank you all for being here this morning. Without your generous support, we'd be meeting in the middle of an alfalfa field instead of a parking lot."

She stopped to let the chortles die down. "There have been a number of changes made since we broke ground. While several were a surprise to me, I'm reminded of something my grandmother used to say." Looking out over the bunting draping the dais, she paused for effect. "When one door slams in your face, you can be sure a window will open up someplace else."

Laughter tittered through the crowd. She glanced down and saw David and his new wife standing below her to the left. With Davey in a stroller, they made quite a family picture. It pleased her that she could watch them now without the bitterness she'd felt for so long.

Blessing Wyatt for the changes he'd made in her life, she searched the crowd for him, and found him at last, standing a little apart. His silver hair shone in the summer sunshine. He watched her with an expression which made it obvious to anyone how he felt about her.

She paused to smile just for him, then her gaze moved over the audience. "The Oakmont Public Library is very dear to me. Likewise, the Oakmont Collection has been very much a part of my life. It's given me a great deal of personal satisfaction to have started it and launched it on its way. Now it's time for me to turn it over to other hands. I'm sure that with Oakmont's continued support, Joe Franklin and the new curator will carry on in my stead."

Liss took a deep breath, and committed herself. "Some time ago, Mayor Upjohn chided me for not getting more involved in local politics. He mentioned my family's past involvement in Oakmont's development, and urged me to follow their example. Joe Franklin said the same thing."

She looked directly at Howard and Joe sitting together on the dais. "Gentlemen, I want you to be the first to know that I am announcing my candidacy for the vacant seat on the city council!"

A moment of stunned silence gave way to applause, loud whistles and yee-ha's. The band struck up a drum roll. Aggie blew her a kiss, letting everybody know that Liss had her full and enthusiastic support.

Wyatt stared open-mouthed at Liss, who stood calmly by the podium assessing the reaction to her statement. Over the sea of heads, their eyes met and held. What a woman. She'd surprised them all. Surprised him, and he thought he was getting to be the authority on Liss Thayer, soon to be Harrow.

His heart brimming, he held his hands up over his head where she could see them, and clapped.

Watching the pleased smile spread across her lovely, delicate face, Wyatt felt his own smile grow until he thought his ears would fall off. He mouthed, "I love you."

She glowed.

Wyatt saw her gaze switch back to the mayor, and followed with his own. Upjohn and Don Simpson had their heads together, speaking quickly. By the look on Joe Franklin's face, Wyatt guessed none of the three men was happy.

Aggie Fairchild looked satisfied. The state senator looked confused at the dedication suddenly turned political rally.

The mayor returned to the podium and rapped his gavel. "Order," he shouted, his voice hoarse over the uproar. "Let's have some order here, folks."

Grinning, Wyatt made his way through the crowd, letting the continuing applause for Liss swell his heart. She belonged here.

This was her town. These were her fellow citizens.

He'd made the decision to keep the plant open mainly for her, even though he denied it publicly. Now he realized just how far-reaching that gesture would be. Together, they'd have the chance to leave their mark on the future of Oakmont.

He reached for her and swept her into his

arms. Oblivious to the crowd staring at them, he said, "You were marvelous! You did just the right thing. There's no doubt at all that you'll win big. You'll be making policy for the library and overseeing the Collection." He grinned. "You outsmarted them all, honey."

He cut off her response with a swift, no-nonsense kiss that had the crowd whistling and applauding again.

She broke away, breathless and effervescent with victory. "Do you mind?"

"Mind? Hell, no, Alice Louisa. You own this town today!"

Her smile grew from modest to outrageously self-satisfied. "Yes, I do."

"What made you decide to do this?"

She waved vaguely. "I'm not sure. So many things came together. Aggie gave me the idea and it just developed from there. I knew I had to do something. My life is here. You'll be here."

He moved to lead her out of the crush of the crowd. When at last he was able to get her into a quiet corner, she pulled his head down and kissed him.

He raised his head and grinned down at her. "You've done it, now. All these people are going to expect you to make an honest man out of me."

She laughed up at him, riding high on her

victory. Taking his hint, she asked, "You remember when I said I didn't want a short-term affair?"

He tightened his arm around her, loving the excitement on her face. "I seem to recall something like that."

Loving the way his silver hair shone in the bright sunlight, she gave in to the impulse to run her fingers through it. "I'm going to exercise my prerogative to change my mind."

His answering smile changed with the surprised look he threw her. "You want an affair after all?"

She shook her head, ash blonde tresses dazzling him as they glinted with her movement. "Do you still want to marry me?"

Wyatt's dark blue eyes lit with happiness. "You betcha, Alice Louisa. We'll make it a lifetime affair."

WATCH AS THESE WOMEN LEARN TO LOVE AGAIN

HELLO LOVE (4094, $4.50/$5.50)
by Joan Shapiro

Family tragedy leaves Barbara Sinclair alone with her success. The fight to gain custody of her young granddaughter brings a confrontation with the determined rancher Sam Douglass. Also widowed, Sam has been caring for Emily alone, guided by his own ideas of childrearing. Barbara challenges his ideas. And that's not all she challenges . . . Long-buried desires surface, then gentle affection. Sam and Barbara cannot ignore the chance to love again.

THE BEST MEDICINE (4220, $4.50/$5.50)
by Janet Lane Walters

Her late husband's expenses push Maggie Carr back to nursing, the career she left almost thirty years ago. The night shift is difficult, but it's harder still to ignore the way handsome Dr. Jason Knight soothes his patients. When she lends a hand to help his daughter, Jason and Maggie grow closer than simply doctor and nurse. Obstacles to romance seem insurmountable, but Maggie knows that love is always the best medicine.

AND BE MY LOVE (4291, $4.50/$5.50)
by Joyce C. Ware

Selflessly catering first to husband, then children, grandchildren, and her aging, though imperious mother, leaves Beth Volmar little time for her own adventures or passions. Then, the handsome archaeologist Karim Donovan arrives and campaigns to widen the boundaries of her narrow life. Beth finds new freedom when Karim insists that she accompany him to Turkey on an archaeological dig . . . and a journey towards loving again.

OVER THE RAINBOW (4032, $4.50/$5.50)
by Marjorie Eatock

Fifty-something, divorced for years, courted by more than one attractive man, and thoroughly enjoying her job with a large insurance company, Marian's sudden restlessness confuses her. She welcomes the chance to travel on business to a small Mississippi town. Full of good humor and words of love, Don Worth makes her feel needed, and not just to assess property damage. Marian takes the risk.

A KISS AT SUNRISE (4260, $4.50/$5.50)
by Charlotte Sherman

Beginning widowhood and retirement, Ruth Nichols has her first taste of freedom. Against the advice of her mother and daughter, Ruth heads for an adventure in the motor home that has sat unused since her husband's death. Long days and lonely campgrounds start to dampen the excitement of traveling alone. That is, until a dapper widower named Jack parks next door and invites her for dinner. On the road, Ruth and Jack find the chance to love again.

Available wherever paperbacks are sold, or order direct from the Publisher. Send cover price plus 50¢ per copy for mailing and handling to Penguin USA, P.O. Box 999, c/o Dept. 17109, Bergenfield, NJ 07621. Residents of New York and Tennessee must include sales tax. DO NOT SEND CASH.

IT'S NEVER TOO LATE FOR LOVE AND ROMANCE

JUST IN TIME   (4188, $4.50/$5.50)
by Peggy Roberts

Constantly taking care of everyone around her has earned Remy Dupre the affectionate nickname "Ma." Then, with Remy's husband gone and oil discovered on her Louisiana farm, her sons and their wives decide it's time to take care of her. But Remy knows how to take care of herself. She starts by checking into a beauty spa, buying some classy new clothes and shoes, discovering an antique vase, and moving on to a fine plantation. Next, not one, but two men attempt to sweep her off her well-shod feet. The right man offers her the opportunity to love again.

LOVE AT LAST   (4158, $4.50/$5.50)
by Garda Parker

Fifty, slim, and attractive, Gail Bricker still hadn't found the love of her life. Friends convince her to take an Adventure Tour during the summer vacation she enjoys as an English teacher. At a Cheyenne Indian school in need of teachers, Gail finds her calling. In rancher Slater Kincaid, she finds her match. Gail discovers that it's never too late to fall in love . . . for the very first time.

LOVE LESSONS   (3959, $4.50/$5.50)
by Marian Oaks

After almost forty years of marriage, Carolyn Ames certainly hadn't been looking for a divorce. But the ink is barely dry, and here she is already living an exhilarating life as a single woman. First, she lands an exciting and challenging job. Now Jason, the handsome architect, offers her a fairy-tale romance. Carolyn doesn't care that her ultra-conservative neighbors gossip about her and Jason, but she is afraid to give up her independent life-style. She struggles with the balance while she learns to love again.

A KISS TO REMEMBER   (4129, $4.50/$5.50)
by Helen Playfair

For the past ten years Lucia Morgan hasn't had time for love or romance. Since her husband's death, she has been raising her two sons, working at a dead-end office job, and designing boutique clothes to make ends meet. Then one night, Mitch Colton comes looking for his daughter, out late with one of her sons. The look in Mitch's eye brings back a host of long-forgotten feelings. When the kids come home and spoil the enchantment, Lucia wonders if she will get the chance to love again.

COME HOME TO LOVE   (3930, $4.50/$5.50)
by Jane Bierce

Julia Delaine says good-bye to her skirt-chasing husband Phillip and hello to a whole new life. Julia capably rises to the challenges of her reawakened sexuality, the young man who comes courting, and her new position as the head of her local television station. Her new independence teaches Julia that maybe her time-tested values were right all along and maybe Phillip does belong in her life, with her new terms.

Available wherever paperbacks are sold, or order direct from the Publisher. Send cover price plus 50¢ per copy for mailing and handling to Penguin USA, P.O. Box 999, c/o Dept. 17109, Bergenfield, NJ 07621. Residents of New York and Tennessee must include sales tax. DO NOT SEND CASH.